# Cold Morning

## Books by Ed Ifkovic

The Edna Ferber Mysteries
*Lone Star*
*Escape Artist*
*Make Believe*
*Downtown Strut*
*Final Curtain*
*Café Europa*
*Cold Morning*

# Cold Morning

## An Edna Ferber Mystery

## Ed Ifkovic

Poisoned Pen Press

Copyright © 2016 by Ed Ifkovic

First Edition 2016

10 9 8 7 6 5 4 3 2 1

Library of Congress Catalog Card Number: 2015949174

ISBN: 9781464205415    Hardcover
      9781464205439    Trade Paperback

Poisoned Pen Press
6962 E. First Ave., Ste. 103
Scottsdale, AZ 85251
www.poisonedpenpress.com
info@poisonedpenpress.com

Printed in the United States of America

*For Pam Ruggiero*
*Susan "Babe" Lessler*
*and Sandra Ruggiero*

*"Women may be whole oceans deeper than we are, but they are also a whole paradise better. She may have got us out of Eden, but as a compensation she makes the earth very pleasant."*

—Lord St. Orbyn in John Oliver Hobbes'
*The Ambassador*, Act III

*"I was so fed up with this hero stuff I could have shouted murder."*

—Charles A. Lindbergh

*"They think when I die the case will die. They think it will be like a book I close. But the book, it will never close."*

—Bruno Richard Hauptmann

# Chapter One

Alexander Woollcott settled back on the old wood-slatted folding chair, wrapped his arms around his tremendous stomach, and groaned so loudly that folks sitting at the end of our long table suddenly jumped, swiveled to stare at him. Oblivious, Aleck ran a plump finger across his gravy-smeared lips, licked the moist fingertip, and grinned at me, his small, round eyes magnified and alive with pleasure behind his Coke-bottle eyeglasses. He struck me as a night owl suddenly blinded by the headlights of a passing car.

"Edna, dear, I've come to an important decision about my life."

This ungainly man twisted on the rickety chair—it creaked and moaned as though trying to escape the heavy load it bore—and waited for me to say something. When I didn't, he flicked a finger against my forearm, impatient.

In turn, I twisted away from him. "Aleck, your decisions usually result in our feuding for months on end."

He smirked as he suppressed a minor belch. "Ah, dear Edna, you really do believe I loom gigantically in the affairs of your humdrum but lavish life."

"A sentence I am tempted to parse, but dare not."

He spoke over my words, one fleshy hip sliding into the woman on his left. I watched her growl and leave the table. He blinked his eyes wildly. "There is so little that you understand about the workings of a complex man."

"When I finally meet one, I'll wire you my thoughts."

He chuckled and pointed at his half-finished plate of food. "Listen, my dear. I may have to convert to—tell me, what is the religion of these wonderful folks here?"

"Methodist, according to the sign on the church above us."

"Well, well. Followers of that delirious John Wesley. Doubtless a well-fed man. But Methodists are puritans at heart, no? They believe in fasting. Or do they?" A deliberate pause as he glanced around the shadowy basement with the long institutional tables covered in much-washed but severely ironed white tablecloths, its faded gingham lace curtains shrouding the tiny windows up by the ceiling blocked the weak noontime winter sunlight streaming in. A drab room, the hint of moldy basement about the place. Freshly painted white wainscoting along the walls, checkerboard tiles dotting the floor. "And I may have to *move* here." He stressed the word, shuddered as though he were Napoleon facing imminent exile.

"To Flemington?"

"A hick town, sure. *Quaint,* to use the redundant word popping up in all the news accounts. But"—he surveyed the food before him—"such exile is worth it, to dine daily in this pedestrian church basement. Succulent pot roast and rosemary-slathered potatoes, and feathery onions so transparent that..." He sighed, closed his eyes, a thin smile gracing his lips.

"But Aleck, you were born in New Jersey, no? Red Bank? Some notorious commune of free-spirit folks."

He grumbled, his voice even whinier than usual. "A house of eighty-five rooms and dozens of folks in everyone else's business. The Phalanx. A father with incurable wanderlust and a love of poverty. My youthful eyes looked to Hamilton College, then to Manhattan, that blessed city. Like any celebrated raconteur, I refuse to cross the Hudson into Jersey swamp land."

"Yet here you are, settling in, salivating over a luncheon produced by church ladies in hairnets and sensible shoes."

Aleck glanced up from his dish, his fork still suspended in air. He rolled gloriously in his seat, his triple chins shimmying. His vaudeville sliver of a moustache quivered under his beak nose. His eyes took in the line of prim and proper women, ladies of the Women's Council, standing behind a counter, ladles in hand, staring in bafflement at the avaricious and chatty folks before them.

Aleck nodded toward them. "Frankly, given the hidden delights of such frontier cuisine, perhaps I should encourage a few more crimes of the century. One is not enough, though Colonel Lindbergh might take issue with me."

"How crass." I turned away but looked back at him and grimaced. "Aleck, you fit right in with the snickering, snobbish crowd out there."

I pointed toward the small windows fronting Main Street. There clusters of visitors gossiped and yelled.

"Ah, Miss Ferber isn't happy with the way the murder trial is shaping up?"

I rolled my tongue into the corner of my mouth. "Miss Ferber is unhappy with a lot of things, and this…this spectacle is the stuff of horrible satire—if it wasn't so sad and dangerous."

"What are you yammering about, Ferber? This spectacle is a journalist's dream. All the elements of one of your melodramatic novels—the blond American hero who conquered the heavens, soloing across the Atlantic to Paris with five sandwiches. *Vive l'Américain!* The ah-shucks country boy pitted against a villainous illegal German monster, an ice-cold megalomaniac with a burglarious history and a consuming jealousy of the world's hero. Lindbergh versus Hauptmann. The power of light against the power of darkness."

"A street brawl, this trial."

"Nor inappropriately—a sporting event."

"And a nightmare for America. Really. Somewhere in Germany a buffoon with a toothbrush moustache is chortling— See. Look. See how juvenile—how barbaric!—the American civilization is."

"I repeat, Ferb dear, you're speaking nonsense." He sneered. "And this Bruno Hauptmann has a lot in common with Hitler, both products of the German surrender of 1918."

"The crime of the century, indeed."

The "biggest event since the Resurrection," H. L. Mencken's sardonic and nasty label of the trial of Bruno Richard Hauptmann, the sole criminal—the lone vulture—accused in the kidnapping of Little Lindy, Charles A. Lindbergh's twenty-month-year-old son, snatched from his cradle in Hopewell, New Jersey, on a windy March night, while his parents sat talking downstairs. A national search that lasted nearly three years, until a German carpenter from the Bronx, an illegal to our shores, passed a marked ransom bill, and the world swooped down on the thirty-five-year-old man. The nation breathed in, thankful that our greatest hero might find resolution.

Now, starting on January 3, 1935, the murder trial in Flemington, New Jersey, a place no one willingly traveled to, especially in the dead of an icy winter, attracted the world's attention. Hundreds of thousands of curious souls, fired up by incendiary Hearst presses and the rabid radio commentators like Walter Winchell, who blathered every Sunday night on WABC about the kraut bastard who took away an angel from America's legitimate hero—the man who flew the Atlantic solo and came home to parades and fame he didn't want. Bruno Hauptmann, assumed guilty until announced guilty.

Even Aleck Woollcott, sitting next to me now, his finger gripping a generous portion of Brown Betty, had his Sunday radio program, "The Town Crier," introduced by a clanging bell. "Hear ye! Hear ye!" Then: "This is Woollcott speaking"—even Aleck told the world that Bruno should be burned in the chair. His grim radio broadcast was followed by the inanity of Burns and Allen and Eddie Cantor. *The Lux Radio Theater.*

"So here we wait," I went on in a low voice. "Madame Defarge knitting the days away."

Aleck dismissed my comments with a shrug. "Our lives for the next few weeks paid for by the august *New York Times*, which covers its daily front page with all the minutia of the trial—and our take on it, the celebrity commentators, mine, yours, and even novelist Kathleen Norris and her daily diary. Look at her."

I faced the doorway. Kathleen Norris had, in fact, just walked in and stood in the entrance, her small frame lost in an oversized wool coat, her head encased in a blue felt cap. The novelist wore a surprised look, her chin tilted upward, as though she'd just smelled something offensive. She nodded at Aleck, then at me, as Aleck waved her over. "I adore her, of course," Aleck began, "but never read her prose. I have enough indigestion."

Kathleen Norris turned to leave, probably choosing to dine at the Union Hotel Café across from the courthouse. The Union Hotel, the one hotel in town, the residence of everyone, including the jurors housed on the fourth floor. As she moved, she bumped into Damon Runyon who lolled against a doorframe, cigarette bobbing in the corner of his mouth, his fedora tucked under an armpit. He glanced back over his shoulder at the departing novelist and shook his head, an amused smile on his face.

A tall, lanky man, with his wiry frame and blue-black beard stubble, a weathered leathery face, and dark shadows under his eyes, he squinted into the large basement, his eyes sliding off my face and landing on the cherubic Aleck Woollcott. His eyes danced as Aleck, an old acquaintance, grunted at him. But Runyon mouthed one word, which he repeated: "Circus." With that, he shrugged his shoulders and swiveled away, disappearing out the door, headed up the wooden steps leading to the street.

I frowned at Aleck. "Our fellow scribbler Runyon is having no fun at this crucifixion."

"What makes you say that?"

"I can read lips. He thinks this…this spectacle—this whole trial, in fact—is a circus. A mockery of American law."

Aleck harrumphed. "He said no such thing. Lord, you are fanciful, dear Ferb."

I leaned in. "I also heard him earlier in the lobby of the Union Hotel as he watched a gaggle of Hearst reporters scurrying about, their voices filled with glee, some of them humming that street chant. 'Kill Bruno!' He said quite clearly, though to no one in particular, 'Why don't we give the man a fair trial? I'm watching the end of American civilization.' A position, dear Aleck, I'm beginning to agree with."

Aleck held up his hand in front of my face. "Prattle on what you will, but this trial has all the markings of a Greek tragedy—the war-ruined, aloof Hun pitted against the down-home blond Greek god. It's positively…well, riveting."

"It is that, I grant you. But we seem to be forgetting a dead child and another life on the line. If we believe in American justice—"

But Aleck broke in, looking around him, taking in the festive diners. "I have to get on. Walk me to the depot, Ferb. Manhattan is still two hours away from this snow-crusted burg."

"You're coming back tonight?"

"Of course. I don't want to miss a second of this drama."

"You dropping off your copy at the *Times*?"

"And yours as well. Your faithful messenger."

I smiled. "An Olympic runner, that's what you are, dear Aleck."

He grunted. "I never run anywhere."

"I know."

"That's why Ford perfected the car and Bell the phone."

"And Carnegie Deli the pastrami and rye."

Like it was a contented pet, he tapped his Buddha belly under the buttoned sports jacket. "Another blessing from a god who believes in taste buds."

I stood and waited for Aleck to shift his body, draping the long black Chesterfield coat over his shoulders like the stupendous cape he favored at Broadway openings, positioning the huge black hat with the wide brim on his head, checking to see whether the ivory cigarette-holder he so favored was in his breast pocket. He tapped an ivory-head cane on the floor.

Outside, we paused on the sidewalk, a wisp of ice crystals swirling in the cold air, clinging to the newly erected telegraph poles. "More snow coming," Aleck whispered, glancing up into the white sky. I pulled my fur collar tight around my neck, shivered, and moved through the folks lingering on the sidewalk. Madness, all of it. Shuffling swarms of excited people, oblivious of the chill in the air, leaned into one another, gossiping, chatting, glancing toward the Hunterdon County Courthouse that dominated the small-town street. Stolid, impervious, that courthouse with its four Doric columns and its colonial cupola, with its seven ancient stone steps, struck me as a humble place to settle picayune disputes among local farmers—yes, his cow did wander into my hayfield—and not the focus of international attention. Surrounded by hundreds of telegraph wires—the Postal Telegraph and Cable Company had fifty operators for its thirty-six wires—messages sent out into the world, three million words a day, I was told—the building seemed to glow from the sleet that pelted it.

Main Street and Court Street swelled with people who moved back and forth, shrouded in winter coats and scarves and furs. Reporters shuttled back and forth out of Hewitt's Cut-Rate Drug Store, many of them groggy from sleeping overnight in their cars because no rooms were available at any price now. Lines of cars, bumper to bumper, idling, puffing smoke into the frozen air, reporters leaning against doors, pads at the ready. Overhead wires were strung from rooftop to rooftop, telegraph and telephone, snaked like the head of Medusa into the upper room of the courthouse where pine boards held operators, shoulder to shoulder, *tap tap tap* night and day. A constant hum in the street, a tremor of excitement that seemed on the edge of erupting into full-blown hysteria. Applause—why?—unbridled laughter, recognition—*hey, Joe, you seen the killer?*

A Rolls-Royce the color of apple cider assumed a place before the Union Hotel and a sleek, expensive woman, her face lost in furs and veils, sauntered out, looked around—expecting what? confession, gunfire, screaming?—and then slid again into the backseat, the uniformed chauffeur holding the door and seemingly wondering what to do next. Mrs. Ogden Livingston Mills from New York, holding a tiny Peke. She must have barked an order at the driver because he hurled himself into the driver's seat and pulled away from the curb. Every day she arrived, a phony subpoena allowing her access to the courtroom.

Aleck and I shuffled past the crowds, with Aleck huffing and puffing. "Lord, it's only juror selection. Not," he stressed, "the big event."

I'd been in Flemington for two days now, ensconced in a tiny room in the Union Hotel, fifty jam-packed rooms, in a room adjacent to that of Aleck, down the hall from Kathleen Norris, in shouting distance of journalists Walter Winchell and Sheila Graham. And so many others, like Raoul de Roussy de Sales from *Paris-Soir*. Lionel Shortt from the *London Daily Mail.* Others were forced to find housing in Trenton, twenty miles away. Hearst's darling, Adela Rogers St. Johns, had secured rooms in a nearby house. Above me were the six rooms where the twelve jurors, eight men and four women, would sleep, though certainly they could hear the beer-woozy blast of journalists and rabble-rousers throughout the night in the tavern below them. They'd eat in the dining room, a curtain separating them from the rowdy press.

Already I balked at the dismal assignment. The *New York Times* scoffed at the frenzy the Lindbergh kidnapping engendered in tabloids like the *New York Mirror*, yet, oddly, planned a daily transcription of the trial. They ran a front-page section called "The Kidnapping Situation," a chronicle of all the kidnappings in America, the so-called "snatch game" that plagued the rich and influential. And, of course, the *Times* commissioned literate commentary from the likes of Aleck Woollcott, Kathleen Norris and—well, me. "Your eye for detail," the editor had wooed me. "The human touch. Stories from the sidewalk."

Well, the human touch these days was, I feared, a little heavyhanded, given the opening days of the trial. This was Circus Maximus, this was Chinese water torture, this was—and I refuse hyperbole here—a paralysis of integrity. At night the poolroom of the Union Hotel, converted into Nellie's Taproom, became a tavern where the rum and local applejack flowed, with the boisterous celebrations of the hundreds of reporters drinking until they passed out. And always—from somewhere in the street—the drunken slobber of a midnight reveler's vaulted scream, "Kill Hauptmann. Die."

A Roman orgy of utter sensation.

Not that Aleck, a man who relished the cruel barb or the sentimental hymn to a dead child, agreed with me.

I'd already told myself I'd stay a few days, perhaps listen to the initial testimony of Colonel Lindbergh, hear what Bruno Hauptmann said in his own defense, and then leave, head back into Manhattan. My editors balked at that, to be sure, but I was not going to be a part of such a travesty. *Isn't this trial so divine, my dear? Positively riveting. Divine, yes, divine! Is that a new mink, darling?* No—not for me, such twaddle. Guilty or not, Bruno Richard Hauptmann was paraded about like a drugged circus animal, the oily specimen in the jar, this startlingly handsome man in the charcoal-gray double-breasted suit, immaculate, his Windsor tie neatly knotted.

At the livery office attached to the local post office—a closet-sized room where drivers drank coffee, did crossword puzzles, dozed, and spat into spittoons—Aleck signaled to a man sitting just inside the door, who immediately scurried toward him. As with other newspapers and radio stations, the *Times* had hired drivers and automobiles to shuttle its writers and editors back and forth to the city—and, as well, to assist writers doing local color research in the provinces, perhaps day-trips to nearby Hopewell, where the baby was snatched, to the Next Day Hill mansion in Englewood, where Anne Morrow Lindbergh's family lived. To anywhere that might yield a gold nugget of throwaway information that would titillate the readership. Long, sleek cars at the ready, with drivers ready to do our bidding.

"Sir." An old man with sloppy Burnside whiskers and a balding red head nodded at Aleck as he buttoned his coat.

"Ah, Willie," Aleck acknowledged him. "Ready to wing my chariot northward?"

Willie grimaced, tilted his head to the side. "Don't know about no chariot, but the time in Manhattan is two hours from now, sure as I'm driving."

Willie Nolan—"William, my name, but my mother called me Willie"—was one of two full-time drivers provided to us, neither of whom pleased me, although Willie was decidedly more offensive than the other, a slick but taciturn young man named Marcus Wood, largely because Willie was a garrulous, crusty man, hopelessly opinionated and certain his shared ignorance need not be questioned. A tiny, twig-like man, perhaps sixty, maybe older, sun-baked sagging leathery skin despite the deep of winter, Willie looked like someone more at home in faded dungarees, with pitchfork and a sprig of alfalfa lodged between his two front teeth, both of which were sadly buck and cliffhanger prominent.

Dressed now in an oversized livery uniform, shiny gold buttons against a navy-blue blazer, a look doubtless mandated by whatever firm the *Times* employed for us, Willie had told us when we first met him that he was a local—"Spent years at a chicken farm a stone's throw away"—hired for the duration of the trial and happy with the ready salary. "Still a depression on the land, you know." But he was bothered by the multitude of ungracious visitors who clogged the back roads and spilled out of the rooming houses and spare bedrooms of the townspeople. "Everything in town filled up, five bucks a night to sleep on a pool table." Then he added, "For me, money for tobacco." A cloud of smoke from a stub of a Camel lodged in his mouth circled his pale face.

Aleck tucked himself into the backseat of the Buick town car. Willie spread a blanket over Aleck's lap, an unnecessary act although Aleck's eyes brightened as though he'd been named prince regent for the Jersey shore.

"I'll be back later tonight," he told me as Willie slipped into the driver's seat. A sickly grin. "Don't wait up for me."

"I'm certain the angry crowd with torches will alert me to your return."

Willie switched on the ignition but glanced back at me, winked. Something I ignored, of course, the foolish old geezer. The other day, rounding us up in Manhattan, he'd informed us that he'd been instructed to keep his mouth shut, not to discuss the upcoming trial, simply to chauffeur us as needed—and immediately he delivered an oration on injustice and American heroism and the fate of an America that allowed such miscreants as Bruno Richard Hauptmann to sneak into our country illegally—and then snatch blond, curly-haired Lindy Jr. from his nighttime cradle. Aleck encouraged him, though I frowned my disapproval—ignored, to be sure. Worse, as we approached Flemington, he sang the radio hit that was popular right after the baby was taken:

*Who stole the Lindbergh baby?*
*Was it you? Was it you?*
*After he crossed the ocean wide,*
*Was that the way to show your pride?*
*Was it you? Was it you? Was it you?*

Then he glanced at us in the rearview mirror. "Sometimes I fall asleep with that melody beating in my head."

"Touching," Aleck had commented.

"Perhaps you should see someone," I'd jibed, and Aleck shot me a look.

So Aleck would be hearing his unending spiel for two hours, I guessed, and I smiled as I headed back to the Union Hotel. Aleck, himself a gossipy chatterbox, lived to break into any conversation and introduce his own topic and then exhaust it. Filling the entire backseat of that expensive car, he would be beet-red and tongue-tied in his efforts to shush the driver who luckily and expertly never took his eyes off the road.

As I turned away, I mumbled to myself, "Let the hanging begin."

At that moment, strutting past the livery depot, his face tilted into the neck of his assistant, Walter Winchell paused. "What?"

"I wasn't talking to you," I told him.

Winchell scrunched his eyes in his small bony face. "Be careful what you say, Miss Ferber. Words can boomerang back and hurt you."

"I know how to use words, Mr. Winchell."

His face flushed. "As do I."

"But my words don't set people on fire."

He paused for a second, glared at me, and turned away. But he muttered something to his assistant who did look back, eyes hard and cold, and I knew I'd added my name to Winchell's celebrated blacklist.

# Chapter Two

Resting in my small room, jotting notes for a column, I stared out the window into the back parking lot. A grove of skeletal trees, a parking lot, a ramshackle storage hut, and an icy back street of squat dull homes of faded white clapboard and green shutters, a street silent now, not a soul in sight. Late afternoon, restless, purposely avoiding the courthouse where jury selection was going on, I walked downstairs through the lobby, still teeming with people, mostly a band of Hearst reporters all talking over one another.

Hearst supposedly had sent a squadron of over fifty reporters and photographers and telegraphers to cover a trial he planned to feature for months. His bureau chief, Eddie Mahar, was standing next to Damon Runyon, the Hearst factotum jabbing Runyon in the chest. "This Bruno guy looks like the new guy over in Germany, the one they call Der Fürher, that Hitler, both corporals in the war, no?" Runyon, stepping away, snarled, "I think we should keep an open mind." Mahar scoffed, muttering, "Nazi monster. I got proof this Bruno praised Hitler to his friends."

Hearst, of course, had already announced in editorials and on front-page spreads that Hauptmann was guilty—everyone knew that. Nevertheless, he had enticed Hauptmann's wife, Anna, impoverished and homeless and in despair, to let him pay a twenty-five-grand retainer for the defense, hiring Edward Reilly, the bombastic Bull of Brooklyn, who bragged that he had a photograph of Lindbergh on his desk but insisted he have exclusive access to her. I found that tidbit a little disconcerting—guilty, guilty, but let me pay for everything…so long as I have rights to whatever salacious story I can extract from the trial.

Anna, staying in Mrs. Opdike's rooming house with her little boy, Bubi, was guarded by a slew of female reporters, including a pesky Dorothy Kilgallen, allowing only the *New York Journal* access to Anna. Kilgallen, twenty-one and dressed like a little girl in a pinafore, had stopped me in the lobby two days ago and gushed, "I loved *Imitation of Life*." When I told her that Fannie Hurst wrote that potboiler, she blanched and walked away.

I sighed. A long trial, I knew, and deep in my marrow I knew the earth had tilted on its axis. Bruno Hauptmann might well be a horrible murderer, but he needed his day in court. This couldn't be good.

As I listened to Eddie Mahar and Damon Runyon spat, Walter Winchell, that tiny squirrel of a man, bustled into the lobby, demanding an answer from a housemaid who was trying to avoid him. She looked near tears. Dapper in a three-piece black houndstooth suit, his black-band fedora tipped to the side, he hammered at the young woman about some nonsense.

As I walked by, he glowered at me. In the dining room, late afternoon, only a few stragglers occupied the tables, hard-bitten reporters jotting into pads. A middle-aged couple, looking like accidental visitors to the hotel, stared vacantly out the front window, neither speaking. A scraggly man in an Associated Press cap was talking to a *New York Daily News* stringer, lecturing him, it seemed. The young man, belligerently indifferent, kept trying to get away, tapping the pocket watch conspicuously displayed in his right hand.

I selected a small table by the front window and watched as the waitress took her time noticing me. She'd been eavesdropping on the conversation of the two reporters. I ordered a cup of tea with a slice of lemon, as well as a slice of the Hopewell chocolate cream pie—as recommended and highlighted in capital letters on the black chalkboard by the entrance. Other tasteless menu items included lamb chops Jafie—named for Dr. John Condon and the nickname he employed as an intermediary between Lindbergh and the kidnapper. Baked beans Wilentz—the prosecutor. And for dessert, ice cream sundaes called Lindys. Nice touch, I thought—as tasteful as public intoxication. As I spoke to the young woman, she stared over my shoulder, gazing out the window at the street.

I cleared my throat. "Miss," I began, "could you also...?" I cleared my throat loudly.

She snapped to attention. "Sorry, ma'am." She spoke in a brittle, crackling voice, vaguely British Cockney. "It's easy to be distracted."

She pointed outside where actress Lynn Fontaine was strutting by, dressed in a leopard-skin coat.

"I'm not surprised. Lots of famous people streaming by in this small village, so..."

She interrupted me. "And you're one of them." She grinned, showing a missing side tooth at the back of her smile, an omission that gave her a comical vaudevillian grin, not reassuring. "The manager"—she pointed over her shoulder at a dapper young man in a wide-lapelled shiny suit standing against a counter, fingertips idly grazing the cash register—"he's Horace Tripp and a sweet tyrant of a boss—I mean, he whispered when you walked in that you are Edna Ferber and I said who and he said *Show Boat* and I said you're kidding and he said..."

I broke into her babble: "Yes, I'm that *Show Boat*, poop deck and all."

That confused her and she glanced back toward the street. "It did ring a bell, you know." A tickle at the back of her throat.

"That's comforting, my dear."

She leaned in, the grin wider now. "Name is Annabel Biggs."

"A pleasure."

She perked up. "Is it really? Well, thank you."

I tapped her wrist. "Dear, it's just something people say."

"Oh, I know *that*. But, you know, being here is like being in the center of the universe."

"The trial?"

She nodded vigorously. "It's like…the Old West. Like in a Western. You head here to make your fortune."

I was confused. "You come here to make a fortune? As a waitress?"

A confidential whisper. "A gold mine, this trial."

"For you?"

Again the conspiratorial glance out into the street. "Especially for me." She swirled around, an awkward pirouette.

"And why is that?"

A loud celebratory voice. "The world is my oyster."

That made no sense to me. "What?" I stared into her eager face. "What?"

Again the loud, insistent voice, though she glanced back at the manager. "Things happening."

"You have a delightful accent," I lied.

That gave her pause. "Born in England, as you can tell." A high cackle, forced. "But I've been in Chicago the last few years, this job, that job. Last job at the Palmer House, all lah-di-dah, that place. Grubbing about." Then her hand shot out to take in the room. "This job. The hotel put out a call for workers and—here I am."

"You wanted to come here?"

A moment's hesitation. "Of course. I mean, the Lindbergh kidnapping. I read every word in the papers. Listen to Winchell on the radio. Everybody's talking about it. The craziest thing in the world, this story." Another pause as she lowered her voice. "I'm…like part of the story."

"What does that mean?"

"Let's just say that I know a thing or two, ma'am." A silly smile.

A woman, I considered, who wanted to be a part of the story—a gossip, perhaps. Fodder for the letters sent back to England.

"And what is that?"

She paused.

"Things." Another hearty laugh, but she stopped abruptly.

I probed. "You like being in Flemington? This sensational trial. The Lindbergh baby."

She drew in her breath, but then her voice trembled. "Things." The word swallowed. "I know things." The slapdash grin of someone bubbling over with a secret she dared not reveal.

I was confused. What were we talking about? "Obviously, you follow the case, Annabel Biggs."

For a second she wore the expression of the town gossip who can't contain her babble, but immediately regrets it. She pulled back, a little nervous. "This is the thick of things here."

"But you said..."

"I'll get you your tea." She backed away. "And that Hopewell pie."

She stopped a few feet away from me, stared back as though I'd violated some privacy, the look on her face baffling: a mixture of fear and elation—a child tempted to reveal something that could get her into trouble. But what?

A quirky-looking woman, this Annabel Biggs, tallish, perhaps five-foot ten or so, big-boned, broad shoulders made more dramatic with obvious shoulder pads under her uniform. Bobbed ink-black hair too cheaply dyed and styled in some imitation of a silent film star, a smear of bright red lipstick on a full, fleshy mouth. Her small dart-like eyes set far apart in an expansive face, but eyes that flashed, intense and searching. A woman not beautiful at first glance, I realized, but somehow eye-catching, the pieces coming together so that she drew your stare. You found yourself marveling at her...I guess the word is *brio*. A life pulse, a charged wire.

Here was a woman who understood her physical failings—her body almost mannish and clumsy, her large hands with bony fingers—a woman whose native and feminine intuition grasped how to translate herself into someone who could haunt you, mesmerize. A young woman who probably intoxicated some men—and repelled others—but knew that some men savored the thrill. Early thirties perhaps, a woman confident, a tad arrogant, and a whole lot sensuous. She moved briskly across the room, disappearing into the kitchen.

Annabel Biggs obviously intrigued me.

As my eyes followed her back into the kitchen, I noticed that the restaurant manager watched her retreating back, a sliver of a smile on his face. He had a droopy-eyed look, as though he'd just awakened from a catnap—his shoulders sloped in the insolent posture of a Parisian gigolo. His lips twitched. A roué, I considered, but a shabby one. I'd seen his ilk in France during the years after the war, and never liked what I saw.

He snapped his fingers and three waiters across the room scurried into the kitchen. He caught me watching him—what was the harsh look on my face?—and rushed to my table.

"Is everything all right, Miss Ferber?" A bow. "Horace Tripp at your service."

"Of course." I stared up into his eager face.

"Is Annabel treating you right?"

I nodded. "A lovely accent, that girl's. A surprise in this out-of-the-way American town."

"Cockney, ma'am."

"I know."

He looked behind him. "My wife is British as well."

"Another Cockney lass?"

"Ah, no. London." He smiled. "Her father was a publican and..." he waved a hand in the air..."without Annabel's street-monger howl."

"That's not very nice."

He bowed. "A little joke, Miss Ferber. Annabel is aware of my...teasing."

"I'll bet."

Annabel returned with my tea and pie, shyly stepping around Horace Tripp. For a moment she twisted her head, dumbly flirtatious, and color rose in his neck, though a hint of a smile appeared.

"Horace," she admonished, "didn't I hear your wife calling you?" These last words came out harshly, clipped, and the redness in his neck worsened.

Two waitresses, stepping from the kitchen with trays of glasses, stopped to watch. Horace waved toward them, then nodded back at me. One woman's head shifted from Horace to Annabel, though the plump one looked confused. "My wife, Martha." The tall slender woman with the blond Clara Bow curls glowered. "And Peggy."

"One happy family."

He looked to see whether I was serious. But I noticed the woman on the left—the wife, Martha—kept frowning as her gaze moved from her husband to Annabel, who relished the moment. Horace, suddenly flustered, bowed again, and stepped away. But as he scurried by the two women, marching into the kitchen, I found myself watching, not his wife's shrewish face, but that of the other waitress, Peggy. Raw jealousy there, a mix of anger and resentment. And I understood in some atavistic way that Horace was somehow involved with Peggy, a woman perhaps ten years his senior. That momentary flicker of a glance—it told the story.

Yet Martha's harsh eye was focused on Annabel, as though she were the Jezebel in the room. "I warned you," Martha hissed into his ear as he passed by her.

He disappeared into the kitchen, past Martha standing straight, arms tucked into her chest. Next to her, rocking from one foot to the other, Peggy did her best to look bored with it all.

Ah, I thought, amused—a kitchen soap opera, spitfire intrigue among the Jersey hash slingers.

But my attention shifted back to the street as the babel of raised voices drifted into the room. A gust of wind blew a cloud of thin snow against the window. On the sidewalk, huddled against the cold, a group of men faced the street. Fists raised, their dark faces scrunched in anger, in unison they roared, "Kill Hauptmann. Kill Hauptmann."

I started, so abrupt and fierce the shouting, so bone-marrow ugly. I strained my neck to see what they were looking at, but at first I saw nothing. From behind me Horace reappeared and with the waitresses peered across an empty table. A few of the reporters stood, and one, laughing, deliberately echoed, "Kill the baby killer. Burn the German."

Nearby a jittery young man with huckleberry freckles and a cowlick grabbed a pad and jotted down something. I'd met him earlier in the lobby as he'd accosted Aleck Woolcott. "My name is Joshua Flagg. From out of the Indianapolis Hearst syndicate," he'd said. "Not a reporter but an observer." That made no sense. Like a show-off child, he introduced himself to everyone there, one after the other, though I noticed he avoided the large contingent of seasoned New York and New Jersey reporters from the Hearst newspapers. Now, like a neighborhood boy thrilled to be invited to a party, he rapped on the icy window and yelled to the men, "Kill Hauptmann." He stood a few feet away from me, almost blocking my view.

"Sir," I admonished, "you're a journalist." Then I added, "Or an observer. Whatever that breed of reporter is."

He ignored me, a macabre smile on his face.

Horace Tripp spoke over my objection. "I fought against the Germans in the Great War, Miss Ferber. American infantry."

"And what has that to do with Hauptmann?"

He waited a heartbeat. "Well, he fought for the Kaiser."

"So what?"

He was ready to say something, but at the moment there was whooping in the street. I pressed my face against the ice-cold window. Joshua Flagg, swaying back and forth, sucked in his breath.

Charles A. Lindbergh was crossing the street, flanked by Colonel Norman Schwarzkopf and Colonel Henry Breckinridge, two of his advisors in the long investigation. Schwarzkopf headed the New Jersey State Police. Breckinridge was a Manhattan attorney, a close friend of Lindbergh. Behind them, in striking military precision, walked four state troopers, men in that curious New Jersey uniform of campaign hats, robin's-egg blue field jackets, and flaring riding breeches with the orange piping down each leg, a Prussian look that took me back to my days wandering through the last breath of the Austria-Hungarian Empire, all that braid and pomp and authority.

Colonel Lindbergh strode in front, his legs moving quickly, obviously the leader, and he wore no winter coat, no hat. Rather, he wore a charcoal double-breasted suit, tightly buttoned, the icy wind rustling his blond, boyish hair. He walked so rapidly the other men struggled to keep up, although Schwarzkopf kept leaning into his side, as though confiding something. I'd never seen Lindbergh before, other than in Pathé newsreels in theaters or pictured on the front page of newspapers, especially after his magnificent 1927 solo transatlantic flight from New York to Paris, piloting *The Spirit of St. Louis* into Le Bourget Airport.

I recalled the *Times'* headline: LINDY DOES IT! The new American hero, glorified, with the emperor's middle name: Augustus. American royalyy, writ large. When he married the daughter of one of the wealthiest men in the world, Ambassador Dwight Morrow's daughter, Anne, the world applauded the man called Slim or Plucky. The Scott and Zelda Fitzgerald of breathtaking aviation, the splendid couple, blond and beautiful. A couple that hid from the world, demanding privacy they could never have. A world that came crashing down when their little baby was snatched from his cradle one windy night.

So here he was, a brisk walker, long strides, a tall, lanky man, slight of frame. I studied his face. A farm boy, I considered: that Midwestern Scandinavian fairness, so pale in comparison to Bruno Hauptmann, the man who was his dark shadow—the brooding German with the deep-set blue eyes that never seemed to blink. A morality tale, this. Black and white, good and evil, the forces of light and the forces of darkness. A miracle play, a mystery play from the Middle Ages being played out on small-town American soil, the awful conclusion probably written in stone from the moment the police nabbed him on that New York street.

Lindbergh stopped in mid-stride in the middle of the street, and a passing car ground to a halt, waited patiently. Schwarzkopf and Breckinridge looked at each other, the four state troopers standing at attention. Lindbergh's look swept the street and briefly focused on the Union Hotel. I was afraid to move my face from the window. Indifferently, his eyes caught mine and I thought: a hayseed, this brave Minnesotan lad, a barnstormer with wrenches and gadgets and propellers, who had lifted himself off the ground and into misery. His head shifted—a profile of a man who seemed helpless, his chin weak and stiff, but a man also, lamentably, callow. A good man who'd taken the wrong turn on the country lane and hated the sense of loss that quaked within him. Now a shabby man boldly approached him, but before one of the troopers could extend a forbidding arm, Lindbergh closed up his face, a look that demanded distance. An impenetrable mask. So the man, flustered, backed away, his face red.

Stillness in the café.

When I turned to look behind me, Annabel Biggs was laughing quietly to herself. Her eyes danced.

# Chapter Three

That night I barely slept. What bothered me, other than the lumpy mattress and intrusive springs and the babble of drunk reporters down the hall, was that street tableau I'd observed: the conquering hero Lindbergh pausing in the winter street, a statue in place, but, worse, my startled realization that the sculptor had forgotten to fashion a face that was—well, heroic. A boy happy to perform airplane stunts at the country fair, surprised by the rapturous looks of the farm girl from one town over. That Lindbergh—not the heroic figure whose image now evoked such sadness in America. What did it all mean? I wondered.

But I supposed what also rankled was Annabel Biggs' mysterious laugh, calculated and giddy, which followed her cryptic remarks as she served me tea and pie.

Five a.m., an ungodly hour to be sitting up in bed, especially in New Jersey. A vacuum of space and time.

A walk, I convinced myself. Back in Manhattan, snuggled in my penthouse apartment on the Upper East Side, I religiously walked each morning, though not at such an ungodly hour— my purposeful stride up Park Avenue, over to Lexington, down Madison, a mile or more, invigorating, thrilling, the streets waking up, the sanitation trucks washing the streets as the garbage men clanged their buckets. Here, in early-morning Flemington, the world was still frozen, time stopped. Here, in Jersey, the citizens slept and dreamed under homemade quilts. Bruno

Hauptmann slept in his cell down the street in the jail behind the courthouse, guarded by a trooper, the shrill light always on, perpetual sunshine. Maybe not slept—I was told that he paced the night away. Back and forth in the six-by-eight cell. A cot, a toilet, a sink. Slippers. Perhaps, like me, he was haunted by the face of Colonel Lindbergh, the father of The Eaglet. Little Lindy. He paced his narrow cell as he waited to be told he was to die. Chain-smoking. A Bible on his cot.

Gazing out my window that faced a back lot of garbage bins and rusted cars, I shivered. The cold seeped through the sills, whistled against the hiss and shriek of the old cast-iron radiators of the room. Bundled up in my fur coat, I wrapped a scarf around my neck, pulled my mink hat over my hair, and tucked my gloves into my pockets. Tundra or not, I was headed for a walk.

"Cold morning," I mumbled to myself as I walked downstairs into the lobby. Flemington would always be one long cold morning for me—a frozen tableau of hoary ice and snow showers and the awful stillness on the landscape. An empty street at that time of day, but within hours impassable, clogged with cars puffing out exhaust, people streaming past, frantic, loud, anxious. The specter of death and judgment covered the trees like a fog. Cold morning: this was a town that could never get warm again.

The overheated lobby was deserted, not even the night clerk in sight. Perhaps he was napping on a cot behind the reception counter. Perhaps Bert Pednick, the owner, believed no one should be up at that hour. As I buttoned my coat, tightening the scarf, preparing to slip on my gloves, I heard a raspy sound from one of the overstuffed chairs in the small area of old couches and coffee tables and magazine racks by the front door. At first I saw no one, but that gurgle erupted again, a man sloppily clearing his throat. The acrid scent of tobacco from a cigar, raw and pungent, as a thin cloud wafted into sight. I stepped closer, and the man lost in the big chair yelped and dropped his cigar, then rushed to retrieve it.

"Christ, Miss Ferber," he bellowed, "you do like to scare a man."

"Ah, flattery so early in the morning." I smiled.

He didn't.

He banged the side of his head. "I must have dozed off."

"Mr. Flagg, I believe?"

He stood and bowed. "Of course, Joshua Flagg. The one and only. I introduced myself yesterday."

"Yes, in fact, you introduced yourself to everyone in the lobby."

He looked around, sheepish. "Well, not everyone." He rubbed his eyes with the backs of his hands.

"What does that mean, sir?"

He whispered, "I'm trying to keep a low profile."

"That's hard to believe." To his puzzled look, I added, "You hurl your name into everyone's conversations."

He ignored that. "Why are you up so early?" He waved a hand across the empty lobby.

"I might just as well ask you the same question. Why are you in the lobby at five a.m., other than trying to commit arson on this old rickety structure?"

He glanced at the smoldering cigar resting precariously on the edge of an ashtray. Now he reached for it, tucked it into the corner of his mouth. "I never sleep. I don't like to sleep. You *miss* things."

"I assume your boss, William Randolph Hearst, demands constant vigilance from his lackeys. After all, this *is* the hour when all the spectacular news takes place."

He squinted. "You're mocking me."

"Yes, I am. But more so the yellow journalism of your syndicate—and leader."

"It's a job." He leaned in confidentially. "I'm on special assignment for the chief."

"What does that mean?"

A tinny voice, which I immediately mistrusted. "I'm Hearst's operative. I'm not one of the fifty or so reporters bustling around here. They got *their* job to do. My job is to…"

"To spy on them?"

He chuckled. "Of course not." A sigh. "Well, maybe a little. But they don't *know* me, that crowd of scribblers. I'm here to catch the story that no one thinks is worth talking about."

"At five in the morning?"

"Well," he grinned, "I *am* talking to Edna Ferber, author of..."

"*Show Boat.*"

Again the foolish grin. "Sooner or later you might have a story to tell me."

"I get paid for my stories."

"Not the ones you want to keep secret."

"And I have secrets you want me to share?"

A long deliberate pause. "You will."

This Joshua Flagg bothered me. At first glance he struck me as a young man, perhaps just in his twenties, with his gangly, slender teenage boy's body, a long drawn face pocked with acne, a red blister on his forehead. A rumpled, out-of-fashion sports jacket, checkered and frayed at the cuffs. The high-school newspaper editor craving the Fourth Estate's wonderful and revolutionary scoop. A simple man, harmless. But as I looked at him, I realized something that jarred me. He was not an eager, albeit nosy, boy— rather, he was much older, maybe even in his thirties. His was a good-looking face, but one that spent too many hours in closed rooms, a worm-whiteness to his cheeks. The deep lines around his weary eyes, the sagging lips, the hard-bitten cynicism in those blue-gray eyes. Suddenly I didn't trust him. My trained nose for news, hammered into me from my days as a nineteen-year-old reporter back in Appleton, Wisconsin, told me something was wrong here. This ferret-like man was up to no good.

"And how do you get on with the other fifty Hearst reporters?" I asked him.

"I don't," he shot back. "I'm not supposed to."

"Perhaps they don't believe you're working for the chief himself."

"They don't." He slapped a grin onto his face.

"Neither do I."

I walked away.

◇◇◇

Outside a blast of cold wind slapped me in the face, and I shuddered. I persisted up Main Street, crossed toward the courthouse and the House of Records, maneuvered my way past Meyer's General Store—with its life-sized cigar-store Indian outside, a carved wooden brave painted a stolid red and black, totally unthreatening—then past Lyman's Barber Shop, Sussel's Haberdashery, then past the quaint post office that also contained the small headquarters for the different livery services that sprang up for the trial. I noticed the long black Buick town car sitting in the parking lot, its windshield covered with an opaque layer of frozen ice slick. Inside the passenger side window, a placard, discreet and with familiar gothic lettering: *New York Times*. Doubtless the feckless driver Willie was in some boardinghouse nearby, most likely talking loudly in his sleep, annoying the other boarders. I assumed someone would eventually and justly smother him with a pillow, maybe the other driver—Marcus Wood, that fashion plate from *Vanity Fair*, who probably spent his nights in local taverns, his fingers running through his Bryl-creemed hair, as he dreamed of becoming the next Valentino.

Quiet, quiet, the morning streets said nothing at all.

Invigorated, feeling better now, my lungs swollen with chilled air, I turned back. It was just a little too cold to be sauntering along. I hurried down a side street, wended my way back, circling behind the county jail, walking alongside the imposing tombstone factory—how ghoulish!—and reached the rear of the Union Hotel. Finally, tired now and ready for a cup of blisteringly hot coffee in the café, I strolled past some untrimmed pale-green juniper hedges and entered the parking lot.

Loud voices assailed me, amplified by the still morning air. I stopped, but saw no one.

A woman's voice blared from the side of a nearby storage shed. Immediately I knew it was Annabel Biggs, that feisty and curious waitress from the café. Her raised voice, thick now with venom, echoed off the metal sides of the shed. "Damn you, Cody Lee."

A man grunted. The sound of spitting. He stepped back from the corner of the shed and came into my line of sight. A faint glow of sunrise silhouetted his large head. A burly man, thick-chested with a bushy moustache and longish hair that peeked out from a woolen pullover hat, he jutted his chin forward, furious. "I don't get you, Annabel. I swear to Christ, I don't get you."

Then Annabel stepped out of the shadows and into the growing morning light, positioning her body inches from the man who towered above her. "I said you gotta stop following me, Cody Lee. I gotta work here, you know." She pointed to the back of the hotel.

"And I ain't got a job to get to?" A voice laced with sarcasm.

"Well, you can haul your truckload of timber to hell, for all I care."

Cody Lee grunted again, swiveled around as if trying to decide what to do. He walked away and rested a hand on a battered pickup truck, a funnel of dark smoke escaping the muffler. I thought he'd open the door and slide in, but he changed his mind, rushing back to Annabel, who faced him belligerently, arms folded over her chest, her face set in a dark frown.

Both were dressed in uniforms. She wore the waitress outfit I saw yesterday, the blue-and-white gingham pinafore with the matching wraparound hatband tucked into her hair. She'd obviously been headed into work but was approached by Cody Lee, himself in a dark brown shirt and blue dungarees, with high work boots. She had draped a light winter coat over her shoulders. He wore a dark brown hooded parka, unbuttoned.

"So this is the brush-off then?" he squeaked out, hurt in his voice.

"I ain't made you no promises, Cody Lee." A trace of delight in her voice. "I got this new job for now. Yeah, we had ourselves a few dances over to Newark, we had fun, but"—she hesitated—"you want something from me you can't have. I *told* you—let's just have fun. I got other things on my mind now."

"Yeah, things."

"Things."

"Yeah, I know," he said in a mocking voice. "Your big plans. You know, Annabel, a little whiskey and you brag about money—big money coming your way. You think I ain't heard you going on about *that*? That's why you're in town."

She looked startled, tilting her head. "I ain't said nothing about that."

"I ain't a fool, Annabel."

"Hey, Cody Lee, we had a few laughs, you and me. Can't you leave it at that?"

A long pause. "No man likes to get dumped."

She pouted. "I ain't dumping you. I'm"—a throaty laugh—"moving on."

"Yeah, moving on to what?"

"I come to America to get rich."

"Yeah, at a time when everybody else is dirt poor and getting poorer."

A shrug of her shoulders. "I got me a map to Easy Street."

"What the hell does that mean?"

She turned away, headed to the back entrance of the hotel, but looked back at him. "Just what I said, Cody Lee. I'm gonna go back to Bradfield in style." She lowered her voice. "And I ain't dragging a guy like you with me. As I say, we had some laughs, you and me. But this girl's got the keys to the kingdom."

"Those letters?"

She jumped, shot back at him. "What about the letters?"

Now a sickly smile from him. "Like I said, when you got a little too much booze in your royal veins, you babble about the letters—or the *magic* letter that opens doors to…to bags of money."

She was furious, storming back at him and punching her fist into his chest, though she immediately rushed away. "Don't you mind about that, Cody Lee Thomas. You just step away from my life now. This trial ain't gonna last forever, and I got me a front row seat—and a salary at the café, to boot. I keep my eye on my future." She flicked a finger at him. "Go back to hillbilly heaven, like over to that tarpaper shack you talk about in the Sourlands hills—or wherever you hail from. Moonshine boy with dirty fingernails."

Suddenly Cody Lee lunged at her, so abrupt a movement that Annabel shrieked. As I watched, he stopped, staring down into her upturned face. He raised his hand and I waited for the slap. But his hand stayed suspended in air, trembling.

Triumphant, Annabel smirked and then, raising her hand in a wide sweep, slapped him across the face. He flinched, fell back.

She started to laugh, a gurgling, dark laugh.

Stunned, Cody Lee teetered, debated what to do, then jumped into the cab of his running pickup, squealing out of the lot, leaving behind a spray of ice and pebbles.

Annabel, immobile, rolled her head side to side and adjusted her waitress cap. She headed into the hotel.

Planted behind a clump of evergreens, witness to the unsettling domestic skirmish, I suddenly realized how cold I was—my cheeks were numb to the touch and my eyes watered. I headed toward the hotel's back entrance, my head swirling with images of that ugly confrontation. Yet as I opened the back door, I sensed movement behind me. Turning quickly, I caught sight of a person sheltered behind a brick wall, the slightest hint of a shoulder, a dark shadow that disappeared immediately. I blinked wildly, focusing—had I imagined someone there? Of course not. Someone had been there, watching, listening, someone who'd probably spotted me trailing after Annabel into the hotel. My heart beat rapidly, fear sweeping through me. I didn't move. I waited. But nothing happened. Not a soul in sight. Hard silence in the cold morning. No one in the deserted parking lot but me, I told myself. But I didn't believe that. I *knew* someone had been there. Watching.

The clerk behind the reception desk looked up as I hurried in, his eyes narrowing. "Ma'am?" A bony young man with plastered-down hair over his forehead, he'd been buttoning his jacket and removing a piece of lint from his lapel. "Ma'am?" he repeated, alarmed that a middle-aged guest was stumbling into the lobby from the back entrance, her cheeks slick with cold.

"N-n-no matter," I stuttered, which of course made no sense, but he wisely turned away, fiddling with the cubbyhole mailboxes behind him, though I noticed a surreptitious glance over his shoulder to check on my level of utter madness.

At that moment a porter snapped open the wide French doors of the café, so I wandered in. Though I smelled roasted coffee, there was no one in sight.

"Hello?" I announced.

The waitress—Peggy, I recalled—peered through the small glass window of the kitchen door, frowned at me, but cracked the door.

"Darling," she said in a warm voice, "we're not open yet. A few minutes."

"Any chance for coffee?" I was shivering.

She looked over her shoulder, said something to someone behind her, and then stepped into the dining room. "Have a seat." A thin but friendly smile. "I can get you a cup of java right now."

I sat by the front window in the seat I'd occupied yesterday, and she placed a cup of coffee before me, then left a small earthenware pitcher of cream and a bowl of sugar cubes next to it. She whispered, "We don't open for a bit, but I got to have my coffee before my shift starts." She chuckled. "I bet the aroma drew you in. Ain't nothing like the pull of coffee."

"It did, indeed." I smiled up into her face. "Thank you."

"Well, you looked chilled to the bone, ma'am."

"I took a walk."

At that moment a clatter of rushed footsteps sounded from the back of the room, and a door at the end of the hall opened quickly. The manager, Horace Tripp, rushed in, his overcoat half off his shoulders, one arm still struggling with a sleeve. A compact man, below average height, he moved with the assured stride of a tall, cocky man. He had the look of a stage-door Johnny, a prominent jawline and flashing eyes—a man who'd whisper sweet nothings into your ear. Now he looked flustered, uncertain, and his eyes drifted from Peggy to me.

He muttered, "I'm late." But he was speaking to no one in particular, though Peggy, glancing back toward the kitchen, nodded at him.

"Miss Ferber, we are not open yet."

"Obviously, you are." I grinned at him, but he shot a look at Peggy.

"The poor dear was numb with cold," she told him.

Horace spoke over her words, ignoring me. "Is Annabel in yet?"

"I'm right here." The door behind him opened and Annabel, running her fingers down the buttons of her uniform as if to check whether any were undone, spoke to his back.

"Where's your wife?" Annabel asked him. "She didn't come with you? We're short-handed today as it is."

He looked at Peggy. "Martha is under the weather."

Annabel grunted. "So she says."

Horace nervously looked at me, then back at her. Then he rattled off a few other names, and Peggy nodded toward the kitchen. "Everybody is straggling today, Horace." His overcoat slung over his arm, Horace walked toward the kitchen door, but he spoke to himself. "It's going to be another long, long day."

Peggy called after him. "Looks like you could use a cup of coffee yourself." The line was surprisingly warm and affectionate, yet somehow a coy plea for attention. He smiled back at her.

"I was outside too long," he explained. "The bucket of bolts I call a car wouldn't turn over this morning."

Annabel sucked in her cheeks and said in a voice so low I could barely make out her words. "Not the only thing he couldn't turn over this morning."

Hearing her, Peggy flushed and she bumped the edge of the table where I sat sipping the steaming coffee, warming my chilled hands around the hot cup.

Ah, I thought, the delicious melodrama continues, act two. *The Kitchen Gods: A Farce*. Adultery in a cold climate.

Annabel rapped her knuckles on my table in bizarre punctuation, then headed to the kitchen. She shook her head and said too loudly, purposely, "Them two. Romeo and Juliet, they ain't." She winked at me.

Sputtering voices drifted out from the kitchen, Annabel's alto rumbling, Horace's voice telling her to pipe down. "*She's* out there." A young waiter I hadn't seen before walked out, a tray of glasses balanced over his head, and managed to place the precarious load deftly on a sideboard. He was startled to see a guest seated in the room Yes, indeed. *She* was undoubtedly out there.

As I finished my coffee, dropping a generous half dollar on the marble-top table, a young boy in knickers and a slough-boy cap rushed in and deposited a stack of newspapers on a table. He spotted me watching him and with an impish grin on his round face, thrust out a paper, executing a little half-step with a flourish. I tipped him a nickel. Standing there, I scanned the headlines of the thin paper, the *Hunterdon County Democrat*. The bold headline caught my attention:

LINDBERGH ARRIVES IN TOWN

And underneath:

*Jury Selection Today*
*Bruno Paces in His Cell.*

A large photograph, center page, showed Colonel Lindbergh stepping out of a Franklin. A pugnacious Colonel Schwarzkopf had his hand on Lindbergh's elbow, a fatherly gesture, protective. Lindbergh was staring to the side, as though surprised by the photographer. His lips were drawn into a thin, disapproving line. Schwarzkopf's eyes—hard, unfriendly marbles—looked into the camera.

But in the upper right corner of the large grainy picture was a tiny inset—Bruno Richard Hauptmann staring into a camera, a mug shot, the size of a postage stamp. A stony expression on his triangular face, the eyes also hard, fierce. A dreadful juxtaposition, the two pictures, looking, indeed, like stamped mail. A postcard sent from the edge of hell.

I tucked the newspaper under my arm and left the café. The lobby was lively with movement now, hustling reporters and guests, a hum of excitement. As I headed to the stairwell, I glanced toward the sitting area. Still nestled into one of the overstuffed side chairs, arms wrapped around his chest, was that annoying scamp, Joshua Flagg, slumped over, asleep. A copy of the *Hunterdon County Democrat* rested on the arm of his chair. I stood there watching him, his chest rising and falling. But he wasn't asleep—that much I knew, because for a second his eyes fluttered, half-open, as he surreptitiously surveyed the room. Most likely he spotted me watching him. Then he tucked his head into his chest, sighed heavily, but I detected a hint of a smile. It had nothing to do with dreaming. He was watching me watch him.

# Chapter Four

The next day, late afternoon, Aleck and I sat in the church basement, the last diners, lingering over coffee and buttery sour cream
cake that Aleck insisted was manna from the gods. He refused to
leave and kept blowing ridiculous kisses to the matronly woman
who ladled out the confection, though she did her best to ignore
the drooling epicure. "Really, Aleck," I chided him, "people will
think you're mad."

"Enviable, that diagnosis. Thus folks stay far away from me."
His stubby fingers stuffed crumbs into his mouth.

"There may be other reasons for that, Aleck."

"Jealousy. A horrible thing, Ferb." He rolled his tongue into
the corner of a lip, retrieving a flake of the crispy pastry. He spoke
with a full mouth. "We sit here while Rome burns."

"And I sit here with you. We should be securing our seats
in the courthouse." I smiled at him. "I do question my own
common sense sometimes."

"My dear, there's nothing common about you."

"Thank you."

He swallowed loudly. "I didn't mean it as a compliment."

"Of course you did. You're simply speaking the truth because
you're dizzy with sugar."

"You can't resist the wisdom I spout at you—gratis, I might
add—because I know my words will appear in the mouth of
one of your dashing heroes. Gaylord Ravenal uttering Aleck
Woollcott *bon mots.*"

I raised my eyebrows and changed the subject. "What happened yesterday? What did I miss?"

I'd spent most of yesterday back in the city arguing with Doubleday. I'd been driven around noon into Manhattan, meeting with my publisher, sleeping at my own apartment, but I'd been squired back to Flemington in time to have lunch with Aleck.

He shrugged. "Jury selection is over, as of this morning. You didn't miss a thing. Opening statements—going on now. Last night Lindbergh himself stepped into the Union Hotel lobby for a minute, his lovely wife, Anne, at his side. The place froze. Anne looked tired, though she smiled at everyone. She has to testify today, this afternoon—maybe. His lawyer Henry Breckinridge was with them. Both disappeared into a back room. Oddly, they were trailed by Walter Winchell, who followed them in. The door closed behind them all, though some hack reporters put ears to the door until shoved away by the clerk. Quite intriguing."

"I don't like Winchell."

"Of course you don't," he said. "He has a radio show, and you don't. People actually read what he writes in his columns."

I ignored that. "And then?"

"Nothing. A half-hour later they all walked out, the Lindberghs slipping into Breckinridge's car, and Winchell retreating to Nellie's Taproom out back to regale lesser souls with his brassy commentary. Strangely, he passed around forbidden copies of the ransom notes, asking opinions on whether they matched samples of Bruno's handwriting, which he also had copies of."

I jostled him. "Aleck, we have to leave this basement. They'll make us pay rent shortly."

He wiped his lips with a napkin, looking longingly at the dessert plate that that held measly crumbs and a slight smear of creamy frosting.

"There was a bit of a flurry early this morning," Aleck continued. "Breakfast at the café was sporadic. No one got what they ordered."

"Lindbergh?"

He shook his head. "No, nothing to do with that. Actually I have few facts, just what the night clerk told me."

I waited. "And?"

"Dear Ferb, you must allow me the dramatic pause."

"Empires rise and fall during your pregnant silences."

He glanced around the room and pointed to a copy of the *Hunterdon County Democrat* on one of the tables. "One of the waitresses who works in the café was strangled by her boyfriend last night."

I caught my breath. "What?"

He leaned over and retrieved a tattered, folded copy of the morning paper. "Perhaps I am the only out-of-towner who peruses this slight rag, filled as it is with dairy production estimates, chicken maladies, and library budgets. There must be something in it, I'm assuming."

I rushed my words. "Aleck, tell me now."

"What the clerk told me—and that was all I heard—was that a young woman got into a brouhaha with her Neanderthal boyfriend, some knock-down-drag-out screaming match right in the café, around six last night, and the argument spilled over into her rooms at the boardinghouse on Blake Street. I gather she was a mouthy broad, dear Ferb, so said the clerk who had no affection for her. But said boyfriend followed her home and, well, strangled her. Her roommate returned from a late shift to find her body just inside the doorway. Dead. As a doornail."

"Tell me…" I stammered, "her name?"

"Edna, why are you getting so het up about this?" But he perused the newspaper and thumbed his fingers on the page. "Here. The bottom of page one, a short squib, easy to ignore."

"Read it to me."

He did, and I trembled. Annabel Biggs had been strangled in her room last night, discovered by a returning roommate, Peggy Crispen, at nine o'clock. Four or five lines, nothing more. Police allege…police believe…police conclude…"Miss Biggs, a new employee at the Union Hotel Café, recently moved here from Chicago where she worked as a waitress at the Palmer House.

Witnesses told police she had a loud confrontation with Cody Lee Thomas, a local man from town. Thomas was picked up at Jeb Stubbin's farm where he lives with his mother and works as a handyman." Thomas now sat in the county jail.

"That's it?" I asked.

Aleck was getting ready to leave. "What knowledge they have, I suppose." He peered at me through his thick eyeglasses, owl-like. "Now don't tell me, dear Ferb, that you *know* these people."

I stammered. "I met her in the café. A loud, annoying woman, cocky, not my cup of tea. And I saw this…this Cody Lee Thomas fighting with her yesterday morning. Early. I was taking a walk."

"Lord, Edna, you're a witness to murder."

"Well, hardly. A fight between lovers."

"Was it something you said to them?"

I ignored that. "Let me read that." I grabbed the paper from him, but the short piece said little else. My eyes swept up the front page: a photograph of Anne and Charles Lindbergh walking with Anne's mother, Mrs. Dwight Morrow, and her younger brother, Dwight Morrow, Jr. The brother looked angry, his hand thrust out, traffic-cop style, at the photographer. A lengthy profile of the young prosecuting attorney, Attorney General David Wilentz, who looked spiffy with slicked-back hair and a broad smile. A short history of the storied Herndon County Courthouse, where the drama was being played out. The brutal death of Annabel Biggs was a random footnote, noted but dismissed.

That rankled.

Aleck nudged me. "Edna, the testimony begins shortly. We have our coveted seats." He withdrew a card from a breast pocket, waved it at me. I noticed it was food-stained, tattered at the corner. He glowed. "Official Pass. Hauptmann Trial. Signed by John H. Curtiss, Sheriff of Hunterdon County." He pointed to a line of boxes at the bottom. An X was checked next to "Press."

"Did you lose yours, dear? These slips of paper are worth their weight in gold."

I scarcely listened to him. "I have something to do, Aleck. You head back into the courtroom. I'll be there shortly."

"Your seat will be taken by—maybe James Cagney. Or Jack Benny or Jack Dempsey. I heard they're all here today."

"They'll stand for a lady."

"I would, too—if I ever chance to meet one." A suppressed belch. "I'll send you a wire when I do."

I hurried to the café, which, at this time of day was filled with folks, every table occupied. A group of men waited to be seated. Standing in the doorway, I searched for a familiar face, but the young waiters rushing about were men I hadn't seen before. I waved, and one approached me, looking irritated.

"A table'll be free shortly, ma'am." He pointed at the waiting men, but didn't look into my face, turning away quickly, headed to the kitchen.

I put my hand out to stop him. "A minute, young man."

He turned back, his voice brusque. "We're very busy."

"I see that. Business as usual."

Perplcxed, he waited. "Yes?"

"May I please speak with the manager, Mr. Horace—" I hesitated. "—Tripp, I believe."

"He's in back."

"I can wait."

But within seconds Horace Tripp flew out of the kitchen, hurled orders as he moved through tables, and approached me. "Miss Ferber?" He bit his lip. "A problem?"

But before I could say anything, the kitchen door swung open, and his wife, Martha, wiping her hands on an apron, joined him, standing so close her shoulder touched his. Her hand reached out and grazed his, though involuntarily he pulled his away. A warning, I thought—she is telling him something.

"I just learned about the sad end of one of your waitresses," I began, watching both of their faces close up. When Horace cleared his throat, ready to say something, Martha cast a sidelong glance at him, then stared directly into my face.

"We've been told by management not to alarm the guests," Horace whispered.

"I'm a guest and I'm already alarmed."

"But why?" Horace wondered. "Did you know…?"

"No, not at all. But we had a brief talk in here, and I…well, I remembered her." I breathed in. "Such a gruesome end. Sad." I waited.

Husband and wife looked at each other. "We only know what the cops told us." Horace's voice was hesitant, scratchy.

"Which is?"

Again the furtive glance, one to the other. Horace stepped closer, and I noticed a bead of sweat on his brow, an imperfection on the nightclub gigolo. But Martha spoke up. "Sorry, Miss Ferber. We don't know much. This Cody Lee Thomas—a man who'd stopped in before, a big man, crude, rough—interrupted her service, though she shrugged him off. They had a brief argument with Annabel finally shoving him away. He made threats—you know how angry people do that." Martha locked eyes with mine. "Men get carried away."

"But what happened?"

Horace glanced around the busy room. "Miss Ferber, I understand you're a reporter looking for a story—and famous and all…"

I was impatient. "Could you please tell me what you know?"

Resigned, he motioned to Martha, and I followed both to a small office. He shrugged, and whispered, "If you insist…"

"Please, sir."

"This is what we know. Cody Lee stormed away. Annabel laughed about it, talked too loudly about it as she talked about *everything*. She…well, she *crowed*—that's the word—crowed that he was a big dummy. But then she went home."

"Where she was strangled."

Martha added, "By Cody Lee Thomas." She grasped Horace's elbow and he looked at her.

"He admitted it?"

She shrugged, her face tightening. She was through with the conversation. "Dunno. I assume so." She started to back away. "We have to…"

"Her roommate found her," Horace went on. A quiver in his voice.

"And she is?"

"You met her, I think. Peggy Crispen. The chubby waitress." This from Martha, who rolled her eyes at Horace, who reddened. "The one who sashays around here."

"May I speak with her?"

Horace bit his upper lip. He cleared his throat. "She didn't come in to work today. The shock, I guess. I mean, you come home and open the door and there is Annabel on the floor. Peggy told me that her neck was twisted...." His words trailed off.

"They were friends?" I asked.

Martha answered. "No, just roommates, forced to room together because every room in Flemington is worth a fortune these days. I don't think they even liked each other."

"Why do you say that?"

Horace shot her a look. "Tales out of school, Martha."

A sarcastic grunt. "You should know." Then, a fake smile directed at me. "Peggy is older than all of us—a decade maybe."

"But I don't understand your interest in all this, Miss Ferber." Horace glanced toward the doorway.

"I'm not certain myself." I offered an anemic smile. "Only that—well, I overheard a bruising spat between Annabel and, I'm assuming, the man they say killed her. Yesterday morning. Early. In the parking lot. I don't know whether to contact the police or..."

Martha broke in, anger in her voice. "A big lug of a guy. Unshaven, a slob. Annabel said he hauls lumber out of South Jersey."

"Well, that does sound like the man I saw."

Horace stepped back. "Then..."

"What did you know about Annabel?" I wasn't ready to leave. "Her family? I know she was British."

They looked back and forth, though Martha frowned. "Not much," Horace said. "We're all new here. Management hired her a few weeks back. I come out of Trenton. She came a day later. Peggy, a week later, don't know much about her either. You know, more staff considering the trial coming up and all." A quick smile. "Then Martha followed me. Newly married, the two of us."

Martha added, "Last summer." She rolled her tongue into the corner of her mouth. "A whirlwind romance, me and Horace." A pause. "None of his secrets shared with me."

Horace hissed, "Martha, for God's sake."

"Romeo," she muttered.

I raised my voice. "But I am curious about something Annabel said to me in the café. Something about her payday— something like that. Like she was expecting some good fortune. Something that she planned for…"

Horace blanched. "She told you *that?*"

I smiled. "A chatty woman."

"Bossy and noisy and loud," interjected Martha, refusing to look penitent when her husband narrowed his eyes at her.

"So you heard it before?"

"She hinted at it—in capital letters," said Martha "She was always hinting about something big coming her way." A smirk. "Then, if pushed, she'd clam up. 'What do you mean?' Said in an exaggerated Cockney grunt. Hey, I'm from England, too. No one talks that way."

"What do you know about her past?"

Horace spoke. "Not much. Her last job was at the Palmer House in Chicago."

"Or so she said." From Martha.

"You doubted that?" I asked.

"She had a lot of stories, that one. And a roving eye." She glanced at her husband. "For weak men with wallets of dollar bills falling out."

Horace had the decency to look embarrassed, this oily Lothario. But his severe face told me the conversation was over. "Perhaps you should talk to the cops," he concluded. "I dunno, Miss Ferber, like pick Cody Lee Thomas out of a lineup or something."

"One last thing, though."

"What?" Martha said, impatient.

"Well, I understand that things have to be business as usual in the café. Yes, I get that. But there seems to be so *little* attention to her murder. That piece in the morning *Democrat* was so...dismissive. A footnote. A woman stopped for jaywalking. Trivial."

"Well," Martha insisted, "she's not the Lindbergh baby, you know." Her British accent became more pronounced as her lips twisted into a snarl. "And she's not exactly Colonel Lindbergh, like an American hero. A big muckamuck."

Her husband added, "And they got the murderer, no? Some rube from the boondocks. A shanty boy."

"No matter, a woman's life..."

"But the matter is over," Horace summed up. "Enough of this. Please." With that he bowed and walked out of the office. Left standing near me, fiddling with a button on her uniform, Martha produced a quizzical smile that led me to believe that the loss of the flirtatious waitress was one less problem she had to deal with concerning her gadabout husband.

# Chapter Five

"Edna dear," Aleck called out as he joined me in the hotel lounge. "You missed a riveting opening of the trial. Whatever is the matter with you?"

"Tell me."

"Well, David Wilentz thundered that Bruno snatched the child, the rung of the ladder breaking, the child smashing its head. Supposition, true, but galvanizing. Then he called Anne Lindbergh to the stand, and the silence in the room was palpable. Even Bruno Hauptmann flicked his rigid head a half-inch to the right. He even tapped his foot, that Bronx alien. She was grace itself, beautiful, dressed in a peach-colored blouse, a black-and-white dotted suit, a small black satin beret. Very Parisian. A blue fox fur off her shoulders. Discreet. Lindbergh himself watched her carefully, on one side Schwarzkopf, the other Breckinridge. Wilentz had her recite the events of March 1, 1932—deciding to stay another day at Hopewell because the baby had a cold, putting him to bed, dressing him in a flannel nightshirt, taking a bath, sitting with her husband who'd returned from the city, the nurse Betty Gow asking if she had the baby, if her husband had the baby. But the baby was gone. When Wilentz finished, defense attorney Reilly realized he'd better tread lightly. 'The defense feels that the grief of Mrs. Lindbergh needs no cross-examination.'" Aleck sighed, seemed on the edge of sobbing. "She was magnificent."

"It must have been unbearable."

"And you missed it, Edna."

"I had something to do."

"More important?"

I deliberated. "As important."

"Impossible, you foolish woman." He pointed a finger at me. "Do you believe in psychics?"

"Of course not."

"I don't believe you. I often picture you sitting alone in your apartment, some witchery chant coming from your gramophone, a shawl draped over your shoulders, a crystal ball before you, as you commune with spirits."

"What is your point, Aleck?"

"I received the strangest note this afternoon. A woman from Hopewell—or at least a farm near Hopewell, but a mile or so from the Lindbergh mansion—she informs me she heard noises the night Little Lindy was kidnapped." He lowered his voice. "She reads cards, she wrote, and a message received said…"

"For God's sake, Aleck."

"But she insists she heard German spoken in a grove of trees."

"And she never told the police this before because…what? She forgot?"

He grunted. "She's visiting her daughter in nearby Raritan. We have an invitation."

"*You* have an invitation. Have fun."

He scrunched up his face. "You must come with me, dear Ferb. Old ladies give me the willies, present company often included."

"Aleck."

"I insist."

"Being imperious is not a good role for you, Aleck. You lack the appropriate gold crown slipping down your forehead."

He burst out laughing. "Proud of yourself, aren't you?"

Aleck insisted we commandeer the town car and dine at the Hawthorne Inn on the outskirts of the township where we'd meet the woman. "I hear great things about the restaurant."

"I don't think the *Times* planned on our scooting around the countryside sampling the local cuisine."

"Local color, dear Ferb. Trials are deadly—at least most of them. I need to spice up my running commentary." A long pause. "Although my column on Anne Lindbergh's grace will move most to tears."

"It'll move *you* to tears, Aleck."

"I do sob at my own gripping prose."

Old Willie was our driver, although he grunted when he was roused from his rooms at Mrs. Olsen's Rooming House. Yet, once behind the wheel as he was tooling out of town into the countryside, he chatted endlessly about the crowds of people streaming into Flemington—the enormous traffic jams as cars inched along. "Save time just to hang the bastard," he concluded.

"You don't believe in a fair trial?" I asked.

"Not when everybody knows what's what."

Aleck was amused. "And what is that?"

"The murder of a baby boy."

"Tell me, Willie," I started, "did you read about the murder of the waitress at the Union Hotel Café?"

"Yep. Heard all about it. It was in the *Democrat.*"

"*Barely* in the *Democrat,*" I snarled.

Willie glanced at me through the rearview mirror. "Your point, ma'am?"

"Annabel Biggs. A woman murdered." My words sharp, hot.

Aleck frowned. "By her boyfriend, I gather."

A long pause as Willie chewed the side of his face. "You know, his ma says he wasn't the one that done it."

I sat up. I touched the back of the driver's seat. "You know him?"

The car slowed. "Not *him*, really. Sort of a big lout, keeps to himself. Folks say he's as dumb as a bucket of rocks. But his mother…she works as a housekeeper on a farm nearby, owner a friend of my brother who lives in Somerset."

"What did she say? Tell me."

He watched me through the rearview mirror. "Well, nothing to me. But my brother tells me his ma was crying and blubbering all last night, says her boy—he's like an overgrown child, that one, and slower than a slug on the mossy side of a tree—he was with her that night."

The news troubled me. "His mother said that? And the police don't believe her?"

A dry chuckle. "What do you think?"

"Did you ever meet Annabel Biggs, Willie?"

"Naw. No reason to."

Aleck was regarding me severely, his eyes popping behind his thick glasses.

"Perhaps his mother is telling the truth," I went on.

Willie was tired of the conversation. "If you say so."

"Well, I don't know, but…"

"A sad woman, that one. I met her a couple times at the general store, lugging groceries back to the farm. A widow, survived a drunk husband and a couple dead children. Burned out of a tarpaper hovel thick in the Sourland Mountains. Back of Lambertville, I hear."

"This Cody Lee Thomas is an only son?"

"The only one that lived." A sigh. "But, as I say, not the swiftest pebble washed up on the beach."

"No matter." I spoke through clenched teeth. "Yes, you've mentioned his stupidity too many times, Willie."

"Can't help a man observing the world around him."

"With compassion, no less."

Aleck glanced at me, a nervous tic in his voice. "What is your point, Edna?"

"Annabel Biggs was up to something larger than a simple misguided romance with a country lout."

Aleck rolled his eyes. "What do you think, Willie?" He inserted a cigarette into his holder and lit it. Smoke filled the backseat.

"Not much. I like to keep my mouth shut most times."

"Yes," I told him, "I've noticed."

◇◇◇

Willie sat in a tavern across from the Hawthorne Inn—"Have myself a cocktail, just one"—while Aleck and I ate supper, a pleasant enough meal made barely tolerable by the presence of Mavis Jones, who, it turned out, should have used her celebrated psychic powers to glean that Aleck and I would discount every word out of her mouth. A fussy old woman with an ancient fur cap pulled over stringy gray curls and a faded Mother Hubbard under a Persian lamb overcoat, she rattled on about the Germanic guttural mumblings she'd heard the night of the kidnapping. "Out on the road what leads to the colonel's mansion."

Of course, she couldn't remember exactly when that was, admitted not knowing a word of German, and, in fact, confessed to living miles and miles from Hopewell—"My sister is a pig slaughterer in the woods"—and—well, would she receive payment for her information? Would Aleck have to use her name? She grinned at him, twinkled her eyes, and mentioned listening to his radio broadcasts when the winds and God allowed enough reception.

Aleck fumed, purposely blowing smoke into her face.

"No, my dear, it would be better if I not mention your name. I believe you already probably have enough humiliation in your life."

"Aleck!" I admonished, but he shrugged me off.

Mavis Jones smiled broadly as though he'd complimented her for her discretion and decency or—God knew what?

"I'll listen again this Sunday," she assured him.

"This is all your fault," I said to Aleck when we got back in the car.

He sighed. "Of course you'd say that."

Aleck's Sunday night half-hour on WOR out of New York City was growing in popularity. Last week he'd interviewed Darius Poor, a crime reporter from the *Daily Mirror*, who'd written about the various mythologies that erupted around the notorious kidnapping. A sprightly, somewhat sardonic, interview obviously caught Mavis Jones' psychic attention. Aleck and Darius made light of the wild rumors surrounding the horrific event, Aleck pooh-poohing three current stories being bandied about: one insisted that the kidnapped baby was *not* Charles Lindbergh, Jr.—in fact, the body was an anonymous child dumped in the bushes to distract the police. That road was a conduit for bootleg liquor, and the syndicate needed to end police searches there. Moreover, the real baby was being raised elsewhere in the vast Republic. Two, that Al Capone and the mythic Purple Gang were instrumental in kidnapping the child. Of course, Capone had publicly offered to help locate the child, should the government choose to release him from prison in Chicago. The authorities scoffed at that. And three, that Lindbergh himself was at the heart of some nefarious dealing because on the night of the kidnapping he was supposed to be in Manhattan addressing the New York University dinner at the Waldorf-Astoria. Instead, he drove back to New Jersey, unexpectedly, forgetting his obligation, in time to be witness to the empty cradle upstairs.

"A maligning of a true American hero," Aleck intoned on air. Darius Poor agreed. "Lunacy in the land."

Of course, that broadcast brought out the loonies and the naysayers and the speculators and—and, well, enter Mavis Jones onto the scene, psychic and hearer of phantom Germanic voices in the wilderness of her scattered mind.

"Your fault..." I repeated to Aleck. "You cracked open the door of the asylum."

Aleck smiled wanly. "I got a good dinner out of the evening."

"What do you think?" I asked Willie, who, I noticed, had been paying attention to our conversation.

"Ma'am, as I say, I keep my mouth shut."

"Yes..."

But he kept talking. "But it seems to me this is only the beginning of the circus."

◇◇◇

That night I sat on the edge of my bed, the radio on, listening to Walter Winchell's radio broadcast. "Good evening, Mr. and

Mrs. America and all the ships at sea…" A clatter of telegraph keys—*tap tap tap*. That signature opening, followed by his staccato voice. Stops and starts, a broken rhythm that gave you a sense of immediacy. Hot off the press, Winchell sitting in your living room inside the Zenith console radio.

In my lap lay a copy of the day's *New York Daily Mirror*, the tabloid rag Winchell wrote for.

Early that day I'd seen the man strutting into the hotel lobby, grabbing the sleeve of the undersheriff, Barry Barrowcliff, as he handed him a note. He threw a sidelong glance at another reporter from the Hearst syndicate and frowned at the Hearst darling, Adela Rogers St. Johns, who was signing an autograph with a flourish. A gaggle of fawners hovered nearby, laughing loudly. At one point Joshua Flagg skirted by him, and Winchell called out to him—"Sir, a minute of your time"—but Flagg kept moving. Winchell leaned on the reception counter, a casual pose as he began a loud screed about his belief that David Wilentz would exact a confession from Bruno Hauptmann on the stand.

So now I listened to Winchell's summation of the day's events of the trial, a rat-a-tat-tat delivery that soon waxed eloquent as he rhapsodized about Anne Lindbergh's testimony, a bathetic encomium to her strength and beauty and resolve. A catch in his throat, he paused so that America could weep with him.

My Lord, I upbraided myself—I am so cynical. What is there about Winchell that so rankled?

He ended with a commentary about the prosecutor David Wilentz, "an advocate for justice," and Edward Reilly, chief defense lawyer, a venerable old jurist, described as a "lackey in the employ of the underbelly of man's reason. Bruno's henchman."

A man with a turn of phrase, that Winchell boy.

I waited as he spoke of little Flemington, of the "hominess" of the old village, of the venerable Union Hotel with its old-fashioned balconies and Victorian gingerbread trim, or the general store that still held a pickle barrel, the life of the average citizen. I waited. Not a single mention of the murder of Annabel Biggs, waitress at the Union Hotel Café. Not a word.

I waited—that poor woman ignored and forgotten so soon. The golden god Lindbergh and demonic monster Hauptmann, the only antagonists in the Greek drama that was playing out against a Jersey backdrop.

I switched off the broadcast, annoyed by his ticker-tape delivery and smart-mouth tone.

I turned to his column in the *Mirror.*

Again, not a word about the murder of Annabel Biggs or the arrest of Cody Lee Thomas.

I lay in bed that night with an indelible image of that waitress—that brash woman filled with mystery, up to some mischief. A woman whose secrets leaked out of her, uncontrolled, dangerous. Perhaps she said something of her scheme, her…pot of gold. Not a woman I could ever like or care to know. Dead now, supposedly at the hands of Cody Lee Thomas, the big, hulking bull of a man who'd towered over her in the parking lot the other morning. I realized I'd have to talk to the police—to tell them what I heard. Not that it mattered—Cody Lee was already under arrest.

But…Annabel Biggs. What about her?

What about her?

Her murder? A life snapped to an end, brutal and raw.

Her life? Her moment?

She needed her justice. I felt it to my marrow.

# Chapter Six

The police station was a squat white clapboard building tucked behind the courthouse, an unremarkable building in need of a coat of paint. A band of light-hearted, jostling reporters loitered on the sidewalk, positioned beneath the windows of the jail. A contingent of Jersey state troopers stood at attention by the front doors, their ornate uniforms making them seem colorful birds of prey. A modest station, I knew, but also the jail where Bruno Richard Hauptmann was housed in back, secure, waiting, pacing his cell, listening daily to the taunts from the passersby outside. "Kill Bruno. Kill the German." That awful chant that erupted every so often, a flash fire of hate that sailed through the crisp January air and through the drafty sills of the station windows.

Inside, disarmed by the sudden quiet, I approached a desk where a dour-looking young man in a wrinkled uniform sat with his legs up, a newspaper draped over his chest. Thick eyeglasses with oversized horned rims had slipped down his nose. A blast of noise from outside broke the eerie silence—a reporter whooping it up—but the man, sitting up, paid it no mind. Nevertheless, I jumped, grabbed at the pearls around my neck—yes, they were still there, my touchstone to sanity—rattled by the awful juxtaposition of street chaos and the tomblike calm within this building.

"Help you, ma'am?"

I identified myself as Edna Ferber. He yawned, and I decided I could not possibly like him, though he showed a fresh-scrubbed innocence in that pale face. "I want to speak to the chief of police."

"The sheriff?" he asked, stroking a thick moustache and running his fingers through his curly hair. "Busy at the courthouse. Can I help you?"

"And you are?"

He sat up, pushed out his chest where a badge identified him as Deputy Hovey Low. "In charge," he added, a smile on his face.

"I'm here about the murder of Annabel Biggs."

For a second he looked baffled, as though I'd broached an unfamiliar subject—and an unworthy one. But then his eyes widened and he nodded behind him. "Got the killer in back."

He started to say something else, but then thought better of it. He flicked his head to a line of hard-backed chairs set against a wall. An old woman sat there, staring at us. Deputy Low frowned at her, and she dropped her eyes into her lap. A skeletal woman wrapped in a thin winter coat, her hands clutching a cloth hat that bore a cluster of paper roses scrunched along the brim. A hat best saved for a summer tea party, albeit one two decades back. Her fleshless face held huge, deep eyes, shadowed.

"Yes, well," I went on, "my visit may not matter, but I feel it is my duty to..." I stumbled. I sensed the eyes of the old woman riveted on me, waiting, waiting. "It's just that I happened to hear a disturbing quarrel of Annabel Biggs in the parking lot behind the Union Hotel the morning of the...the killing...and it was nasty and...the man..." I faltered, unsure of myself. I didn't like to be so rattled—not an image I cultivated in myself, fearsome reporter that I always insisted I was. But—those eyes on me. I shot her a look—she wasn't blinking. "This Annabel was a battler, I think, sort of loud and..." Again, I stopped, unsure.

Deputy Hovey Low reached behind him and removed a sheet from a folder resting on a filing cabinet. He handed it to me, though his fingertips held onto it too long. "This the man you seen?"

Dutifully I nodded. I was looking at a recent mug shot—full-face and profile—of Cody Lee Thomas. That severe face, almost insolent, angry. But also bewildered—at least as he was being booked. I flashed immediately to the much-publicized mug shots of Bruno Richard Hauptmann, that same hard-boiled penetrating stare, almost mesmerizing—but without the bafflement Cody Lee couldn't mask. Hauptmann's innate intelligence demanded you look at him. Poor Cody Lee wondered why anyone would want to. "Yes, that's the man."

"Yeah, we got lots of reports of them two battling it out in public like silly fools. Water and gasoline, them two. Sparks fly. I guess she was a firecracker and he was..." He stopped as he focused on the old woman who was sitting up straight now, her face drawn and still.

"I thought it my duty..."

But Hovey Low was through with me, settling back into a chair and holding out his hand for the mug shots. "Case closed."

"Are you sure?" I asked.

That bothered him. "Yep."

"A confession from Cody Lee?"

"Dumb as an ox, that one." He smirked as he reached for a wad of chewing tobacco. "But no, the man says he ain't done it."

*Ain't done it*: the words echoed in my mind, a curious ungrammatical rhythm that was immediately so dismissive and—wrong.

I wasn't through. "In my brief exchange with Annabel Biggs in the café, she struck me as a woman with"—I paused—"a larger purpose. Cocky, sure of herself, a woman who *planned* something." I stressed the word. "A woman who set her sights on..." Now I stopped, held by the bleak look on Low's face.

He wagged a finger at me. "The girl is dead, ma'am."

"I know that, sir."

"And her killer sits in back." A sickly smile as he worked an unpleasant piece of tobacco into the corner of his mouth. But again he glanced at the old woman who watched me closely. He looked away and frowned. "I'll tell the sheriff you stopped in."

I was dismissed. Irritated, I swiveled, turned back to say something, but Deputy Low had buried his face in the newspaper. He was reading the funny papers, I noticed. The Katzenjammer

Kids. I read over his shoulder. "Gas Buggins." "Dickie Dare" with Cranky Joe. Delightful, I thought. Slapdash buffoons with exclamation points in the balloons over their heads. A childish smile on his face as he moved his lips.

I walked out in the cold morning sunshine and stood on the sidewalk, stared at by attentive state troopers. The spent light bulbs from the photographers' cameras littering the sidewalk popped as folks stepped on them. As I walked into the street, I heard movement behind me.

"Miss Ferber."

The old woman had followed me out of the jail.

In the biting cold air she stood too close to me, her trembling face inches from mine. You saw a pinched woman, a starved barnyard pullet, tiny with so little flesh on her old bones, a caved-in face the color of parchment. Maybe late sixties, with that look of someone who had struggled through a raw, niggling life, the years dropping away, unnoticed, unwanted. I suppose it was her eyes: a washed-out cornflower pale blue, but haunting the ferocity in them belying the resignation the rest of her body communicated. She stood there, silent, one hand moved to her stringy hair and tucking a loose strand under the old-fashioned cloth hat with bunched-up roses. For a moment she shivered, her chin dipping into her chest.

Then, surprisingly, that same hand slowly reached out and grasped my forearm. Though I wore my fur coat, insulated against the cold day, her touch was electric, a bolt that made me gasp.

"Yes?"

"I'm Cora Lee Thomas." A strangled whisper escaped her throat. "Cody Lee's ma." She pointed back to the jail, her fleshless fingertips suspended in the air.

I didn't know what to say, so I said nothing.

"They won't let me see my boy until Sheriff Curtiss returns. I been waiting all morning."

"That's unconscionable."

She squinted at me. "Don't know what that's about, but they promised me."

"You wanted to talk to me?"

She nodded. "I heard you in there." Again, she pointed back to the jail.

"I'm sorry, Mrs. Thomas. I know I spoke against your son, but..."

She broke in, heated. "No, no, don't. You done what you got to do, Miss Ferber. And"—she actually smiled and I noticed a missing tooth that made her look frail—"it was what everyone tells them. Cody Lee and that Annabel woman was like hateful cats tucked under a blanket in a straw basket. Sooner or later the claws come out."

"And yet they saw each other."

She scoffed. "Strange words, them ones. 'Saw each other.' My Cody is a foolish boy—man, of course—but one long given to boyish infatuations. All his life, and him thirty-five next Tuesday. A girl looks at him and he...like melts. This Annabel, she..." One of the reporters monitoring the jail stepped closer, peering at the two of us. A passing car backfired, and someone applauded. Another reporter joined the first, watching me, perhaps hoping for any tidbit of Lindbergh fodder.

"Buy you a cup of coffee at the drug store?" she asked in a low voice.

She pointed to Maynard's Drug Store a few storefronts over. I nodded.

Inside, the soda fountain counter was packed, a few folks swiveling on the stools checking us out. Reporters, mainly, because I recognized one from a Milwaukee news syndicate. He glanced at me, recognizing me, and then at Cora Lee Thomas, whom he didn't. His eyes drifted down her shabby coat, her withered face. He turned away. Cora Lee strode to the back of the drug store, chose a marble-topped ice-cream parlor table by the kitchen door, lost in the shadow from the brick wall, and sat down with her back to the customers. I slid into a chair opposite her. We said nothing as I ordered two coffees, mine with whipped cream, the waitress never removing the pencil tucked into her hair, just nodding and walking away. "Black," Cora Lee yelled after the waitress. "But real hot, please."

"Tell me what you want," I began.

A long sigh that broke at the end. "No one believes my Cody Lee is innocent."

A heartbeat. "And you think I do?"

She smiled thinly. "Yes."

"But why?"

She shrugged. "I heard you talk of Annabel in there. You didn't *like* her."

"But that doesn't mean I don't believe your son killed her. There are hundreds of people I dislike, some I actually despise, but I don't believe they should be murdered." I smiled. "Tempting as it sometimes is for me."

She shook her head back and forth. "You showed up there. The jail. Something bothered you." She drew her lips into a razor-thin line. "He was with me that night, Miss Ferber. And the sheriff won't believe me." She locked eyes with mine. "You will."

"Why?"

"You're not a fool."

"Tell me."

"Let me tell you first about Cody Lee, my boy." She took a deep breath. "A good boy, but always a slow one. A kind boy. Gentle. Trusting."

"What are you telling me?"

"Only that he's the kind what has a heart easily broken. Like he meets a girl and he thinks—well, I'll marry her and we'll have children and..." She threw back her head. "It never works out." Her eyes brightened. "Like some foolish girl who goes to a dance and comes home and dreams of cottages and white picket fences. Well, that's my boy."

"Where are you from?" I wondered about the accent, a mixture of country twang and clipped drawl.

"We come out of the Sourland Mountains, back of Princeton. Tarpaper shack and dirt roads and coyotes and mountain lions. Near to where Colonel Lindbergh built at Hopewell." She clicked her tongue. "Back then you could climb a fir tree and see the roof of his house. Before the tragedy. My husband hauled lumber like Cody Lee does. A little bootlegging, some. But the Depression stunned the land there. A fire one night, real bad. My husband died, my children were long gone then, dying young, except for Cody Lee. Him and me—all that's left. I got me a cousin down here who says an old farm couple need a housekeeper and a handyman." She grinned. "Mother-and-son team, one size fits all."

She stopped talking as the waitress placed two cups of coffee on the table, then backed away.

"Tell me about Annabel Biggs."

For a moment her face closed in, her mouth sagging. "Cody Lee mostly helps out at the farm, keeps the outside humming. Old couple—the Myersons own it, too old to do anything now—so Cody does the lifting, as needed. Winters, like now, like his daddy, he hauls timber up to the mills in Trenton. One night, back down here, outside of town, he stops for a beer at this roadhouse. The Oak Tavern, a speakeasy now legal as all get out. That's where he met this Annabel, fresh to town. She's hired because of the trial. I guess they sort of liked each other, leastwise that's what he told me, but he's a quiet sort, painfully shy around girls, even though he's now thirty-five years old. Two girls in all his life, both fickle, walked away from him and he mooned over them for years."

"Annabel?" I prodded.

"Well, yes, Annabel, she likes him, looking for a guy to take her around—buy stuff. I mean Cody Lee is big and tough-looking, that rough face, but a nice smile and dimples—and kindness women can pick up on right away. Like a puppy that catches your eye, makes you smile."

"They went out?"

"They seen each other a lot for a few weeks, I guess. I mean, I know the little cash he got hauling lumber disappeared at the roadhouse. He'd pick her up in his old pickup and off they'd go."

I sipped my coffee. "You ever meet her?"

"Once. Like when he was taken with her, he brung her to the farm. All the whistles in a mother's head start to go off. A gold-digger where there was no gold to dig. You know what I mean? She struck me as a shifty girl biding her time. Looking for fun and games until she was ready to move on. Her eyes were always looking over her shoulder—at the horizon."

"Why? What did she say to you?"

She thought for a second as she ran her fingertip along the rim of the cup. "It warn't so much *what* she said, Miss Ferber, it was the *way* she was. I don't know how to explain it, but it was like Cody Lee was a play toy, like one of those wooden toys you pull along on a string. Head bobbing, eyes bulging. She liked the dumb attention from him. I seen her teasing but in a mean way. She ain't a nice woman, her with that British accent and all. That was clear to me. It was also clear that she didn't care for him."

I sighed, sipped my coffee. It was cold. "But he fell for her."

"Yeah. Big-time. A lummox, that boy."

"What did you mean by her looking at the horizon?"

"Well, the one time I seen her I asked her why she moved out of Chicago. She said something about being in Flemington for pay dirt."

"Meaning?" Echoes of my own conversation with her in the café bounced in my head.

"Well, at the time I thought she meant because, you know, everybody coming here to make money because of the trial. The hotel adding staff. Like the boys in the street selling souvenirs, like those little wooden ladders that look like the one against the Lindbergh house. Little boys hawking them on corners. That sort of thing. Lots of jobs open in the restaurants and rooming houses. Silver dollars jingling in pockets."

"But that's not your final thought?"

She shook her head. "No, I felt she was up to something. You know how you get a feeling in your gut?"

"I did, too." I tapped my fingers on the table. "This was a woman with a purpose."

She stared into my eyes. "I don't understand."

"Well, frankly, I don't either. My gut, I suppose." Idly, I stirred the coffee with a spoon. "You said Cody Lee is innocent."

Her voice took on force. She leaned in and I smelled her stale breath, dry, a hint of rosewater on her neck. "I told the sheriff, but no one listens to me. Cody Lee and Annabel battled at the café around six that night, so he storms off, but the manager and this other waitress, Peggy, they told the police Annabel was there till seven, her shift over, when she went home. Seven, Miss Ferber."

"So?"

"They *seen* her till that time. So Cody Lee was back at the farmhouse *before* seven, twenty minutes or so before, riled up, yes, but *there*. I remember looking at the grandfather clock in the parlor when he come in, his face red, his neck muscles throbbing, angry as all get out. But I made him some root tea, and the two of us sat in that parlor and listened to the seven o'clock news come on the radio. In fact, we sat there for a couple hours. I remember him chuckling over *Fibber McGee and Molly* until Cody, he—he tunes in Paul Whiteman." Her eyes got moist. "He likes the soft music, he does." At ten we had more tea and some cookies I baked and we turned in. He *never* left the house, Miss Ferber."

"So he couldn't have murdered Annabel."

Her palm slapped the table. "Not 'less he be in two places at one time."

"You told this to the sheriff?"

She nodded rapidly. "And he said it ain't proof. Just me, a mother lying to protect a murderous son."

"No one else saw him?"

"The Myersons are old, asleep in their room on the other side of the farmhouse. No, just us two."

I closed my eyes. "My God."

She waited a moment, then reached out to grab the back of my hand, squeezing it. "Do you believe me, Miss Ferber?"

I said nothing for long time, simply stared back into that lined, horrible face, with unblinking eyes. Finally, tilting back my head, I told her, "Yes, actually, I do."

And I did—all the inklings of something amiss with Annabel Biggs gathered together like iron filings drawn to a magnet, and I knew then that this old woman could not lie to me.

Her eyes teared up and she sat back, her shoulders sagging. "Thank you." She drew in her breath. "My blessed Jesus. At night, in bed, I stare into the darkness and feel—helpless."

"Wait, Mrs. Thomas. I'm not sure what I can do."

She glanced up at the clock over the soda fountain and started. "I have to get back. I have to see Cody Lee. The sheriff..." She stopped. "Miss Ferber, will you come with me?"

I hesitated. "I don't think..."

"Someone besides me, Miss Ferber. My boy needs to see somebody besides me. They gave us a court lawyer but no one else."

I nodded. "Yes, I will."

Again she tapped the back of my wrist. "A blessing from God, you are."

"Yes," I mumbled, "folks who know me are already engraving that on my tombstone."

She took me seriously. "They should."

I drew my tongue into my cheek. "Probably sooner than later. My enemies."

"You have no enemies." Said loudly, simply.

"Of course I do. That's how I know I'm alive."

She eyed me curiously as she dug into the patent-leather purse she'd deposited on the seat. I held up my hand. "Let me," I told her, placing two quarters on the table.

Back at the jail, the sheriff hadn't returned—"Delayed, you know," Deputy Low muttered, then added sarcastically, "There *is* a murder trial going on, you know." But he'd telephoned and told Low to allow Cody Lee's mother a good half hour.

Hovey Low eyed me suspiciously. "But you was just here, lady."

"Observant," I noted. "I like that in an officer of the law."

"So what do *you* want?"

"I'm a friend of Cody Lee's mother." I pointed to the woman who nodded at me. "I'm assuming I can visit as well." I took a stride forward, as though to push past him, and the man, sty-mied, backed up, actually half-bowed at me.

We sat in a small, windowless room, a long table and three chairs, the walls painted a dreary deck green that must have induced immediate confession, the door open so Hovey Low could sit in a hallway chair, tilted up, his feet on the doorjamb, yards away but feigning indifference.

The deputy led Cody Lee in, leg shackles hobbling his steps.

Cody Lee Thomas had an unshaven chin and uncombed hair in need of a trim. Dressed in green prison fatigues, institutional slippers on his stockinged feet, he was an overgrown boy, a heap of a lad dumped into a chair. His eyes alarmed me: dull gray, shadowy, drained of life. Here was a man felled by events he couldn't really grasp, the stolid ox lumbering in a meadow startled by the sudden rainfall. An ungenerous description, I freely admit, but not an unsympathetic one: Cody Lee Thomas was the victim of a malevolent god that spat him out and then assumed he'd graze in a faraway field. He looked like the neighborhood boy you always liked but never left alone with the scissors. He smiled wanly at his mother who made a big show of introducing me.

"Her name is Edna Ferber."

I realized that Cora Lee had no idea who I was, and probably assumed I was a field reporter for one of the New York dailies—which I was, sort of—or a dilettante visitor to the trial, one of the powdered women in furs and diamonds whose drivers tooled up to the Union Hotel, women who did lunch and murder trials for diversion. She'd never heard of me. Now ordinarily I'd be a tad offended—after all, I was the author of *So Big*, which had won the Pulitzer, and I was the fairy-tale godmother of the hugely popular stage musical *Show Boat*—but...so be it...vanity had no place in this awful room.

He mumbled a greeting at me, perplexed as to why his mother had dragged in the middle-aged woman with the three strands of pearls, the careful spit-curl perm, and an ostentatious fur coat that was one season out of style—at least on Madison Avenue.

"She believes that you are innocent," Cora Lee told him.

He grinned at me. "I am."

"I know." My own emphatic words startled me.

His face got cloudy. "How, ma'am?"

That stopped me. "Because I believe your mother cannot lie."

He nodded quickly, agreeing.

A grunt from the hallway, Hovey Low marking time.

"We only have a half hour," I said quickly. "Talk to me about Annabel Biggs."

His eyes softened, his lips trembled, and for a moment he closed his eyes. "I don't know what to say."

"You cared for her?"

He nodded. "Yeah. A lot. I mean, we only went out a bunch of times but we…you know, we laughed a lot. She was *fun*." A heartbeat. "For a while."

"But you fought with her."

He bit his lip. "Yeah, a lot. She was a wild cat, that one. At the end. I mean, out of the blue she said the fun and games was over."

"But why?"

He looked puzzled and scrunched up his face. "You know, it was real strange. She said something like—'The trial is starting and I gotta focus. Got no time for you.'"

"That makes little sense."

He shrugged. "That's all she talked about. The trial. The kidnapping—the murder. That is, when she had a little too much gin at the Oak Tavern, the roadhouse out on Elm Road."

"Tell me what she said."

His hands shook as he lit a cigarette, for a moment watching the smoke rings drift upward. His fingernails were broken, dark, ragged, the fingertips yellowed from nicotine. Surprisingly slender hands on so big a man—and I shuddered, imaging those long graceful fingers around Annabel's neck.

"She said she was here for the trial. A little secretive. I asked her why she left a good-paying job in Chicago—she said it was a fancy-schmancy hotel there—and she winked at me. 'Big money.' So I said, 'How so?' I mean, a job as a waitress is about the same."

"And what did she say?"

Listening closely, her hands resting in her lap, Cora Lee echoed my words, "What did she say?"

"Most times nothing, but then she'd brag about some big payoff. One time she whispered, 'Lindbergh, Lindbergh' like a song you got stuck in your head, but when I asked her what was what, she clammed up. But once she said that blackmail is a tool that gotta be used like a pointed gun. That made no sense."

"Maybe it makes a lot of sense," I said.

He glanced at his mother. "I dunno."

"Annabel Biggs came here for reasons other than generous tips," I added.

Cora Lee looked over my shoulder into the hallway where Hovey Low watched us. "She was up to something."

Cody Lee went on. "She could be loud and noisy and pushy and…and she, you know, liked to bat her eyelids at guys. But it was all a game. I think."

My heart raced. "But talking of Lindbergh? A payoff? But what?"

"Yeah, but she never got to talking about it much. Too much gin and she falls asleep in the pickup." His mouth flew open. "Wait. I remember—laughing, real silly, she said something about letters. A cousin's letters. 'Secrets from the pot at the end of the rainbow.' Her words. Made no sense to me. Strange, no?"

"We ain't gonna ever know," Cora Lee interjected, her voice weary.

I sat back, thought about his words. "But it does confirm my suspicion that she was ready for some windfall she thought she'd get."

Cora Lee spat out, "What she got was being strangled."

His mother spoke the words so quickly that Cody Lee winced, his shoulders sagged.

Looking at him as he sat slumped over, his face wide with confusion, I realized how some woman might find him irresistible. The mooncalf eyes, the wispy hair slipping over a high forehead, the sudden dimples, the sheer bulk of him—the boy in the man's body, but still harboring a child's air of wonder. A seductive, lethal combination, perhaps a very real allure to a pernicious woman like Annabel Biggs, the local boy with the keys to a pickup. Some men were like chocolate sundaes, consumed with gluttonous delight but then forgotten when you left the ice cream parlor. Cody Lee Thomas was the perennial huckleberry boy bringing the cow in at sunset. Annabel, bored, wanted him to take her to the dance.

Hovey Low surprised us, standing in the doorway and rapping impatiently. "Time." He pointed to a wristwatch. "The court lawyer gotta come later. Time."

Cody Lee's mother was in a rush to leave, slipping on her coat and gloves, kissing him on the cheek but turning away quickly. She disappeared into the hallway, but I stood there, flummoxed. I trailed after Hovey Low, watching him lock Cody Lee in a cell after unlocking the leg shackles. He opened the door to let Cora Lee slip out into the main room. Suddenly Hovey touched my sleeve, an impish grin on his face. "Come."

He led me back down the corridor, past Cody Lee's jail cell, where I came face-to-face with two Jersey state troopers sitting on chairs. They didn't look happy to spot Hovey and the confused woman at his elbow.

"Look." Hovey Lee pointed past the indignant troopers.

I found myself staring into a small cell where Bruno Richard Hauptmann stood, looking back at me, his hands gripping the bars of the cell, his face glaring at us, stony and severe. He'd been holding an unlit cigarette through the bars, waiting for a light, but now drew back his arm. The cell was brilliantly lit, perpetual daylight, and I knew the lights were never turned off. He lived under that shrill sunshine. Hovey chatted briefly with a man he identified as Hugo Stockburger. "Speaking German," Hovey told me. "If Bruno says anything in kraut talk, he writes it down." Hugo nodded at us. Hauptmann did, in fact, say something I didn't catch—a low, guttural sound.

He watched me, curious. Our eyes held, and I stared into the narrow, triangular face, that shock of muddy blond hair, neatly parted, slicked back. The high chiseled cheekbones. But what mesmerized me in that awful instant were the deep-set, blue-gray eyes: an awful intelligence there, caginess perhaps, willful and determined, a little cocksure. He was searching for something in my face. A tight, muscular body, sinewy and lithe, he had a raw masculine sensuality. The movement of his arm raised up, grasping the bars, seemed a deliberate calculation. A man who believed he could charm the devil, this one. The hypnotist in prison garb. I caught my breath, stunned by the deadly virility. I pivoted away, bumping into a wall, my hand reaching out to secure myself. I turned to catch Hovey's amused eye, which I deeply resented.

The state troopers grumbled as they stood, stepping in front of the prisoner.

I staggered out, Hovey's stupid laugher following me into the front room. Cora Lee was nowhere in sight.

# Chapter Seven

That afternoon I accompanied Aleck as he made an excursion to Hopewell to survey the Lindbergh homestead. We'd seen the awful pictures of that white home, stark, unfinished against a winter landscape, newsreel renderings that included that preposterous makeshift ladder placed against the side of the house, its top rungs below the window of the baby's nursery—the point of entry for the kidnapper. Aleck wanted to describe his own visceral reaction on encountering the home, where no one now lived, the Lindberghs in seclusion at Anne's mother's Next Day Hill mansion or, once in Flemington, staying outside of town. The Lindberghs would never return to that Hopewell mansion.

"Edna dear," Aleck said as we cruised along, "you're awfully quiet this afternoon."

I hadn't told him about my visit to Cody Lee Thomas and, of course, my sudden encounter with the most hated man in America, Bruno Richard Hauptmann. Frankly, I didn't know how to frame my words, at a loss to sort out the welter of mixed emotions that flooded me in the cramped police station and jail. Bruno—an ordinary man illuminated against a backdrop of national frenzy. Bruno—I saw a dead man.

"A sleepless night," I lied.

Aleck eyed me curiously, not trusting my words.

Our driver was Marcus Wood, and I thanked God for that. Willie's insistent rattling voice, like hail on a corrugated tin roof, would have driven me to distraction. Instead, Marcus was a driver who rarely spoke, his eyes always straight ahead as though expecting disaster. A smooth, careful driver, he nevertheless had the casual flippant air of so many young men in a hurry, those jazz-age, zoot-suited boys who twenty-three skedooed their skittish girls into the backseats of Model T Fords. Marcus was probably in his early thirties, a dandyish sort who had abundant black, oiled hair, a hammered Leyendecker jaw, and watery blue eyes that I found utterly charming.

Nattily dressed in a double-breasted uniform that looked better on him than on the ancient Willie, Marcus breezed along, often nodding his head as though listening to a popular radio ditty in his head. He often seemed off in his own thoughts. Addressed once about the road conditions—the traffic out of the small town was bumper-to-bumper, and maddening—he didn't answer, and I realized he wasn't listening to us. That disturbed me, but I still preferred his indifference to Willie's buttinsky tactics. At one point, slowing behind a milk wagon, he pointed to a movie marquee at the Palace. *Murder in the Clouds,* starring Ann Dvorak and Lyle Talbot. He twisted his head to the left, smiled to himself, and mouthed the word: *ironic.* It certainly was.

He'd driven for us once before, a short spin somewhere out of town, and at the time Aleck had fussed. He later insinuated that Marcus was too good-looking to maneuver a car safely. "I don't trust young men who remember too fondly the dandyish world of Rudolph Valentino." He'd added, "The wave of a young girl from another car and you and I are smashed to smithereens against an inconvenient tree."

I didn't care—I enjoyed his classic profile, that turned Roman nose and jutting chin and Arrow Shirt-model looks. True, he seemed out of place silhouetted against the drab Jersey landscape of ice-frosted trees and wasted farm fields and sagging Cape Cod bungalows.

Unfortunately we arrived at Hopewell near dusk, though the January sunset of red and orange and yellow ribbons provided a postcard backdrop for the stark white Romanesque-styled mansion set against the dark woods. In a remote part of Jersey, this home was ten miles north of Princeton, true, but really tucked into the inaccessible wilderness of the Sourland Mountains. I thought of Cora Lee in her tarpaper shack deep in the woods nearby. Poor, grubbing farmers. The whitewashed fieldstone and stucco home, with its high-angled peaks and gabled slate roof, seemed a throwback to a medieval fortress. An incongruous white picket fence sloped down the driveway.

Aleck scribbled some notes about the desolation—"Why would Colonel Lindbergh choose so distant a spot to build—and the openness? Lord, you can walk up to the mansion without preamble."

"Which someone did," I remarked.

"It's so open," Aleck repeated.

I stared through the gathering darkness. The mansion was largely dark, but lights were on in some rooms. The light in the upper nursery, I noticed—how well I remembered that shot from the newsreels. That ladder placed up against the white stucco. Now a line of state troopers blocked the front entrance, and a burly trooper, standing at the ready, watched us closely. His hand was raised: no further.

Marcus braked the car.

Aleck began reciting the opening lines of a column I knew he was writing in his head. "On a windy March night, three years ago, a lone kidnapper, carrying a homemade ladder, slipped across the bleak yard of Colonel and Anne Lindbergh."

I broke in. "Melodramatic, Aleck."

"But true."

"The court has to prove Bruno Hauptmann was here. Otherwise there is no case. Witnesses?"

Aleck cleared his throat. "A baby lay in his cradle, sleeping, tucked in."

"I can't imagine a single man, a stranger to these parts, approaching the house," I said.

"Well, he did."

"Too many unanswered questions. How did he know where the nursery was? The Lindberghs had never been at Hopewell on a Tuesday night. Who told him? How did he know one of the shutters was warped and couldn't be locked? Colonel Lindbergh said he heard a crack—like a rung of a ladder snapped—while he sat downstairs. It was nine-thirty or so at night—four or five people awake and moving about the house. Why wouldn't Bruno wait until everyone was in bed?"

Aleck was annoyed. "Stop this, Edna. What are you, his lawyer?"

I fumed. "I'm asking intelligent questions."

"A lone vulture, that Bruno. He wanted to destroy an American hero. The Lone Eagle."

"Why were all the prints wiped clean in the nursery? All of them gone."

Aleck burst out, "Enough!"

"An inside job," I mumbled, "and the state police trampled on the evidence, neglected to make an imprint of the one footprint in the mud, didn't measure tire prints. Colonel Schwarzkopf…"

A phony laugh from Aleck as he tapped Marcus on the shoulder. "Enough. Turn around."

The car moved.

"Marcus, my lad, would you live in such a home?" Aleck asked.

Marcus flicked his head back and smiled. "These days I live in one room in a rooming house on the edge of Flemington. I bet the foyer in there"—he pointed back to the mansion—"is bigger than my room." He glanced back at me. "And across the hall from me is Willie who snores like a locomotive in a tunnel."

"But would you live in such a house if you had all the money in the world?"

Marcus deliberated for a moment, taking the question too seriously. "No."

"Why not?" Aleck persisted.

"People who live in such houses…" He changed the course of his sentence. "People who have too many rooms are always lonely."

"Let me write that down," Aleck roared.

"Aleck, for God's sake," I said.

But Marcus was smiling broadly, enjoying the moment. "I'm afraid I heard that somewhere. I never say anything original."

"Neither does Aleck," I hummed.

Aleck let out a loud whoop, and I smiled.

Back on the road, I watched light sleet falling on the road, and asked Aleck, "Do you realize there was *no* mention of Annabel Biggs' murder in the press today?"

He'd been lolling with his eyes closed. "That's because they have the killer."

"I'm not so sure."

He narrowed his eyes at me. "Now what does that mean?"

"Remember Willie said his mother was his alibi."

He squinted, interested. "Of course, Ferb, a mother believes her son."

"Who knows if he really did it?"

"Edna, this has nothing to do with you."

"Oh, but it does. A woman murdered, then dismissed."

Aleck tapped Marcus on the shoulder again. "Marcus, my good man, did you read about the murder of the waitress at the Union Hotel Café?"

"Yes, a small piece in the *Democrat*."

"You read it?" I wondered.

"Well, Willie kept talking about it to a lot of the drivers."

"Did you ever meet her?" I asked.

He scoffed. "Drivers don't eat in that café." He glanced back. "A hot plate in my room."

"You have family around here?"

"Up to Newark."

"Not a hometown boy like...Willie?" I asked.

Now he chuckled. "Not quite. Hayseed and manure...and smelly cigars. Willie has the country in his bones."

"And you don't?" From Aleck.

"When this trial is over and the money dries up, I'm back to a city."

"What city?" From me.

"Well, any city'll do, but Newark is a start."

"The trial can't last forever," I commented.

For the first time he looked back into my face and the car swerved onto the shoulder of the road. "Hauptmann has to die," he said, flat out, seething.

"What?" Aleck bellowed.

"An illegal immigrant here to take jobs from American-born citizens. Come on, think about it. A depression in this country."

"But you think he is guilty? And he has to die?" Aleck asked.

"Being illegal shouldn't be a death sentence," I offered.

"Yeah, but murder should."

"If he did it."

Again the dismissive laugh. "Oh, he did."

"You don't like foreigners?" asked Aleck.

"Foreigners everywhere. Look at this Annabel woman. She came here to these shores looking for…" He paused.

"Opportunity?" I ventured.

"Yeah," he said snidely, "opportunity. That's the word, I guess. Her and Hauptmann and millions of others. She should have stayed in England. He should have stayed in Germany. In prison there."

"But why?" I asked.

He glanced back, puzzled. "Hey, America is a dangerous place." He snickered. "Come to New Jersey and they'll murder you."

"Hauptmann?"

"Yeah, they're gonna kill him, too."

"You're a grim young man," I said.

"No, ma'am, I'm a guy who looks at the world straight on. You learn that by driving a car. You can never take your eyes off the road."

Aleck looked perplexed. "If you do, what happens?"

"They'll get you. They always do."

Aleck shot me a look but lapsed into silence, tucking his head into his chest.

# Chapter Eight

Peggy Crispen was expecting someone else to knock on her door. A short rap as I glanced at Aleck at my side, and the door flew open, a smiling Peggy ready to say something. Aleck was catching his breath after walking up the one flight of stairs in the boardinghouse. Peggy clutched the sweater she had draped over her shoulders, pulling it together and holding it at her neck, as though she'd been surprised in the process of dressing. Or undressing. She jumped back, the smile disappearing.

"I don't understand," she let out.

"Miss Crispen," I began, "a few moments of your time?"

But she was looking at Aleck and not at me, and muttered, "What is this about?"

"Hello, we've met before in the café. I'm Edna Ferber, and this is Aleck Woollcott. We're writers from New York and…" I stopped because her face closed in, her eyes shrouded. She turned back into the room, as though to flee, but finally looked back, tapped her foot impatiently, and grumbled.

"I ain't talking to any more reporters."

"You've talked to reporters?" That surprised me.

"This Joshua Flagg guy keeps knocking, says he needs to…"

Aleck broke in, his voice silky, a twitch at the corners of his lips, a twinkle in his eyes. I got alarmed by the sudden transformation as he rolled his head back and forth, some feeble mimicry of a *bon vivant* on the town. "My dear, we don't mean to bother you, but our concern is *real*. This sad story, a young beautiful woman, a stranger to our shores, murdered by a rejected boyfriend, well, it must be traumatic for you, I'm sure." He went on, insipid drivel doubtless appropriated from a tattered copy of *Rebecca of Sunnybrook Farm* or *Pollyanna*, but I could see Peggy softening, her body relaxing, her shoulders dropping, her head inclined coyly. A little amused, I gaped at Aleck, this overflowing man with the soft woman's hips and waterfall chins, a man who usually generated no such masculine heat, none really, a notoriously sexless raconteur of the old Algonquin Round Table, who had long eschewed romance and intrigue. Obviously he'd missed his calling—he should have been starring on the Broadway boards.

He had fought me about visiting the hapless Peggy Crispen, who'd shared a room with Annabel Biggs. On the stroll over he'd stressed that I was out of line.

"But why?" I'd insisted.

"There is no reason to visit this…this Peggy Crispen."

"She was Annabel Biggs' roommate—and a waitress who worked with her."

"So what?" He'd stopped to catch his breath. "You're already covering *one* story, Edna. The one the *Times* is *paying* you for. This cheap murder is trivial stuff."

"I need to look into this story."

"For what reason?" Exasperated, he pointed a finger at me. "Backwoods fornication is never original."

"Really, Aleck."

"Lascivious louts and wanton waitresses." He grinned. "How Victorian parlor of you."

Yet he'd agreed to accompany me, though hesitantly, insisting the wayward corners of small-town Flemington, once we departed from Main Street, were havens of immoral behavior and unseemly conduct. "I was in France during the Great War," he told me. "I've seen the dregs."

I'd rolled my tongue into the corner of my cheek. "Well, I haunt the echoey alleys of Broadway, Aleck, where you maintain your warren. So I know firsthand the darkness at the end of the tunnel."

"You think you're clever, my darling. Please leave *that* to me."

Peggy Crispen occupied a small room on the second floor of a yellow clapboard-sided roominghouse a few blocks from the Union Hotel, a residential street behind the Women's Exchange, whatever that was. A rundown building with peeling boards and hallways painted too many times so that dark, caked-on paint made the corridors cave-like, uninviting. A threadbare carpet on the stairwell, unraveling at the edges. A loose handrailing, · the squeak, squeak of old steps. The nervous *yip yip yip* of a dog somewhere in the building. The aroma of burnt onions from a first-floor room.

Peggy bowed us into the small room. Faded floral wallpaper—were those gigantic hollyhocks speckling the walls?—the seams splitting. A shabby wool carpet over rough oak boards. An ancient dresser someone had painted a sad orange. A curtain rustled as a breeze seeped through the old, rickety windowsill. A flophouse destination. I felt sorry for Peggy. Two single beds across from each other in the room, one doubtless belonging to the late Annabel. Sloppily made, covers uneven, both beds covered with knotted chenille spreads. A suitcase resting on the coverlet. A small pine table and two chairs by the window. Peggy spotted me looking at the suitcase on the bed, contents spilling out.

"I been packing some of her belongings," she pointed out. "Don't know what else to do." A shrug, helpless.

"No relatives?"

She stared at the suitcase. "Nobody's come forward. The landlord ain't no help."

"My dear, are we interrupting anything?" From Aleck, not me.

She smiled at him as she jerked her shoulders toward the two chairs. "Sit, I guess."

Aleck settled his tremendous body into one of the chairs, which creaked and shimmied. Carefully, he balanced himself, then reached into a pocket to extract a cigarette holder. Peggy nodded toward a pack of Lucky Strikes on the table, and he took one, inserted it. Peggy reached for one and lit hers and his. "Miss Ferber?"

I shook my head. "No, thank you."

"Well," Aleck said to no one in particular, "I may end up on this sad floor." The chair groaned.

For some reason Peggy tittered at that and tossed him a quick, approving wave. He beamed at her.

"Were you expecting someone?" I asked disingenuously.

Her eyes watched me closely. "No, why?"

"Well, you seem dressed for an…engagement."

And she did. A powdered face, a trace of peach rouge on her cheeks, garish bright red lipstick on her full lips. She'd pulled her hair into a precise French twist, graced with an ivory clip. A chubby woman, perhaps in her late thirties or early forties, with a round moon face and round hazel eyes exaggerated by a line of dark kohl, she'd squeezed herself into a dress designed for a smaller—and decidedly younger—woman, a cocktail dress sequined at the bodice, a glittery hemline, the kind I used to spot on the now-departed flappers dancing all-night marathons at Rose Land. Her plump upper arms pushed at the seams, threatened to break free. Dark-complexioned, a hint of the Mediterranean about her, close-cropped bobbed hair, out of fashion.

She stammered, "I'm stepping out later."

"Well," I said slowly, "we won't keep you long."

She perched on the edge of her bed, her knees together, one hand under her other elbow. Nervous, she fidgeted and inhaled the cigarette, blew a circle of smoke over her head. Aleck, watching, waved his cigarette holder, sending his own cloud of smoke into the air. Giddily, he smiled at the woman. When she smiled back, I noticed a smear of lipstick on her front tooth.

I smiled at no one.

"Were you close to Annabel?" I asked.

She answered by looking at Aleck. "No. Well, sort of. I mean, we didn't *know* each other until we had to room together. In this *dump*. Space and all—because of the trial. Everybody charging an arm and a leg for any room they got in this town. The hotel put us together. I mean, we worked together—talked."

"You liked her?"

"Not at first." She debated her answer. "She was noisy and interrupted everyone. A little showy. A young woman, you know, happy with herself. But, you know, being in this room with her, I got to know her."

"She arrived from Chicago, right?"

"Sort of. England, somewhere, I guess." A little grin. "That irritating accent those people got." She looked into my face. "What's this all about? I mean, they got the guy, no?"

"I'm trying to satisfy a curiosity," I told her.

"That makes no sense."

Aleck chortled. "Indulge the woman, my dear. It's easier to answer her questions than to ignore her. She'll eventually go away."

I ignored him. "Miss Crispen, I just want to get a clear picture of who Annabel was. After all, she was murdered. She had a life. She should have some justice, no?"

Again, she answered by looking at Aleck. "Well, they got the guy."

"Cody Lee Thomas," I stated. "I met him. What did you think of him?"

She took a long time answering, drawing in her cigarette, watching the red glow, and then extinguishing it abruptly in a clamshell ashtray.

"A hick, that one. A rube."

"Did he come here? To these rooms?"

She swung her head back and forth. "Never. Not allowed. But I seen him at the café. At first he's stopping in to pick her up after her shift, all lovey dovey, cooing at each other, the two of them, but then she tells him to scram, and war breaks out. You heard about the arguments at the café?"

I nodded. "I witnessed one unpleasant skirmish in the parking lot. There was no one around."

Except for that shadow, I thought. The flash of movement.
A person there.

"Well, then you know he was a pest. Mooning like a lovesick
boy. Sort of embarrassing."

"Is that why you didn't like him?"

She giggled. "He's a hick. Simple as that."

She glanced toward the door. I expected someone to knock.
At one point she half-rose, fidgety, then settled back down. Aleck
sighed out loud, unpleasant, though Peggy cast a warm glance
at him. He smiled back. But when she looked back at me, that
look disappeared, replaced by a stern, disapproving expression.
A woman obviously taken with the rotund Aleck. And with little
patience for the severe spinster hurling untoward questions at
her. She waved a finger at him. "You're on the radio. I thought
I knew your voice. I listen…"

"My dear," Aleck bowed, "a fan."

"But did Cody Lee Thomas kill her?" I interrupted. "Such a
murder seems extreme…."

She held up her hand, her voice now a whisper. "She told me
that Cody Lee said he'd kill her if she left him."

My throat went dry. "Well, that doesn't sound like him."

Aleck shot me a look. "Edna, really. Such romanticism on
your part. You don't *know* the man. He's not…"

I bit my lip and addressed Peggy. "She may have been lying
to you."

She clicked her tongue. "Be that as it may, I told the cops
what she said." She pouted. "They was happy to hear my story."

"Good Lord."

While Aleck nodded his approval, she went on, her words
more forceful now. "I had to. I mean, she says he threatened
to kill her, and then I come back here after my shift and she's
there"—she pointed to a spot by the door—"and she's lying in
a heap, her neck twisted." A tick in her voice, a swallowed sob.

"Was the room a mess?"

"What do you mean?"

"Things strewn about? Anything taken?"

"Well, she was still wearing her ring, but I know she said it was a real gemstone—like a sapphire—but I can tell paste, honey. Woolworth's bargain bin all the way." A faraway look came into her eyes. She stood and walked over to Annabel's dresser. She swung back, puzzled. "Annabel was always reading these letters she saved."

"Letters?"

"Yeah, a stack of them."

"And?" Echoes of Cody Lee mentioning letters…but what did that mean?

"They ain't here now."

My pulse quickened. "Someone took them?"

"Who knows? Maybe not. Maybe she put them back in the drawer." She pulled open a top drawer. "She always kept them here." She drew her lips into a thin line. "Nope. Gone." For a second her eyes flitted around the room, nervous. She bit the corner of a polished nail.

I looked at Aleck. "What does this mean?"

He arched his hands. "Obviously, the murderer took them, Edna."

"I know that," I said, irritated. "But what does it *mean?*"

"You're assuming a lot, Edna. This could mean nothing."

"Or something. There was no reason for Cody Lee to take them."

Aleck addressed Peggy. "Were they about him?"

She moved to the window and looked down into the street. "I don't like this talk. All of this." Her eyes got cloudy. "I think someone was following her. I mean, one time she said she felt there was always someone in the shadows, watching."

"Cody Lee?" From Aleck.

She shook her head and sank into a chair. "Naw. Leastwise I don't think so. She said she felt it when they were together sometimes. Like a shadow nearby that moved away when she got near." She shivered. "I told her it was a ghost." She looked down at her hands. "I'm not liking any of this. I'm getting spooked." Her voice shaking, she looked down into her lap, but, in an unguarded moment, twisted her head to the side. "I really have to go out…"

"Looks to me like you are ready," I said.

She didn't like that. "I like my privacy."

A figure in the shadows. The one I saw—that cold morning when I overheard the spat in the parking lot. A shadow? A lurker? Someone waiting to kill her. To take some letters? What did all this mean?

I shifted the direction of the conversation. "Did she like the job at the hotel?"

"She liked the money, but she said she was gonna quit in a bit."

"Why?"

A sliver of a smile. "Oh, the old gravy train coming in."

"Meaning?" From Aleck.

"She came here because someone was gonna give her big money."

"But who?"

She wasn't listening. "And she told me I'd get some of it. If I helped her out."

"Help her out how?" Aleck sat up, interested.

Again a barely whispered word. "Lindbergh."

Silence in the room.

The sound of footsteps in the hallway.

Aleck cleared his throat and leaned in. "Peggy, my dear, you're not telling us something."

She tossed back her shoulders. "Don't matter no more anyhow. She's gone. Whatever gravy train was coming in now is long gone from the station."

"But what about Lindbergh?" I asked. "Yes, she came here for a job—because of the trial. The opportunity…"

The look on her face stopped me, hard, haughty. "You just don't get it."

"Then tell me."

"She said she knew something that was gonna get her big money."

"From Lindbergh? Blackmail?"

"Dunno." Another shrug. "I mean, she could've just been crowing big-time—like she was a braggart. Put a little liquor in the broad and, well...I only got bits and pieces when she was a little, you know, tipsy. She could get chatty then. Like she couldn't keep her mouth shut. Like it spilled out of her. She *had* to tell someone. Bubbly. Then, sober the next morning, she denied everything. 'You ain't heard me right.' That's what she said to me."

"Tell us what you remember."

"I don't know if..."

Aleck's voice got sharp, insistent. "Who wrote those letters, Peggy dear?"

She debated what to say but finally, in a small echoey voice, she muttered, "Violet Sharp."

My head swam. I looked at Aleck, who was slack-jawed, eyes bright. "Violet Sharp?" he repeated.

She nodded. "Yes. Violet Sharp." She trembled. "The one in the newspaper."

Violet Sharp. Aleck and I exchanged knowing glances.

Anyone following the Lindbergh kidnapping understood how explosive those two words were. Violet Sharp, a girl who figured prominently back in the days immediately after the kidnapping. She'd been the downstairs maid at the Dwight Morrow mansion in Englewood, New Jersey. Charles Lindbergh had insisted his servants—and those at his mother-in-law's mansion—*not* be interviewed, trusting them, insisting they be left alone. The state police, under Colonel Schwarzkopf, initially suspected an inside job, largely because Charles and Anne usually spent the week at Englewood and only weekends at Hopewell, their unfinished homestead. But because Little Lindy had a bad cold, Anne called to say they'd be staying in Hopewell and could the chauffeur drive the nurse, Betty Gow, to help care for the baby? Violet Sharp took the call at eleven-thirty that morning. Somehow, then, the kidnapper knew the Lindberghs were staying in Hopewell.

Despite Colonel Lindbergh's adamant stance, all the servants were routinely interviewed, and were compliant and cleared.

But Violet posed a problem. She was agitated, uncooperative. And the newspapers made much of her evasions. She couldn't recall where she'd been that awful windy night, at first saying she was at the movies in Englewood, then changing her story. She was with a man named Ernie, no last name, and two of his friends. Then she said she'd been to the Peanut Grill, a speakeasy in Orangeburg, New York, but drank only coffee and danced a bit—back home by eleven.

An attractive brunette, given to flirtations, Violet Sharp shifted from cooperation to belligerence. At twenty-seven, she'd emigrated from England to Canada in 1929 with her sister, Emily, in the United States nine months later at the YWCA in Manhattan. Mrs. Morrow hired her, and liked her, though other servants said she was moody, sometimes hysterical, often coy and mysterious—a woman who savored her time away from the mansion. During the course of three interviews she'd changed: a precipitous drop in weight, some forty pounds, the once-plump and sassy girl now cowering and jittery. She fainted at an interview. Her decline began with the discovery of the baby's body.

Colonel Schwarzkopf believed she'd been the informant—unwittingly or not—alerting the kidnappers to the baby being in Hopewell that night. He sent Inspector Henry Walsh to do another interview. Walsh, a blunt, threatening officer, had little patience with the evasive Violet, who, during a previous interview when she'd gotten hysterical, still managed to smile and wink at a secretary as she left the room. The police didn't trust her.

She vowed not to be interviewed again. When officers arrived at the mansion, she rushed upstairs, mixed powdered silver polish into a glass of water—a concoction containing cyanide chloride, a milky-white liquid—and walked down the stairs, a gurgling sound from the back of her throat, where she collapsed. She was dead.

Dwight Morrow, Jr., summoned by a servant, carried her body up to her bedroom.

Mrs. Morrow, in talking to the press, said Violet had "simply been frightened to death."

Colonel Schwarzkopf announced to the press that her suicide confirmed his suspicion that she had knowledge of the crime against Charles Lindbergh, Jr.

Lindbergh himself rejected the idea.

Violet's sister, Emily, who had been employed nearby at Constance Chilton's home, had applied for a visa to return to Tult's Clump in England on March first, the day of the kidnapping. On April first, four days after the ransom was delivered, she sailed back home. She never informed the authorities. Back in England she told the indignant press that the police had hounded her innocent sister. "Death by Third Degree," screamed the *London Daily Mirror*.

Violet remained one of the nagging mysteries of the kidnapping saga, unanswered.

The London press still clamored for answers.

The British Consul sent flowers to her funeral.

"Violet Sharp?" I said again, breathless.

Peggy nodded. She pointed to the top of the dresser, now empty of the letters she'd mentioned. "She wrote them letters to Annabel, Violet did."

"But why?"

She blinked wildly. "A secret she told only me. They was cousins from England. They grew up together—Annabel and Violet and Violet's sister, Emily, the one who skedaddled back to England before the cops could question her."

"Oh my God," exclaimed Aleck.

"Indeed." My word was swallowed.

Aleck was muttering to himself. "But what did Violet tell her cousin?" He fumbled. "I mean…well, blackmail? How?"

Peggy sighed. "She didn't like to talk much about them, the two sisters. I guess Emily and Annabel didn't like each other—but Violet liked Annabel. I asked her if Violet was… like murdered. Not a suicide. It seemed strange to hear that a young girl would kill herself like that. But then Annabel started to cry. But she said no, Violet was always a temperamental girl, melodramatic, a little crazy."

"But the letters had to be important if someone took them?"

"*Maybe* took them," she stressed. "Maybe Annabel got rid of them and I didn't notice."

"Do you believe that?"

"No." A simple, emphatic response. "Not really."

"Then what?"

Aleck softened his voice and reached out a hand to pat the back of Peggy's wrist. She melted. "What did Violet reveal in the letters? What do you know? And how could it lead to a payoff now for Annabel? Did she expect Lindbergh to pay her money? For what? Silence?"

She looked toward the door and walked to a mirror to check her makeup. When she spotted lipstick on her tooth, she reached for a tissue and dabbed at it. Her tone addressing Aleck was confidential. "Look, I guess Violet liked to go to roadhouses back in the day when there was Prohibition and such. But she got this infatuation for some guy who lived on another rich estate nearby, some wealthy friend of the Morrows. One of the son's old friends—the son named Dwight Morrow—a guy who used to come around. A handsome devil-may-care smooth-talking fool, money dripping out of his pockets, but a real Casanova, that one. He wooed the girls and then said goodbye. I guess Violet caught his eye one night. Like she'd flirt even with the rich guys. She was a pretty young thing, I suppose, with that British accent that American men get dizzy over, though she was a little plump—like yours truly." She beamed at Aleck. "Some men like a little meat on the bone." A stiffled giggle. "Anyhow, she said that this rich guy and Dwight took her in a roadster to some speakeasies."

"What was his name?" I asked.

Hesitation. "I don't want to get him in trouble."

"His name," I insisted.

"Blake Somerville. But you can't repeat that to *anyone*. You know, his father was, like, the lieutenant governor of New Jersey. They own, like—like, these oil refineries on the shore—that give Jersey that sickening smell. But real rich, that family. That's what

Annabel said." She paused, looked toward the door. "I mean, Violet could have been making up the story. She was a maid, for God's sake. Rich boys don't take maids to roadhouses." A pause. "Well, maybe they do, if you know what I mean. But it could be nonsense, something you write in a letter to impress your poor cousin. Violet, Annabel said, had these flights of fancy."

"But I can't connect the dots," I said. "How could Annabel arrive in Flemington with the goal of blackmailing Charles Lindbergh? How would she get at him? And what information would he *pay* for?"

Peggy waited a long time. "Well, Annabel said someone in the Morrow family…like, *knew* something. Something Violet confided—it was worth its weight in gold, she said. And Colonel Lindbergh would *not* want his wife, Anne, and her mother embarrassed. It would mean Colonel Lindbergh made a mistake when he shut down the interviews at first. Doing that, you know, led to a sad ending. I mean, the Morrows are Jersey royalty, for Christ's sake."

I nodded at Aleck. "So Annabel was going to use the letters to get Lindbergh to pay money. To buy her silence. There must have been something in the letters about the kidnapping. Something that involved the Morrow estate."

Peggy breathed in, finished now, her eyes staring at me. "No, I…"

"You what?" said Aleck, gently.

"I don't wanna say no more." Peggy stood up. She was shaking. "I made a mistake here."

Aleck poured on the charm. She'd stepped toward the door, but he stretched out his hand, tapping her wrist affectionately. It took some effort on his part. "There was more in the letters, right?" he coaxed her.

"Not *them* letters."

"But what?" I said too loudly and she grimaced. Her indifference to me—perhaps dislike?—bothered me, but of course I lacked Aleck's mysterious allure.

"Peggy, my lovely dear…" From Aleck, not me.

"There was one letter she wouldn't show me."

"Why not?" he asked.

"Insurance, she said."

"It was with the others?"

She shook her head. "Never was in the pile." A sly grin. "I checked once. She let me read those letters, sort of proud of them. Like her place in history, sort of. But one time she waved this other letter at me, the last one before Violet offed herself with that silver polish. Maybe she carried it with her. Or she hid it. She said it was the key to the vault."

Involuntarily I spun around, searching the corners of the room. "Here?"

"I guess so."

"Did you find it?"

A sigh. "Never gave it no mind because of her, you know, murder. That spooked me. I forgot about the letters—*the* letter. The whole thing was dead with Annabel."

"Then it's here?"

"Dunno."

"Well…"

"We have to find it, dear," Aleck whispered.

But at that moment there was a loud rapping on the door, and we all jumped. Unfortunately, I emitted a Victorian scream worthy of a heroine in *Tempest and Sunshine*. I flushed, horrified.

Peggy rushed to the door, although she paused to primp herself in the mirror before turning the knob. But conscious of Aleck and me nearby, she inched the door open slowly, probably with the purpose of concealing the visitor in the hallway. Her escort for the evening? Someone who'd be quickly shooed away.

"Christ, not you again."

The door flew open.

Joshua Flagg stood there. "Excuse me, Miss Crispen…"

He stopped abruptly as he peered into the room, looking past her, flabbergasted to discover Edna Ferber and Aleck Woollcott sitting primly on the chairs, eyes focused on the annoying young Hearst upstart.

"I told you not to come back," Peggy roared at him. "I ain't talking to you. I ain't got nothing to tell you. Annabel's killer is in jail. You gotta leave me alone." She looked back at us. "Christ Almighty, my room is like Grand Central Station today."

Sheepish, sputtering, Joshua stepped back and disappeared from view. His hasty footsteps galloped down the stairs.

# Chapter Nine

The letter.

"Aleck, you have to get that letter."

"Edna dear, this obsession of yours."

"Did you hear me, Aleck?"

"I'm not deaf, and your voice usually has the timbre of a train whistle roaring into a station."

"Then you'll do it?"

He smiled maliciously. "That woman finds me charming. Alluring, if you will. A novelty for me, titillating though unwanted."

"And a form of madness."

He chuckled. "Jealousy, my dear."

"You'll do it?"

He nodded "A glance from me and she wilts like a morning glory in the afternoon sun."

I ignored that. "Good." I tapped his sleeve. "Now, Aleck."

We were sitting in the lobby of the hotel later that night, though it was difficult to concentrate because of the hullabaloo and stampede of eager feet. Reporters everywhere, bumping into one another, occasionally glancing at the two of us as we sat quietly in the plush armchairs, each with a cup of coffee on a side table.

"Now," I repeated, "you know Peggy is searching that dismal room for the hidden letter. Tearing off the wallpaper. You do know that, Aleck? You could see it in her eye, that panic, that urgency."

"It's late—she seemed to be waiting for a suitor to knock on her door. I mean, she sent us packing after that Joshua fellow fled down the stairs."

"Yes—and while I was in the middle of a question."

"You're always in the middle of a question, Ferb."

"Be that as it may—go. She may be back home now."

"What makes you certain she'll reveal its contents to me?"

I sucked in my lips. "You flatter her, lisp at her, flutter, and twinkle those night-owl eyes of yours. A hint of cheese strudel on your breath—I have no idea. For some reason she finds you—to use your word—alluring." I looked around the room. "There must be something foul in the tap water of New Jersey."

"Women have found me attractive, dear Ferb." A sloppy grin. "You know, all the things I really like to do are either immoral, illegal, or fattening."

"Do you find her attractive, Aleck?"

A pause. "You know the answer to that."

"I thought so."

"But the attention of women for a man like me is a rarity—a solar eclipse, if you will—that must be cultivated."

I nudged him again, harder this time. "Then go cultivate."

He stood but looked down at me. "I imagine men never find you alluring, dear Ferb."

"They'd better not if they know what's good for them."

"You scare men away." He chuckled. "But you don't scare me, my dear." He pointed a finger at me.

"I repeat—only men, Aleck. Only men."

◇◇◇

Early the next morning I took my usual walk, the streets still dead, though the bitter cold cut short my stride, yet I paused in the back parking lot, empty now, recalling that spitfire spat of Annabel and Cody Lee. The wind whistled along the eaves of the hotel, drifted through the crevices of the metal storage shed, and I lingered, listening to the ghosts that swirled and eddied there. Chilled, numb, I returned to my room, showered, dressed for the day, and scurried into the café. Aleck was already there, a cup of coffee before him as he chatted with a waiter.

"You're late." He spotted me and motioned to a seat.

I mouthed the word "coffee" to the waiter as he rushed away.

"Tell me." I looked into Aleck's face.

"My, my, not even a good-morning buss on the cheek." He inserted a cigarette into his holder and purposely took his time lighting it.

"Tell me."

"A knock on her door and again the disappointment in her face—for a moment, at least. Her expected suitor, I gather, the one she'd perfumed and powdered herself for, never showed. But she was overjoyed to find me rapping on her door."

"The letter, Aleck."

Aleck peered over his eyeglasses, which teetered on the edge of his nose. He contemplated a cinnamon roll on a plate before him, one fingertip touching the sweet frosting. He licked it with approval. "I may have to order another."

Bitingly, I said, "I'll order you a…gross, Aleck. Tell me."

"A couple glasses of wine late in the evening at a hideous log-cabin tavern called, forgive me, Edna, the Dew Drop Inn. The hoi polloi refuses to avoid egregious puns. Can you tell me why?"

"Can you tell me why you're blathering about nonsense?" I smiled. "What don't you want to tell me?"

"As Peggy and I nestled into a food-stained booth, torn with springs disturbing my derriere…"

"Please, Aleck."

"She went on and on about hearing me on the radio. The Town Crier. My comforting tones, she called them."

"Aleck!"

"Anyway, she did locate that letter, right after we left—after, that is, Joshua Flagg interrupted and she showed both of us out. She wasn't happy about the letter."

"Did you read it?"

He shook his head. "She refused to show it to me, though she did reveal some of the contents. She found it, remarkably enough, hidden behind a loose floor panel in that hideous room. Behind Annabel's bed."

"Of course, she already knew it existed."

"Yes, Annabel had hinted at some of the scandalous contents. And its contents *alarmed* her. Thank God for the Dew Drop Inn."

"Tell me," I insisted.

Aleck's fingers wrestled with the cinnamon roll, although he still gripped his cigarette holder. "Let me first say that poor Peggy now is frightened. Somehow the murder of Annabel and our visit and the talk of the letters from Violet Sharp—and, to be truthful, the mention of Charles Lindbergh and the kidnapping—all became a jumble in the same mathematical equation—well, she's added all these elements together in the test tube of her mind, and she's…afraid."

"But of what?" I asked.

He shook his head. "Of Cody Lee Thomas."

That stunned me—unexpected. "But he's in jail."

"No matter. She'd got this idea that he'll break out of jail."

"And what? Kill her?"

"I know, I know. It makes no sense. But she says he's a brute."

"He's a gentle man."

Aleck peered over his eyeglasses. "Really, Edna. You do sentimentalize the most loathsome of the male species."

I ignored that. "There has to be something else."

"Well, yes. Cody Lee is safely out of the way. To me, he's not part of the nonsense Annabel believed, by way of Violet's own fantastic imagination. But she thinks someone else is involved with the kidnapping, maybe a friend of his—and possibly around."

"Preposterous." A waiter glanced out the small kitchen window, then disappeared. I leaned in, confidential. "Just what did Violet Sharp say in that final letter?"

He sucked in his breath. "Explosive, my dear, but dear Peggy is hesitant to tell all."

We locked eyes. "But she told you enough."

"I *am* a charming man."

"And the generous purveyor of a bottle of wine in the...Dew Drop Inn."

"Please, those words sound bleak coming from your novelistic mouth."

"Tell me."

The manager, Horace Tripp, walked briskly out of the kitchen and stood, arms folded, watching us. He didn't look happy. Nearby tables began to fill, but he paid them no mind. Rather, his glare suggested he was solely focused on Aleck and me. Out of the corner of my eye I could see his head flick toward us, curious, though when I looked in his direction, he twisted his head away so quickly it was almost comical. The vaudeville comedian with exaggerated stage business. He picked a piece of lint off his morning coat.

Aleck, pausing in his story, noticed him. He leaned in, nodded at me, and said loudly, "The manager cannot take his eyes off us."

But I was impatient. "Finish, Aleck. What did Violet write to Annabel?"

Aleck scratched his head, deliberated. "I'm piecing together the words, some of which were delivered from a drunken if provocative mouth. Her delivery was like scattershot from a faulty shotgun. But do you remember how she told us that someone in the Morrow household was the key to her fortune?"

"Yes, of course."

He spaced out his words slowly. "The *reason* Annabel believed her fortune now lay in Flemington had to do with Colonel Lindbergh's schizophrenic brother-in-law, Dwight Morrow, Jr."

"What?"

"I know, I know," he went on in a hurry. "But that could be stuff and nonsense. I gather the friend Violet often talked about, this Blake Somerville, the wealthy cad, was someone Violet thought she loved. According to Peggy, Violet—leastwise Annabel's rendition of her scattered cousin via the letters—was a pretty girl, but flighty, given to infatuations and romances and...

and sexual flings that she feared Mrs. Morrow would discover. A girl who, as they say, liked a good time at parties."

"But what does this have to do with the kidnapping?"

"Let me get there. Violet mentioned Dwight Morrow's intense dislike of his brother-in-law, Charles Lindbergh. The young man—the only son in the family—adored his older sister Anne, resented the famed aviator squiring her away into an international world of flight and fancy. Not only that, but Lindbergh used to make fun of him. Dwight suffered emotional breakdowns, hallucinations, and such, and he even refused to attend the lavish wedding of the two."

I shook my head in disbelief. "But you're not saying *he* was involved with the kidnapping of the baby, are you?"

"I'm only telling you what Peggy gathered from talks with Annabel. Violet liked roadhouses, especially in those dry days of bootleggers and rumrunners, and she craved the attention of men, especially the dipsomaniac butler named Septimus Banks. They were butlers and townsmen and livery grooms, plebians, the help, but Blake Somerville swept her off her feet, a slick operator, charming, moneyed, amoral."

"And?"

"According to Peggy, in the long last letter, Violet insisted Blake played into Dwight's dislike of Lindbergh, played up the young man's resentment of his family. He felt he'd been duped out of fifty grand in his dead father's will, that his severe mother was cruel to him. To his face she once called him 'the family tragedy.' Violet was amused by Blake's suave manipulation, his power over people. Blake wanted to help Dwight get back at his family."

"You're not saying *he* orchestrated the kidnapping of the baby? Preposterous."

"That's where Peggy begged off, dear Ferb. She suddenly got scared talking to me—I guess I should have ordered another bottle of cheap wine at the Dew Droop Out, or whatever it's called. Her last words before she became a clam—she mumbled about a stupid prank gone wrong."

"A prank? Preposterous."

"I guess Violet described Lindbergh as an ah-shucks country boy at heart, a simple man who liked to play stupid pranks, especially on his family. One such prank supposedly was to hide the baby in a closet for a short time from his wife and the nurse, Betty Gow."

"Preposterous."

"You have to stop saying that, Edna. At least not so loudly. You're like a parrot in real pearls."

"This is a fantastic story."

"Keep in mind Violet liked to make up stories, according to Annabel. A *liar.*"

"Still and all…"

"You've read the biography, Edna. Lindy is a hero but a country boy at heart. A simple jokester."

I frowned. "I know the stories—how he thought it funny to splatter mud on folks watching him taxi his plane. Substituting gasoline into the water jug of a pilot so that the man had to be hospitalized."

"Boyish stunts."

"Done by a *man*, Aleck. I've read that Betty Gow, discovering the cradle empty, pleaded with Lindbergh, 'Do you have the baby? *Please don't fool me.*' My emphasis here, Aleck. She thought he was playing a game—again."

Aleck wasn't happy with me. "That meant nothing." He made his round eyes into slits. "Violet Sharp was a storyteller."

"There's more, right?"

I looked around me. The room was filling up, and Horace Tripp was rocking on his heels, his steely eyes on us.

Aleck sat back in his chair, blew a smoke ring into the air. "Violet wrote in that letter that Dwight Morrow *hated* the baby, but Blake…well, Blake didn't love anything but idle game-playing. Blake Somerville was a few years ahead of Dwight at Amherst College, dropped out, drifted back in, but the real contact happened when both were confined to Montclair Manor for treatment."

"What is Montclair Manor?"

"I gather it's a loony bin for rich folks."

"So Dwight and Blake…"

"Rediscovered each other, old neighbors, and Blake wooed the impressionable Violet and…"

"And Annabel came to believe they were instrumental in snatching the baby?"

Aleck didn't answer for a minute. Then, slowly, "This is a stretch, Edna. If you ask me, it's a lot of hooey. Violet was a troublemaker, an hysteric, and a fable-maker. Peggy wouldn't go on except to say that Violet was rattled after the baby disappeared that night, made a frantic visit to her sister, Emily, across town, who in short order boarded a boat back to England. I gather Emily was also a guest at roadhouses with this Blake, a man who obviously liked to entertain the help, if you know what I mean. Then Violet, questioned three or four times by the state police, killed herself."

"My God." I breathed in. "But there is no proof."

"None whatsoever. Just Violet's rambling in that last letter, now tucked away in a different place by Peggy."

"She has to give it to the police."

Aleck laughed. "I don't think she'll be doing that."

"But if the letters were stolen, except that one, the odds are Cody Lee Thomas is innocent. What would he care about all that business at the Morrow mansion? But it means someone else knew about those letters."

"Don't make too much of this," Aleck said.

I spoke over his words. "This Blake Somerville intrigues me. He sounds very Machiavellian, some slick Jersey Iago twisting the disturbed Dwight Morrow for some sick pleasure."

"But Edna, this sounds to me to be Violet's warped fancy. A series of exaggerations in letters to Annabel in Chicago."

"And yet Annabel believed it—she left the Palmer House and came to Flemington, hoping to cash in, to blackmail Colonel Lindbergh to save the reputation of…"

"Of his wife's distinguished family?"

"It all seems unrealistic."

"Look around you, my dear. It's one more piece of the convoluted jigsaw puzzle—this circus of a trial, the madness in the streets, this *danse macabre* of insane reporters looking for any tidbit to scoop the others—this is a Hogarth etching being written in Jersey."

"We need to do something."

Aleck held up his hand. "Oh, I don't think so. Who would believe such a—I'll use your word here—preposterous story? Cody Lee threatened Annabel with death, and he's behind bars. A lover's quarrel turned deadly. Annabel is dead. Violet Sharp is dead. Dwight Morrow and Blake Somerville are rich, privileged young men, insulated from the real world. Should we accuse... imagine the outcry."

"But the letters?"

"One letter, Edna. The others gone. And that one insane—and probably fictitious—letter is in Peggy's hands, tight-fisted. She told me she plans to burn it."

"What? She can't."

"Who is to stop her?"

"Evidence."

"Of what?"

I stammered. "Of...of..." Wildly, I ran through the words: murder, kidnapping, mayhem, chaos, farce.

"Maybe they talked about a stupid prank, Edna. Just idle talk. Like: 'Hey, let's think of a way to rile that aviator hero.'"

"That went wrong."

"If they actually did anything, which I don't believe for one second. You're not thinking sensibly, Ferb. It was not a plot hatched in the Morrow mansion. Don't get carried away, my dear. This isn't some Grimms' fairy tale, the wicked brother-in-law. It was really Bruno Richard Hauptmann. I mean, think of the amount of evidence collected against the German monster. A man who hid the ransom money in a makeshift garage, who spent it willy-nilly in a time of great Depression, a man who was identified by witnesses, including Jafsie, Dr. Condon, the go-between. Eyewitnesses, Edna. Bruno the carpenter and his makeshift ladder. A man who…a man who is on trial for murder."

I held up my hand. "Enough. I know the drill. It's restated in every editorial. But no…not enough. There's a tale here that needs unraveling, Aleck. The letters tell the story. Cody Lee has nothing to do with this."

He glowered at me. "There is no story, Edna. Just the fanciful nonsense of a troubled girl." He watched my face closely. "And what do you propose to do?"

I spoke over his words. "Tell me about this Montclair Manor?"

"I know nothing about it. A mental hospital in the hills of Jersey, across from the Hudson."

"For rich folks."

"Poor folks who are bonkers have only the walls of their bedrooms."

A rustling as Walter Winchell strolled in, an entourage of cub reporters and sycophants surrounding him. He paused for a second to glance down at us, and Aleck nodded at him. He was going on about something—I heard him thunder, "You can detect criminality in the eye corner" or some blather like that—and he slid into a chair, waiters hovering, coffee poured, homage paid.

"We need to leave," I told Aleck. "The floor show is going to begin."

Aleck bubbled over. "Why do you dislike that man so?"

"He's a horrid little gossip monger, venal and spiteful."

"That's what I like about you, Ferb dear. No room for moderation. Everything black or white."

"That's because people are good or bad. One or the other."

"You don't really believe that."

"Sometimes I think I do."

As we readied to leave, the manager suddenly stood near me, clearing his throat.

"Yes, Mr. Tripp?" I asked.

"Yes, call me Horace, please."

"Yes, Mr. Tripp?"

He lowered his voice. "I cannot help wondering," he stuttered, struggled with his breath. "I...yesterday, I...I saw the two of you walking out of Peggy Crispen's room at the boardinghouse."

I looked around. "Is she working today?"

That flustered him. "She sent word to say she has a headache. She won't be in."

"A pity," said Aleck. "An attractive woman, sensible."

Horace could make little sense of that, a puzzled expression on his face. He looked over his shoulder. "Well, you two were in her room, yes?"

"Annabel's former room," Aleck interrupted.

"Yes, well, I was wondering about it. It's none of my business, of course, but she does work here and I am responsible for..." His voice took on a hushed, raspy tone. "Is there a problem?"

"Why were you at the boardinghouse?"

"I..."

The kitchen door swung open and his wife, Martha, appeared, rushing up, her hand tucked under his elbow. "Horace, one of the cooks needs you."

Flushed, stumbling, he tottered back and bumped into a chair. But I was watching his wife's face: cold, cold, the lines around her mouth crimped, rigid. And her eyes flashed a horrible look that was both angry and hurt.

I watched Horace's retreating back. Of course, he'd been the visitor Peggy Crispen had been expecting in her room, the reason she was so dolled up, the reason she was surprised when the pesky reporter Joshua Flagg rapped on the door. She had been expecting her lover, the philanderer Mr. Tripp. And I now wondered if the two-bit kitchen Romeo had also wooed Annabel Biggs.

# Chapter Ten

A freezing morning, six a.m., unable to sleep, I bundled up but faced wind squalls, ice pellets, abandoning my walk within minutes. A blizzard had covered the town during the night. I watched horse-drawn sleighs hauling milk to the Union Hotel. When I walked into the hotel through the back entrance, I spotted Peggy Crispen standing in the hallway, dressed in her waitress uniform, her winter coat draped over her arm. She was trembling.

"Peggy." I approached her, alarmed.

She shook her head. "No. Leave me alone."

"What? What happened?"

She was disoriented, swaying back and forth, moving her head wildly, searching the empty hallway.

"I don't know what to do."

I grasped her elbow. "Tell me what happened."

Her eyes were glassy, faraway. Focusing, she offered me a thin smile. "Last night when I returned to my room, the door was cracked open. I *know* I latched it when I left. I always do. But it was open."

"Someone broke in?"

She nodded furiously. "Yes."

"What did they take?"

Silence, trembling lips, then a slight gasp. "Nothing." She closed her eyes. "I think—nothing."

"Then what?"

"They pulled open drawers, overturned furniture, ripped the seams of my clothes, dumped my makeup on the floor, smashed dishes on the shelf."

"Did you call the police?"

"Well, I started screaming, a neighbor came rushing in, called the owner from downstairs. He called the police."

"And?"

"They asked me what was taken. When I told them nothing, they backed off. The cop did, I mean. He smirked at me. The landlord was there and they talked about how it was where Annabel was strangled." She looked into my eyes, terrified. "Do you know what he said to me? He said, 'You gotta be careful.' That's what he said. Like it was nothing. Then he said, 'Maybe someone read about the murder and thought the place was empty and could find something to pawn.'"

"That's feeble," I told her. "And unacceptable."

She bit her lip. "Then they all went away, and I was left to pick up the pieces."

"What do you think, Peggy? Who?"

She spun around, as though fearful someone lurked in the shadows, stalking her. So quick her movement that I also jumped, swung around. Nothing: no one: silence. But a chill ran up my spine.

Slowly, her words a low hiss, she squeaked out, "It was the letter."

"The letter," I echoed. "Did they find it?"

She didn't answer. Thrusting out her arm, she pushed against me, hurried down the hallway, dragging her coat along the floor. I called after her, but she never looked back.

I debated knocking on Aleck's door, but changed my mind. Instead, I went into my room, showered, dressed for breakfast, and checked my notes. I needed to be in the courtroom that morning because the *Times* expected a column from me. I needed to record what I saw. "The human interest angle," my editor had stressed over and over. "We'll handle the legal stuff, reprint the daily transcript, but you and Aleck will provide the local color."

Aleck had whispered to me after we left that luncheon in Times Square, "We've been hired as scribbling gladiators in a Jersey Circus Maximus."

"Yes," I'd answered, "let the blood-letting begin."

But what intrigued me now was not so much the dynamics of the courtroom—the bluster and swell of young Attorney General David Wilentz for the prosecution and the old-style fire-and-brimstone of the defense attorney Edward Reilly. No, what fascinated were the sudden bits and pieces of Annabel's ill-fated move to Flemington and her connection with the Morrow and Lindbergh households. Idly reviewing my notes, I scanned the press articles I'd been given in a folder, all dating back to the night of the kidnapping. In particular I read that Violet Sharp had left the Morrow mansion at eight that night, going with an "Ernie"—no last name—and two of his friends to the Peanut Grill roadhouse, returning at eleven, her return witnessed by old Mrs. Morrow herself. Though Violet stumbled on delivering the truth—movies, not roadhouse—she later changed her story.

Ernie, I thought. And the Peanut Grill roadhouse in Orangeburg. Montclair Manor, the den of madness somewhere in New Jersey. The Morrow siblings. Anne, beloved wife of the hero. Dwight, disaffected only son, in and out of mental hospitals. And this…this mysterious Blake Somerville whom Violet adored, the rich young man who routinely seduced and manipulated and cajoled—and somehow was at the heart of all of this.

Yes, Aleck pooh-poohed it all as a vain girl's folly, but not so fast. That was the story I wanted to explore.

Aleck, though he might balk, would have to be Sancho Panza as I tilted at windmills.

And now the moment with Peggy Crispen in the hallway.

Cody Lee Thomas sat in a jail cell, probably in shouting distance of Bruno Richard Hauptmann, both men accused of murder.

Someone did not want the truth to come out, and I didn't believe it had anything to do with Cody Lee. Someone had strangled Annabel Biggs to cover up another crime. Perhaps someone had stolen the incendiary letters, if—the awful if here—they'd actually been stolen. Perhaps that burglar now realized that there was another letter that would implicate—might turn the law's pinpoint focus away from the hapless Bruno. Or somehow not only him but others as well. The gang of kidnappers that Colonel Schwarzkopf often talked of. *Used* to talk of—because these days his press statements focused only on Bruno, the lone wolf. The arrest of Cody Lee Thomas was happenstance, perhaps fortuitous—but it didn't end the story. The existence of the letters—and the suicide of Violet Sharp—told me that.

Aleck wasn't at breakfast, though everyone else in the world was: Adela Rogers St. John was pontificating about how her father, the storied jurist Earl Rogers, would have dealt with the trial. She'd made clear her allegiance to Hearst with her condemnation of Bruno Hauptmann. A fashion plate, each day of the trial she'd appeared in a different Hattie Carnegie outfit, designed especially for her. She looked good in the rotogravure. Now, sharing coffee with Walter Winchell, she nodded as he snarkily announced that Judge Trenchard, the seasoned jurist who presided, was a personal friend and "an American, to boot." He added, "That says it all."

Well, of course, it said nothing at all, as I glared at him, pulled in my disapproving cheeks. Unfortunately, he caught my look. He actually grimaced, the look of a menaced dog ready to bite.

I looked for Peggy Crispen, but she was not in the café. A band of waiters and Martha Tripp moved among the diners, though Martha looked distracted, her face flushed, slopping a glass of orange juice onto the floor, ignoring it, and then ignoring a customer's call for more coffee. She kept glancing toward the kitchen door, her countenance icy. Finally, his face as stern and flushed as his wife's, Horace Tripp followed a waiter out of the kitchen, his hands holding a tray of cereal bowls. He mumbled some words into the neck of the young waiter, who turned, stumbled, then apologized for something he had done. His garbled, loud "Not my fault" sailed over the room, and Horace's frown deepened.

I called him to my table. "Mr. Tripp." I waited as his eyes scanned the room.

He approached me. "Miss Ferber?"

"An hour ago I bumped into Peggy Crispen in the hallway, distraught. She mentioned a burglary in her room. She was frightened and…"

He interrupted me. "Peggy has been canned."

"Fired?"

Sarcasm in his voice. "Another way of putting it, I'm afraid."

"You let her go?"

His eye got wide. "Me? Of course not. We're short-handed as it is. Lord, with the loss of Annabel Biggs, we had to scramble." He stopped, unsure of his indiscretion. "I'm sorry. I'd don't mean to talk of this."

"What did she do wrong? When I saw her, she was obviously headed into work this morning."

He surveyed the large room again, but lowered his voice. "The management found fault with her. I gather she was weeping in the lobby, distressed, became agitated, her face splotchy with…with that makeup she wears, and when she ran into the kitchen"—he pointed behind him—"she had a loud argument with Martha."

"About what?"

Walter Winchell looked up from his table and eyed me suspiciously. Adela Rogers St. Johns was polishing a rhinestone brooch on her lapel.

"I was doing something else. Martha called attention to Peggy's disheveled look, her weepy face, and Peggy babbled about a robbery, which alarmed us, of course. I rushed over, but Martha lost her temper and accused Peggy of"—again the furtive glance around the room during which he caught Winchell's censorious eye—"questionable behavior. Peggy snapped, actually slapped my wife. *Slapped* her. All this, of course, in the kitchen, thank God, but loud enough to entertain the early-bird reporters who jumped up. Mr. Lawrence, the head boss, who'd followed the noise, dismissed her at once."

"Where is she?"

"I assume she's home. If only she wasn't so…hysterical."

"Back to her room?"

Again the sarcasm. "Where else?"

His tone annoyed me. "Perhaps she could catch her breath in your own rooms, sir." An unforgiveable remark, perhaps, but joyous for me to deliver.

His face blanched, his jaw dropped with the suddenness of a cartoon character, a clattering of teeth, and he half-bowed and darted away.

From behind me a voice roared, "Good work, darling Ferb. You do know how to eviscerate a man." Aleck slid into a chair opposite me.

"I have lots of practice with you."

"Ah, a glib breakfast rejoinder that goes for the jugular."

"That wasn't the part of your body I was referring to."

"Brava, Ferb. Much better. You must have laced your coffee with a squirt of bathtub gin you salvaged from a hip flask during your flapper days."

Enough of this. "Aleck, Peggy has been fired. Someone broke into her rooms and ransacked them."

His eyes widened. "Oh, my God. The letter?"

"I never got an answer from her."

"The poor dear. Well, I must…"

A chair slid across the tiled floor from another table, tucked itself between us, and Joshua Flagg looked from me to Aleck. An odd smirk covered his features, his face clownish. He was a dangerous chameleon, I realized—last time I thought him peculiar-looking, a face off-kilter, a crooked jawline and a pointed nose. Today, fresh scrubbed, his hair trimmed and his moustache shellacked, he was caddishly handsome. He would be the young man you nostalgically remembered when you were safely married and away from him.

"Ah, the intrepid reporter for Hearst."

He shook his head. "No, not a reporter. I told you. An aide."

"A spy who tells everyone his business," Aleck offered.

A twinkle in Joshua's eye. "Words, words, words."

"That's all we have," I noted.

"I doubt that," he said to me. "You have a curiosity."

"And evidence for that is?"

He sat back, rolled his tongue over his upper lip. "Observation. The trained eye of a world observer, a bright fellow as myself."

"Like our visit to Annabel's room—and Peggy's?" I forced him to look into my face. "By 'our' I include you, sir, rapping on the door and then running down the stairwell like a spooked kitten."

He chortled but there was nothing funny in his laugh. "A mistake on my part."

"Mr. Flagg," I began, "I don't seem to recall inviting you to our breakfast table, and yet here you sit, tucked in between us like an orphan begging for a spot at the dinner table."

"I never beg."

"You are now, sir."

"I guess I am."

"So what does Hearst's peripatetic reporter want from us?"

He waved his hand in the air. "I'm not a reporter. I'm an aide…an assistant."

"So what do you need assistance with?"

He faltered, his neck getting crimson, a bead of sweat on his brow. "Just that…"

Aleck was impatient. "Speak up, fool, for God's sake."

He rushed his words. "I was wondering what you two are on the trail of?"

"Meaning?"

"Miss Ferber, you were spotted visiting Cody Lee Thomas in jail. A common murderer, below contempt. Rumor has it you even stared down Bruno Richard Hauptmann." I started to say something but he held up a hand. "I mean, you were allowed to see him close up. No one else can."

Aleck was making a clicking sound. "Edna, what? You did *what*? You visited the jail? And didn't tell me?"

"A memory lapse, Aleck."

"What are you up to, dear?"

"Nothing, Aleck. A chance meeting—with Hauptmann."

"Chance?"

"It was an act of amusement by the deputy, sir, someone having fun with me. I was supposed to quake and shiver. I suspect Hovey Low believes women are cowering simpletons. He didn't know that I interviewed craven murderers in old-time Milwaukee when I was barely in my twenties."

"Nelly Bly with a beer stein," Aleck sneered, still annoyed.

Joshua ignored Aleck. "Then you two were cozy in Annabel Biggs' room right after she was murdered. Talking to Peggy, the waitress, the chubby girl who keeps telling me to get lost."

"What do you want from her? And, I repeat, from us?"

He breathed in and whispered, "There's another story going on here. Annabel and this dead Violet Sharp were related."

I stiffened. "How do you know that, sir?"

"Annabel got a little tipsy in a roadhouse one night, and the gal liked to rattle on and on about a pot of gold just out of reach. She said too much—hinted that Violet Sharp—that suicide on the floor of the Morrow mansion that everyone still wonders about, especially the defense team for Bruno—told her something."

"Well, the secret obviously died with her. With Annabel, I mean."

"Did it?" A sharp, penetrating gaze, his dark gray eyes shiny.

"I had one brief conversation with the girl, Mr. Flagg. She served me coffee."

"And yet you visit her murderer and then her roommate."

"I'm a reporter. I follow leads."

Aleck harrumphed. "Where is this going?" He pouted. "Why have I been kept in…darkness?"

Joshua sat back, stretched out his legs. "I'm trying to find out what you know, lady. Annabel and Violet and…and even Violet's sister Emily. The three Fates, as it were. Somehow they got mixed into this cauldron of kidnapping and ransom money and death and German illegal aliens to our shores."

"Well, I don't understand it either," I concluded.

"Are you sure?"

I sat up straight. "I'm not in the habit of lying, young man. That's the truth."

His eyes swept the room. He nodded in the direction of Walter Winchell. "Pompous little ass, wouldn't you say?"

"Well," I smiled, "we agree on something." A heartbeat. "But that's not why you're sitting with us—to malign a prominent radio personality and hack writer for the *Mirror*."

He grinned. "I don't miss an opportunity to mock my superiors."

"That must require an enormous amount of your free time."

He laughed out loud.

I understood now why he was sitting at our table. He feared we'd stumbled on a piece of a puzzle that was his concern. Or he didn't *want* us to fit the pieces together. He wanted to know what we knew. Either he harbored some horrible secret and was afraid we'd also caught on, or he lacked some details and hoped we'd supply the missing information. A scurrilous young man, a shiftless sort. He was smiling at me now, attempting to woo me. I stared into his face. "I think it's time you left us alone. My coffee is cold."

When he started to say something, I turned aside. Finally, he walked away.

# Chapter Eleven

Aleck and I crossed the street toward the courthouse and showed our passes at the entrance—red for journalists, white for officials, yellow for telegraphers. We were shown to our seats in the packed, hot room. The narrow winding stairs led up to a gallery where spectators and reporters gaped, admitted first come, first served. A high-ceilinged room with yellow walls, large windows on either side and behind the judge's dais. Old church-pew benches lined the walls, folding chairs appropriated from the Flemington Fairgrounds. Reporters scribbled on pine boards—no typewriters allowed. Five hundred folks were jam-packed in the room, and I noticed one man, his overcoat bulky and pitched to his side, concealed the lens of a forbidden camera. The judge had ordered no cameras, no newsreels, but the click and blip of mechanical noises surfaced as we waited.

Attorney General David Wilentz was trying his first criminal case. A young man, probably in his thirties, a rail-thin handsome man with a slender dark face, shiny black hair, he'd stepped into the Union Hotel lounge the day before dressed in a snazzy suit, a pearl-gray felt fedora with the brim snapped down in front and to one side, a velvet-collared Chesterfield overcoat, a white silk scarf encircling his neck. But now standing before the judge, he wore a simple blue suit, a stiff, high-collared white shirt, and an understated striped tie and handkerchief—the country lawyer gone to court.

He spent the morning thundering about the quality of lumber, his witness a "wood expert," a scholar who had a lot to say about the various types of wood that compose the kidnapping ladder—and one piece in particular that Wilentz insisted—he hammered home the idea, his facile voice rising as he faced the jury—came from Bruno Hauptmann's own attic.

"Impressive young man," I whispered to Aleck.

The testimony was countered by the celebrated defense lawyer Edward Reilly, a fiftyish man, towering with a massive stomach, a man who dressed in a formal dark morning coat, a white carnation in his buttonhole, striped gray trousers and white spats, a Biblical prophet bullying the witness who refused to back down. His elegant attire was emphatically out of place in this small-town courtroom. This could not work to Hauptmann's advantage, a fact I whispered to Aleck.

Aleck whispered back. "The man's a drunk. He may be drunk now."

The scuttlebutt in Nellie's Taproom suggested that Reilly had been falling-down drunk the day after New Year's and, at one point, had danced around a flagpole on Main Street. Surrounded by a changing bevy of busty women he called "secretaries," he was being paid by Hearst—in fact, Reilly confided that he didn't like Bruno Hauptmann and let another lawyer, Lloyd Fisher, do the interviews with the suspect. Reilly met with Bruno for a matter of minutes. With his ruddy face, his reeling posture, and his circus antics, Big Ed spent his time at a local tavern during the trial's lunch break.

As Wilentz thundered on, his finger pointing at Bruno Hauptmann, the accused stared at him, face rigid, chin up, spine erect. I watched the room, jotted a note or two. Spectators, bored with the laborious details of the science of lumber, did crossword puzzles, flipped through the pages of a movie magazine, one old woman knitting a sweater. A juror chewed tobacco with an intensity that would shame a cow and her cud. Another juror, a plump woman with pin curls, yawned and nodded to someone in the gallery.

A crowd of spectators had bunched at the back, and I was surprised to see Horace Tripp standing behind a smaller man. As Wilentz finished up, I followed Horace's gaze. He was staring at Bruno Hauptmann. He never seemed to blink, so intent was his glare. When Wilentz remarked that Hauptmann had been a soldier in the Great War, a man who served the Kaiser and fought American servicemen, a man trained to kill, a heartless machine-gunner, Horace actually let out a gruff cough. Of course, I knew he'd fought in the war, had returned bitter, and had no doubt that the illegal German immigrant who sneaked onto our shores and massacred a hero's baby...well, that man had to die. I was so enthralled by the back of the room—Horace's eyes finally found mine and he made a helpless shrug that made little sense—that I missed Wilentz's closing remarks, though Aleck, jotting something in his pad, broke the tip of his pencil and matter-of-factly reached over and took mine from my hand. I let him.

As the lawyers bickered over some legal fine point, I sized up Bruno Hauptmann as he watched his wife, Anna, sitting on the side. Bruno was dressed in a loose, double-breasted gray suit, a handkerchief neatly inserted in his pocket, a careful slicked-back haircut. With his penetrating blue eyes, that chestnut hair, his high cheekbones, pointed clean-shaven chin, he struck me as emotionless—severe, stoic, sullen, an alarming blankness in his look. An arrogant man, I thought, one who was looking with contempt at the proceedings, a man who did not believe he'd be found guilty.

At one point Colonel Lindbergh twisted in his seat, said something to Henry Breckinridge, sitting at his side, and Bruno flicked his head for barely a second. He refused to look at the aviator. Sitting four chairs away from Bruno, Lindbergh had none of the spiff and polish of the well-groomed Bruno—he sported a gray suit without a vest, a frayed shirt cuff, chaotic hair. When he moved, a coat seam looked ready to give. But that same movement revealed the .38 in a shoulder holster under his jacket.

At four-thirty, Judge Trenchard called it a day. As Bruno was led out, he mumbled some words to his wife. It looked like he said, "Don't worry."

Anna Hauptmann trembled. A plain-looking woman with strawberry blond hair, a drab hausfrau who struck me as an odd companion for the matinee idol husband, she was dressed in a simple navy-blue dress with a cowl neck, a small black felt hat over sensible curls. A white medal hung from her neck on a black ribbon. I recalled such women in the Bavarian market-place—sturdy, buxom, earthy, washed-out eyes, and clipped words. Strong-jawed, unattractive.

She watched as Bruno was led out by a state trooper.

David Wilentz, gathering his papers, then stepped into the aisle.

The spectators applauded madly.

◇◇◇

In the early darkness as snow showers cast halos around the streetlights, I took a walk. Aleck had gone back to his room to write his column, but I begged off. The horrid spectacle of the courtroom ate at me. The laughter rocking the courtroom, the jeering, the applause, the merry jostling crowds, the fur-decked society folks who spotted friends from Manhattan and waved across the room as the judge made an announcement, and then demanded silence. A party, this, and a wonderful time for so many. And Anna Hauptmann, that dowdy, confused wife of an alleged killer, occasionally stared back, wide-eyed, at an America she could never understand. Her eyes showed bafflement, some resentment, and finally absolute wonder.

I strolled slowly, lost in muddled thought, vaguely aware of groups of people shoving by, heading to supper, turning into taverns. The Candy Kitchen had a line of customers buying bags of sweets. The Blue Bow Tea Room placed a "today's special" sign in the window: "German chocolate cake." At least this was not as tasteless as the Union Hotel Café featuring "Hauptmann Pudding."

A snow flurry surprised me, and I spun away from a blast of sharp icy air. At that moment, wiping flakes from my face, I spotted someone standing in the entrance of a building. Peggy Crispen, bundled up in a threadbare winter coat, a scarf wrapped around her neck. Not her own roominghouse, I noticed, which was two or three doors down, but a small clapboard-and-brick building that housed a haberdashery on the ground level, now closed, the lights switched off. Peggy stood on the stoop, shivering.

"Peggy, for God's sake." I rushed to her. "You're dying of the cold. What in the world?"

Her voice was tinny, faraway. "I don't know, Miss Ferber. I'm afraid to go inside. I'm afraid...I..."

"But you can't stay out here. You'll die of the cold."

I reached out my hand and touched her elbow, but she shook me off. "I know. I will go in. But not yet." She glanced down the street, and I noticed her eyes settled on a small tavern, a spotlight illuminating the façade. The White Birch Tavern. A door swung open and a trio of partiers strolled out. The sound of music from a jukebox, a country-western ditty. The strum of a fiddle.

"I gotta think what to do."

"Come with me, Peggy. I'll find a place for you. You can't..."

Suddenly her hand flew out at me as she spoke through clenched teeth. "Go away. All of you. Goddammit. I just wanna be left alone. None of this ain't supposed to happen. None of it is my fault. I don't know these people...these stories...Annabel's nonsense. Now it all falls on me, and...and, someone keeps knocking on my door."

"Who is it?"

"I don't know. I won't answer. Then the phone rings in the hallway and someone yells it's for me. I won't come out. That Joshua fellow lingers on the street, watches for me, bothers me."

"I heard you were let go at the restaurant."

A loud, phony laugh. "Yeah, that was coming. I point the finger at Martha. It ain't my fault she's married to a cad, that man who won't leave you alone."

"Did he and Annabel...?"

That surprised her. "No, she had no liking for him and made that clear. But Martha thought she did—*her*, not me. Big laugh. Me, the fat one. She doesn't trust Horace. But, you know, I thought he'd fight for me. Help me keep my job. He just stood there and watched them humiliate me. Now what am I gonna do? No money, nothing." She swayed in the doorway and let out a sob.

I hesitated but went on. "You were seeing him in secret, Peggy?"

A harsh laugh. "A funny way you put things, Miss Ferber. A secret that was no secret because he crowed about every conquest. I let that fool into my life because I was lonely in this godforsaken town, and I don't know why. A little flattery and a few dollars spent on me at the bar. Nobody around that I could be friends with. Just people I meet in taverns who can't remember my name the next day. But Horace, well, he wooed me. I knew he was married but I didn't care." Shaking from the cold, she drew back into a corner as a blast of wind shook her.

"You knew that couldn't have a good ending, Peggy."

"He's suave and slick and says these nice things. I'm a fat girl without a mirror."

"Still."

"You know what he told me, Miss Ferber?"

"What is that?" I waited while she rubbed a handkerchief across her nose.

"He said he was gonna leave Martha when the trial was over, and I said, 'Will you take me with you?' And you know what he did? He laughed like a crazy fool, and he said, 'Men like me don't marry girls like you.'"

"Lord, what did you say?"

A throaty laugh. "That's the sad thing. I looked at him and said, 'Yeah, I know.' And I still let him follow me home. I'd sneak him into the room." She stepped away from the stoop. "Please leave me alone, Miss Ferber." Still shivering, she tottered down the sidewalk and disappeared into the tavern.

# Chapter Twelve

Colonel Charles Lindbergh took the stand.

Someone at the back of the courtroom applauded but stopped abruptly when someone else shushed him.

I thought of Damon Runyon's muttering that first day—a circus, this trial. Runyon, in fact, was sitting a row behind me, arms folded over his chest and glaring across the room, as though waiting for something egregious to happen. As we all waited for the morning to begin, watching the celebrated aviator moving to a chair, the atmosphere was titillation and sputtered glee.

Opening night on Broadway, I thought: a hum of anticipation and the swish of fur and beaded purse and elegant dinner jacket. For, indeed, it was celebrity time in the packed room: Ginger Rogers, Frederic March, and Jack Dempsey. Earlier, a Rolls-Royce had pulled up to the curb and a jeweled matron stepped onto the sidewalk and waited to be looked at, led with suitable salaams into the inner sanctums. She'd been subpoenaed—not that she'd testify today, but that meant she'd be guaranteed a seat.

When Judge Trenchard walked in, I expected quiet—instead, there was a low rumbling of joy. The show was about to begin again.

Colonel Lindbergh looked at ease on the witness stand, sitting with crossed legs on a hard-backed chair, a slouch to his posture, his head tilted to the right. A lock of that infernal blond hair slipped down over his forehead, and for a moment he tossed back his head, willing it back into place.

Bruno Hauptmann refused to take his eyes off Lindbergh.

Everyone was waiting for Lindbergh to name Bruno the killer. Yesterday's testimony had been riveting, true—but routine. Now David Wilentz led Lindbergh through the blow-by-blow events of the awful night—his return home from the city, dinner with Anne, chatting with her in the living room when he heard what sounded like a slat of an orange crate snapping against the side of the house. He never investigated, assuming it was the wind.

"Was it the sort of noise that would come with the falling of a ladder?"

"Yes, it was, if the ladder was outside."

They discovered the baby missing. "I was reading in the library, and Miss Gow called to me in a rather excited voice and asked me if I had the baby."

"What else?"

An envelope on top of the radiator. Wilentz waved it then—and the note inside. Wilentz read the fearsome ransom note, stumbling over the garbled English and the fragmented sentences.

Throughout the long morning and afternoon sessions, I kept an eye on Bruno Hauptmann. David Wilentz repeatedly pointed at him, forcing Lindbergh to stare at the accused. A sullen look on his face, suspicious.

Bruno, Bruno, Bruno.

The word echoed in the chamber, ominous, dangerous, ugly.

Each time he thundered Bruno's name, a barely audible hiss rolled through the crowd, raw, angry. The judge looked up, seemed ready to admonish the crowd, but simply stared.

At lunchtime, I watched Lindbergh leave with Anne, Colonel Schwarzkopf, and Colonel Breckinridge, and the crowd outside howled like banshees and pushed and shoved. "Hang him! Hang him!" When the sheriff opened the back doors, reporters who'd been forced to remain inside, now were anxious to wire or phone in the morning's proceedings and pushed over one another, shoving, yelling, sheaves of paper spilling out of their pockets, as they raced to the streets or upstairs where a room of telephones and telegraphs had been established to facilitate reporting to the hinterlands.

I walked with Aleck to the church basement for lunch. Knowing his rapacious love of the good ladies' bounty—today's advertised special for fifty cents was roast chicken with parsley-buttered potatoes and peach cobbler with homemade vanilla ice cream, a menu Aleck had whispered to me during one of the lulls in Charles Lindbergh's testimony. Aleck bounded down those well-worn wooden steps. His tiny hands dropped a half dollar into the plate as though tithing ordered by Biblical scripture.

◇◇◇

Late that afternoon I found my mind wandering, speculating. News accounts all noted that Hauptmann never used the name "Bruno," even though it was his given Christian name. He was known all his life as "Richard." His wife supposedly didn't know his given first name. Some of his friends called him "Rich"—so American, so back-lot baseball. But the press had latched onto "Bruno" with a vengeance. Why? I wondered. So many news accounts kept referring to him as "the German" or "the alien" or the "illegal stowaway" or "the monster" who'd invaded our shores. Perhaps "Bruno" smacked more of an outsider, the ethnic pariah. So what if his wife and friends knew him as "Richard"? He'd become the notorious "Bruno" forevermore.

So, as I watched Hauptmann stare at Lindbergh, I realized there were two Hauptmanns at war in Flemington, two differ-ent men. Bruno, the inhuman violator of a hero's family, cold, ice in his veins, the solo perpetrator of the heinous crime. And Richard, the affable Bronx carpenter who was the proud father of little Manfred (ironically named after the Great War's German aviator hero, Baron Richthofen, the Red Baron), the man who swam at Hunter's Island in Pelham Bay Park with friends, drifted in his canoe while strumming his mandolin, had birthday cel-ebrations, went to the movies, waited for his wife to finish her shift at Frederickson's Bakery in order to drive her home. The young family man, fashioning a life under the bright sun of the American Dream.

Bruno or Richard—was there a third man who embraced both? Maybe.

A man caught with fourteen grand of ransom money hidden in his makeshift garage floor.

A man who lied about the money. Who told many lies. Who blamed it on the dead German friend Isidor Fisch—little Izzy—who'd returned to Leipzig and promptly died of tuberculosis. "The Fisch story," the papers glibly termed it. The man with the consumptive cough had left suitcases and a shoebox with Bruno. Supposedly he owed Bruno money for a shared business venture, trading in furs. When there was a leak in the attic, the box on a shelf got wet and Bruno supposedly discovered the cash. He didn't know it was ransom money, he claimed. He freely spent some—he never hid his face when he did so—and hid the rest from his wife. He traveled to Maine, Florida, Canada, but no ransom money surfaced there. Why not unload it there? Why just New York City? I wondered about that.

A Fisch story, they called it in court. A killer. A kidnapper.

Lindbergh was talking about the second ransom note.

*Dear Sir, We have warned you not to make anything public or notify the police. Now you have to take the consequences.*

Bruno Richard Hauptmann watched, and I watched him. And I watched his wife, Anna.

At one point Walter Winchell, seated directly behind the prosecution table, jotted something down on a pad and slipped it to Wilentz, who paused in his questioning of Lindbergh, glanced back at the reporter with a trace of annoyance in his face, and nodded. Winchell sat back, satisfied, though immediately he began jotting another note. Wilentz dropped the first onto his table, and I wondered whether his next questions to the aviator were, in fact, supplied by the intrusive reporter. When I looked to see Judge Trenchard's reaction, there was none. He was tapping a pencil as he watched Lindbergh cross his legs, lean back, and consider a response.

Well, of course, I thought—Walter Winchell was so often seen at old-time speakeasies and Broadway openings, chit-chatting with those fawning around him, sometimes jotting down what I assumed were dazzling witticisms and satiric thrusts and handing them to his acolytes. Rumor had it he hung around with Owney Madden, a Hell's Kitchen mob boss. Why should the murder trial be any different?

David Wilentz's voice dropped, and the aviator leaned forward to hear. At that moment his double-breasted blazer opened and I spotted the small revolver.

I nudged Aleck. "The gun."

"So what?" he said.

"In court?"

"Perhaps he's going to shoot the man who stole his baby."

"And you approve?"

"It will save the taxpayers a fortune."

"And be a miscarriage of justice."

"No one would care."

"I would. This isn't the Wild West, Aleck. He isn't Billy the Kid. Wyatt Earp." I stammered. "Hopalong Cassidy."

His eyebrows rose. "Hopalong Cassidy? He never existed."

"You get my point."

"He's trying to make a point."

"Which is?"

"He's not a man to be fooled with."

"Maybe he'll shoot Walter Winchell, who is clearly the prosecution's amanuensis. You did see that creep slip Wilentz a note?"

"That surprised me, I admit."

"Maybe I should slip Bruno Hauptmann a note."

Aleck ran his tongue into his cheek. "I'm surprised you haven't already. A mash note scented with your cloying gardenia perfume."

I turned my back on him.

Judge Trenchard called it a day.

◇◇◇

Back in my room, resting on the bed, I skimmed through a folder of articles supplied by the editor at the *Times*. Yes, all the minutia of the daily trial fascinated me, especially watching the celebrated Lindbergh, arguably the most famous and popular man in America—in the world?—slowly and methodically recount the unimaginable horrors of the past few years. But what had come to fascinate me was the chronicle of Annabel Biggs and her cousin Violet Sharp. *That* dynamic. *That* puzzle. I reread articles from the immediate days of the kidnapping, the iterated questioning of the skittish and volatile Violet Sharp, the frightened young British girl who crumbled before the authorities.

Something had happened in the Morrow household. But what? A prank, planned, according to Peggy. A prank that involved Dwight Morrow, Jr.'s involvement with Blake Somerville—and Violet Sharp, who obviously had a fascination with the mysterious man. But what? A prank to kidnap the baby—make-believe? Make the child disappear from home? Ransom money handed over? But was it just a foolish barroom game they played—and Violet believed it? Or had they really done it? A fake kidnapping of Little Lindy that went awry? Impossible. Dwight and Blake at Amherst College. Then meeting again at an insane asylum in Montclair? Impossible. Violet's confession to her cousin in a series of letters, and the last one the most explosive—a letter missing now or destroyed. Letters that brought Annabel Biggs to Flemington to extort cash from Lindbergh. Blackmail. The sacrosanct Morrow family—Dwight, the shunned son. That seemed farfetched, but...Annabel now murdered, and not by Cody Lee Thomas. That much I knew. And her room violated again. Those letters possibly taken. Hard to know. A letter searched for and found by Peggy Crispen, an innocent victim of the drama, now scared out of her wits.

Violet Sharp. A suicide.

But did she still hold the answer?

How did Bruno Richard Hauptmann figure in all of this?

I reread an article that talked of Violet's activities the night of March 1, 1932, her visit to a roadhouse with Ernie Miller and another couple. They drank illegal beer. She drank coffee. Only coffee. Why? Ernie was asked. He didn't know. In fact, he didn't know anything about her. He'd been driving on Lydecker Street in Englewood and spotted Violet and her sister, Emily, walking. Thinking he knew them, he stopped, and, flirting, invited Violet to go out. No, no, she said, but gave him her number. One time—the night of the kidnapping.

Ernie Miller. He might have the answer.

I was late meeting Aleck at the Puritan Restaurant down the street. He was seated at a table by the window and had already eaten. Peeved, he pointed to the remains of a chocolate cake. A smear of chocolate rested ingloriously on a plump cheek.

"Saving that for later?" I asked him.

"Edna, Edna, the problem with our conversations is that I find myself waking up in the middle of them."

"Ernie Miller." I stared into his face.

"Now you're speaking in tongue." A pause. "Singular."

"He's the one who took Violet Sharp to that speakeasy the night of the kidnapping."

"We all know that, Edna." He signaled to the waiter for another piece of cake. I ordered baked chicken, though I wasn't hungry. "And he's scheduled to testify for the prosecution in an upcoming session."

"But he may have information on this…this cockamamie tale that Annabel spun—the rich boy's prank, although I hardly think 'prank' is the proper word here."

"If prank it were, Ferb. To my thinking, Annabel and Violet exchanged giddy schoolgirl letters, imagined romances and imagined wealth and outright nonsense. *Nothing* of that happened."

I broke in. "You don't believe that, Aleck. Annabel was murdered."

His mouth was stuffed with cake. "Yes, by the country hick named Cody Lee Thomas, dirt under his nails and hayseed in his buck teeth."

"No, he didn't do it."

Aleck waited a long time. "Edna dear, you're like a vaudeville skit in which one end of the horse rides west, the other east."

"I need to meet with Ernie Miller."

Aleck choked as he sipped coffee. "Impossible."

"You have more power at the *Times*—on Broadway—than I do. Find me an address. Set up a meeting."

He banged a fist on the table. "I will not be a part of this."

"Frankly, I don't want you there. You scare children."

"Obviously not enough." He winked at me.

"They told me to follow up human interest leads, the *Times* did. This is one."

Aleck got serious, his fingers gripping a cigarette and slipping it into his ivory holder. "Leave this alone, Ferb."

"No, I won't."

"I will not speak at your funeral."

"And why not?"

"A waste of my words. There will be no one there to hear my eloquent lies."

"An empty room has never stopped you before."

He sighed. "I'll see what I can do. But no good will come of this."

"I don't suppose it will. Nothing about our sojourn in Flemington can possibly have a happy ending."

He nodded to the entrance. "Look what the cat allowed in."

Joshua Flagg had walked in, but he dragged a foot. A white bandage covered one eyebrow. There was a bright purple welt under a swollen eye.

"I know Hearst employees bring out the worst in folks but this?"

Aleck snickered. "It's a delightful story. Edna, you obviously missed it."

"Tell me."

We watched Joshua Flagg spot us, deliberate approaching, then deciding to slink out the door, so hasty a move he careened into a customer, who cursed him. Aleck relished gossip, so he cleared his throat, glanced around him, and spoke loudly. "I heard it from one of our drivers, you know, Marcus, the good-looking one you can't seem to take your eyes off."

I cut in. "For God's sake, Aleck."

He adjusted his eyeglasses, and his small eyes seemed enlarged now, unblinking. With that round plump face and those circular thick glasses he was a caricaturist's ultimate dream: the cherubic owl. "Anyway"—he stretched out the word—"Marcus told me Joshua was loitering around the depot where the drivers bide their time waiting for famous folks like us to snap our fingers. Anyway, Marcus said Joshua wandered in, nosy as hell, and started asking questions of old Willie, our other favorite driver. The one you ignore."

"And you admit to finding an annoying chatterbox."

"Words last. Beauty fades."

"So does my patience, Aleck."

"Anyway, I gather he demanded Willie tell him where he'd driven folks, in particular, us."

"Us!" I exclaimed.

"Exactly. Actually, *you*. He seemed inordinately curious about *your* habits, my dear. I don't know why he didn't ask me. I've seen all your bad habits." Aleck flicked ashes from a cigarette into a tray. "I'm always ready to tell the world about Edna Ferber's social lapses."

I bit my lip. "Just what is he up to?"

"A spy, I'm sure. Old Willie, despite his slippage into senility and excessive verbiage, turns out to be a wiry sort, filled with gusto and verve. Like one of your unrealistic oil riggers in *Cimarron*. When Joshua asked one question too many, Willie punched him in the face and knocked him against the wall." He smiled. "Hence the injured bird we just spotted looking for a nest."

"I may start to appreciate Willie," I said. "But I wonder what's going on. You and I are not the subjects of any story line."

"Maybe something's going on that we don't see."

"That thought scares me, Aleck."

"Don't expect me to protect you from that scamp, Ferb. My weapons are words, not fists."

"If he forces me to parse a sentence at gunpoint, I'll dial your number."

◇◇◇

The next morning Colonel Lindbergh took the stand again. Ten a.m., promptly. His wife wasn't with him today.

David Wilentz had him recount the reddish clay marks discovered in the nursery. The footprint outside the window. A man's footprint that the police neglected to measure. The homemade ladder. Letters to Dr. Condon, "Jafsie." The arrival of the baby's sleeping garment in the mail. Riveted, the spectators were waiting for the moment when Lindbergh heard the voice of the kidnapper.

Yes, the drive to St. Raymond's Cemetery in the Bronx, waiting in the car while Dr. Condon went by himself to deal with the man who called himself John. Cemetery John. The payment of the fifty-thousand-dollar ransom.

As he sat some three hundred yards away in the car, windows rolled up, Lindbergh heard a thick guttural German voice call out.

"I heard what was clearly a voice calling from the cemetery, to the best of my belief calling Dr. Condon."

Wilentz paused. "What were the words?"

"In a foreign accent. 'Hey, Doctor.'"

"Since that time have you heard the same voice?"

"Yes, I have."

Another dramatic pause.

"Whose voice was it, Colonel, that you heard calling, 'Hey, Doctor'?"

"It was Hauptmann's voice," Lindbergh emphasized.

Turning his head, he stared into Bruno's face.

Bruno's body jerked in his seat. The guards on either side of him stiffened.

I looked toward Aleck, who sat enthralled, mouth open. Two and a half years after the kidnapping, I considered, and Lindbergh insisted he'd recognize that voice anywhere. Two words, yelled from a distance in a dark night graveyard.

The room was silent, hypnotized. Glances swept from Lindbergh to a stoic Bruno, eyes locked on his accuser.

The empty hole of time that followed his pronouncement seemed endless and yet a flash of a second.

Looking at the unmoving Bruno Hauptmann, I understood to my marrow that he would die in the electric chair.

# Chapter Thirteen

Willie drove me into Manhattan late the next afternoon. I'd scheduled a meeting early that evening with Ernie Miller, set in motion by someone at the *Times* who knew someone who knew someone else. Ernie Miller, a little rattled at the invitation, agreed to meet me at an Italian bakery on Arthur Avenue in the Bronx. He was also promised a crisp twenty-dollar bill, that, my editor informed me, was my own responsibility.

Willie was unusually silent as he cruised along, which surprised me.

"Willie," I began, "I understand you had a little scuffle with Joshua Flagg."

He twisted his head around, a thin smile on his face. "Word spreads, no?"

"Your fellow driver Marcus told Aleck Woollcott."

"Ain't my proudest moment, I tell you."

"Sounds wonderful to me. I think that reporter—or whatever he is—is of questionable morals."

He rubbed the side of his nose and debated what to tell me. "Don't know about that, ma'am, but I do know I don't like no folks nosing around and demanding attention."

I waited a heartbeat. "I hear that he was curious about where you drive us—in particular, me."

The car slowed and Willie bent his head over the steering wheel. "For a quiet guy, that Marcus yammers up a storm."

"Well, it *does* concern me, Willie, wouldn't you say?"

A long pause. "Guess so. I never got to ask him the *why* of his question because my temper got the best o' me."

I leaned forward and tapped the back of the driver's seat. "What do you think, though? Why the question?"

Willie glanced back at me. "Hey, we drivers got a job to do. I think he believes you are onto a story that *he* wants to know about. And he got the idea"—he said *idear*—"that the drivers is like them—poor folks ready to spill the beans on our customers."

"But all the reporters are here for the same story, no? The trial of Hauptmann for kidnapping and murder."

He cut me off, his words rushed. "He asked me if I drove you to Englewood."

"Next Day Hill? The Morrow estate?"

He nodded. "I told him no, but he said something about that gal what killed herself."

I sat up. "What?"

"Dunno. Just that name, thrown out like that." He snickered. "Then we got into it."

I banged one fist into the palm of my hand. Violet Sharp. Joshua Flagg was pursuing—or monitoring—the same story I was. Hence his pursuit of Annabel and now her roommate, Peggy Crispen.

Willie was mumbling about something.

"What?" I said into his neck. Under his chauffeur's cap his drab grayish hair looked unwashed, scruffy.

"All this is stuff and nonsense when everyone should be planning the execution of that scoundrel Bruno."

"I know, I know—you're convinced he's guilty. We've heard you before."

His head swung around and the car drifted to the right. "And you ain't sure?"

"That's why we are having a trial, Willie."

"All show, ma'am. If I had my way, he'd been strung from an oak tree in the center of town. And then a party thrown afterwards."

"Well, perhaps then we should be thankful you're not the sheriff in town."

He glanced into the rearview mirror. I made eye contact: anger there, stoniness.

Well, I told myself, I discovered a way to curb Willie's garrulous tongue, although I probably created yet another soul who'd like to wring my slight and powdered neck. With the three strands of real pearls.

"We are allowed to disagree, Willie." I spoke into the silence.

"That's your opinion." His words were clipped, final. His grip tightened on the steering wheel as we sailed into Manhattan.

◇◇◇

At my Park Avenue apartment I checked in with my housekeeper, who was surprised to see me traipsing in, rushing around. I checked my mail, drank a cup of coffee, and was thankful my mother was out shopping. She'd frowned on my taking the assignment in Flemington—"You're a novelist, Edna, not a tabloid scribbler. And that trial, that evil German killer—evil, evil, evil."

"It's for the *New York Times*," I'd told her.

"No matter. Sometimes they like to sink down into the mud and wallow around, that paper."

"The *Times?*"

"Wake up, Edna."

After my coffee I caught a checkered cab up to the Bronx. The driver balked at the destination, but I'd rapped impatiently on the glass barrier between us, and he became appropriately docile. I'd sent a moody Willie back to Flemington, although he informed me he had to deliver some reporters from the newspaper back down to the town. "Willie's gadabout service," he summed up.

I'd be staying overnight in the city, but Marcus Wood would collect me at six in the morning for the trek back to Flemington, arriving in time for the trial.

At seven at night, the streets dark and shadowy under bright streetlights, a wispy fog of sleet swirling in the air, I stepped out onto a busy sidewalk. Arthur Avenue, the roustabout heart of Little Italy in the upper borough. Despite the painful cold and growing threat of heavy nighttime snow, people pushed carts through the cluttered sidewalks, an organ grinder stood outside a small café and sang a Neapolitan ditty. As I strolled by, he extended an arm, thrusting a tin cup at me. I ignored him. "O Solo Mio" was never a favorite of mine. There was a price to be paid for offending my eardrums. Had he had a trained monkey, I might have offered a pittance. After all, the poor creature needed to be fed.

Ernie Miller had chosen the rendezvous, a corner eatery he favored called Mamma Lucia's. He knew people there, he'd told the editor at the *Times*. Home territory.

"Sounds suspect," Aleck had told me. "You know, Edna dear, there are still persistent rumors that the Mafia and the crime bosses stole that baby. Kidnapping is a favorite pursuit of the mob. The snatch racket. Irving Bitz and Salvatore Spitale and all that sorry crowd. Lindbergh even invited Mickey Rosner, a notorious *capo*, to Hopewell, thinking the underworld would get his baby back. Or so the rumor goes. Lord, Lindy gave Mickey a copy of the first ransom note, which doubtless allowed every extortionist to jump into the game."

"I don't think the Mafia is going to rub me out, Aleck."

"I know. They've refused the thousands and thousands of lira I've tossed their way."

"And Ernie Miller doesn't sound like he's a native of Palermo."

"Really? Ernesto Millerini? I knew him as a lad, playing stick ball on Mulberry Street." Aleck laughed until spittle seeped from the corner of his mouth. I waved him away.

Now Ernie Miller was waiting for me at a back table, and he didn't look happy. As I walked in, he stood, waited until I looked around and caught his eye, and he waved me over.

"Mr. Miller?" I approached the table.

He nodded. "I don't know why you wanna talk to me."

"I talk to a lot of people. I'm a reporter."

He had a raspy whine to his voice. "But I don't know nothing. I told the cops everything. You know, I met Violet Sharp one time, really, I mean, I met her walking and then, well, we went to the speakeasy. One time, almost three years ago, and now I gotta be on the front page of the newspapers." He mopped a brow with a large handkerchief and slipped back into his chair.

"Thank you, Mr. Miller. I know you had nothing to do with…"

He spat out, "Damn right. Nothing about a kidnapping. But people—they look at me now and point me out." His lips trembled. "My life will never be the same."

"Yes, it will," I assured him. "Once this is over and you've had your say, you'll get back to your life of…"

"Of what? I'm a bus driver from Closter, New Jersey. A simple guy."

He bunched up his face. He was a tall, willowy man with sloping shoulders, a shock of fair hair cut in a tight military style. A freckled, pale face, long and bony. Dressed in a misshapen wool sweater, faded blue and green, some threads loose at the collar, he stared at me with hard, gray eyes that reminded me of a child's playground marbles. Rough hands, weathered, a scar across the back of his right wrist, which he fingered nervously. Then, reaching into the pocket of a worn gray overcoat he'd slung over the back of the booth, he took out a pack of Old Gold cigarettes and tapped one out, lit it, and closed his eyes dreamily, relaxing.

"Mr. Miller?"

His eyes popped open. "I was just thinking."

"About what?"

A wistful smile. "About the way fate hands you a rotten hand."

I pursed my lips together. "Tell that to Bruno Richard Hauptmann."

The wrong words to say, doubtless—he froze, looked away, checked to see whether diners at a nearby table heard me.

"For Christ's sake, Miss Ferber. You do know how to make a man jump."

"Yes, I pride myself on that talent."

"What?"

"Never mind."

I reached into my purse and extracted a twenty-dollar bill. "For your troubles."

He grabbed the bill and tucked it into the cellophane of the pack of cigarettes, though his fingers lingered on the paper, tapping the money. "A man has to get by, you know." A nervous smile. "Charlie Chan smokes Old Gold, you know. I seen the ads on the billboards."

"Nice to know."

"Ain't it, though?" Again, he tapped the money. "This damned Depression and all. Roosevelt says…"

A waitress came to take or orders: spaghetti and meatballs, garlic bread, and wine. Miller smiled as I ordered for both of us.

"I'd like to ask you a couple questions."

He drew his lips into a thin line. "Yeah, I assumed that."

"Tell me about Violet Sharp."

A heavy sigh. "I told it all already."

"Again, please. Humor me."

He looked over my shoulder. "Well, you musta read about what I told the cops. I mean, I went to them when I read about it. They were surprised."

"Tell me."

"I was driving one day and I thought I recognized this girl, so I stopped. We thought we knew each other, but she…like, gave me her number. And I called her. I liked her. You know, that highfalutin English accent, real charming. And she was a flirt, that girl. I mean, she worked for prim and proper folks, but she liked her good times. So I called her up and suggested we go to the movies or to a speakeasy back then when you couldn't—like, drink."

"Of course, that's why she first lied to the police—or forgot. She said she went to the movies, not the speakeasy."

"Well, Mrs. Morrow is old-fashioned."

"And Violet wasn't?"

He grinned. "She was a little flirtatious. I mean, she'd wink at guys walking by."

"She got hysterical when the police questioned her."

"Yeah, I read all about that. They interrogated me and my friends. The four of us went out. Catharine Minners and Elmer Johnson. Easygoing friends. We had a good time, the four of us. She acted like she liked me. But she liked to talk—she told outlandish stories to us."

"About what?"

"Oh, about how rich people act, phony-like. She liked to put on airs."

"Why?"

"I read that when the cops finished talking to her and let her go, she winked at a secretary sitting there. The police caught that."

"Yes, I read that. But that could have been nervousness or, I don't know, she thought, well, this is finally over with."

He got serious, leaned in. "But she wouldn't have anything to do with kidnapping. That was the night it happened. She was with me and my friends from eight till we dropped her off at the Morrows' at eleven. Even Mrs. Morrow told the police that Violet served dinner up till eight and she saw her return at eleven. She wasn't in, you know, Hopewell or anything."

"That doesn't mean she wasn't involved in the kidnapping."

He started. "Why?"

"Well, Mr. Miller, she knew that the Lindberghs had decided to stay one more night in Hopewell and not return to Engle-wood—that the boy was sick. Anne Lindbergh called the house and reached Violet that morning, asking that Betty Gow be driven to Hopewell to help out. Violet *knew* that. Perhaps she called someone."

"Like Hauptmann, the German guy?"

"Someone. Someone had to know the Lindberghs had changed their plans."

A spurt of anger. "Violet was not that sort of girl."

"You don't know that. You only met her once."

"I was gonna call her again but, well, the kidnapping sort of changed the way things are. Especially for her."

"Were you surprised at her suicide?"

He nodded vigorously. "God, yeah. I mean, she was filled with life, talked of going back to England with a pocket full of savings. She'd been squirreling cash away. She had plans."

"Do you think the police scared her?"

He deliberated a long time. "They terrorized her, them cops. They pushed her, threatened, went after her over and over. They probably accused her. I mean, she just got out of the hospital having her tonsils out or something. She was weak, nervous. God, the kidnapping must have thrown everybody off. And then to have them cops down your throat like that. She was the sweetest thing."

I agreed. "A sad story, that ending."

"Tell me about it. Damn cops."

"But her name is going to come up now at the trial."

"Yeah, the defense is gonna say it was an inside job."

I waited a heartbeat. "Maybe it was."

His voice rose sharply. "But not by her. Maybe some other servant. The nurse, Betty Gow. What about that chauffeur, that guy named Ellerson, who drove Betty to Hopewell? Everyone seen him around the Fort Lee speakeasy—the Sha-Toe—where the gamblers hang out, lots of bucks thrown around." He stopped talking as the waitress placed food on the table. Miller poured wine into a goblet, then broke off a crust of thick bread, munched on it.

"Some folks say Violet had a lot of romances," I said.

"Yeah, I heard that. So she saw a few guys. Nothing serious. She was a nice girl. Christ, at the speakeasy that night we all had beer and whooped it up. Violet had a cup of coffee. Imagine that. In a speakeasy drinking coffee."

"Why?"

He rolled spaghetti around a fork and swallowed it. "I don't think she wanted Mrs. Morrow or the other servants to smell beer on her breath. Jobs are hard to get in the Depression, you know. She wasn't no fool. But she liked to go out. So what? We're young. That's what young people do, Miss Ferber."

"I vaguely remember." I smiled at him.

He eyed me curiously, gauging my humor. "I bet."

"What did she talk about that night?"

"I can't remember. I mean, we covered everything. She *did* like to talk."

I broke a crust of bread and took a sip of wine. "She must have mentioned the Lindberghs. She worked for wealthy people. Anne Morrow had married the most famous man in the world. The American hero."

"Well, we all knew that. We kidded her about that, and I could tell she was tickled. But I guess Lindbergh sort of ignored her at the house. Yeah, they talked, but he…like looked right through her. I sensed she didn't care for him that much. She said he was a little—like a hick. Blew his nose into his hands. He spit all over the place—a hayseed. He was mean to Anne—told her to shut up once. Called her stupid. Got ice cold. God, how we laughed at her stories. Anne, the wife, well, Violet liked her a lot." A long pause. "And she even mentioned the baby…how cute he was, blond curls, stumbling around the house, babbling baby talk."

I shifted the conversation. "Did she mention Anne's younger brother, Dwight?"

He bit the inside of his mouth. "Funny that you mention his name. I hadn't thought of that."

"What did she say?"

"I know exactly what she said. She thought he was a little odd—like he had some emotional problems, was always breaking down, being sent away, trouble for the family. Unstable. I guess his mother ignored him, favored the sisters all the time. He was quiet most of the time, she said. But he saw things, like visions. His mother would walk by him, like he wasn't there. But Violet liked him. He was nice to her."

"How do you remember that?"

"Because she got all moon-eyed talking about this friend of his. God, I can still see her. She didn't say much, because I got to frowning. After all, she was with me that night. But I guess he was this wealthy neighbor, flashy as all get-out, some slick operator that ordered Dwight around like a puppet. But she said he was real kind to her, sought her out. Smiled at her a lot. My friends was real curious, her living the high life at the mansion. But not me. I shut her off, angry a bit, saying she was a fool to listen to some rich guy with coins in his pocket. A slick car in the driveway."

"Was he around a lot?"

"I dunno. As I say, I cut her off. A guy don't need to hear that malarkey from a girl he's taking out on the town." A sly smile. "Even if she only orders coffee."

"Did she mention his name?"

"Maybe. I don't know."

"Blake Somerville?"

"You got me. Could've been." A pause. "I remember that she said those guys used to go to the Peanut Grill in Orangeburg sometimes. I think that's what she said. I never seen them, and I went there a lot."

"They go with her?"

"I doubt that, lady. Two rich boys with a servant? Come on."

"Possible?"

He drained his glass of wine, sat back. "Naw. I think Violet liked him because he talked to her, yeah, but he always was... like this fast talker." He gulped, "Yeah, I remember now, she said he was a thrill-seeker. I said, what the hell does that mean? And she said, 'Poor people don't understand that rich people like to do things for the thrill of it.' I tapped her on the arm and told her, 'Yeah, we poor folks, and that includes you, Missy, got no time for thrills.'"

"What did she say to that?"

"I dunno. I stopped listening. Rich people and their lives bore me."

"But she obviously enjoyed rich people."

"Yeah, and look where it got her."

"Tell me about this Peanut Grill."

"A ragtag speakeasy then, hidden under trees and paying off the cops. Mafia types all over the place. Everybody went there. Popular with the crowd from the Bronx from over the Hudson. The Palisades. Tappen."

"Why do you say that?"

He leaned in, confidential. "I told the cops I seen that guy Isidor Fisch there once. Leastwise I think it was him. I mean, they plastered his picture all over the papers."

I sat up. "Hauptmann's corrupt business partner? The one who Bruno said dropped off a shoebox with the ransom money?"

"Yeah, the one who skedaddled to Germany and died of TB there. Supposedly, according to Bruno hisself, Isidor never told him the box was filled with fourteen thou. 'Keep it safe.' Yeah, sure. So creepy Bruno found the money, so he said, and started spending it left and right. The trip to Germany for the missus, an expensive radio, spy glasses—how convenient!—and a new dark blue Dodge sedan. And him never working again after he *found* the money. Isidor was a con artist, true, a man who lied and tricked people. That's how Bruno got caught, stupidly spending the ransom money. Not too bright, Miss Ferber."

"Maybe his story is true."

"Yeah, and I'm the King of England."

"But you saw Fisch?"

He picked up his empty glass and stared at it. "Like, maybe. I guess Isidor was known throughout the Bronx and down into Jersey, working one scheme or another. Selling animal pelts, I heard. But I remember him from one night there because he was loud and made a fool of himself."

"How so?"

"He come there with someone. But he tried to pass a counterfeit bill to the bartender, who bagged him good. They started yelling at each other, and that's how I noticed him. The bartender knew him—called him Izzy. They threw him out on his...rear end, pardon me, Miss Ferber."

"I know what a rear end is, Mr. Miller."

Color rose in his face. "Sorry about that."

"You tell this to the cops?"

He shrugged. "Yeah, but I guess lots of folks told them they seen Isidor or Bruno here and there…taking a subway, walking in the cemetery. Strolling down the street. And I'm not sure."

"Of course you're sure."

He nodded. "Yeah, I suppose I am." He watched me closely. "After he left, the bartender—hey, I know the guy, he's Joe Morelli, a buddy from work years back—he tells me this guy Isidor deals in hot money."

"Hot money? I don't understand."

He checked to see whether any diners nearby were listening. He lowered his voice. "Like counterfeit or stolen money. Like he buys it from someone, not at face value 'cuz it's trouble, dangerous, and he starts to unload it. You know, pass it here and there. The seller makes a safe buck—Izzy has all the risk. He makes a buck or two. It's dangerous but Isidor was a swindler, slippery as an eel."

"Is there any chance Violet Sharp knew Isidor?"

"I don't think so. Why would their paths cross?"

"True." I thought of something. "I wonder if he ever came with his friend Bruno?"

"No."

"How can you be sure?"

"'Cuz I talked to Joe after Bruno's arrest and all. Christ, it was all over the papers—his mug shot. He said he'd remember if Bruno ever walked in. It never happened."

"But he remembered Isidor."

"As I say, everyone sooner or later bumped into Isidor. But you had to keep your hand on your wallet when he was around."

"But Violet…"

He held up his hand. "I gotta go, ma'am. I think I talked enough. You know, all this scares the willies out of me, this talk. Christ, a baby died, Isidor died back in Germany, that butler Ollie Whately at Hopewell died, Violet died."

"Yes—" I started, but he was already sliding out of the booth.

He spat out the words. "And this Bruno fellow is gonna die."
He stood up, waited for me to hand the waitress a few dollars,
though he looked embarrassed that I paid the bill for dinner, and
he placed his fedora on his head, pulled down over his forehead.
He tipped it jauntily, and smiled, half-bowing. "My friends say
I talk too much."

"I'm not complaining."

We walked out of the restaurant together and he said good
night again, thanking me again for the twenty dollars. He offered
to call me a cab, though I refused, bidding him good night. He
headed north to a subway stop.

Standing under a streetlight, gazing up at the light snow drifting across the murky lights, I breathed in. A beautiful night, but
bone-chilling. I stepped into the street to hail a cab.

Shivering from the cold, I pulled my scarf closer, covered my
lower face, and turned away from a sudden blast of sleet. Distracted, I searched up Arthur Avenue, but saw no familiar taxi
lights. I walked down to the corner, hoping the busy intersection
was a better place to grab a ride downtown.

A squeal of tires. A horn blared. I swiveled in time to see a
dark car careening from the opposite side of the street, a speeding car that maneuvered in front of another car—another blast
of angry horn—and, to my amazement, the car sped across the
busy avenue and headed toward me.

Instinctively, I panicked, jumped back onto the curb but
not in time to escape the fender of the car that grazed my side.
I fell against the bumper of a parked car, staggered a second,
righted myself, and watched the errant car, which didn't pause
but headed south, blaze through a red light, now back on the
correct side of the street. I gasped for breath.

"You all right, lady?" a man yelled out.

I stammered, "Yes, I..."

"Hey, maybe it's me, but it looked like that car was aiming
for you. Bull's-eye."

"I don't..."

He laughed. "You got some enemies in this part of town, lady?"

I didn't answer. My eyes followed the taillights of the black car that was a block or two south now. It sped through another red light. Horns blared. A woman screamed.

# Chapter Fourteen

I barely slept that night, the brutal image of that shadowy car and unseen driver kept slapping me awake. I'd doze off, then sit up suddenly, snapped awake by a machine barreling toward me, purposeful, deadly. In the morning, showered but still droopy-eyed, I drank a cup of steaming coffee, ignored the conversation of my mother, and then went down to the lobby after the doorman called up to say my ride had arrived. Six a.m., the city waking up, and the town car idled in front. James opened the door and I slid in.

"Good morning, Miss Ferber." From Marcus, a little too cheerful for the hour.

I wasn't alone. In the rear seat sat two staff members from the *Times*—a photographer I knew as Sammy and Irma Selz, a talented young woman who did line drawings and got on my nerves because her caricatures of me always depicted me as a wild-eyed martinet. She once drew me with a lariat flying high about my head. Annie Oakley with a pronounced Semitic nose.

I decided to sleep during the two-hour trek back to Flemington, though I feared Miss Selz might sketch me with my head lolling, mouth agape, puddles of drool gathering on the corners of my lips. And, given the scare I'd experienced last night, she'd probably catch the tension in my brow, the twitching of my hands in my lap. Worse, I'd probably babble in my sleep, some garbled nightmare that would be used to regale the editorial rooms of the *Times* for days on end. I didn't care. I dozed off.

◇◇◇

At the Union Hotel, Marcus graciously extended his arm as I lumbered out of the car. He whispered, "You look tired, Miss Ferber."

I smiled. "A troubling night."

That puzzled him. "A night in Manhattan always enchants me."

"Yes, well, that's not the word I'd use for last night."

Aleck Woollcott was waiting for me in the lobby, sitting in the reception area, a cloud of smoke around his head and a plate of sugar doughnuts nearby. He toasted me with a cup of coffee. "Right on time, dear Ferb."

I leaned in. "Aleck, someone tried to kill me last night."

He scrunched up his face. "Again? Edna, you have to stop annoying people."

"I'm serious, Aleck. A car crossed traffic and bumped me."

The smirk disappeared from his face. "This is true, Edna?"

"I swear." A heartbeat. "Or I assumed it's true. Perhaps it was an accident, a wayward car, out of control, some drunken maniac, but I felt its driver was purposely aiming toward me."

Aleck leaned over and patted me on the wrist. "Edna, perhaps this…caper of yours has now assumed dangerous proportions."

I snarled, "But what? It's not a caper. I'm asking questions. For God's sake, Aleck. The story of Violet Sharp…"

He stopped me. "It's obviously too raw a story still. There are too many loose ends here." He struggled to stand. "Are you attending the trial?"

"Not this morning. I'll be in my room. You can fill me in later at lunch. Or this afternoon."

An hour later, refreshed with breakfast, I walked to the depot and found Willie polishing a town car. I engaged him for late that afternoon, although he remarked that Kathleen Norris had suggested she wanted a ride to Trenton for an interview. "But" he leaned in, "that lady novelist never leaves town. She's glued to the courtroom and Nellie's Taproom, afraid she'll miss some choice morsel of gossip. The bourbon and applejack crowd likes to chatter. So I don't expect her to bother me today. It's just me today. Marcus is off. He likes to get out of town—too many people in the small town, he says—and drink rum Coke in a country inn where no reporters ever go. Me, well, I like the crowds, the excitement, spotting Colonel Lindbergh strolling by, even seeing that Bruno Hauptmann led across the street to the courtroom, him all spruced up with that new fedora, sullen like a beat puppy, shuffling between the state cops. They should dress him in rags."

"Anyway," I interrupted, "five o'clock?"

"I'll write it down now, ma'am. Car's all yours."

Unless, I thought, Kathleen Norris actually does demand a journey out of town. A friendly woman, Kathleen Norris was. We'd shared a moment in the lobby, and she'd slipped me the copy for tomorrow's *Times* column. My eyes had caught the lines:

> "The big story is on its way to every corner of the world."

Then:

> "There is a steady deepening tension and a steady increasing horror in the Flemington courthouse as the most unfortunate man in the world makes a fight for his life."

For a moment, reading those lines and watching her eager but humble face, I was sadly jealous. I wanted those lines to be mine. Well, maybe not. She was actually a warm, likeable woman—and much too pleasant to spend a lot of time with because such genuine affability strained the muscles used for smiling. Niceness is best applied in small, manageable doses.

When I sat with Aleck at lunch, I outlined my plan: an early evening spin to the Peanut Grill, a place that intrigued me. "Perhaps you'd enjoy the ride?"

Aleck wasn't happy. "Really, Edna. If someone takes a potshot at you, they'll probably hit me. I'm a much larger target."

"But your infamous cutting remarks have given you a tough hide no bullet can penetrate."

"Ah," he grinned, "the insulation of the choice *bon mot?*"

"Exactly."

"Well, that doesn't really comfort me, but, yes, I could do with a drink and a look at a place stupidly called the Peanut Grill. Perhaps Violet Sharp etched her initials into the sticky woodwork." He reached for a cigarette. "Lord, my dear, this wild goose chase you're on."

"Clues, Aleck." I thought of my conversation with Ernie Miller, which I summarized to Aleck. "I want to meet a guy named Joe."

"Don't we all," Aleck muttered.

"Tell me what happened at the trial," I began.

Aleck discussed the morning testimony. David Wilentz began his stream of witnesses calculated to place Bruno at the Lindbergh estate—a crucial bit of courtroom stretching. Otherwise—what proof was there? Circumstantial? The morning session, according to Aleck, featured craggy old Dr. Condon, the nicknamed "Jafsie," the ruddy-faced gentleman who'd delivered the ransom money in the Bronx cemetery. The doddering old man, self-important and bombastic and garrulous, was entertaining, Aleck said. Early on, during a police lineup in New York—twelve burly cops with no accents, and one tiny unshaven man named Bruno—he'd hesitated. He'd refused to identify Bruno at the time. "He is *not* the man. He resembles the man. I can see a resemblance, but I cannot swear to it." Odd, given that he'd spoken face-to-face with "John" for an hour. But on the stand, though Wilentz was visibly nervous, Dr. Condon emphatically named Bruno as the man he met in the cemetery.

"Just how foolish is Bruno, then?" I now said to Aleck. "He wears gloves at the kidnapping site, conceals his identity a number of times, and then talks straight-on for an hour, undisguised. Really, Aleck!"

"Well, the doctor made a show of it, what with announcing that the Bronx was the most beautiful borough in the world."

A sigh. "Then he pointed at Bruno and said—yes, that's 'John.' With his gigantic white moustache and a black bowler on his huge body, he seemed a circus performer."

I checked my watch. "Let's go. The afternoon session begins."

A tedious afternoon. Although Aleck nodded his head in agreement as witnesses against Bruno Hauptmann streamed past, I found myself wondering: Amandus Hochmuth, a frail eighty-seven-year-old man who claimed he saw Bruno speeding by in a car at Hopewell three years back, yet seemed myopic, squinting through cataracts to focus on a photograph displayed before him. The speeding man had a bright red face, he insisted—and everyone turned to look at Bruno: pale white, pasty. Someone tittered. He tugged at his gray Van Dyke goatee, and tottered down to place a hand on Bruno's knee and pressed down hard, probably to avoid toppling over. The tip of his beard grazed Bruno's forehead. Very dramatic, if ridiculous. The reward money, I thought. A siren's awful lure for mountain folks. Bruno muttered, "*Der Alte ist verrückt.*" The old man is crazy.

Worse, an illiterate mountain man from the tarpaper shacks in Sourland, a bumbling sort, easily rattled, recalled a strange man wandering through the woods at Hopewell, a man some three years later he insisted was Bruno. Others testified that the witness was a chronic liar, and only had the wonderful recollection when reward money materialized. A fool, I thought, unconvincing.

A third witness, Joseph Perrone, was the taxi driver in the Bronx who delivered a letter to Dr. Condon. When he walked down and touched Bruno on the shoulder, Bruno roared, "You're a liar."

Perrone had identified Bruno in another New York lineup that included two cops, one in uniform.

"Circumstantial evidence." I jotted in a note to Aleck. "Is Wilentz serious?"

He scribbled back. "Nitpicking, Edna." He took back the sheet from me and added, in barely legible penmanship, "Like your current pursuit of the elusive and departed Violet Sharp. Circumstantial evidence."

"I rest my case."

◇◇◇

Willie made a grunting sound as he pulled the town car in front of the Peanut Grill, parking it a little too close to a bank of pale green yew bushes speckled with ice-hoary red berries. We sat there, the three of us, as Aleck poked me in the side, whispering loudly, "The site of our first date. Do you remember, Edna, my love?"

"No," I shot back, "your memory is slipping, dear Aleck. That was the dessert table at the Algonquin, if I remember correctly. And your cheeks were puffed out with chocolate éclairs."

He chuckled. "We looked into each other's eyes."

"Yes, when you pledged your love to…chocolate."

"A love of chocolate is enduring. A love of you is fickle."

Willie was still grunting, his fingers fiddling with a cigarette he was about to light. "You folks gonna jaw the afternoon away in the backseat like two schoolgirls over Francis X. Bushman?"

We got out of the car.

The Peanut Grill struck me as a frontier cabin, a sloping roof of tired, moss-stained shingles, an ice slick at the eaves, tiny windows the size of a folio page. Peeling clapboards painted a ghastly forest green, the boards sagging, some slipping, nails giving way. Over the front door—built of a wide slab of rough, unsanded pine with wrought-iron handles—a crudely painted sign: The Peanut Grill. For some reason someone had added an "e" in black crayon to the word: "Grille."

"Ambience?" I said out loud.

"Very *Tobacco Road*," Aleck announced. "I can already feel the mildew seeping into my heart."

Inside was no better, though thankfully the late afternoon shadows and the faint lighting gave the interior a monastic feel. Plank tables and barrel-stave chairs cluttered a sawdust-splattered floor. A long oak bar ran the length of the room, a glass tier behind it, with etched mirror and, for some reason, a cheap chromolithographic print of a Conestoga covered wagon being attacked by savage Indians. Perhaps, after all, we were in Wyoming. Or, at least, frontier New York.

"Does Manhattan really exist?" Aleck mumbled.

"It's only a state of mind, anyway," I told him.

There was not a single customer in sight. A man stood behind the bar, busy wiping glasses and stocking the glass shelves. He turned suddenly, shielding his eyes at the burst of sunlight from the opened front door. "We're not really open," he called to us.

"Well, we're not really here," I announced.

A woman was wiping down tables. "What does that mean?"

"We came to talk, not drink."

The man glanced at the woman. "Mostly people come here to do both." He stepped out from behind the car and approached us. "We're closed Mondays," he said. "Says so on the sign outside. Door should have been locked." He wore a simple smile. "But can I help you?"

"Are you Joe?" I asked.

That puzzled him. "Joe?" A pause. "Oh, like the man who works weekends? Joey Warehouse. That ain't his last name, but he works…never mind…an older guy, walrus moustache, real fat face."

I interrupted. "I've never met him, but a friend of his named Ernie told me to ask for him."

"Well, he ain't here. Sorry." He turned away.

"But perhaps you can help us."

He turned back. "Suit yourself. Park yourself down in those seats. Be with you in a second."

So parked we did, though Aleck made a fuss over the wobbly chair he chose, teetering on the edge, his tremendous bulk shifting like a seismic ocean current, and I noticed the woman eyeing him nervously. Settled in, breathing heavily, Aleck reached for his cigarette holder and inserted a Camel. He struck a match. He snapped his fingers as he called to the woman who was now stacking glasses on a sideboard.

"Does this mean we can't drink? I will have a brandy. And a dry martini for my woman friend, the former head of the Upper East Side Temperance League and All-Around Street Litter Patrol."

The woman watched the man who shrugged and said, "All right."

When she went up to the bar, I noticed she winked at him, and he smiled broadly, turning away. Young lovers, I thought, playful and happy to be alive. When she returned with the brandy and the martini—I watched the bartender deftly pour from a bottle, his wrist dramatically exaggerated—she said, "Here you go." An accent, decidedly Irish. "And you are from Europe?"

"County Cork." A half-bow. "Mary Louise, though my friends call me Marielle. Mary L. M-a-r-i-e-l-l-e is how I spell it. Understand?"

"It's not that complicated," Aleck said.

She pointed to the bartender. "He's Charlie. From Newark."

Charlie, dragging a rag across the bar, bowed with a flourish.

An attractive couple, mid-thirties perhaps, she with a pointy freckled face and washed-out brown hair. He with a high forehead over sleepy blue eyes and a pronounced chin, a mouth with a mess of wrinkles around it. A broad-chested man, short, a street fighter with a bit of a scar under his left eye. They looked like they belonged together.

"You two plan on getting married?" I asked, disingenuously.

That surprised her, and she blushed, hurled a sidelong glance at Charlie, who chuckled. "I guess we are now." He pointed playfully at Marielle. "Gotta listen to the customers, no?"

Laughing, embarrassed, she shook her head back and forth.

"Well, you should," I said.

Marielle seemed pleased. I was the yenta she'd hoped for—a role I savored.

Aleck eyed me suspiciously. "Edna dear, why must all of your talks lead to matters amorous? The title of your biography will have to be—*Nothing Risqué, Nothing Gained.*"

I ignored him.

"You two married?" Marielle looked from Aleck to me.

Aleck spat out his brandy, choked, dropped his cigarette holder. "Please," he howled, "can't you see I'm a man of utter discernment?"

That confused her, so she turned away and chose not to answer.

Enough of the tomfoolery, I thought. Willie would shortly be leaning on the horn, impatient. But I knew I'd won over these two young souls.

"We're reporters," I began. "I'm Edna Ferber and this is Aleck Woollcott."

Marielle sputtered. "Lord, Mr. Woollcott, I listen to you Sundays on the radio. Charlie, you know who this is? The Town Crier." Charlie shrugged. "You're so funny."

"Edna Ferber has written novels," Aleck began slowly. "Doubtless you haven't heard of her."

Marielle shook her head. "No, sorry."

I plunged in. "No matter, my dear. We're researching the Lindbergh kidnapping case." Marielle's face fell and she glanced at Charlie, who also attempted to look solemn. "We know that Violet Sharp, the maid from the Morrow estate who killed herself, was here with Ernie Miller the night of the kidnapping."

Marielle's face closed up. "Yeah, we talked to the police already. They asked about it. We said, yeah, the four of them were here."

"You remember her?"

"Well, yeah. I mean, when she spoke she had that English accent, and she heard my Irish one, and we laughed and she told me her name."

"That night?"

A heartbeat. "Well, no. She was here before when I was working one night. Waiting tables. We talked and all."

"She was a regular?" I wondered.

She nodded. "Well, not a regular. But she liked the place."

"A drinker?"

"That was strange. Always coffee. Strong, black. No sugar. Like she was afraid. But everyone else with her liked a shot of whiskey and a beer. That was when we were a speakeasy. So we had to be careful."

I held my breath. "She came with others?"

"Well, that one time with that guy and his friends. You know, the night of the kidnapping. That was what the cops asked about. But she came a few other times with two guys. The rich boys."

"Rich boys?"

Marielle pulled up a chair and sat down, resting her elbows on the table. "Well, you know how she worked for the Morrows. Everyone did. She talked about that. Real proud of it, as she told me. She *loved* working there. And one day she comes in with their son, a boy named Dwight. I'd seen him before because he'd stopped in with friends. But she introduced him as her boss, then she giggled."

I was perplexed. "Isn't that strange, a servant coming to a speakeasy with her employer?"

She looked toward Charlie, who stood behind the bar, grim-faced, uneasy. "Maybe so. Hey, in those days all sorts come into a speakeasy. It was like a place to go, no matter who you are. I mean, she was respectful and all. She even called him Mr. Morrow. I remember that. I thought it odd. He's drinking with his friend, and she's acting like she should serve them."

I waited a second. "His friend?"

"Yeah, another rich guy. He came a lot. Dwight, now and then, and he always looked lost. Like he shouldn't be here. Now don't get me wrong. Violet Sharp only came a few times, maybe. I can't be sure. But it was clear she had a hankering for the other guy."

"And he was?"

"Blake something. That's what he said to call him. He let everyone know he was rich, come from a great family and all. I mean, he made like he was friends with the owners of this place. Maybe he was. Angelo Riscinito, his name." She whispered now. "He was cronies with regulars, guys named Irish Pete and another we called The Chink." She dropped her voice even lower. "Mobsters out of Mulberry Street." A sudden smile. "They don't come here no more—now that we're legal."

"Dwight?" I prompted.

"Dwight kept his mouth shut, the few times he was here, talking quietly to everybody, real polite to me, but Blake boomed and roared."

"What did he say?"

"It wasn't so much *what* he said, but the *way* he said it. That was one good-looking man, let me tell you, slick as all outdoors. Suave, like a movieland star. Dressed to the nines, hoity-toity, slicked-back hair all shiny and polished. Pointed black Italian shoes. A diamond stickpin. Always an expensive cigarette holder between his fingertips."

Charlie walked out from behind the bar and slid into a chair. He'd been listening to the conversation. "I didn't like him," he added.

"Why is that?" asked Aleck.

"He looked down on everyone. Even the Morrow kid, who was like a dumpy kid you beat up on in school. Treated *him* like a servant. Get me this, do that, stop talking, listen to me. He ruled the roost, that one."

Marielle spoke up. "Dwight was meek, like a follower."

"You say Dwight rarely came here?"

"Yeah, not much."

"Did you tell this to the police when they talked to you?"

Her eyes got wide. "No, should I have? All they asked was about the night of the kidnapping. Everything was about Ernie Miller. So she came with her boss two or three nights. Nobody's business, and it ain't related to killing that baby. That I'd bet on."

"What did the police ask you?"

Charlie answered. "They also wanted to know if she was here with Bruno Hauptmann or Isidor Fisch. They flashed pictures of both of them. I never seen this Bruno, tell you the truth. Isidor, yes. But I don't think Violet Sharp knew either one. Leastwise, as I saw. She sat with Dwight and this slimy Blake, very polite like, proper. Not smooching or cuddling, but I could see this Violet had it bad for Blake."

"How did he treat her?" I asked.

Charlie sighed. "Like he was this matinee idol and she was a shop girl swooning over him. He liked that, I could tell." A long pause. "She was a fool, that girl."

"Tell me about Blake," I said.

Marielle smiled. "A charmer, but real phony. Disloyal."

"Why do you say that?"

"He came here one night, got a little plowed with the rotgut they served then." She looked at Charlie apologetically. "You know it's true, Charlie. Back then. Anyway, I overheard him blarneying this girl he was with. I never seen her before. But he's talking about Dwight, calling him a simp, a milquetoast. How when he snapped his fingers, Dwight would jump. Then he said Dwight was in a nut house just over the Hudson in New Jersey. That he *worked* at the nut house and that's how he met him." She looked into my face. "That confused me. Here he's acting like a rich boy, a friend of Dwight from another wealthy family, and then he says he worked in a nut house. Nothing added up. But I figured he was just making things up."

Charlie added, "One of the customers told me that Blake was the black sheep of his family. He wasn't allowed to go back home. He lived in New York, was even an actor on Broadway for a bit, worked as an elevator operator in some hotel somewhere, who knows? A spoiled, rich boy who got thrown out by his parents. He kept coming back—his mother loved him—but daddy kept sending him into exile." Charlie laughed out loud. "In his thirties and he's still playing the bad boy. Toot-toot-tooting the night away on the pennies in his pocket. Always looking for a good time. Thrills."

Marielle was eager to add something. "God, I just thought of something funny. I mean, we all knew Dwight was the brother-in-law of Lindbergh, but he never talked about it. Like it was a forbidden topic. Blake once told someone that Dwight hated Lindbergh."

"Do you know why?" From Aleck.

Marielle grinned wide and winked at Charlie. "Lindbergh likes practical jokes, I guess. It seems one time he sent a letter to Dwight when he came back from college up in Massachusetts. Christmas break, after finals, I guess. There was a formal letter telling him he'd flunked his courses and he was on probation. Dwight got real depressed, crying and all. I mean, his whole family went to that school, it seems. Daddy and all. It turned out that Lindbergh put that letter together. When Dwight found out it was a fake, he refused to come home for weeks."

"Did he confront Lindbergh?"

Marielle nodded. "Dwight's a tiny man, you know. He shoved Lindbergh, who's real tall, and Lindbergh just laughed and laughed."

Charlie looked confused. "But all this got nothing to do with the kidnapping. Or Violet Sharp. Ernie Miller ain't involved. They got this Bruno fellow with the ransom money hidden in his garage. Really."

I glanced at Aleck. "Most likely not. Curious anecdotes about the famous."

"Tell me something," Aleck said. "After the night of the kidnapping, did Blake or Dwight come back here?"

Both shook their heads, but Marielle answered. "No, all the staff talked about that. The police came and talked to us about Violet and Ernie and *that* awful night. No one mentioned Dwight. No reason to. Lots of rich boys come here. They bring rich girls who get drunk."

Charlie broke in, "Bring poor girls who get drunk."

Marielle sat back. "No, this place became No Man's Land for that crowd. For lots of folks—except for the crazies who read about it in the papers."

"Blake disappeared?"

Both nodded.

I looked at Charlie. "You said that Isidor Fisch used to come here."

Both nodded quickly. "Yeah, a bad apple," Charlie noted. "But we told the cops about that. They did ask about Bruno. No one ever saw him, true—but Izzy, yes."

"What can you tell us about him?" I asked.

Charlie said nothing, but went behind the bar and returned with another brandy and another martini. "On the house."

He sat down. "As I was saying, we read about Isidor in the paper afterwards, like his connection with Bruno. But he was just a slimy little con artist, a little Jewish weasel, who sized you up. Could he get a dollar off of you, that kind of look."

"He was a sick man, I remember," Marielle added. "Always coughing in your face, spitting up on the floor. It's a wonder we ain't all in a TB ward somewhere."

"Who was he with?" Aleck asked.

Charlie tilted his head, thinking. "Well, I only spotted him a couple times. He tried to move some fake bills, and he was told not to come back."

"Hot money?" I asked, and Aleck's eyebrows rose.

Charlie grinned. "You know about hot money?"

"I know about a lot of things."

Aleck stared at me. "Edna, what in the world?"

Charlie explained. "Isidor was a sham. He claimed he traded furs or pelts, was a skilled fur-cutter, worked with this Bruno guy, but I only read about that later. A gambler, he was, a nervous Nelly, always pacing the floor, watching people. He moved money around. Bad money. Hot money. Fake and real. Tried to get folks to invest in a pie company that never existed—I read that it was all fake, like he even had a fake letterhead printed. A cheat."

"Did he ever mention Bruno?" I asked.

"Not in my earshot. And I told the cops I never seen Bruno in here. Never. We talked about it afterwards. Izzy probably played Bruno for a dupe. Maybe Bruno was in on it, maybe he knew the money was hot—maybe even from the kidnapping. Bruno strikes me as a greedy man, cold, anything for money. But Isidor lied about his business ventures. That's what the papers said. This scheme, that one. Lots of money in his pocket, or none at all, begging for a quarter."

Marielle went on. "Maybe Bruno ain't lily white in this story, but I bet he was tricked by Isidor."

"Who drops off a shoebox of fourteen grand and then boards a boat for Germany?" Alex wondered.

"Where he dies. Tough luck." Charlie shrugged his shoulders. "Somebody said he was blackmailing Bruno because Bruno was here illegally. Maybe he did."

Marielle summed up, "Fourteen grand, hidden by Bruno. And they're saying he did it alone. Come on. Think about it. Then where is the rest of the fifty grand ransom? Tell me that. Ask Isidor. Oh, you can't. Probably hidden somewhere in an attic in Germany. Or in somebody's pocket right here in America."

I stood. "We have to get back. We have a driver waiting."

"He's paid to wait, Edna. They also serve who sit and wait." Aleck glanced toward the doorway.

"Enough, Aleck."

Aleck stood, arching his back. "So be it."

When Aleck took out his wallet, Charlie waved it away. "On me."

Marielle addressed Charlie. "Were you here the night Blake came in with this guy, a wiry man who annoyed everyone."

"Isidor?" I asked.

"No, I told you I never saw them together, those two."

"Go on."

"A quirky guy, short, fawning, rushing up to Blake and then rushing away, getting him drinks, laughing at anything he said. That night Blake was dressed for dinner, white cravat, a black cutaway jacket, like he was going to a cotillion at a country club. But this other guy was sloppily dressed, a Hooverville hobo."

"They were together?"

She nodded.

"They walked in together. And Blake called him by a name."

"What?" asked Aleck.

"Johnny. I remember that. But Blake at one point sidled up to him and hissed, 'Keep your mouth shut, Johnny. You talk too much.' I remember that."

"But what was he talking about?"

"Dunno."

"No ideas?"

"It had to do with a girl."

"Why do you say that?" I asked.

"The only thing I heard was Blake angry as hell, spitting into Johnny's ear. 'Make sure Emily is on board. You hear me?' But that was it. Blake wasn't happy with the guy and they left real quick."

"That was it?"

"Yeah."

Marielle smiled and waved us off.

◇◇◇

Sitting in the backseat of the car, Aleck said in a low voice, "Isidor Fisch?" He stared into my face. "A new player on your stage."

I pointed to Willie's head. "Later."

Willie had been fiddling with the wipers as a light snow fell, but when Aleck blurted out the name, he sat ramrod stiff, head pressed against the rest, inclined. Nosy, the man, of course.

I nodded at Aleck. We rode in silence.

But on the ride back to Flemington, Aleck was restless, bothered. Finally, in an angry whisper, he said, "Edna, I fear you are seeking a murderer who is anybody but Bruno Hauptmann."

Willie twisted in his seat.

Again the heated whisper, "I fear you're going to the other side."

"There is no other side, Aleck."

A snide tone in his voice. "Bruno's not one of your romantic heroes, Ferb dear. He's not Gaylord Ravenal jumping onto a show boat to woo the ingénue."

I faced him. "Are you out of your mind, Aleck?"

"No, but I fear you're going to go out on a limb. And somewhere a man is sharpening his saw."

# Chapter Fifteen

The telephone in my room jarred me at seven. I'd overslept—I wanted to be up before six, dressed for a walk in the cold morning—but I found myself dreaming of tons of hot money falling from the sky, a disturbing image that was alarming because I couldn't breathe under that avalanche of illicit cash.

Cora Lee Thomas spoke in a hesitant voice. "Miss Ferber, my apologies for the...the call."

"That's all right. Tell me."

"Could we meet for coffee? I know you are busy and all... with the trial and..."

I glanced at a clock on the nightstand. "Where?"

"There's a little diner down from you, the Maple Leaf. Nobody goes there but townsfolk."

"Give me ten minutes."

When I arrived, she was already sitting in a back booth, steps from the kitchen. An early-morning eatery, noisy with the pleasant hum of men and women headed to work: milk and bread and egg delivery men, all chatting, back-slapping, downing hot coffee and toast, joking, teasing, then rushing off. Everyone, it seemed, was on a first-name basis. *Hey, Linda. New work boots, Jack? Mary, another cup of java. You seen* It Happened One Night *at the Palace, Mabel? That Clark Gable.*

Cora Lee, spotting me, waved, and a few heads turned as I walked back. I was an outsider, clearly, a tiny woman in the long and expensive fur coat and sable hat, a woman who touched her three strands of pearls nervously.

"Thank you," Cora Lee whispered. She shook my hand.

A waitress walked over and I ordered coffee with a dollop of whipped cream.

"We ain't got whipped cream until they do the pies later on."

"Plain cream then," I said.

"I should think so." A click of her tongue and off she went.

Cora Lee was smiling. "Now you've given her something to yap about all day."

I smiled back. "I don't think people talk about things I do, Mrs. Thomas."

She twisted her head to the side, amused. "Miss Ferber, I know who you are now. A writer. I bet you get tongues wagging all over your Manhattan."

That gave me pause. My Manhattan. I liked that.

As I sipped my coffee—delicious, hot with a hint of bitter chicory—I began, "Tell me why you called."

She sat back, debated her first words. "I don't got anyone else to talk to—I mean, someone who believes me." She looked over my shoulder. "I thought long and hard before I dialed your number."

"Tell me."

She breathed in. "I heard yesterday from the lawyer—he's this young guy they appointed, but he never looks me in the face so I know he don't believe me—well, he told me some guy has come forward to the police. Now this guy lives on the same floor of the boardinghouse as Annabel, a guy who travels a lot, a drummer of women's dresses, he said. He was leaving that night and seen a man move out of Annabel's room, not fast but sneaky and bent low. A bulky man, big like my boy, bundled up for the Arctic, he says. Scarf around most of his face. But he says he glimpsed some of the face, and then watched him slink down the stairs. He seen a flick of the guy's head." She swallowed. "They showed him a picture of Cody Lee and he said it's him."

"My God."

Desperation in her voice, her words rushed. "But it ain't true, Miss Ferber. He gotta be lying through his teeth—or mistaken. He seen someone else—it had to be. I told you—Cody Lee was with me. The man is wrong."

"But what now?"

"They're gonna do one of those lineups, you know, have my boy stand with some others and see if this guy can pick him out, you know, all of them dressed in winter clothes."

I tried to reassure her. "Perhaps he can't make an identification."

She dipped her head into her chest and said in a low voice, "No, you know how it works for poor folks." Then, breathing in, she went on. "Now they got this photograph of a scratch on Cody Lee's forearm, a long scratch they seen when they brought him in. It looks like Annabel fought him. They said she did. They found a bit of blood under her nails. But Cody Lee got scratches all the time. Lord, he hauls lumber. He got scratches on his legs, his shoulders. Black-and-blue marks."

I took a sip of coffee and watched her. "I don't know what I can do, Mrs. Thomas."

A sliver of a smile. "That's not why I asked you here, Miss Ferber. You can't do nothing. I know that. But"—she gazed toward the doorway, unblinking—"I just needed to *talk* to someone. I catch me a bus every day so I can visit him—there's no one else." She stopped, abrupt. "No one."

I patted the back of her wrist. "Any time. Of course. I'm someone who believes you." I thought of something. "Maybe I *can* do something. Let me call a lawyer friend of mine in New York. Perhaps another attorney can see this differently."

"No." Her hand up in my face—so shriveled, skinny, the nails bitten to the quick. Her face fleshless, haggard.

"I'd like to do this," I said.

Again, louder. "No. The money."

"Let me worry about that."

Her eyes got wide and glossy. "Lord, Miss Ferber..."

"There are no guarantees, Mrs. Thomas."

Then she started to say something, but her voice broke. Sobbing, she dipped into her purse for a handkerchief, but in her fumbling she spilled the contents: a few coins, a comb, a house key, chewing gum. A crumpled pack of cigarettes. She scrambled to gather the items, but they slipped away from her. Finally, distraught, she sat back and closed her eyes. She was whispering, "Oh my Jesus! Oh my Jesus!"

◇◇◇

Aleck and I slid into the backseat of the town car, and Marcus, offering blankets for our laps because the car was cold, looked unhappy that we refused his gracious offer. Night had fallen early, a whisper of snowflakes swirling in the air. We were headed to Princeton where Aleck had scheduled an early dinner with a professor he planned to interview on an upcoming Sunday night radio program. At the last minute, at my prompting, he'd invited me, though he confessed the professor's wife had wanted to meet the author of *So Big*.

Judge Trenchard had adjourned the trial for the afternoon, and the automobiles were bumper-to-bumper leaving and entering town, a gridlock with horns blaring and fists raised and curses hurled as out-of-town drivers attempted to move. "Zero miles per hour," Marcus had moaned. Unfortunately, Aleck had been delayed at the hotel so we'd ended up in the unmoving queue, which didn't please Aleck—he repeatedly tapped Marcus on the shoulder as though he were Pegasus and could fly us over the roofs of the cars. But Marcus also seemed flustered, his neck stiff, largely because some hot-shot reporter in an old tin lizzie had edged in front of us, nearly sideswiping our front fender.

"Calm down, Aleck," I begged him. "Your face is beet red."

"I don't like being late for meetings."

"Then perhaps you shouldn't have lollygagged in your room while Marcus and I sat in front."

"It's all right, Miss Ferber." Marcus looked back. "Mr. Woollcott is a busy man."

Aleck smiled. "See, Edna. People understand me. Do you hear that?"

I ignored him, gazing out at the sidewalks jammed with enthusiastic strollers. Laughter broke through the closed windows of the car, a raucous blurt that seemed profane. In the nearby jail, Bruno Hauptmann could doubtless hear the silly hurrahs, the chanting. "Kill Bruno." That mantra rarely stopped. Children called it out loud as they hawked grainy photographs of baby Lindbergh, or "authentic" autographs of Lindbergh, or cheesy replicas of the notorious ladder. Even wisps of blond hair supposedly cut from the dead baby's head. Boys in knickers and winter slicks pounded on car windows. One attacked our car. "Wanna buy a bar of soap from the courthouse bathroom?" he asked. Marcus shooed him away.

"Look there," Marcus pointed. "Brayer's Pool House." We stared at a weathered sign over the storefront, cluttered with sloughing men, a wisp of steam seeping out from a vent. "Every night they throw down blankets on the slate-top tables and rent the space to reporters and visitors for a buck a night."

"You're kidding," I said.

"That isn't anything," Marcus went on. "The floor of the grocery is covered with blankets, people huddled by the rows of aged cheese and packaged dried peas and beans. An old lady sits awake all night, a grandmother, they tell us, watching that the city reporters, boozy from a night at Nellie's Taproom, don't slink over and nibble at the groceries."

We idled, exhaust from the automobiles clouding the air.

Aleck grumbled. "This is madness. A small town like this acting as if it's Times Square. The nerve."

"Aleck," I assured him, "we'll get there."

He slipped a pocket watch from inside his vest and tapped Marcus on the shoulder with it. Marcus, concentrating on the street, jumped, slammed on the brakes. His lips moved, a silent curse we were not supposed to hear. I didn't blame him.

"Marcus," Aleck went on, "why would you do this for a living?"

Marcus looked into the rearview mirror and smiled. "What else would you have me do?"

I spoke up. "You could become a drama critic for the *Times*. They pay you for idling and daydreaming in your seat at the Selwyn, third row center."

I detected a smile from Marcus as he moved his fingers through the hair at the back of his neck. The chauffeur's cap slipped to the side.

We sat, inched forward.

Aleck was craning his head against the side of the window. "Look there," he said excitedly.

A half block ahead, standing on the sidewalk, a state trooper had stepped into Main Street and was signaling to a car in the line ahead of us. "Anne Morrow Lindbergh," Aleck stated.

I peered out the window. Two or three cars ahead of us, stuck in the abysmal traffic jam, was a long black town car, and standing alongside it was another state trooper, impatient that nothing was moving. Standing on the sidewalk, the Morrow party was waiting for it. Anne stood next to an older woman swathed in furs and a monstrous velvet hat with sweeping veils. Mrs. Dwight Morrow, obviously. Her arm cradled her daughter's waist, with Anne leaning in, saying something. "That young man pointing in our direction…" My words trailed off.

Aleck pushed his face against the window. "Of course. Anne's younger brother, Dwight Morrow, Jr."

Dressed in a bulky Chesterfield overcoat open to the wind, an elaborate fuchsia scarf loosely draped around his neck, the small man wearing an incongruous pince-nez looked impatient. I recalled his face from the news photographs. So here was the brother mentioned in Violet Sharp's letters to her cousin Annabel. So here was the troubled young man, victim of bouts of depression, perhaps even schizophrenia, the young man mentioned in the same breath as the slick operator, Blake Somerville. Dwight Morrow, the prankster. The supposed prankster. The reason Annabel had taken a job in Flemington—supposedly to extort cash from a grieving Colonel Lindbergh in order to protect the illustrious Morrow family. Dwight Morrow, Sr., a few years dead now. Ambassador to Mexico, wealthy partner in J.P. Morgan, on the fast track to becoming President of the United States—until a premature heart attack felled the man. Here, his hand raised against a swirl of snow, was the surviving son, a weak reflection of that mighty man.

I exchanged a glance with Aleck. "So that's Dwight."

He nodded. "In the flesh."

"No one said he was in town."

Aleck was amused. "I didn't realize you kept abreast of the comings and goings of the wealthy and privileged in town."

"True," I said, "but where is Colonel Lindbergh?"

"Perhaps he's in the town car guarded by the state police that's stalled in traffic."

To my horror I spotted a young man, maybe nineteen or twenty, dressed in a slough boy cap and burlap jacket, moving across the sidewalk, hawking hot dogs in a carnival voice. A haze of snow covered his shoulders—and the hot dogs he offered. He even rapped at the window of the limousine, though the state trooper, standing on the other side, barked something at the lad, who scurried away.

"A circus," I said. "Despicable."

We inched along.

Aleck fumed. "Goddamn it to hell." Dumbly, he jabbed Marcus' shoulder, a sudden move that didn't please Marcus. I could see color rise in his neck.

Suddenly there was a break in the opposing traffic, and Marcus flicked off Aleck's hand, swung the car into the other lane, causing an approaching car to screech, the driver slamming his brakes. "Enough of this," Marcus yelled. "Mr. Woollcott, I hear you."

The car roared across the street, slid between two jaywalkers, turned down a side street, and Marcus grinned like a mischievous schoolboy. "There's more than one way to get out of this town."

His eyes off the road for a second—another squeal of brakes as a rickety old Ford tried to cut in from a parking spot. Surprised, Marcus leaned on the horn. The man cursed us loudly, unmistakably, through his closed windows, and Marcus, I could see, was tempted to return the favor. But, of course, he didn't.

Aleck did that for him, a volley of *damn you* and *go to hell* tripping happily from his lips. Marcus, back straightened, approved.

But, of course, the roller-coaster ride caused me to slip across the backseat, slam into Aleck's cushy side and mandarin tummy. He frowned—"Really, Edna, such intimacy in front of a stranger"—as I bounced back against the door, a rag doll in the hands of a madman.

"Thank you, Marcus, but I prefer to arrive at my destinations in one piece."

He bit his lip and refused to face me. "I'm paid to drive—not *sit* with you."

Aleck applauded stupidly, but we found ourselves immediately snarled in another traffic jam. Obviously others had conceived the same useless plan. Eventually, of course, we crept out of town, Aleck sweating and harrumphing, Marcus silent now, and I—I wished I'd remained in my hotel room reading a novel by anyone but Kathleen Norris.

Aleck was reciting poetry to me. "'I like to see it lap the miles and lick the valleys up.' Or, in my version, I like to crawl the miles long to pick my spirits up. Much better than dear Emily, the spinster of Amherst you must have known in your childhood, Edna."

"Yes, dear Aleck, but…" I stopped, gob-smacked. "Aleck!"

He turned, alarmed.

I sputtered, "Emily."

"Yes, I know who wrote that poem. Emily"—still the sly grin—"Bronte."

"No," I hissed, "the waitress at the Peanut Grill yesterday, Aleck. That man mentioned a girl's name. Emily."

"I was there, Edna. I have a good memory."

"Obviously not good enough."

"And why is that?"

I whispered into his neck. "Violet Sharp's sister is named Emily. Annabel's cousin. Another maid, but one who scooted back to England right after the kidnapping."

He stared into my face, his eyebrows raised. "Edna, Edna, where are you going with this madness? You're running off into a madman's wonderland."

So I ignored him for the remainder of the ride, pouting a bit, which I regretted, but thinking. Aleck paid me no mind, though he kept telling Marcus to step on it. A noisome refrain: *I'm late I'm late I'm late.* Marcus ignored him. In Princeton, of course, we were gloriously late, the tweedy professor peeved and serving us cold chicken and informing Aleck that he'd reconsidered an appearance on Aleck's radio program, but perhaps in the future. Aleck fumed, but the professor's wife, joining us, seemed inordinately interested in me and went on and on about *So Big* and *Show Boat* until Aleck, furious, struggled to his feet and announced, "This show has closed out of town."

And with that he headed to the car where Marcus, dozing over a newspaper, apologized for something he didn't do.

The ride back to Flemington was icy, Aleck now and then beginning some cruel jibe, fashioning some nastiness but never quite finding it.

When Marcus dropped us off at the Union Hotel, his eyes narrowing at Aleck who was huffing and puffing, I strode on ahead, tired of the childish man. I felt a headache coming on— and probably a colossal feud with the argumentative Aleck. Our skirmishes were the stuff of Broadway legend. But Aleck, primed for an argument—I understood the signs: the flicking of his tongue against the side of his mouth, his index finger twitching against his nose, his walk a pronounced and prim waddle, his cheeks the color of blood—trailed after me.

I skirted by Nellie's Taproom, already bursting with noisy drinkers, and stepped around the mongrel black-and-white dog—called Nellie—whose presence helped name the make-shift tavern, a dog that, I'd heard, received twenty fan letters a day from the American heartland. I walked into the café where I spotted Horace Tripp slumped in a chair. Aleck, ready for a fight, followed me in. Past the dinner hour, only a few tables occupied, but Horace sat with his head dropped into his lap, a cigarette burning in an ashtray at his elbow. He looked up, and I saw a ravaged face, deep lines around his mouth, bloodshot eyes. He lifted a hand in greeting, but his arm shook as he dropped it back into his lap.

"What?" I demanded, stunned.

He said nothing but looked into my face, vacant-eyed.

Aleck walked up to him and leaned in. "What, Mr. Tripp?"

His head fell to the side like a doll's head loosened from its strings.

"Tell me." I softened my voice.

"Peggy Crispen is dead."

Stunned, I shut my eyes, saw flashes of brilliant light, jagged waves of scarlet and white. My head swam, and I gripped the rail of a chair.

"Tell me." Louder now.

"They found her body a little while ago. Outside of town on a country lane. She—she *froze* to death."

I shivered. "What?"

His voice gained strength. "The sheriff was here a while ago. He didn't know she no longer worked for us." His voice hardened. "That the hotel canned her." But then the droopiness returned, his eyes moist. "He said someone driving by saw her curled into a ball by a bank of snow, coatless. Christ Almighty. She had no overcoat on. Like it was summer. He said they think she was drinking at the place down from her room, somehow wandered out, took the wrong turn, and wandered away from the town. No one saw her."

"Without her coat?" I asked.

"I know, I know."

"My Lord," I said, slipping into a chair.

He looked into my face. "How can that happen? Someone must have seen her, no? People don't wander without a coat in freezing weather. Someone must have driven by. The sheriff said she was probably drunk. She—he said people knew her at this tavern nearby."

I looked at Aleck. "Another death."

"She froze to death, Edna."

"Like Annabel. Dead."

Aleck spoke in a clipped voice, close to my ear. "It's not a murder, Edna. Get that notion out of your head. She was a frightened woman, afraid of her room, probably spending the night in a bar. She wandered away."

I drew my lips into a thin line. "I can't believe that, Aleck. It's just not—possible. Too much has happened in that one room. Annabel's murder, the burglary, the letters, and now this."

Aleck spoke through clenched teeth. "Stop this now."

Horace, watching us, stood and frowned. Slowly, he shuffled through the kitchen door, and I heard a pot clang onto the floor. I stood. "This day is over," I told him. "And not well."

As I turned to leave, the kitchen door swung open. I expected to see Horace returning but instead Martha stood there, her arms folded over her chest.

"Martha," I began, "I heard the horrible news from your husband."

Fury laced her face. "Poor Horace. Now he'll have to find a new dalliance to annoy me with."

"Really, Martha. A woman has died a horrible death."

She laughed an unfunny laugh. "And there will always be a new one. It's the nature of the beast."

"Surely…"

She turned to go back into the kitchen, but she looked back at us, a grotesque smirk on her face. "Two down. Imagine that. Maybe it was something he said to them. Or *did* to them. Or didn't do." A thin high cackle. The door slammed behind her.

# Chapter Sixteen

Peggy Crispen. Dead.

Frozen to death. A body lying against a snowbank in the frigid night. Impossible. When I closed my eyes in bed, I saw her scared face as she stood, bundled and shivering, in the doorway of a building near her own boardinghouse. Frightened out of her wits, that woman, afraid of the space she'd rented during her sad sojourn in Flemington. Not only had she discovered the strangled body of her roommate, a numbing horror, but then found her room ransacked, again violated, and finally, cruelly, she lost her job. Dead. Peggy Crispen. A woman who found herself embroiled in a drama she had no part in creating. And now dead. Drunk, wandering away from town. Impossible.

Early morning, unable to stay in bed, I walked to the boardinghouse and knocked on the first-floor apartment door of the landlord. A shuffle of feet from inside, the snarl of a dog, and an old man stood in the doorway. "Yeah?" He was adjusting paint-stained dungarees, bunched at the work boots, tucking in a yellowed undershirt that bore one or two cigarette burns near the collar. Again, the cigarette-smoker's rasp, "Yeah?" He peered at me through myopic eyes. "You ain't the plumber."

"I certainly am not."

"He's late."

"I'm on time."

That tickled him, a twist of his lips as he grinned and threw back his head. I saw a broken tooth and a blackened one, both of which gave him an oddly jack o' lantern look, though the long, wrinkled face, pockmarked and splotchy, belied that festive look.

"I'm Edna Ferber, a writer."

"All booked up. Doubles, triples. I got folks sleeping in the hallway, ma'am."

"No, no, I'm not looking for a room." Then I added, unnecessarily, "I have one at the Union Hotel." His eyebrows shot up at that. A coveted habitation, that hotel. "I have some questions about Annabel Biggs and Peggy Crispen."

He stepped back, silently nodded me in. "I got some coffee on. I suppose you'll take a cup." He motioned me to a dumpy chair, currently occupied by a fat orange-matted mongrel who did not plan on sharing the space. But a flick of a wrist from the old man and the beast toppled to the floor, yawned, eyed me through rheumy eyes, and slunk into a corner.

"I'm Pervis Trumbull," the old man said, extending his hand. "I figured someone gotta talk to me about them sorry girls."

"Why?"

"Nobody murders nobody in Flemington, leastwise in my long memory—and I been here seventy-seven years now. Papa fought for the Union against the South. Wounded, he was. And now that hillbilly strangles poor Annabel and people just nod like she died of the flu or something. Not fair, let me tell you."

"Well, I feel the same say, Mr. Trumbull. All the sensation of the Hauptmann trial lets folks ignore—"

He cut in. "Making a lot of us folks rich, but I can't wait till everyone goes away."

"Too many people here?"

"Craziness, all of it."

"I agree."

Again, he broke in as he snapped a Lucky Strike from a pack and lit it with a long wooden match. "That trial shoulda been in Trenton. Not here. Lord, they put two airplane landings not one hundred yards back of this house. Buzz over my head when I'm sleeping. We got this young mayor, John Schenk, who thinks it's good for business. And it is. But I'm not complaining."

I smiled. "Sounds as if you are."

The same deferential chuckle. "My wife, now dead these twenty years, used to say if I didn't complain about things I got nothing to talk about."

"Mr. Trumbull, could you talk to me about Peggy Crispen?"

That startled him. He got up, stumbled to the kitchen with the cigarette drooping from his lips, and poured two cups of coffee. He placed one in front of me and nodded at a small pitcher of milk. I helped myself. Hot, savory, thick. Perfect.

"Annabel Biggs is the story, no?"

"But Peggy's death bothers me."

He scratched his head. "I ain't following you, ma'am."

"Two women in the same room, both now dead?"

He bit the inside of his lip, managed to sip coffee while dragging on a cigarette. "But Annabel was killed." He pronounced the word *kilt*.

"Yes, but Peggy was afraid to return to her room here. The break-in afterwards."

He waited a heartbeat. "Yeah, I know. I seen that. I talked to her. Sad, sad girl, didn't know what to do, what way to turn."

I watched him over the rim of the cup. "Yes, the police have arrested Cody Lee Thomas for murder. They consider that case over and done, but to me there is so much mystery with Peggy's death—frozen to death in a bank of snow deep in the night? A horrible death, and strange."

He shivered. "Sort of shook me when they brung me that news, ma'am."

"So, yes, Annabel's murder intrigues, but Peggy's bothers."

"I see what you mean." He sat back. "She was a sweet one, that Peggy."

"And not Annabel?"

Another drag on his cigarette. "I don't like to speak ill of the dead, always been warned against it, but"—a feckless grin—"I seem to be doing it all my life, especially since at my age, going on seventy-eight this coming May, I got lots of dead folks around me, and some deserve being spoken of poorly."

"However…" I prodded.

"Annabel was a just little too loud for me. Not that she made a ruckus in her room. I don't mean that. I wouldn't have tolerated it. This is a quiet house." He grinned. "A little overcrowded these days, but so be it. I mean, she liked to swagger around the hallways, collaring strangers, boasting of this and that. In your business, yammering about the trial and the coins in her pocket from waitressing over to the Union Hotel. But she's the type what got under your skin, speaks too close to your face, eyes burrowing into you, tell me, tell me, tell me. And you ain't got nothing to tell her, frankly."

I smiled. "I guess you didn't care for her."

"Not a question of liking anybody. I didn't trust her. Struck me as someone up to scheming. You know, the shifting eye corners, that cloudy look? Late with her rent so I had to pound on her door. You know what I mean? She told me she was out of here the day they threw the book at Bruno Hauptmann."

I nodded. "She had her sights on something beyond Flemington."

"One way to put it. But a pretty gal, that's for sure. In a hard diamond kind of way, you know—all sharp edges and razor cuts. That bright red lipstick girls wear nowadays—called them hussies in my day. I had no idea why she took up with that tar-paper boy, Cody Lee Thomas, him following her around like a puppy dog, the two of them yelling at each other in the street like barnyard animals. Him from the Sourlands—frontier where Negroes and Indians married folks running away from the law. Annabel tells me how she told him to get lost, don't let him near the house, and he took it real bad. Then he kills her. Sooner or later somebody was gonna kill a girl like that."

"Did you see him that night?"

"Nope. Over to my daughter's in East Amwell. Spent the night listening to *Amos 'n' Andy* on her new Zenith. Come back to find Peggy and the cops running up and down the hallways like chickens with their heads cut off."

"You liked Peggy?"

"What's not to like about her? Always polite to me. Laughing girl. She talked to me. Young folks look through old folks, you know that. But she was kind of lost, you know."

"What do you mean?"

He struggled with his words. "Well"—he stretched out the word—"she was always looking up. Or around. I seen her on the sidewalk and someone walks by and she looks at them, like waiting for someone to be her friend. A lonely look on her face. Sort of broke my heart. A plump girl, that Peggy, so fellows didn't smile at her."

"I think the manager of the café was fond of her."

He scoffed. "Yeah, I seen that Casanova slipping around here. Stopping in at her room. When I caught him, he tells me he got to tell her about something about work. Lying to me. I don't allow no fooling around in my house—I'm a Presbyterian elder myself—but I know it goes on. That man played on her loneliness. One time I saw them whispering on the front stoop, and he bustled away. You know what she said to me? 'That man only knows how to lie.' Smart girl, but weak. She let him into her life. Him a married man."

"She was afraid to stay in her room after the murder."

He nodded. "Yeah, but I told her it was over and done. The scum in jail for good. But then somebody broke in. That never happened in my house before. And that set her off, dizzy and fretting. She was gonna move out, but where you gonna move in Flemington these days? You can't. She had to stay put for now."

"Did you see her the night she died?"

"Early on. Yeah. I'm walking home and I seen her going into the Smiler's Tavern on the corner. Lots of locals meet there. The owner is a no-account Methodist. I don't drink, and a young girl ain't got no business in a tavern. A single woman. Well, any woman. Do you drink, Miss Ferber?"

"A cocktail now and then."

He squinted his eyes. "Comes from living in a big city, I bet."

"You bet. A big city is one of the reasons I drink."

"Real funny. Anyway I go to bed around nine, but I checked the furnace first. I seen her walking up the stairs. She calls to me, a little tipsy, I think. But what do I know? I say good night and she tells me she's plum tuckered out. She was out looking for a job that day, chance of being a waitress at Smiler's Tavern. I wait till I hear her close her door, latch it shut. I could hear the snap of the lock. After the robbery, I put another lock on, made her feel safe. I go to bed."

"So she most likely didn't wander drunk from that bar into the countryside," I said, mainly to myself. "She came home."

"Not 'less she went back out again. And I doubt that."

"But there was a reason she left the room later that night."

"Maybe she had to meet someone."

"Or maybe someone got her to leave."

A quizzical look on his face. "That seems unlikely, Miss Ferber."

"I don't think she left alone."

"But why?"

"That's what I intend to find out."

◇◇◇

Back at the Union Hotel I heard my name called out. Cora Lee Thomas was sitting on one of the wing chairs by the reception area, her chair turned away from the front window. A tiny woman, she looked lost in the oversized chair, but she'd also tucked herself in, as though hiding from the reporters drifting down from their rooms, her head pressed against the back of the chair.

I walked over. "Mrs. Thomas."

She glanced around the lobby, already filling with people. "I've never been here before. So fancy a place. I didn't know if I could sit here."

I smiled. "You're perfectly welcome here." I slipped into the wing chair next to her, turned it so I faced her. "Has anything happened?"

Her eyes got moist as she fumbled for a handkerchief, dabbed at them. "I'm sorry."

I held her hand. "What happened?"

A helpless shrug. "They held that lineup I told you about, Cody Lee standing with these other guys. He says he was the only stocky guy, and so the drummer identified him." She stared into my eyes. "But that's impossible. So...so then they told him to confess, and he wouldn't. I don't know what that meant, but they said someone has come forward who says he *saw* Cody Lee and Annabel together in the doorway, arguing. But that had to be a different night. I mean, they argued at the café earlier that night, but he left. She kept working her shift and then went home."

"Where someone strangled her in the room."

Cora Lee shuddered and echoed my words. "In the room." A heartbeat. "He didn't follow her home because he was with me."

"You know I believe you, Mrs. Thomas."

She nodded, a wistful smile making her ragged face come alive. "That's why I'm here, I guess. You're the only person who believes me." She surveyed the lobby. "I wanted to thank you because I got a phone call from this lawyer from Manhattan who said he's a friend of yours. He's sending a friend who practices criminal law down here in Hunterdon County, an old school chum of his, a good lawyer, Yale Law, he said, his name is Amos Blunt, he tells me." Now a wider smile. "Thank you."

"No matter."

She looked away, sheepish. "He told me you said you'd cover the...you know."

"I told you not to worry about that."

She interlocked her fingers and drew them up to her chin. She sucked in her breath. "People ain't that kind to other folks anymore, Miss Ferber. With the Depression and all, it's...like cutthroat out there."

"I believe you when you say that Cody Lee is innocent."

Emphatic, her hand tapping the arm of the chair. "Yes, he is."

"But there's something else you want to tell me. I can tell."

Bashful, she glanced away, then tilted her head toward her lap. She wouldn't look at me. "Cody Lee got himself a temper like his father, sad to say. And he's restless in that cell, banging into the bars. So I guess he had a little shoving match with the jailer."

"Oh Lord, that's not good."

"I *told* him that. 'What's the matter with you?' I yelled at him. 'You ain't looking good that way. They'll think you're a violent man, no respect for authority. For laws.'" Her voice fell to a whisper. "When he hit the jailer, he heard that Bruno Hauptmann yell something at him in German. Like he heard the whole thing."

"What did he say?"

She rolled her head back and forth. "My Cody Lee don't speak German, but the jailer, he told this Bruno to shut the hell up."

"Did he?"

"He did. But the jailer made fun of him, saying to Cody Lee, 'Even that baby killer is a better prisoner than you.'"

◇◇◇

The café got still when I walked in after the morning session of the trial ended. Aleck sat alone by a window seat, motioned to me, but the look on his face suggested he'd rather be sharing a convivial sandwich with Lizzie Borden. A table of Hearst reporters, huddled nearby, stopped mid-sentence and mid-bite as I moved by, their eyes accusing.

"Pariah," Aleck said too loudly as I sat down.

I spun around to take in the packed room. Lowell Thomas was chatting with Margaret Bourke-White, both watching me. Douglas Fairbanks was sitting with Clifton Webb, both signing autographs, and thus paying me no mind. Worse, Joshua Flagg sat with his back against a window in a chair set apart from the table, as if he'd been exiled. And, perversely, he was pointing at me, a silly grin on his face. Walter Winchell, wearing ridiculous dark glasses tipped up onto his forehead, was holding court with three others at his table, and his rat-a-tat ticker-tape voice flowed over the heads of the other diners. "Incredible." At least I believe that was the word he hurled my way.

Of course, I understood the reason.

A copy of that morning's *New York Times* lay on different tables, opened to an inside page. In fact, Aleck cavalierly shoved his copy toward me, his fingers anxiously tapping the page. I saw my byline under the provocative headline: "Violet Sharp, A Cautionary Tale." The editor's headline, not mine, I hasten to add. I'd submitted it as "Violet Sharp, A Woman of Secrets." My editor Marvin Loeb said it lacked verve. So does my editor.

No matter the wording, the content of the piece obviously infuriated folks.

My first line: "The world should never forget Violet Sharp."

No chance of that, these days—in this Fourth Estate gladiators' ring, all the reporters maneuvering for blood and a scoop.

What I'd done was assemble what few facts we knew about the sad life of the servant in the Morrow household who killed herself rather than be interrogated one more time by Inspector Walsh of the New Jersey police. An abbreviated character sketch of a pretty young girl, described as a little plump but with lovely eyes, maybe an overbite, a woman who came to America to enjoy a better life—one who planned to return to her native England with cash in her pocket to help her parents. A young woman who liked to dance and go to the movies and to frequent illegal roadhouses. Nothing unusual there—most young folks did so in that restrictive era of Prohibition. Innocents all. An innocent abroad. But a young woman caught in the horrible fabric of the Lindbergh kidnapping, swept into the confusions of guilt and mistrust and accusation. It was too much for her. The first "insider" accused by Colonel Norman Schwarzkopf, who stated his conviction that she was party to the kidnapping, although he later changed his mind.

A familiar story, a few years old now, but brought back into the light by the current trial. A profile of an aborted life. I wondered in the last paragraph if Violet Sharp had died with a secret.

But obviously I'd overstepped some line.

"Edna, how could you?" From Aleck, stewing and eyeing me over the rim of his coffee cup.

"I'm a journalist."

"You're a provocateur."

I chuckled. "Rather extreme, no, Aleck?"

"Look around you, my dear."

I did: censorious eyes, frowns, pursed lips, the claque of disapproval.

"Edna, your portrait of that sad suicide deflects from the horrors of the crime at hand. You've opened a raw wound. Everyone is reading between the lines—you're impugning the aviator himself. Everyone is focused on Hauptmann and Lindbergh, and you pen some melancholic song to a dead beautiful girl. Edgar Allan Poe you are not."

"Aleck, I didn't mention any of the"—I dropped my voice to a whisper—"the business with Annabel and the letters from cousin Violet to her. There's no mention of Dwight and the Morrow household. Certainly nothing about Blake Somerville and Violet's infatuation with him."

I watched his face carefully. He drew his lips into a tight line, flicking his head as if to suggest I might be overheard. "You mention her sister, Emily—her flight back to England."

"So what? All I did was write about a young woman's sudden place in the whirlpool of a national tragedy. It's a morality tale. The common man suddenly, well, thrust onto the front page. Out there. A girl horrified."

He dismissed me with a wave of his hand. "You're talking nonsense."

I looked around. "I really didn't expect my article to create such a furor."

"Thousands of words are produced every day, Edna. A million words a day are telegraphed from Flemington. Every scrap of information on Lindbergh and Hauptmann, real and imagined, makes its way into the press. But, as you've noticed, all the sympathies are with Lindbergh and the Morrows. With Charles and Anne. I myself described Anne Lindbergh on the witness stand as—as a wistful Madonna."

"You're a sentimentalist, Aleck."

His jaw dropped. "Your focus on the dead girl suggests… well, secreted information, a story not fully told."

I stormed, "Well, Aleck, that's exactly how I view it."

He thundered back, "But that's wrong."

"Who are you to tell me I'm being ridiculous?"

He sighed. "Edna, we are friends."

"You sound doubtful."

A thin smile as he adjusted his tiny glasses on his cheeks. "We've had our bitter moments, our battles royal, but I do get protective of your rash behavior. On occasion."

I seethed. "I've never done a rash thing in my life." A pause. "Save, perhaps, befriend you."

Aleck eyed me curiously, silent, one hand fingering the cigarette holder he'd extracted from his breast pocket. Instead, he struggled to stand, though he announced in a loud voice, "Nevertheless, I will accompany you tomorrow, as planned. Your capricious pursuit of nonsense. It'll do me good to leave this sad hamlet for greener pastures. I've appropriated Marcus and the car tomorrow. Marcus is ours for the whole day. A foolish venture, but nevertheless I promised you I'd arrange things."

"Thank you, Aleck."

Tomorrow, a quiet Sunday, I planned to visit Montclair Manor, the asylum where Dwight Morrow and Blake Somerville had been patients. Earlier Aleck had told me he knew a retired nurse who lived in the area. He'd make a few phone calls, set up a meeting. "Frivolous," he'd told me, but I persisted. In an aside he'd said, "She took care of Zelda Fitzgerald there. She violated that confidence, and doubtless she'll violate every other confidence. A couple of free front-row theater tickets, and the woman will do electric shock on Helen Hayes. Which would enliven any party, frankly. The woman has few scruples. The two of you should get along famously. I'm only going because I want to watch the two of you engage in a battle of wits."

Quietly, "Thank you again."

"Marcus will call for us at seven. I told him to appropriate a road map. For all his Valentino looks, the lad is a provincial—he knows only Trenton and Newark and workable parts of Manhattan. Montclair is wilderness to him."

I repeated, "Thank you."

"But don't expect me to be pleasant on the long, long ride."

"I wouldn't expect the axis of the earth to shift."

Aleck lumbered out of the café, leaving me alone at the table. As he walked by Walter Winchell's table, I noticed the pesky reporter wave to him, as if in recognition of Aleck's decision to abandon the heretic Ferber.

I sat alone, nursing a cup of coffee and feeling strangely triumphant, isolated from that swelling, gaping crowd. Horace Tripp walked by, a sheaf of menus in his hand, and he glanced down at me. I started to say something—another expression of sympathy at the death of Peggy, perhaps—but he was looking away. When the waiter asked me what I wanted to eat, I said nothing. Just coffee. A table for four with me alone, sipping a cup of lukewarm coffee. He didn't look happy.

A short time later Walter Winchell rose, and his entourage trooped out ahead of him. He lingered, shuffled near my table, and, unbidden, dropped into the chair Aleck had vacated.

"Can I help you?" I asked.

"The question is, can I help you?"

"You first." My winsome smile broke at the edges.

"I read your piece in the *Times*," he began. "We all did. Probably Colonel and Mrs. Lindbergh. Colonel Schwarzkopf. It smacked of rampant sentimentality, some sob sister posturing on your part. You depict this—this Violet Sharp as some faded ingénue from one of your romances. Why is that, Miss Ferber? The only thing lacking would be harps playing and angels singing her to heaven."

"Leave her to heaven."

"What?"

"A line from another writer. Shakespeare. I don't think you've heard of him."

An unhappy grimace, his tight ferret's face distorted. "All I'm saying is that this trial is being watched by the whole world. Colonel Lindbergh is a genuine American hero, beloved, revered. Honored."

"And I respect him."

"I wonder about that." A snide twist of his lips. "I do."

"Well, that's your peculiar failing then."

"Bruno is a monster."

"But Violet Sharp was not."

"But you are suggesting that she had something to do with the kidnapping."

I sat up. "I never said any such thing."

"The mention of her name—singling her out, especially harping on the police questioning—its harshness…"

"Because she died a horrible death."

"She was an hysteric." He nodded toward his sycophants, clustered nearby.

"Really?"

A snicker. "Something you should understand."

I remained silent.

He stood. "You know, Miss Ferber, there is an awful price for nonconformity."

I waited a moment. "Words I can hear Adolf Hitler saying to his robotic SS minions."

He flushed, stammered, "How dare you?"

"We are in a democracy. Innocent until proven guilty."

"That doesn't include Bruno the German."

"Nor obviously me as well."

"Nonconformity." He stressed the word.

"I know. I heard you. Nonconformists, even in a democracy, are a small club of enlightened souls. A small club, but a refreshing one. There's a certain liberation when you break away from the herd of fat, grazing cows."

"Be careful." His final words, hissed, fierce. He tapped his fingers on the table, planted his feathered fedora on his head, adjusted his dark glasses, and left the café.

I sipped my coffee. Looking down, I wanted no contact with anyone, but someone was hovering over me. Joshua Flagg had left his seat in the corner and had approached my table.

"Now what do you want?" I asked.

A blank expression on his face, his eyes dark and unblinking. "That Winchell fellow is a strange man."

I fumed. "Is that why you've approached me? To tell me what I already know?"

A devilish smile now, dark and cruel. "You're playing a dangerous game, Miss Ferber. Dangerous."

"What are you saying?"

"I've said it. Dangerous."

With that he scuttled out of the café.

I sipped coffee. Cold now, filmy and dark.

Distracted, I heard yelling in the street. The state police officers were walking the jurors back from their lunch, sheltered as they were at the end of the dining room, lamentably in earshot of the talkative reporters on the other side of the curtain. Walking in a straight line, tense, shoulders bumping, the six men and four women, bundled up against the cold, moved toward the courthouse. A daily ritual, this awful passage from courthouse to hotel and back again. And, as usual, crowds of people lined the street, blocked the street and sidewalk, watching, watching. Cameras snapped photographs, newsreel footage rolled, but no one dared address the jurors. The stern eye of the state police made that certain.

But as they moved across the street, the chanting began.

"Kill Bruno. Kill Bruno. Kill the kraut."

*Kill the baby killer.*

*Kill him.*

*Burn him.*

The voices rose, swelled, broke in the icy air, overlapped and became thunderous.

*Kill Bruno.*

*Kill.*

As I watched, one of the defense lawyers, Lloyd Fisher, hurried to the doors of the courthouse, opened them, and Anna Hauptmann, looking dowdy in a bulky black cloth hat and cheap coat, brushed by him, her shoulders hunched.

Someone in the crowd spotted her and the crowd shifted toward her.

"Kill her. Kill her."

*Let her die.*

*Kill her.*

# Chapter Seventeen

Aleck grumbled as I entered the lobby. "Edna, the car is waiting. Must you dawdle?"

Outside, exhaust spewing from the long car, Willie stood with the back door open.

"Where's Marcus?" I asked him, and Aleck raised his eyebrows. He mouthed the words: foolish woman.

"With his wife over to Trenton."

"Marcus is married?"

"So am I," Willie said. "You surprised?"

Aleck leaned in. "Miss Ferber was hoping Marcus would be available for the next Hollywood version of *Show Boat*. Gaylord Ravenal behind the wheel of a chariot of the gods."

"Quiet, Aleck. Willie has yet to step on the gas and already you're annoying me." I turned to Willie. "Do you have children?"

"Everybody has family, ma'am. It's what you do in New Jersey. I got grandchildren older than Marcus."

"Hear that, Edna? Procreation as diversion among the swamp-and-toxic-fume people."

"Shut up, Aleck."

I slipped into the backseat and Aleck toppled in beside me.

"Sunday in Flemington," Willie sighed. "Last Sunday over sixty-thousand sightseers clogged the streets. Already the crowds are gathering at the doors of the courthouse. On Sunday the sheriff allows visitors access to the halls—madness I can't fathom.

While state troopers stood guard last week, lines of them, alert, unhappy, well, folks used pen knives to whittle slivers from chairs and tables, tried to secret spittoons under bulky coats, tucked toilet paper in purses, some carving initials in benches. Kilroy was here. Fistfights broke out. They sat on the judge's dais, shuffled through the jury box—'Hey, John, get a picture of me'—or sat in Bruno's chair and made buzzing sounds as if they was being electrocuted."

Unfortunately, in my opinion, they weren't.

"I know," I said to his back. "Craziness."

"Human stupidity still amazes."

Aleck rolled his eyes at me. "Yes, I agree. Craziness is trooping off to this mad house with you, Edna."

I'd assured my editor at the *Times* that I was pursuing an angle on the kidnapping. Faced with his doubtful look, I'd mumbled, "Violet Sharp." My article had engendered hateful mail and furious telephone calls. But my magical words energized the young man, and he nodded approval. He told me, *sotto voce*, that one of the managing editors—whose mother had been one of the haughty Knickerbockers—had spent recuperative time at Montclair Manor, a short visit, where he'd followed Zelda Fitzgerald around the hallways, peppering her with infantile questions about Scott's *Gatsby*. She never answered. "It's the domain of the very rich and the very disturbed."

Aleck and I lapsed into silence, his dislike of our adventure obvious, but Willie found the backseat stillness unbearable, and a few times, shifting his scrawny, ancient body in the seat, he began a ramble about the stark winter scenery, the cold weather, and the awful fog that settled on the hills. He volunteered a remark about the superiority of New Jersey over New York, though Aleck's egregious belch at that moment slammed Willie into a confused silence. Not to be silenced, Willie chronicled his disaffection with the Roosevelts, in particular Eleanor. "No one likes a pushy dame."

"Really, Willie," I pleaded. "Enough."

We held eye contact as he looked into the rearview mirror. "Don't mean no offense, ma'am."

"And yet it seems your only talent."

He shut up.

As the car turned into the grounds, Montclair Manor struck me as a Gothic backdrop for a chilling British parlor drama: stark Tudor turrets, hemlocks leaning on the slate roof, creeping ivy withered under the harsh blast of January. Small leaded glass windows dotted the façade. The grounds were darkswept now, ice-tinged, and even at midday I could detect faint illumination seeping through, though most of the buildings seemed forbidden, if not abandoned.

"Lord, Aleck," I told him. "Such a building could only exacerbate any depression I had."

A ridge of old mansions high on a hill that overlooked the distant Hudson River, the gigantic homes of moneyed Robber Barons now transformed into clinics, hospitals, charity organizations.

Aleck was peering out the window. "Please behave yourself, Edna. They have the power to hold us there."

"It's for the rich, Aleck."

"My point exactly. You qualify. I don't. I will be compelled to scrub the toilets."

The front door swung open, a creaky whine, and I expected to see Mary Shelley jotting notes on a steno pad for a sequel to *Frankenstein*. We were met by a tall stringbean of a man dressed in a charcoal morning suit with a carefully appointed ascot and a matching light-blue handkerchief peeking from a breast pocket. So tall was this man that he had to bend dangerously as he endeavored to shake our hands. "I'm Thomas Colby, the director. I've been told to expect your visit." Another bow, precarious as he swayed a bit, and then a toothsome smile. Too many teeth in so tiny a mouth. "Such an honor to have such famous guests." Then, without pausing, "We understand you're doing research for an article on mental aberration and its successful treatment."

I sucked in my breath. "Well…"

Aleck jumped in. "You are correct. *The New York Times*, you know."

"Oh, I know."

Aleck shot me a look. *Careful, Edna.*

"Mark Jamison called ahead, of course. He's on our board. A friend to our institution."

"A wonderful friend," Aleck went on. "We were at Hamilton together."

"So I understand."

Which, I knew, was how this questionable visit had been orchestrated. Aleck called a friend from his college days, someone connected with the *Times*, and the machinery had been oiled. A few other surreptitious phone calls that touched base with Mark Jamison's sister, whom Aleck had never met. A casual lie about the purpose of our visit, a journalistic ploy that skirted some ethical boundaries...

Director Colby ushered us in to a reception area where coffee was waiting. He dipped and swayed as he poured for us, although he never asked us if we wanted any. He nodded toward a plate of dry, unappetizing cookies, which I shunned but Aleck immediately reached for, swooping up two at a time. Both disappeared into his mouth, though he was compelled to wash them down quickly with gulps of hot coffee. "They are good, no?" Colby intoned and I wondered if he intended satire. I doubted it. But I noticed he touched not a one.

He sat there stiffly, his long flamingo legs drawn up almost to his chin, his eyes watching us. A drip of unnecessary drool seeped from the corner of his mouth and, in a flash, a large geographic tongue flitted out, captured the vagrant spit, and made it disappear. I stared, wide-eyed, enthralled. A Dickensian character, this Thomas Colby, but accommodating, suddenly producing expensive colorful brochures touting the effects of any stay at the institution.

"I understand Zelda Fitzgerald was here for a brief visit," I said, though I immediately regretted my words.

He looked flustered and glanced away at the ceiling as if to check that she was not hiding there, and announced, "Issues of confidentiality, my dear Miss Ferber. You do understand."

"Of course."

"Lord, Edna," Aleck sympathized, "I'm surprised your family allows you out in public."

I smiled weakly.

A discreet knock on the door, and Colby looked up, irritated. "Oh, yes, of course." He hesitated. "Nurse Smith will give you a tour."

We walked through a common area, a recreational lounge, and a library, and I saw not even one patient.

An hour later we thanked Colby and left the grounds for lunch at a small coffee shop, The Copper Kettle, as planned. We met Mark Jamison's sister, a retired ward nurse who'd agreed to talk with us.

Alice Jamison was a small, fussy-looking woman, late sixties perhaps, dressed in a crisp cardigan sweater and a butterfly brooch, sensible polished black shoes, her gray hair pulled into a severe bun and her nails bitten to the quick. When we shook hands I noticed thin lines of dried red at the edges. Alice Jamison had a quirky smile, mischievous, the town scamp who'd metamorphosed into a middle-aged gossip or town crier. As we walked into the eatery, she caught my eye and offered a quick, furtive wink, conspiratorial. I knew I was going to like this woman.

No one from Montclair Manor ever frequented the place, she told us.

"Too many farmers in overalls and five-cent cigars."

Which suited me fine. At midday the tiny eatery smelled of savory cheese and fresh baked bread, the raw hint of rising yeast and aromatic coffee beans. A long counter did, indeed, exhibit a gaggle of locals, none however in overalls but all chummy and joking, men and women from a local brewery affectionately teasing the red-faced counter boy, a lad who stuttered and guffawed and seemed to be having the time of his life. We sat at a back table, a crisp white tablecloth covering it, and ordered the specialty of the day: homemade Belgian stew, advertised as a concoction of shredded roast, peas, carrots, and diced potatoes. It was, to my delight, the perfect meal for a cold, blustery day.

Alice sat back, smacking her lips after the last sip of coffee, her wadded napkin dropped onto the table. "Of course, I haven't been at the Manor for a while. Things change." A hint of a smile. "And now I can tell tales out of school. I suppose you two didn't travel here for a commentary on the latest research in psychiatric methods."

Aleck grinned. "Always of interest to Edna, true...but no."

Alice leaned in. "My brother tells me you're in Flemington at the Hauptmann trial."

"That's true," I told her.

"Does this have anything to do with that?"

I debated what to say, but demurred. I wanted no repercussions. But her wide, eager face demanded the truth. Or, rather, some part of the truth.

"I'm researching the family background. Particularly Anne Lindbergh's side, the Morrow family. So rich and famous, so prominent in the headlines now. A family that long shunned tabloid scandal—a father predicted to become President of the United States—and now finds itself smack-dab in the middle of it. Who are these people? I wondered."

She caught my eye and twisted her lips. "Dwight Morrow, Jr."

Startled. "What?"

"I'm not a fool."

"I never said you were." I smiled back at her.

She waited a heartbeat. "I've been reading your pieces in the *Times*. Both of yours."

"And?" I waited, anxious.

Again that mysterious smile. "Mr. Woollcott, you have a jaundiced view of the defense team."

"And I?" I wondered.

"You, Miss Ferber, have a jaundiced view of the prosecution."

"Interesting," I said. "I'm trying to remain impartial."

"You're not doing a good job of it."

Aleck whooped it up, enjoying himself. "Alice, my dear, you are like your brother."

"Yeah, I've heard that before."

"He never let me get away with anything at Hamilton."

"He still talks of the time you played Lady Macbeth."

I howled. "Really, Aleck?"

Aleck grumbled, "No one did it better."

"Oh my Lord," I chuckled.

"Really, Edna." He nodded at Alice. "Go on. Point out Edna's myriad faults. Her horrible bias. Her wilting before the shrine of Bruno."

But Alice backtracked. "No, not true. All I'm saying is that Miss Ferber enjoys—maybe that's the wrong word—*likes* exploring the darker side, the underbelly, accused." She breathed in. "I loved your piece on Violet Sharp. I'd forgotten about her. You made her come sadly alive, Miss Ferber. No one took note of her emotional turmoil. You refuse to let that troubled girl be forgotten."

"Thank you."

"But I'm not saying you name her as suspect—or guilty. She is just—there. A happenstance of history, the accidental victim."

"Exactly."

"And what about me?" Aleck preened. "I write, too."

She broke in. "You talk of procedures and opinions and evidence and authority and state police methods. You made Anne Lindbergh and Charles Lindbergh statues—the wife is a Madonna to you, and the husband is an icon. Statues in a frieze. Miss Ferber talks about people."

I waited a second. "Dwight Morrow, Jr."

"Yes," she hummed. "The real reason for your visit here. The Morrow family. So little has been written about the siblings." A shrug. "No reason to, really."

"Yet fascinating," I added.

She watched me closely. "I agree."

"So?" Aleck went on. "Tell us."

For a moment she gazed off. "Tales out of class, forbidden, but"—her smile belied her schoolmarm hairdo—"I'm among friends." She sat back. "I liked Dwight quite a bit. Respectful, shy, humble almost. Always polite and stepping out of your way."

"He sounds like a good house pet," Aleck noted.

Alice frowned. "Quite a sense of humor as well, that Dwight. Sardonic, quick. Then, other days—boorish, impetuous."

"Did the Lindberghs visit him here?"

She shook her head back and forth. "Nobody visited here. It was like…this whole business will not be discussed."

I went on. "His sister Anne?"

"As I said, no. The strange thing is, Dwight talked about her all the time. I gather he'd been obsessed with her, the favorite sister, doted on her, she on him. But when she married the aviator, everything shifted. The imperious mother liked her three daughters—and not him. That was clear. The whole family was troubled with health problems. The father had a misshapen arm and battled migraines and depression. High-achievers, all of them. Looked out from that mansion over the Palisades, and they crumbled. Elisabeth had a weak heart, Anne hid in her room, and Dwight went to Groton where he had a breakdown. A stutterer who heard voices. Dwight continued to have problems, in and out of care, patterns not unfamiliar in that family, I hear tell. But a sweet man, I need to tell you that. I *liked* him."

"Sounds like a sad boy."

"It's very easy to dislike many of the patients—not because of their illnesses, which often are bizarre, but because they come from a life of privilege. Their mental condition sometimes made their demands impossible—but they viewed us as—well, the help. But Anne's marriage to Charles turned Dwight upside down, depressed, sullen, hidden away, explosive. He avoided the wedding."

"Dangerous?"

A long pause as she bit her lip. "Only to himself."

"Montclair Manor wasn't the only place he was sent to?" Aleck asked.

Alice nodded. "Problems in Amherst, a mysterious fire in his dorm. He was sent to Stockbridge, the Riggs Foundation for

Psychopathic Diseases, another wealthy enclave. A mysterious fire there, and he was moved to Beacon, New York. The Craig House. A sad boy, a lump of clay who still had baby fat—and wore a pince-nez, just like his dead father. Then he ended up here for a year."

"Diagnosis—schizophrenia?" Aleck asked.

She nodded. "He thought he was a lighthouse that forgot to send out light. He called himself St. Peter, and then said he was *all* the saints. He believed he was himself the very classmates who tortured him."

"Sad, sad," I said.

"Hallucinations."

"But then he got better, right?" I said. "Sent back home?"

"Of course. When he didn't have his spells, when the hallucinations ended, he was a bright, responsive, a pleasure, a good student at Amherst."

"That's right. He was at Amherst when the Lindbergh baby was taken."

"He was no longer here, of course. He'd returned to school." She grinned. "He worked for Al Smith's campaign for president—to spite his Republican family who were Hoover advocates. He refused to return home when news of the kidnapping broke—I heard he stayed in his rooms." Alice narrowed her eyes. "I think I know where this is going, Miss Ferber. I mean, your interest in Dwight."

I hedged. "I'm interested in how the family deals with the kidnapping."

She studied my face. "Of course, his relationship with Colonel Lindbergh."

Aleck interjected, "Edna does character studies, I'm afraid. Sometimes they have nothing to do with the heinous crime."

"I can talk for myself, Aleck." I turned to Alice. "Yes, it's true that I am interested in the dynamic of the Morrow family."

"Well, yes, Dwight had no liking for his brother-in-law. I can only tell you that he'd mutter and fuss about things the Colonel said, often not even to him. Lindbergh is everything Dwight is not: tall, handsome, famous, charming. And, worse, he swept Dwight's sister away from that insolated household, not too long after the venerable Dwight Sr. died suddenly. Dwight was the man of the house for a moment, but, sadly, he was still a boy. He couldn't protect his beloved sister from the menace of the lone eagle swooping down on Englewood."

"But they never had words."

She swung her head back and forth. "Dwight would never have words with anyone. He'd hide in a book in the library rather than tell you to your face what needed to be said."

"But he must have told you things?"

She waited a second. "Of course. Things that made me sympathetic to him."

"Like what?"

"He said Lindbergh gave him candy that was really a laxative. He slipped a stink bomb into Dwight's glove."

"True?"

"I believed it." Alice squinted. "You know, you can't use lots of what I'm telling you."

"I assume that. I'm looking for—flavor."

"Go to a soda fountain," Aleck quipped.

I looked at Aleck. He wasn't too happy with the tenor of this conversation, but I knew he wouldn't be: my probing encroached onto sacred and patriotic territory, inviolable. The boy aviator had flaws—and egregious ones.

"Have you heard enough, Ferb?" he said bitingly.

I hadn't. "What about Dwight's friends here?"

"Well, patients don't really make friends. Temporary, enforced, begrudgingly. But"—her eyes lit up—"of course there was Blake Somerville. You know the Somervilles of New Jersey and Pennsylvania. Political forces. The bankers. Blake had been at Amherst a few years before Dwight, I think, but he was at Montclair Manor when Dwight entered as a patient."

"Tell me about Somerville."

She smiled. "A singular creation, that one. The kind of slick confection who preys on the weak. But he already knew Dwight,

I guess, or at least their families have estates near each other in Englewood. At first he acted as big brother but his touch was lethal. I don't think I ever disliked a man so much, and my job is to heal. That was impossible."

A chill ran up my spine. "Tell me."

"He acted, well, sort of messianic, a man who craves followers, but for no other end than some personal satisfaction. Handsome, suave, glib, a fast talker, he drew you in, attracted you, but then inevitably, after a bit, you saw the devil under the flash of his eye. Mischief, often cruel and vicious."

"His malady?" I asked.

A crooked smile. "Probably his family just wanted him out of the house." A dismissive wave of her hands. "He sucked Dwight in, of course, and Dwight listened to everything he said."

"A close bond?"

"An *evil* bond. Blake has little emotion, so he didn't care for Dwight—or anybody. One of the doctors said he viewed Dwight as an experiment. He'd set him off to do pranks—to foul up the works."

"Like?" I probed.

"Well, for one, Blake and Dwight would slip into a patient's room, hide things, and watch the patient go bananas. Or he'd tell a patient a family member had died, and he'd watch the hysterics. We caught on to a few of these—someone saw—but I'm sure he did many more."

"How did Dwight play into this?"

Aleck was fiddling with her napkin, unhappy. He cast a dark eye on me, which I ignored.

"His patsy. His stooge. He directed Dwight to do such and such. Then the two would sit in a lounge and howl and slap their knees and yell out. If Blake got reprimanded by the director, he'd find a way to blame Dwight. 'You know how he is, sir,' he'd babble. 'Unstable.'"

"Where was his family?"

"Well, ultimately I heard that they disowned him—wouldn't allow him back at the estate. He terrorized, he stole money, he pawned jewelry, he—he manipulated, turned brother against sister. That sort of thing. Not for any end but the thrill of it." Her index finger wagged at me. "That's it. A man born to wealth who lives for a vicarious thrill. Nothing else matters."

"How long was he here?"

"Not long. But twice. He disappeared for a year or so. I heard he tried to become an actor on Broadway, even had some parts. I mean, he had the looks and this radio-announcer kind of voice. But I doubt if the stage could hold him. Before he came back here—before the family disowned him—that is, I heard he had this old Park Avenue lady in his power, milked her savings account. Then her children stepped in. When he was here the second time, a brief time, Dwight was no longer here."

"Back at home?" I asked.

She nodded. "But Blake had a new acolyte. An absolutely frenzied young man, a few years younger, had been admitted. The son of an editor on the *Chicago Tribune*, I recall. Blake became his hero. In fact, the young man altered his own appearance, shellacking his hair so that it sparkled, dressing the same way, approximating Blake's casual walk—he had a way of sauntering that suggested he was taking his time headed to the Saratoga races at tea time—and even using Blake's expressions. Blake employed a lot of flapper era jargon—like *bee's knees, cat's meow, oh you kid.* Artificial and purposeful. When he used those expressions, he always had a superior tone, as though challenging you to remark on the language being passé. But when this young man used that language, it sounded sad and lonely, echoes of his mentor. Blake would tap him on the shoulder and say things like, 'There, there. Someday you'll be a shadow of the real me.' Whatever that meant."

"His name?" I asked.

"Is that important?"

"Probably not, but…"

"Ezra Cilley."

"That's a real name?" Aleck asked, grinning.

"What finally happened to Blake?" I wondered.

Alice sat back, finished with the interrogation. "He walked away."

"You mean out of Montclair Manor?" Aleck asked, flummoxed.

She chuckled. "It's not uncommon. These are rich folks. Yes, we have a locked room, places for electric shock, other kinds of therapy, but most wander the halls like ghosts of their former selves. They demand—or their families do—a lot of freedom. One day Blake put on his street clothes and walked off the grounds."

"Did anyone find him?"

"Well, a few phone calls, but his family wanted no part of it. He was dead to them."

"And so he's disappeared?"

"As I say, he slipped out the door and kept walking."

# Chapter Eighteen

Willie was impatient to head back to Flemington, but my mind raced with the information Alice provided. The day had turned damp and raw, a pocket of ice fog settling over the roads, so Willie crept along, reassuring us he would return us safely. The more he assured—he did go on and on, nervous weather forecaster—the more I planned my funeral. The fog lulled him, made him melancholic. The car drifted. I repeatedly tapped his shoulder. "Willie." He hummed laments about long drives he'd taken that ended in—disaster. "Nice touch," I whispered to Aleck. A long day, this, so I wanted to return to my rooms, soak in a hot bath, call for tea and a cold plate, and drift away.

But first I needed to talk to Aleck. I pointed out a roadside diner. "Coffee," I breathed. "Coffee."

"Cake," Aleck responded, a gleam in his eye.

"That, too."

Seated in the art deco diner, all polished chrome and country-western jukebox and cracked red leather stools, I began, "Aleck, tell me what you think."

He shook his head vigorously. "No, no, dear Ferb. This is your out-of-town preview. You're the writer and director, if not the star. Yes, it'll bomb in New Haven, but you have to have your way."

"Aleck, stop talking."

His small eyes got wide. "You just asked me what I thought."

"I didn't really mean it." I smiled winsomely. "Actually, I plan on telling you what I think."

"But I can read your mind."

"I doubt that." A heartbeat as I scanned the grimy menu and mumbled to the waitress, "Coffee with whipped cream. Or any cream. Banana cream pie." As she turned away, I said to him, "There's a story here. Dwight Morrow and Blake Somerville—and, lamentably, Violet Sharp. And perhaps even her sister, Emily, now safely hidden away in merry old England."

Aleck held up his hand. "Before you go on, I want to register my objections to this day."

"You don't have to, Aleck. I read the expression on your face all day long." I fiddled with a spoon on the table. "I think we have to take Violet's letters to Annabel seriously." His eyebrows shot up. He grumbled. I continued, "Indulge me, Aleck. Don't you think there is something about this story…this Blake Somerville? An intriguing player in this drama."

Aleck frowned. "But you're making a huge and impossible leap from the Morrow household and this vagabond trickster to the kidnapping of Little Lindy."

"I'm simply suggesting that we think about what Annabel believed—based on letters from her cousin. How else do we place Violet Sharp into this? She had an infatuation with a dangerous man, someone who knew how to manipulate folks, like Dwight and Violet."

"We don't know that."

"Yes, we do. Violet was seen with them."

"So what?"

"So Annabel understood that Dwight harbored a dislike of Lindbergh, documented—a well-placed dislike, if you ask me—and this disowned rich man maneuvered him into some foolish prank. That last letter talks of a prank"—I deliberated, pausing—"maybe to hide the baby, get money, then return the boy."

"Maybe."

"A prank that Dwight perhaps thought disruptive and pesky. To get under Lindbergh's skin. Payback for Lindbergh's pranks on him. But I think Blake Somerville thought it great fun."

"Rather maniacal, no?"

I tapped the table. "That's my point, Aleck. We're dealing with a man who is amoral, who lives for the hunt, the thrill, the sensation."

"But a real baby died, Edna." He stabbed a piece of cake. "Not some mental game-playing, some fantasy maybe, they talked of."

"That's where the plan fell apart. Everything was in place. Perhaps the sister Emily, living nearby…"

"Stop, Edna. All the evidence points to Bruno Hauptmann. The *real* kidnapper. Not some rich boy fantasy as told by a lovestruck maid."

"Hauptmann? Circumstantial evidence, all of it."

"True, but…"

"But can you see this stranger approaching the Lindbergh home by himself, carrying a ladder, at eight or nine o'clock at night? Not even midnight, with everyone sleeping. Wouldn't you wait until everyone was asleep? Charles and Anne are downstairs talking. Servants are around. The nurse in and out of the nursery. How did he know they'd be there that night? They were supposed to be at Anne's mother's home. Chance? Really? So this lone man slams a ladder against a wall, climbs up, walks into a dark nursery he's never been in, and pulls the baby out of the cradle. What if a nurse slept in the room? What if she walked in? What if someone glanced out the window and spotted a ladder? Nine o'clock at night. No one sleeping yet. And where would he bring the baby after he tottered down that ladder? A hotel?"

"No." Aleck's voice rose. "Hauptmann planned on killing the baby in the cradle. Right there. There would be no noise."

"No." But I faltered. "So he carried a dead baby down the ladder?"

"And a rung snapped. The sound Lindbergh heard. Maybe the baby was in a bag, soon to be buried nearby in a shadow grave."

"One man, a stranger to that huge house, doing all this?"

"Are you saying that Dwight and Blake kidnapped the baby that night? Based on Violet's nonsense?"

"I don't know what happened. I doubt if Dwight was part of the event. I can't see *him* climbing a ladder. After all, he was back at college. Remember that he refused to return home the next day. He stayed in his rooms at Amherst. But perhaps Blake executed the kidnapping. Perhaps Dwight knew, and Blake was fed information from Violet, who'd learned the Lindberghs were staying at Hopewell that night."

"You're forgetting something else. A ransom note left behind, Edna. Obviously written by a German immigrant struggling with the language. German punctuation. The dollar sign *after* the amount. As in Germany. The use of German words like *gute* and *haus*. Misspelling *boat* as *boad*. *Note* for *not*. You've read the ransom notes. Fifteen or so of them. German. Barely literate."

I deliberated a second. "An act. Someone purporting to be a foreigner. Part of the plan."

"You're stretching, Edna."

"I'm looking for a pattern, Aleck."

"Hauptmann fits the profile. German, German, German."

"I know."

"And he had over fourteen thousand hidden in his garage. Documented ransom notes—gold certificates. He'd been passing money left and right."

"Well, Bruno claimed he didn't know it was ransom money. The serial numbers were published in the press. Would Hauptmann be so foolish to hand out bills he knew were recorded? He bought gas with one, pulling his automobile into the station and not hiding his face. His license plate. The prosecution insists Bruno is cagey, a maniacal killer who planned every detail alone. If Bruno was so careful, why become so—so cavalier later on? 'Here, take this gold bill I got as ransom money. Remember what my face looks like.'"

Aleck got quiet, then said, "Dr. Condon handed over the ransom money to a German." A deep intake of breath. "A goddamned German."

"Maybe."

His voice rose, harsh. "What are you saying?"

"Keep in mind that Blake Somerville was an actor on Broadway."

Aleck howled. "Really, Edna. Really?"

I slammed my fist down on the table. "Yes, Aleck. Really."

He dropped some coins on the table and signaled he was ready to leave.

"We shouldn't try Bruno for the sins of the Great War. You know as well as I do that there's a strong anti-German sentiment in the country, Aleck."

He settled back in his seat. "And rightly so. The brutality of the Kaiser and his minions is documented. I was *there*, Edna. American solders were slaughtered in that war. And now Hitler—meetings of the German-American Bund in Manhattan."

"My point, Aleck. We have a dislike of all things German, which is understandable. Lord, you can't say *frankfurter* anymore."

"*Hot dog* is more American."

"Yes, I know. Everybody knows that. I said *gesundheit* to a woman in the market and she snapped at me."

Aleck would have none of it. "Bruno Hauptmann was behind this. Resentment of the American aviator hero."

"Well, that may be true. But he was not alone. Maybe he's just guilty of greed—extortion, him and that pathetic con man, Isidor Fisch. We may never know."

Aleck's voice broke. "Enough, Edna."

"You're getting angry."

Aleck locked eyes with mine. "I *am* angry. With you. You are headed up the wrong street, my dear." He hissed his words. "Your monomaniacal obsession with Annabel's murder and her preposterous story has clouded your vision. Schoolgirls with fairy tales they write to each other."

"No."

He held up his hand. "Enough."

"I…"

He snarled. "Are you rehearsing your next diabolic column with me now? Will I find these words echoed in tomorrow's *Times*? Didn't your encomium to the dead beautiful Violet satisfy your lust for notoriety?" A high laugh. "I can see it now. Here's a headline for you—A Violet Wilted." Then in a tinny singsong voice he warbled, "Roses are red, Violet is dead."

"You're not funny."

He stood and was thrusting his arm into the sleeve of his overcoat. "I'm a forthright man, a little bizarre, admittedly. I'm considered the wittiest man in America, Edna."

I bit my lip. "And often the most unkind."

He left me sitting in the booth. I sipped my coffee slowly.

Back in the car, I asked Willie why he hadn't come into the restaurant for coffee.

"Got me a bag of the wife's gingersnaps." He held up a paper bag, wrinkled and folded over. "And besides I seen that you two needed to have a chat about something. You was both all jumpy and twitching."

Aleck chortled. "Words that have never been used before with the estimable Edna Ferber."

When we were on the road, Aleck faced away from me, but I could tell by the flushed neck and the red spots on his cheeks that he was boiling. Finally, a half-hour into the ride, he glanced furtively at me, a mischievous glint in his eyes, magnified by the owl-like eyeglasses he wore, as he leaned forward in the seat, addressing Willie.

"Tell me, Willie, my friend, what do you think of Miss Ferber's wide goose chases?"

"Ain't my business. As I was saying to Marcus just yesterday, these excursions pay for food on my table."

"But let me ask you this—what do you think of Bruno Hauptmann?"

"I already told you."

"He already told us," I seethed, "back at the start of the trial. He believes Bruno is guilty."

"That I do, now more than ever."

That surprised me. "Why more now?"

"I hear folks talking in the bars at night. I listen good. That ladder, for one."

"A shoddy construction," I noted. "Bruno is a seasoned carpenter."

"And he got them eyes."

"Tell me," I prodded him.

He caught my glance in the rearview mirror. "Cold, like steel balls. That man ain't got no emotion."

"Yes, a severe man, arrogant..."

"No, he got iron his veins. Not blood."

"Still and all, a man..."

Aleck broke in. "A killer of babies."

"One, possibly, Aleck. Just one. And the jury is out."

"The war done it," Willie snapped.

"What?" From Aleck.

"I read that he was dragged into the Kaiser's army when he was seventeen. A boy. Impressionable. Made him a machine-gunner. A boy. They turned him into a monster, that's what war does to boys."

"Good point." I said.

His voice cracked. "My only son—he fought in the war. The American side, of course. He came back someone I don't know. He stares off into space—blubbers. Now he's gone off to California, left a wife and kid behind. The war is a bitter teacher."

"I agree, Willie," but I added, "A young man's bones not fully formed yet. Not yet a man. A boy, subjected to the horrors of that war. He was gassed, in fact."

"But that ain't no excuse," Willie insisted. "When he got back home, yes, the land was bare and people starved, so he took up crime. He climbed a ladder to break into the mayor's home. He robbed women with baby carriages at gunpoint. He took their loaves of bread. He escaped from jail." His fingers punctuated the remarks by drumming the steering wheel. "Look at his eyes, Miss Ferber."

"I have."

Aleck smirked. "As well as thousands of other women."

"Hard, as I say. Marbles."

"So the workings of the trial mean nothing?" I asked him.

"Meaning?"

"Meaning he's already convicted?"

"Yes, ma'am. They're going through the motions. The only thing left is to burn him in the chair."

I shivered. "Hardly American, Willie. We have laws. Innocent until…"

"Guilty. Plain as the nose on your face."

Aleck was laughing. "The common man has spoken."

I glared at him.

We arrived back at Flemington as darkness fell, and I wanted to grab a bite, draw a hot bubble bath, and surrender to a good night's sleep. A few stragglers stared at us as we stepped out of the car, but Aleck lagged behind, signaling to another reporter from the *Daily Mirror* that he'd like a few words. They'd shared a space when Aleck wrote drama criticism for *The New Yorker*. I waved good night and left.

But I was drawn to the noise coming from Nellie's Tavern and glanced in. A rowdy crowd of tipsy reporters and hangers-on. But what alarmed me was the laughter. The sequestered jurors on the floor above, two to a room, listening to the chants from outside—that incessant "Kill Bruno" that rarely disappeared—but also the glib pronouncements of the reporters, bored and drunk and happy, on the floor below. Kill Bruno? Was that refrain etched onto their brains and souls? I hoped not.

Suddenly some wag stepped into the center of the room and bellowed some doggerel that mocked Bruno's misuse of the English language, his bowdlerized phraseology, his garbled German-laced English.

> *Is das nicht ein ransom note?*
> *Ja, das ist ein ransom note.*
> *Is das nicht peculiar?*
> *Ja, it's damn peculiar.*
> *Peculiar*
> *Is das nicht ein singnatue?*
> *Ja, das ist ein singnature.*

Everyone roared, thrilled, glasses raised. Above them the jurors sat through the long Sunday.

I moved on to my room, dispirited. Echoes of that verse played over and over in my head.

Suddenly I thought: *Three blind mice three blind mice see how they run see how they run they all ran after...*

Did you ever see such a sight in your life?

In the upstairs hallway, as I searched for my key, I gazed out the window into the quiet street below. Under the streetlight Horace Tripp loitered. He threw back his head, enjoying the moment, probably something said by the vivacious woman hanging onto his arm, a woman definitely not his wife, Martha. As I watched, Horace tucked his arm around the woman's waist, and I imaged her giggling because she tossed her head coyly. Horace was dressed for a Broadway matinee, I thought: a fur-collared Chesterfield overcoat, unbuttoned, thrown over a dark gray double-breasted suit. His black-and-white patent leather shoes sparkled, his careful spats shimmered. A dandy, this one, a low-rent Jersey playboy out on the town. A man who'd wear a tuxedo to a barn dance and then wonder why he didn't fit in. The man who loved women—and there always was a new one waiting for his touch.

He nuzzled his face into the young woman's neck, and she squirmed.

I found my key. Bedtime.

# Chapter Nineteen

The crowd swelled, stood on shoulders, cursed, begged, and bribed the sheriff. Two men jostled for a spot on a hot cast-iron radiator.

"Bruno Richard Hauptmann, take the stand."

Aleck and I sat shoulder to shoulder on benches on the side, staring into the excited faces of Ginger Rogers and Sheilah Graham, both dressed for a Hollywood premiere in furs and diamonds.

Hauptmann walked quickly to the seat, sat down, crossed his legs, and looked surprisingly at ease. A guard stood behind him. The overhead light caught the high cheekbones, the small mouth, the celebrated triangular chin mentioned so often in news reports—"How like the police composite drawing," the *Daily Mirror* rhapsodized. "A photograph, if you will." Those deep-set riverbed blue eyes under carefully combed muddy blond hair. A charcoal double-breasted suit that fit his wiry, muscular body snugly, perfectly.

A matinee idol, this one, the darker negative of the farm boy Lindbergh in his ill-fitting suit and soft, slack face. The heavy, this Bruno, in a nineteenth-century melodrama. Do not hiss the villain! But of course everyone did, but not in the courtroom, although a man near me muttered, "Look at him, the killer." A low hiss seeped into the room from the gallery, unnoticed by the judge.

Bruno leaned back, almost a wise-guy smile on his face, which was not a good idea. Here, I realized, was a man who fully expected to be exonerated because, as he would tell everyone in earshot, he was innocent.

Innocent.

When he opened his mouth, people leaned forward, attempting to grasp every syllable of the heavily accented voice. A low, thick rumble, a man in full possession.

The questioning began.

Defense lawyer Reilly's pepper-shot questioning—Bruno in Germany, in the army at seventeen, twenty months under fire on the Western Front, his return home at nineteen, his struggle in the impoverished Germany. His convictions and his illegal entry into America. Bruno smiled at the memory. Thrifty, a hard-worker. "I opened right in the beginning a bank account." His marriage two years later to Anna Schoeffer.

On and on, through the morning and the afternoon, the hammered-home testimony, as he came off a little bit self-possessed. A smile. The story of his life in the Bronx.

"On the night of April 2, 1932, after you came from your work in the neighborhood at six o'clock, did you leave your home?"

Charles Lindbergh sat up straight, glared. He'd testified that he'd been at St. Raymond's Cemetery that night, sitting in a Ford coupe, and heard Hauptmann yell, "Hey, Doctor" to Dr. Condon. The ransom delivered.

"No, sir," Bruno stressed.

"You were at your apartment all the time?"

"All the time."

Aleck whispered to me, "No jury of fatuous women would ever find such a man guilty."

"Rather presumptuous, no?" I shot back.

He snickered, coughed a bit. "And you'd be the foreman of that jury, rah-rah-rah pom-poms hurled into the air. You go, Bruno!"

I smiled thinly. "Aleck, you understand so little about women."

"What woman does not wish to be told she is desirous? He *does* that with his mesmerizing stare."

"You curse him because of his looks?"

"You forgive him because of them." He went on. "He gets mash letters, that man. Love tokens. Seventy-five letters a day at the jail—schoolgirls who swoon, supporting him, astrologers predicting a happy future, autograph requests—even an invitation to a barn dance in Arkansas when he's freed. But leave the wife at home." He glanced around the room to find Bruno's wife, Anna. "She probably gets hate mail."

I stared at the sad woman, her face tense, her eyes hooded. She wore a simple blue dress, the kind you'd wear to shop for groceries. She kept her eyes on her husband, fearful, though now and then her gaze drifted out the window. Of course, she knew she'd have her turn up there, her own fresh hell. "She does. But not for the simplistic reasons you're giving."

"Watch the women in the room," Aleck said, swiveling around in his seat. "The rapture, the awe, the beatific glory oozing from heavily rouged faces."

"Quiet, Aleck. People are looking at you."

"They're looking at Bruno."

"Quiet."

He sunk his head into his chest. "'The law is a ass.'"

"Nicely original."

"I didn't say it was." One last remark before he turned away. "I do realize that you knew Dickens personally."

The long day ended when Judge Trenchard adjourned court at four-thirty.

◇◇◇

The court resumed the following morning, Bruno fresh, lively, spiffy in his double-breasted suit.

Bruno's attitude surprised me: cocky, almost flippant, a man who emitted an awful sense of superiority. Rigid, brusque, his responses tight and clipped, he showed little humility or fear.

I glanced at Charles Lindbergh sitting four chairs away, and noticed a trace of color rising in his cheeks. His eyes never left the defendant, but it was hard to interpret his look: a blankness, as though he needed to regard Bruno as a cipher, a stranger who got in his way as he walked by.

Watching Lindbergh, I noticed the line of men gathered at the back wall. A reporter was bent over, illicitly recording the proceedings, though no one seemed to care. Another was using the back of a colleague to jot down notes. Lynn Fontaine, dressed in a cranberry-colored suit with rhinestones in her hair, looked back and spotted lounge singer Helen Morgan, and she yelled, "Darling, darling, oh Helen. I made it today." The judge looked down, frowned, and slammed his gavel. Bruno never looked over, intent on Reilly's questioning. Bruno's alibi—Isidor Fisch and the shoebox.

"Before he sailed, did Fisch leave anything with you for you to take care of while he was away?"

"He left two suitcases."

"What else?"

"Four hundred fur skins—Hudson seal."

"What else?"

"A little box."

The ransom money in the broom closet. Fisch died. The water leak in the attic. The discovery of the money.

The kidnapping.

"On the night of March 1, 1932, did you enter the nursery of Colonel Lindbergh…?"

"I did not."

"….and take from that nursery Charles Lindbergh, Jr.?"

"I did not."

A rustling behind me, a reporter cursing another. I looked back. Horace Tripp stood in back, shoulder to shoulder with the mysterious Joshua Flagg. For a second I thought their standing together was accidental because the room that normally held two hundred had easily five hundred souls gasping for space. But as I watched, Joshua whispered something to Horace, who nodded, whispered something back, and the men shared a conspiratorial smile. Yes, I told myself, they could still be strangers—albeit Flagg spent much of his time in the café and doubtless Horace had engaged him in talk before—but there was something about the exchange: an intimate camaraderie, some shared wisdom, old friends who understood each other.

What also intrigued me was that Horace was wearing the same formal attire I'd spotted him in last night as he stood under the streetlight with the woman who was definitely not his wife—the same out-on-the-town garb with white spats and the elegant Chesterfield overcoat slung over his forearm. But he looked a tad dissolute, his hair not shiny and slicked over now, his face drawn and gray, and some of the pearl buttons on his tuxedo shirt seemed misaligned. I took all that in as he stood there, showcased under the shrill overhead light. Had he traipsed over to the courthouse from his midnight rendezvous?

Joshua Flagg wore a wide-striped suit jacket, vaguely zoot suit from a backwater vaudeville review, with a garish purple tie, poorly knotted. A diamond stickpin caught the overhead light, and I wondered whether it were real. If so, it would be the only genuine thing about the enigmatic man.

"I ask you again," Reilly went on. "Were you in Hopewell, New Jersey, on March 1, 1932?"

"I was not."

Reilly pointed to the notorious ladder.

"Did you build that ladder?"

Bruno, a voice filled with scorn. "I am a carpenter." A moment passed. "Looks like a music instrument."

The spectators howled.

"On the night of November 2, 1933, did you go to the Sheridan Square Theater in Greenwich Village?"

"No, it is my birthday."

Walter Winchell made an audible sound. The movie at that theater was his own *Broadway Through a Keyhole*. The cashier had identified Bruno as the man who flicked her one of the ransom bills, then fled.

"I was never there."

Judge Trenchard called a recess for lunch, and the sheriff led the jurors out the side door, guarded by state troopers, headed across the street to the Union Hotel. Watching their retreating backs while at the same time trying to catch a glimpse of Joshua Flagg and Horace Tripp—both lost now in a crowd of pushing men and woman—I stepped into an aisle and found myself face-to-face with Anna Hauptmann as she was being escorted out by defense attorney Lloyd Fisher.

We stopped, the two of us, inches apart, the sleeve of my dress brushing against her forearm.

"I'm so sorry," I burst out.

But in that instant, leaning forward, the woman caught my eye. Doubtless startled by the penitent look on my face, she offered me a melancholic smile, so fleeting it might not even have been there. But she also mumbled words that sounded like *ja ja ja*, adding, "It is all right" in a soft German-accented voice.

I stood there, paralyzed, as the attorney pushed at her elbow, and she disappeared past me.

From behind Aleck shoved. "For God's sake, Edna, I thought you were going to embrace her."

I looked over my shoulder at him. "A horrible moment, Aleck, the sadness in that face."

He rolled his eyes. "Really, Edna. A murderer's wife."

Walter Winchell stood a few feet away, removing the dark glasses he wore in court. Why? I'd wondered. The sunshine of fame too penetrating? Now, arms crossed, he glared at me as though I'd committed some foul act in his presence. His shoulders bunched up, he swung around and said something into the ear of Colonel Lindbergh's friend, Henry Breckinridge. Both men then swung back to stare at me.

I raised my hand in a short deprecating wave.

Aleck pushed me forward. "Must you be a cynosure, Ferb? This isn't a traffic stop."

While Aleck scurried to the church basement to get lunch, I waited at the entrance to the county jail where, within minutes,

I met Amos Blunt, who introduced himself as the lawyer I'd hired for Cody Lee Thomas. I hadn't told Aleck of my jailhouse meeting during the lunch recess, mainly because I knew I'd be met with his blatant derision. His generous and toxic bile was often too much to entertain.

Amos and I spoke for a few minutes about the lawyer I'd called in New York, an old friend and his classmate at Yale.

"You come highly regarded," I told Amos.

He shrugged that away. "Miss Ferber, I've already met with Cody Lee, of course."

"And?"

"He's his own worst witness."

I caught my breath. "Why?"

"He seems resigned to a fate he doesn't deserve. When I ask for witnesses, for evidence, for—for anything to bolster his case, he becomes quiet, turning away."

"I believe he is innocent."

A wide smile, infectious. "So do I. I've spoken with his mother. She's not a woman capable of lying."

"But that is not hard evidence, is it?"

"Not by a long shot. My instincts—and obviously yours— count for little against the power of a good liar."

A thin, dark man, youngish, though his balding head aged him. Horn-rimmed glasses covered misty hazel eyes, a prominent Adam's apple bobbed as he spoke with a reedy, though pleasant, voice. He struck me as a no-nonsense lawyer. I liked that.

"What about the witnesses against him?"

"Well-meaning folks, and therefore the most dangerous. I sense they're mistaken in their identification, but convinced they could never be wrong."

I shivered. "A deadly combination."

Inside, squired to a meeting area by Hovey Low, whose grimace suggested he was none too pleased to interrupt his lunch with such a frivolous visit, Amos and I sat with a shackled Cody Lee Thomas. The long days behind bars had taken an awful toll on the young man: a ghostly pallor, a hangdog expression, a sloppy morning shave that suggested indifference, the sad-eyed look of a beaten pet.

Amos had scheduled a brief visit, in some ways to please Cora Lee, who'd profusely thanked him—and me, too—a simple card left in the mailbox at the hotel. But also because Amos hoped my seeing him would spark some life in him—make him aware that he had another advocate besides his mother.

Amos did much of the talking, and Cody Lee nodded, perfunctorily, obediently, but said little. Amos reviewed the statements of the witnesses, and Amos surprised me by telling Cody Lee that he'd spoken with an old farmer who had come forward to say he'd seen Cody Lee driving his pickup off the town road and into the long driveway of the farmhouse where he lived with his mother. The old farmer was certain of the time: quarter to seven. He knew that because he had to be down the road at a church meeting and he was already late. Fifteen minutes late. He'd checked the gold watch piece tucked into his vest pocket. Amos quoted the man, a twinge of country in his phraseology. ""The watch I wear ain't never wrong. No siree. I seen that Cody Lee. For certain.'"

Annabel Biggs had been murdered after seven when she returned from her shift at the Union Hotel Café.

So Cody Lee had been safely back home. With his mother. As, indeed, she'd told me.

Cody Lee nodded at Amos. "Like I said." Barely a flicker of life in his voice.

I was impatient. "Cody Lee, help us out. You must have an idea who killed Annabel."

"No."

"When I overheard you and Annabel arguing behind the hotel early that morning, I sensed someone in the shadows. Someone watching."

He squinted. "Yeah, I always felt someone was watching us."

"But who?"

He shook his head, dropped his shoulders.

"What did you think when you heard that Peggy Crispen died?"

He scratched his head. "Nothing." A heartbeat. "No, that ain't true. I thought—yeah, she drank a bit, like the rest of us. But Peggy ain't no heavy drinker, leastwise so she gets drunk and wanders without her coat into the fields and freezes to death."

"Do you think she was murdered?"

My words surprised him, as they did Amos, whose mouth flew open.

"No reason to think that, ma'am."

"Miss Ferber," Amos began, "I wonder what you're saying here."

I held up my hand. "A curiosity, her death. It made me wonder. She was a frightened woman. A break-in at her room. A sense of danger." I changed direction. "Cody Lee, tell me about Horace Tripp."

"The guy at the café?" A sliver of a smile. "Romeo in the sticks."

"You call him that?"

"Annabel called him that—him and the ladies."

"Peggy, no?"

"For one. Annabel laughed about that."

"What did she say?"

"That he was this seedy guy, swaggering around and thinking the women, you know, fall at his feet."

"And did they?"

He looked into my face. "That's surprising. They did. He got this way about him, so Annabel said. I never seen it. He didn't like me coming around. He told me I smelled of cow manure and pig slop."

"How dreadful."

He grinned. "Maybe I did."

"Let me ask you this, Cody Lee. You were seeing Annabel, but did Horace ever go after her?"

A long silence, tense. Finally, biting his lower lip, he said, "Yeah, I knew about that. But Annabel said no, put him in his place, but I seen them together once or twice. We fought about it. 'I ain't married to you, Cody Lee,' she yelled at me. 'But he's married,' I yelled back. She don't care. But it don't matter. A fling, maybe. Then Annabel don't like him. Then he and Peggy got tight. I mean, Peggy really liked him a lot. Sad girl. Annabel don't like no one but herself."

"And yet Horace was married to Martha."

"I never got that one. Playboy from the big city, Horace was. Annabel says Martha shows up and says they're married. She just met him a short time back in New York, it seems. Martha put up with all that from him. Why? I asked Annabel. Do you know what she said? 'Martha made the mistake of falling in love with a scoundrel. Such women are doomed.' Imagine that."

It was time to go, Hovey Low signaled, clearing his throat and leaning on the doorjamb.

Cody Lee rushed his words. "Martha and Peggy had this fight one day. I mean, they came to slapping each other. Martha said Peggy better watch out."

"And what did Peggy say?"

"Only that Martha better keep Horace locked up in the kitchen."

I stood. "You cared for Annabel, Cody Lee, didn't you?"

My words startled him. Actually they startled me.

His lips trembled. "I guess so." Then, throwing his hands into the air, "Don't matter now, does it?"

Outside, standing on the sidewalk, I thanked Amos Blunt, but my words were drowned out by a swell of raised voices behind me. A band of chattering reporters was trailing after Anna Hauptmann and Lloyd Fisher as they headed for the jail door. A state trooper held them back, clearing a path, and Anna, tripping slightly, looked frightened.

As she skirted by me, who admittedly stood there mesmerized, she stopped. That same haunted look we'd shared in the courtroom earlier that morning.

Mindlessly, I reached out my hand. "Hello."

Her lawyer nudged her along, but she hesitated, stared into my face. In a thick German accent she said, "I saw you inside." A bland, unlovely face, swollen eyes. Her hand waved back toward the courtroom. One of her Hearst-appointed guardians, a tough-looking woman, sidled near us, put her hand on my shoulder. I stood my ground.

I stared at the beleaguered woman, felt a surge of sympathy as I recalled how that mongrel street crowd had screamed "Kill her! Kill her!" the other day as she passed.

"How are you doing?" I said quickly, my words hollow.

She smiled. "All right."

I smiled back. "You sure?"

Her eyes got wide. A fatalistic shrug. She pointed to the sky. "*Gott in Himmel.*"

The lawyer said something into her neck, ignored me.

"How is your little boy?" I asked. "Manfred?"

Her eyes got moist. "Bubi. We call him Bubi. He is with my niece. But...*danke.*" Her hand reached out and touched my sleeve.

"You must be strong woman."

Fiercely, "I am a strong woman."

We stood there, the two of us, helpless, with nothing more to say, though I wanted the moment to last. Her lawyer, exasperated, snapped at her, and she moved into the jail. Stunned, I waited, but turned to face the motley reporters surrounding me as a photographer snapped a picture. His fedora had a cardboard strip attached: *New York Mirror.* I walked away. My shoes crunched discarded camera bulbs on the sidewalk.

# Chapter Twenty

Attorney General David Wilentz approached Bruno Haupt-mann. The grilling began, step by step, tearing at Reilly's defense.

"You were never in the Lindbergh house, were you?"

"No, sir."

"Certainly not?"

"Certainly not."

"You never went in there and took that child out of that room, did you?"

"No."

Bruno fidgeted, sat up, slumped down, uncrossed his legs, but his tone betrayed his contempt for Wilentz.

"This is funny to you, isn't it? You are having a lot of…"

"No, absolutely not."

"You are having a lot of fun with me, aren't you?"

"No."

"You think you're a big shot, don't you?"

"No. Should I cry?"

"No, certainly you shouldn't. You think you are bigger than anybody, don't you?"

"No, but I know I am innocent."

"Yes, you are the man that has the willpower, that is what you know, isn't it?"

"No."

"You wouldn't tell if they murdered you, would you?"

"No."

"No. Willpower is everything with you, isn't it?"

"No, it is—I feel innocent and I am innocent and that keeps me the power to stand up."

"Lying when you swear to God that you will tell the truth. Telling lies doesn't mean anything."

"Stop that!"

"You see you are not smiling anymore, are you?"

"Smiling?"

"It has gotten a little more serious, hasn't it?"

"I guess it isn't any place to smile here."

Wilentz mimicked Hauptmann's voice. "'I am a carpenter.'"

"I am."

"That was funny, wasn't it?"

"No sir, there is nothing funny about it."

The defense lawyer stood and addressed the judge. "I think this has gone just about far enough. I mean this patent abuse of the witness."

At quarter to five, Judge Trenchard adjourned for the weekend. Bruno, wiping his face with a handkerchief, looked exhausted, his lips trembling.

The trial would resume on Monday.

Walking out I overheard Jack Benny quip, "What Bruno needs is a second act."

◇◇◇

Early that evening, resting on my bed, I switched on the radio in time to hear Gabriel Heatter summarizing the day's proceedings on WOR. Routine, methodical, and embarrassingly partisan, the popular announcer became anecdotal, mentioning an off-hand remark to him by actress Joan Blondell ("Such real drama, Gabriel. Real"), an approving nod from Jack Benny, and a steely glare from Damon Runyon, who sipped coffee by himself at a table at the Union Hotel Café and frowned on folks who approached him. "Including me," Heatter added. Not surprising, I told myself. Any word with you—an innocent comment about the weather or the size of the portions the Methodist ladies served—well, it was fodder for the insatiable hunger America had for any news from Flemington.

But as I reached to switch off the radio, Heatter added, his voice heavy with wonder, "Everyone is talking about the encounter of Bruno's loyal spouse, Anna, that German *hausfrau* with the pancake face, and Edna Ferber, in town to chronicle events for the *New York Times*. In court Miss Ferber—you all know her because of *Show Boat*, of course—said a few words to the woman in passing. And then the two spoke on the sidewalk as Anna Hauptmann headed to the jail. Scuttlebutt on the street—that is, the gossip of that Hearst sweetheart Dorothy Kilgallen, who wonders what the acerbic and peripatetic novelist is up to—is that folks are not happy."

Angry, I twisted the knob of the radio. Unfortunately it broke off in my fingers.

Well, I wasn't happy with Heatter, that bombastic blowhard of the airwaves.

I was unhappy with him, and Dorothy Kilgallen, the mouse-like woman in the schoolgirl pinafores who once confused me with Fannie Hurst.

My withering look at the time attempted to bore into her soul, though, sad to say, she still lived.

Aleck knocked on my door.

"Edna, I can't go to dinner with you this evening."

"And you're telling me this for what reason?"

"I come with a caveat, but I pray you will not kill the messenger."

Aleck was dressed in his overcoat, an undersized bowler atop his head, his round eyeglasses perched on the tip of his nose. Vaguely Charlie Chaplin, I considered, though Chaplin never had such round bulbous cheeks and that wealth of cascading chins.

"Tell me."

"I am your friend, my dear." But his tone suggested otherwise. A hint of growing anger.

"That remains to be seen."

"Winchell is down in Nellie's Taproom, and because he is a

simple man whose brain cannot employ more than one thought at a time, well…his topic is…you. You, dear Ferb."

I smiled. "Singing my praises?"

"Well, hardly. We all saw—I was at your elbow, Ferb, witness to your undisguised heresy close up—your brief and gaudy exchange with the Hauptmann woman."

"Her name is Anna, Aleck. She has a name."

"The wife of a murderer. A baby killer."

I was ready to slam the door in his face. "So she must be painted with that same brush?"

"You bed down with killers, you cannot expect mercy from a forgiving world."

"Really, Aleck. You can't believe that."

He adjusted the hat on his head. "No matter what I believe, but Winchell is a force, as you know, an arm of the prosecution. You did notice him slip another note to Wilentz today? Vile, that man. He had coffee with the Lindberghs. With Colonel Schwarzkopf. With Colonel Breckinridge. His inventive in the *Mirror* is odious."

"But," I interrupted, "you still feel the need to tattle, send on his gossip about me."

"Only because it will be broadcast on the air waves and in his morning column in that horrendous rag."

I turned away. "Thank you for the warning, Aleck. I can survive Walter Winchell. I survived a laborious dinner with Herbert Hoover at the White House during which he talked of nothing but his digestive tract. After that life is easy."

"Make light of it, Edna, but Winchell isn't alone."

"I know. I heard Gabriel Heatter yammering about Dorothy Kilgallen's little sermon."

"And Adela Rogers St. Johns, the trumpet for Hearst."

"We've yet to hear from Kathleen Norris, our fellow correspondent."

A mischievous smile. "I have. She's sitting at Winchell's round table now, laughing that fake little-girl giggle she thinks is charming, Lady Guinevere to his Sir Galahad. Or his Sir Mordred. Whoever the dark knight was—is."

"I read her piece on Anna Hauptmann, Aleck." I reached behind me for the *Times*. "Let me quote a delicious line. 'How long should a woman stick to a man, anyway?'"

"But you and I have always liked Kathleen—not her *writing* but at parties…"

"Good night, Aleck."

◇◇◇

An hour later, famished, I dressed and walked down into the lobby, though I skirted out a side door, intending to dine alone at the Puritan Restaurant down the street. I didn't want company, and bundled up in a thick wool scarf that covered my face from the biting wind and sleet that blew across the dark night street, no one paid me any mind. The usual contingent of reporters and photographers stood outside the hotel, cigarettes tucked into ice-cold mouths.

But I couldn't walk into the restaurant. Gazing through the front plate-glass window, I saw that the tables were filled, with two reporters from Fox Movietone News standing by the front door waiting for a table. Too much conviviality, too much raucous cheer, and I dreaded hearing the street jury condemn Bruno one more time.

I walked back to the hotel. I'd brew myself a cup of tea on the hot plate and munch on a package of soda crackers I had in my purse. A young boy tapped me on the shoulder and offered me a small replica of Bruno's ladder, a shoddy piece of wood tied with a blue ribbon. "A quarter," he told me. I ignored him but thought of Bruno's defense—the ladder looked like a musical instrument—cross pieces, not rungs, uneven notches, cleats that resulted from a dull plane. Hauptmann: "I am a carpenter."

A sudden gust of sleet slammed into my face—the forecasters predicted a blizzard that night, two or three feet of snow—and I turned into a doorway, catching my breath. My eyes watered and I regretted venturing out of the hotel.

As I stood there, a young man stepped out of the doorway of a small office building across the street from me. He was hatless, and his long leather overcoat was unbuttoned, though the collar was up, tight around his neck. Self-consciously he adjusted the affected pince-nez on his nose. He paused under a streetlight, gazed up and down the street. I drew in my breath: I was looking at Dwight Morrow, Jr. There was no mistaking his face, spotlighted under that light. He appeared to be anxious, looking left and then right. At one point he withdrew a pair of gloves from a pocket and slowly put them on. He rubbed one cold cheek with his hand.

I watched, transfixed.

A few cars streamed by, none hesitating, but he didn't seem to be readying to cross the street. I expected he was waiting for a ride.

A car idled at a stop sign near me, and I saw Colonel Lindbergh in the driver's seat. The new Franklin, the car he often drove around town. He was having an animated conversation with the man in the passenger seat, Colonel Norman Schwarzkopf, who was pointing something out to Lindbergh. As I watched, a figure in the backseat bent forward, his own hand extended toward the front of the car. Colonel Henry Breckinridge. The three men were having a lively discussion, idling too long at the stop sign. A car pulled behind them, closed in, but then swerved around Lindbergh's car, beeping an irritated horn. Colonel Lindbergh turned away, ducking his head down.

My eyes shot to Dwight Morrow, positioned on a diagonal corner up ahead. He was looking in the opposite direction, searching the next block, waiting.

Colonel Lindbergh's car cruised forward, but slowly, and the sleek automobile pulled alongside Dwight. For a moment the car hovered, all three occupants peering at the young man who suddenly stared at his brother-in-law, a look of astonishment on his face. He started, but immediately turned his body away, hunching his shoulders and dipping his head into his chest.

Colonel Lindbergh gunned the engine and the car flew ahead, spitting back sleet and ice and pebbles, a screech of tires as ice pellets covered Dwight's coat. The car disappeared down the street, its taillights pinpoints of red in the gathering darkness.

When I looked back at the street corner, Dwight Morrow was gone.

# Chapter Twenty-one

Monday, Tuesday, Wednesday—Bruno on the stand. Over seventeen hours. For eleven of those hours Wilentz assailed him. Brutal, sarcastic, angry, snarling—all to the end of getting Bruno to fall apart—to confess. It never happened. On Wednesday Bruno left the stand, looked at the jury, found the face of the plump woman juror with the bad cold—and smiled at her.

That afternoon, at twilight, Marcus drove me to Manhattan. I hadn't told Aleck I was leaving, but he'd seen me headed out with an overnight bag. I'd be staying the night at my own apartment, catching a ride back with Willie the following noontime. He had to pick up Kathleen Norris who was speaking about the trial before a women's club near Gramercy Park.

Later that night George Kaufman picked me up in a taxi at my apartment, and we headed to Yorkville, the old German neighborhood in the Upper East Side.

George was looking spiffy in a dark black suit with a red bow tie, oversized, and his signature pompadour seemed more treacherous than ever, a steep Alpine ascent up that high forehead. His huge thick glasses magnified his small brown eyes as he sat back in the taxi, stretching out his long, spindly legs in the scant space available.

"Edna, Edna," he hummed, an elfin smile on his face.

"Thank you for setting this up, George."

"You always surprise me, Edna, your adventures into mysterious lands!"

"Yorkville is steps from your apartment, George. Hardly the uncharted hinterland."

"I know, but I expect fireworks whenever we travel together."

"Nonsense." I looked out the window at the dreary winter Manhattan landscape. "A pleasant dinner with an old man whose accent will most likely be impossible to understand."

He laughed. "I'd have thought that your short time in jittery Jersey would have allowed you to fathom any dialect, given the harsh, tin-can drawl of folks south of the Hudson River."

"Aleck is from Jersey."

"Aleck was discovered, full grown and pudgy, in a satin-lined jewelry box owned by a Russian princess." A pause. "Who smoked perfumed cigarettes from a long ivory holder."

The last time I had dinner in Yorkville I'd been with George and his wife, Bea, and we'd gone to a familiar Germany eatery, Otto's on Eighty-sixth Street, a tiny, gaslit hole-in-the-wall that served the best sauerbraten and Weiner schnitzel. But since then the atmosphere of the neighborhood had shifted—not for the better. Moss Hart reported that Otto's, also a favorite haunt of his, now displayed a black-and-white profile photograph of Adolf Hitler in the front window, and the table by the front door was filled with strident pamphlets touting the glories of the German-American Bund, whose meetings were held locally—and were loud and drearily anti-Semitic. A fundraiser had been held there to raise money for Hauptmann's defense, mostly decent German immigrants, but news reports suggested Nazi supporters maligned David Wilentz—sneeringly calling him "Wilentsky the Jew." The pro-Nazi Friends of New Germany.

"So the Weiss Deli on Eightieth?" I asked George now.

He nodded. "For obvious reasons." A sober expression on his face. "Old Man Weiss recently told me he opened his deli one morning and found a swastika smeared on the front door. Weeping, he told me that. His sons scrubbed it off, but he fears he may have to close."

I was furious. "But this is America."

"Edna, Edna. You are the world's last and most wonderful idealist. You expect the world to be good and beautiful and true."

"Yes, I do."

A twist of his head, affectionate. "That little girl from Appleton, Wisconsin, marching out into the world to slay dragons."

I smiled. "These days I'll settle for the end of a bombastic buffoon with a toothbrush moustache."

The taxi pulled in front of the dim-lit deli, the "e" in "Weiss" blacked out, and a cardboard placard at the bottom of the plate-glass window announcing a Saturday night special of brisket with gravy. A wonderful idea, I considered, though this was not Saturday.

"The name of the man we're meeting here?" I asked.

"His name is Josef Brenner, an immigrant from Munich, Germany, back at the turn of the century. His father was a rabbi, but he's been a handyman at one of the tenements in the neighborhood. His son is Marvin Brenner, a whiz kid assistant director on Broadway shows that Ziegfeld produces. You've probably seen the son scooting around Schubert Alley a thousand times. Bea knows his wife, a girl named Leah from Riverdale, and a few phone calls were made." A shrug of his shoulders.

"Bingo."

"A sweet young man. He told me his father knows the heartbeat of the Yorkville neighborhood, the lifeblood of the Germans, both Jewish and those not so lucky."

I grinned. "Are those his words?"

"Of course not. I write my own material."

Jacob Brenner was already seated in a booth at the side of the deli, his body half inclined out into the aisle, peering at the doorway, anticipating. When he spotted us, he stood, half-bowed, and smiled broadly. He wore ivory-blue dentures that didn't fit his mouth, and I was reminded of the stolid farm women outside Milwaukee who prided themselves on those unnatural ivories.

"A pleasure," he began. "Two famous people, my son says. So I believe him."

George laughed. "The perfect introduction."

Dressed in a bulky green cardigan and corduroy pants bunched at the work boots, a slough boy cap on the seat next to him, a plaid hunter's jacket hanging from a hook, Jacob Brenner was eager to chat. A tiny, wiry man, his sparse hair white with patches of iron gray, he had a bony, long face with weepy, red-rimmed eyes. A bushy moustache, dangerously close to being an old-fashioned handlebar configuration, spread from one pink cheek to the other. When he raised his hand to take a sip of dark beer from a stein, his hand shook, the beer sloshing around but never spilled.

We ordered corned beef on rye sandwiches with potato salad and cole slaw, though Brenner insisted he'd already eaten at his daughter's home. "I live with her now," he told us, adding, a twinkle in his eye, "and a no-good husband but three beautiful granddaughters. A reason to get up in the morning."

As I nibbled on an appetizer of toast smeared with liver paté, he reached out and took a sliver of bread from my plate. "I'll try that."

George's eyebrows rose. "One doesn't take food from Miss Ferber's plate."

He ignored that.

"Tell us about Isidor Fisch," I started.

George's phone call to Jacob's son had let him know what I wanted to know—any information about Isidor Fisch, the deceased German Jew who, Bruno Hauptmann claimed, had left the fourteen thousand in ransom money in a shoebox in Bruno's closet and then conveniently died of TB in Germany. The "Fisch story," the glib reporters termed it. But I wanted to understand who that strange man was—how he fit into the scheme of things, if he did. The sickly, tiny man who hung out with the muscular, athletic Bruno. He'd been seen at the Peanut Grill, although not with Violet Sharp and Dwight Morrow and Blake Somerville. Yet...I felt it to my marrow that Isidor Fisch held some answer to the mystery that Annabel Biggs had set in motion.

Jacob's eyes got wide, alert. "You know, I met that man a few times, no more. I can tell you that. Never thought he'd be... mentioned in the newspapers. Oy, this whole Hauptmann trial."

"How'd you meet him?" I asked.

"So he was around. I take care of a building up the street, I sit on the stoop, and he visits someone on the third floor. He'd stop and chat in the doorway, had a lot to say, but he never looked you in the face, that one. A schemer, that Fisch guy."

"So he was known?"

He waited a bit. "Well, certain folks *get* known, if you know what I mean. They're…like the folks someone will point out and say, 'Look at him, the weasel with the shifty eyes. Hold your hand on your wallet.' So the face sticks in your memory."

"A dishonest man?"

"Hard to say, but that was the thinking. That is, some days. He'd swagger around with cash in his pocket one day, a new hat on his head, suede gloves, and once even a walking stick like he's John D. Rockefeller. Then he slinks around, begging for dimes for the coffee shop or the subway, saying he's dirt poor. He goes to the shul in ripped clothes and begs the rabbi for a dollar."

"Was he always sick?"

He nodded. "Coughing, coughing. 'Get to a hospital,' folks yelled at him. Cough, cough. Spit all over the place. He'd pull out a handkerchief that could wipe out a whole country."

George smirked. "A delight."

Jacob took him seriously. "Well, he could be, some said. A young, good-looking guy, smart as a whip, he had his friends."

"In the German community?" I asked.

"Yeah, here, but mostly up in the Bronx. I got me a few friends who run buildings up there. After his name is all over the papers, linked to this miserable Hauptmann fellow, we all talk over beers. Everybody got a Isidor Fisch story."

"Tell me yours." I was impatient.

He eyed me suspiciously. "I don't know why this is important."

I measured my words carefully. "I'm doing background stories of the trial, as I think you were told. His is one of the backgrounds. Just who was Isidor Fisch?"

He laughed and eyed my paté. "Izzy Fisch. I suppose it's hard to put him into one box. Folks up in the Bronx say he was a wanderer, living here, living there. A real mensch sometimes, give you the shirt off his back. Other times, like I said, a grubby *schnorrer*."

A beggar.

"What do you know about Bruno Hauptmann?" I asked.

Jacob ran his tongue across his lip, looked around the room. "Never heard of him before the…kidnapping."

"Never?"

He shook his head. "Never. Absolutely. Everybody says when we talk, 'Who is this Bruno?' Somebody said they seen him at parties, he called himself Dick. Dick Hauptmann. This Bruno is…is a stranger." He drummed a finger on the table. "But that one guy, he said Bruno liked to spend money. Costly suits. Expensive radios, trips, nice car. And him not working."

"He says he made money in the stock market," I said.

"Yeah, I know."

"No connection to Isidor?" George asked.

"That one guy—keep in mind he's a storyteller, that one, you should hear the whoppers he spins—anyway, he says he seen them together at Hunter's Point. Picnicking, swimming. Isidor paddling a canoe with Dick Hauptmann sitting back like a king."

I laughed. "Nice image."

Only George smiled.

"But with Bruno's picture in the paper, the mug shot, lots of folks say, Yes, I knew him. He was here, he was there." He looked over my shoulder toward the street. "You know, the Germans is rallying around him. There are people on street corners with buckets, collecting money for the Hauptmann Defense Fund. Maybe for Anna and the poor little boy. Meetings in the clubs uptown. Germans—even the German Jews"—he pointed at himself—"scared of what's happening. I don't mean the Hitler craziness. That's what it is—madness. But you know that. I mean, after the Great War and the Kaiser and the dead American doughboys, well, Germans got to look over their shoulders in this country. They say that Izzy Fisch went back to Germany to get his parents out, but he died."

"Do you think Bruno kidnapped the Lindbergh baby?" I asked.

"He could have, ma'am, but folks around here think that's nonsense—a man climbing in a second-story window and walking into a nursery what got no lights on and dragging the baby out from the crib. But who knows? Stranger things have happened, yes?"

"But I'm sensing you're not that keen on Hauptmann."

He sat back, eyed the remaining piece of toast on my plate—I pushed the dish closer and he snatched it up, a smear of paté glistening on his lower lip—and finally said, "If you ask me, him and Isidor got ahold of the cash. The ransom."

I sat up. "Tell me."

Suddenly Jacob looked uncomfortable, fidgeting with the frayed sleeve of his sweater, pulling on a loose thread. "Well," he drew out the word, tentative, "well, Isidor was what we call a survivor. Day to day, he does this, then that. A schemer, and some of it is outside the law. You know, the bad times since the big crash in 1929 turned good people into them that skirt on the edge of things. Isidor is one of them. He keeps his ear to the ground, hears about deals and schemes, and he's there, ready to play the game."

"Like what?" From George.

"Hot money." A sigh. "You ever hear of that?"

"Actually I have. And about Isidor."

"Well," Jacob faced George, "say you got a ton of money you gotta unload. Like it's counterfeit or stolen or like the gold bills Roosevelt made everyone turn in to the banks. Well, say you got you a ransom of fifty grand and you can't circulate it freely. So a man like Isidor buys it from you, sometimes ten cents on the dollar. The thief gets his bundle, free and clear to spend, no cops trailing him, and then Isidor got to move it somehow underground to make his profit."

"And you think Isidor did that?"

A shake of his head. "So they say."

"Could Isidor have been the man who took the ransom money from Dr. Condon in the cemetery—the notorious 'Cemetery John'?"

"Could be. But he's more the slippery weasel rubbing his hands together behind the wall, and then counting his change."

"But Jafsie—Dr. Condon—says the John he talked to coughed a lot."

"As they say, who knows? The man is dead now."

"But Bruno Hauptmann?" George wondered. "Is it possible he got the fourteen or fifteen grand from Isidor?"

"Yeah, he claims Isidor left it there, but I'm thinking he knew what was in that box. He was part of the deal."

"But not a kidnapper?" I asked. "A greedy man trying to make a fast deal?"

"Can't say one way or the other."

But I was thinking out loud. "A dupe, in many ways."

"Yeah," Jacob concluded, "simple greed can make a man into a patsy."

"But we have no proof," I went on.

Jacob stared me in the eye. "From what I read, they don't seem to have any real proof that Bruno Hauptmann climbed that ladder that winter night."

"Not a single fingerprint. Over five hundred on the ladder and not one was his."

"But," George noted, "he's probably gonna die for the crime."

Jacob bit his lip. "They gotta kill someone for killing that innocent babe. People say the country owes it to Lindbergh after what he done for us. Might as well be Bruno."

I shuddered. "Unjust."

Jacob rustled in his seat, ready to leave. "Somebody gotta pay for what them Germans did to American boys."

◇◇◇

After Jacob said good night, George and I lingered in the deli as the owner began closing up—"Take your time, folks"—sweeping the room and dimming the back lights. He sprinkled sawdust on the floor. For a few minutes George and I simply stared at each other, neither talking. Then, quietly, I told him my thoughts about what was happening in Flemington. Trusting him, I had telephoned him during the week, filling him in on the story of Cody Lee Thomas and Annabel Biggs and Peggy Crispen—and my faith in what Cody Lee's mother had told me.

"Innocent, George," I said now. "And before I left this morning I had a note from the lawyer, Amos Blunt, telling me that Cody Lee's being transferred to nearby Trenton to stand trial, moving his case away from Flemington. None of this is good. All this, George, is somehow mixed up with the Lindbergh kidnapping, the events in the Morrow household, but I can't pull it together." Finally, tired, I said, "George, my instincts tell me..." My voice trailed off.

He held up his hand. "I can read your mind, Edna."

I smiled. "I know you can." I thought of something. "Did you ask around about Blake Somerville? His supposed stint as a Broadway actor?"

He nodded. "I called some directors, agents, anyone I could think of. No one has heard of Blake Somerville, the small-time and short-lived actor."

"Perhaps a stage name?"

"If that story is true."

"I guess so. But I need to find out more about him."

"I've put the word out, Edna. If anyone knows anything, they'll get back to me. You know how many bit players there are in our world."

"We're all bit players, George."

He pointed a finger at me. "Some folks get bigger bits than the rest."

"And he had to have an agent, right?"

"Unless it was some role down in the Village in a back room. Experimental, who knows? An unfathomable Strindberg translation."

I shook my head vigorously. "No, not this man. His ego *demanded* Broadway."

"But a bit part?"

"Nevertheless Broadway."

"Well, the word is out." He gathered his gloves, ready to leave, but glanced over my shoulder.

"Wait. What's the matter, George? You look ready to tell me something."

He grinned. "I guess you can read my mind as well."

"Not much of a challenge, frankly."

"Very nice."

"You know what I think of your mind." I smiled. "Well?"

"Aleck has been calling me."

I breathed in. "I'm not surprised."

"He's not a happy man these days."

"He's not a happy man *most* days."

"No, actually you're wrong. Aleck enjoys his life these days, holding court as he luxuriates in his bathtub, beating folks at cribbage, fashioning an atrocious pun as he reclines on his sofa, his left leg curiously tucked under him. You've seen him in his glory. He was always the lonely fat boy in the corner, a little too girlish, dressing up in college in women's clothes so people would laugh at him, but he was miserable all along. Now, he's a celebrated raconteur, a popular radio personality…"

I broke in. "Tell me what he said."

"I gather your columns in the *Times* have aroused some dissent." A broad, toothy grin, savored. "Which, I told him, is what columns are supposed to do."

"Did you read today's column?"

"Yep, my dear. Your incisive attack on those who view the trial as a society event, the women with the minks and Rolls-Royces, the pearls, the laughter. Edna with a social conscience."

"Exactly."

My morning column dealt with the way in which the rich and famous found the trial a wonderful diversion from the cash flow of their Manhattan lives. I wrote, among other things, "It is considered chic to go to the Hauptmann trial." Bruno—"the line his body makes from shoulder to ankle as he sits there is fluid, graceful. A painter or sculptor would be pleased with it."

But the face of a corpse. His voice as dead as his face. My parting salvo, a snide remark about our sloppy jurisprudence that played into the diabolical hands of good old Herr Schicklegruber.

"All the mink coats were saying to the Saville Row topcoats and burgundy mufflers, 'Hel-lo, dar-ling! How are you! Isn't this divine? Isn't it wonderful?'"

I added, "It was horrible and sickening and depressing and wonderful, and it made you want to resign as a member of the human race and cable Hitler, saying, 'Well, Butch, you win.'" Now, staring at George, I repeated that line.

"I know, Edna. I read it. Everyone read it."

"I cringe when some sable-clad matron screams out 'Divine!' as she buys a cheap souvenir of that infamous ladder."

He bit his lip. "Aleck said you're not making friends there."

"That's not my problem, George."

"Winchell is on the warpath."

"Again not my problem."

I reached for the check, squinted at the amount, and opened my purse.

"He wants me to convince you to temper your comments. They see you as pro-Hauptmann,"

"But I'm not." A silly grin. "I'm anti-carnival and circus and kangaroo court. I want fairness. Did he really expect me to obey his command?"

He laughed. "Or that you'd listen to me?"

"I know what they're saying, George, but Lindbergh is so worshipped…"

He spat out, "That Bruno Hauptmann has not a chance in hell."

"My editor at the *Times* told me to write human interest pieces, to flesh out the lives of the players. That's all I'm doing."

"I don't believe that, Edna."

A heartbeat. "Neither do I."

"Something stinks there, Edna. We all know that it's an unfair trial."

For a second I closed my eyes and felt like sobbing out loud. "Bruno may be guilty as all get out, but he shouldn't be railroaded. A fair trial, George. I look at Germany, and Hitler and his storm troopers, and think…in America, it's different. It *has* to be different, George. Otherwise how are we *different* from that monster over there?"

He sighed and stood. "I don't think that's possible in Flemington."

"Neither do I." Now I was crying. "Neither do I."

# Chapter Twenty-two

The alarm clock jarred me and I sat up in bed, facing a window slicked with ice crystals. Five a.m., still dark out, a faint white light at the horizon seeping in, giving the rooftops I glimpsed a misty halo. Bundled up, gloves in hand, I walked through the deserted lobby and began my morning stroll. I needed to walk because I needed to think. Another column due for the *Times*, a tedious routine I was weary of, but the trial was coming to an end.

A smattering of questionable witnesses for the defense, a motley assortment of charlatans and carnival sidekicks who did nothing to bolster Bruno Hauptmann's defense. Indeed, just yesterday, watching Reilly mindlessly not challenge the fact that the discovered body of the baby was definitely Little Lindy, his assistant lawyer Lloyd Fisher yelled, "You are conceding Hauptmann to the electric chair," and stormed out of the courtroom, to which Bruno added, "You are killing me."

The identification of the baby's remains was controversial—were they Little Lindy? So much decay…so much police bungling…

Reilly was never his best after drinking his lunch nearby. So as Wilentz skewered the testimony of the defense witnesses, I watched Bruno Hauptmann's rigidly stoic face. A twisting of his head and a flash of irritation suggested his own bafflement as to why Attorney Reilly allowed such dreadful testimony. So be it, the winding down. The awful denouement of a tragedy, not Grecian, to be sure. More Jersey kangaroo.

I walked through the cold morning streets, not a soul out but me, the way I liked it. And my mind sifted and parsed and deliberated—and, finally, realized the anger I'd been experiencing was gone, replaced now by a deep sadness.

Yesterday the *Times* had purposely and cruelly, so I considered, run my column alongside Aleck's own piece, a conscious juxtaposition that highlighted the different viewpoints he and I had been evolving. A firestorm erupted in the hallways of the Union Hotel. My gentle piece, "Anna and Anne: Two Mothers in Flemington," was a bittersweet sketch of the two women at the heart of this case, both with the same first name, really, both mothers of boys, both facing horrible loss. An elegiac piece, intended to focus on the common ground the women shared. Yes, Anne was born rich and privileged, old American stock, Jersey royalty. Yes, Anna was a poor German immigrant who survived a brutal war and a struggling penurious life in the Bronx. The lives of women seen through the cockeyed prism of national headlines.

But Aleck's column was a strident condemnation of Bruno Hauptmann, a sneering assault on the evidence the defense presented, and a conclusion that only the electric chair would even the score. "Bruno made that ladder with his own hands and it was to be the death of him." A paean to Colonel Lindbergh—"America craves a hero just as parched earth craves the rain"—and, incidentally, rhapsodic praise for Anne Morrow Lindbergh. Aleck made comparisons of Hauptmann with Hitler, an insidious slap in the face. "Like Adolf Hitler, with whom he has a lot in common, he is a recognizable neurotic by-product of the German surrender of 1918." His opinions, of course, and he is welcome to them.

But buried in the short piece was a veiled attack on…me.

Me, Edna Ferber. He bemoaned women journalists, in particular "one very familiar to me, indeed, long a friend," but called them—called me—"sob sisters whose misguided adoration at the shrine of Bruno clouds the reality, fawning novelists who sentimentalize and thus forgive."

My fingers trembled as I read those words.

Worse, my own column, admittedly sentimental and romantic, seemed to bolster his argument—and I looked silly, a condition I despise in women and refuse in myself.

I walked, my pace quickening. My breath froze in the crisp air.

A horse-drawn milk wagon lumbered by, and I smiled— 1935, the triumph of the age of the machine, a line of parked automobiles on both sides of the street, some chugging smoke as the drivers warmed them up, but the farmers carted milk as though it were 1835. The butter-and-egg man. The bread man. I felt a sentimental tug of my heart. I was a little girl back in Appleton, Wisconsin, sitting on our front porch on North Street, watching Peter McClusky's son Joe dropping off a quart of milk and a quart of heavy cream. Peter—Petey—the boy I danced with at Ryan High School.

By the time I walked back to the hotel, the sun was up; a few cars crept along, motors humming; and workmen passed by me, tipping their denim caps courteously. I was feeling better.

As I always did each morning that I walked, I paused in front of the boardinghouse where Annabel and Peggy had lived, my silent tribute to the two women I refused to forget about. That story still roiled in my brain and needed an ending. But this morning, lingering there, wrapping my cold arms around my chest, I heard banging and clanging on the side of the building. Nosy, I turned into the driveway and discovered that someone was rifling through boxes of trash. In the dim light, shadowy in the tunnel between two buildings, a figure was hunched over, tossing debris onto the ground, so intent that he did not notice my presence.

"Christ Almighty, man," A voice yelled. The landlord stormed from the back entrance.

The intruder, startled, rushed away, empty-handed, and ran in my direction. He nearly bumped into me as I stood there, transfixed, and I came face-to-face with a red-faced Joshua Flagg.

"Mr. Flagg," I sputtered, "what…?"

But raising a hand as though to push me out of his way, he barged past me, letting out a fierce grunt that reminded me of a trapped animal suddenly freed of its shackles.

"Just who are you?" I yelled to his back.

He ran down the street, a weaving wobble, left, then right, as though trying to avoid a hail of bullets.

The landlord wasn't pleased to see me in his driveway either. "You," he yelled.

"Well, yes, me, Mr. Trumbull."

"What do *you* want?"

I stammered, "I was walking past, heard the clamor, and watched that man rifling through your trash."

He glanced down the street, but Joshua was no longer in sight. "Trash day, this day," he said by way of an explanation.

"What?"

"I put out the trash on Tuesdays."

My eyes shot to the lopsided cardboard boxes piled next to some galvanized pails. "What was he doing?"

He'd started to back up, ignoring me, but now he turned. "Well, I finally cleared out that room a couple days back." He pointed to the boxes. "Ain't got no relatives I can locate—or care to locate. Sheriff says throw it all away. The murdered girl and the one what froze in the snow. Old clothes and movie magazines and snapshots and tubs of makeup and little else of value. A bottle of whiskey I got for my troubles." A nervous smile. "A few bucks in their purses with their makeup and such. Owed me rent for the room, them two. After the fact." He eyed me challengingly. "Due me, that money, wouldn't you say?"

"I couldn't care less, sir. But I'm intrigued by what that man thought he'd find in the trash."

"He come around before, asking to go into the room." A harsh laugh. "He's crazy, that one. One more reporter, I guess, but I told him to get lost." He shrugged his shoulders. "So what does he do? He waits till I haul out the trash and he's there like a tenement rat climbing over the crusts of bread in the garbage."

With that he tossed me a slight wave and turned away. Over his shoulder, he smirked, "You ain't planning on going through the trash, is you, lady?"

"I've seen enough trash for one day, sir."

"Meaning?"

"Meaning it's time for my coffee."

◇◇◇

In the café a waiter was placing white linen tablecloths on the tables, smoothing them out with deliberate care. He looked up as I strolled in and gave me a toothy smile. "You look frozen to death, ma'am." A boy perhaps seventeen, gangly in his uniform, the pants too short as though he'd outgrown them since coming to work that morning, cowlicky hair and pimply face. And that farm-boy grin. I liked him immediately.

"I am."

"The cure is coffee."

"With fresh whipped cream," I added.

He stopped short. "Oh, I heard about you." But he rushed off to the kitchen.

Sitting behind me at a corner table was Horace Tripp, his back against a wall as he stared across the room. I wouldn't have noticed him but for a raspy sigh that made me look back. I caught his eye. He stared through me. Wearing his white linen jacket, unbuttoned, which surprised me, he slouched in the seat, his elbows on the table and his gaze glassy. As I watched, he snapped out of his reverie, spotted me focused on him, and tossed back his head. "Well, well, Miss Ferber."

"Mr. Tripp." I nodded at him. "You seem unhappy."

A whiskey laugh that went on too long. "I just got sacked."

"Fired? Really?"

He bit the corner of his lip. "Yeah, I walk in and the boss says it's time to go. And me already dressed in my monkey outfit with the fake smile plastered on my face."

"And I thought you loved your job."

Suddenly his face collapsed, his mouth sagging. "Funny thing is, I did. I…" His words trailed off.

I stood. "May I join you?" But I was already walking toward his table, even though it was clear my words alarmed him, his hand flying up to stop me. I wanted to talk with him.

Sarcastic, a tilt of his head. "Have a seat then."

"Thank you." I sat opposite him. "I'm sorry."

He seemed to be gauging my comment, distrustful, but then, breathing in, he simply said, "Thank you."

Sitting there, a tad disheveled, his careful hair now uncombed, he seemed less the suave Lothario slinking around the café, his leering eye sizing up available women. Now, to my surprise, I found myself admiring his looks, that pronounced Leyendecker chin and those high cheekbones. A wisp of gold in the corners of his gray eyes, quite appealing and utterly dangerous. A sleek, expensive man with the slightest suggestion of a glutton's paunch as he stretched out in the seat. But a charmer, this one.

"What happened?"

"Why do you want to know?" But he smiled as he spoke.

"I'm a nosy writer. A phrase that in itself is redundant."

That puzzled him but he let it slip by. "My wife." Said, the two words hung in the air, explosive, loud.

"Martha?"

A sliver of a grin. "I only have one wife, Miss Ferber."

"But many romances."

"Good for you, Miss Ferber. Kick a man who's down."

"One of my specialties, George Kaufman once told me." I stared into his face. "I always thought you saw such dalliance as a touchstone of your manhood."

"Again, Miss Ferber, another salvo."

"I'm sorry, but I have little patience with men who cheat on their wives."

He broke in. "I can't help myself." A pause. "But you don't want to hear that, do you? I can see you readying another shotgun blast to my ego."

"Tell me what happened?"

"I thought Martha understood." He held up his hand as he

saw me opening my mouth. "No, please. Anything I say is going to inspire you to…"

"Inject truth?"

"Yeah, truth. Let's go with that word." He covered his chin with his hand, and when he dropped his hand into his lap, his lips were trembling. "Sooner or later she would leave me."

"How long were you married?" I asked.

"We just got married. I mean, six months ago. A whirlwind romance in Newark, if such things can actually happen there. A short time in Manhattan looking for work. Both of us headed here to the Union Hotel Café for this job…this trial."

"How long did you know her?"

"A matter of weeks." A deep sigh. "Impulsive, that's me. She fell for me, would you believe? She begged for marriage. I thought, well, maybe it's time."

"So now she's divorcing you?"

His voice became fierce. "I don't give a damn about her or this job. It's that she's been real vindictive. She went to the sheriff."

I sat up. "About what?"

He debated telling me, drumming his fingers on the table. Finally, resigned, he said, "She told him that I snuck out of the café after Annabel left work—that I disappeared for a half hour."

"Did you?"

He wouldn't look into my face. "No, it's a lie."

I banged my fist on the table. "No, I think you're lying to me now."

A half-hearted chuckle. "The thing is…well, I *did* leave but not—I swear, not—to hurt Annabel. Why would I strangle her?"

"Where did you go?"

"That's not important."

"It will be for the sheriff."

He threw back his head. "I don't think the sheriff gives a damn. He's focused on electrocuting Hauptmann and he's got that mountain hillbilly in a jail cell. I'm sure he thinks Martha is just a spurned woman."

"Has he spoken to you yet?"

He shook his head. "No. But Martha told management that I was involved romantically with Peggy and even Annabel and…" A fatalistic sigh. "They have little patience with that."

"But why would Martha want to get you involved in a murder?"

A long pause. Finally, "Because she actually thinks I killed Annabel."

"What?" I spoke a little too loudly. "But why?"

"Because Annabel spurned me, if you want to know the truth. We had this…well, moment, foolish on my part, stupid on hers, but she wanted no part of me. She made that obvious one night in front of Martha, and we had a knockdown fight over it. I mean, me and Martha. But Martha thinks I can't stand to be rejected, and so…"

"So you killed Annabel."

He laughed. "Preposterous, no?"

"Actually, no. Men have killed for less than that."

"But not me."

I waited a moment. "How do I know that?"

He stood now, reaching for an overcoat that he'd draped over the seat, glancing toward the kitchen door and tugging at the sleeve of his jacket. "I won't be needing this jacket. The funny thing is this, Miss Ferber. Martha was *not* working that night. She left at seven, like Annabel. She was headed right home. She was supposedly at home. But she knew I slipped out of the café that night because, well, she was in town. She spotted me. The question is, what was she doing that night? Maybe she strangled Annabel."

"Do you believe that?"

"I've seen her angry. I've seen her jealous. That says it all."

With that, he half-bowed self-consciously and left the café, though he glanced again toward the kitchen. Just as he walked out, he slipped off the white linen jacket and hurled it onto the floor.

◇◇◇

I dawdled at the table for an hour, loath to return to my room, asking the waiter for a pencil and paper, scribbling thoughts and observations for my next column—my last column, I'd decided.

The waiter periodically refilled my cup, served me a corn muffin slathered in apple butter, poured me a glass of fresh-squeezed orange juice. Each time he approached the table, he hesitated, as though fearful he was interrupting me. But I found his tentative behavior endearing and sweet. His name was Miles, he told me when I asked him. Which, he said, he hated. His mother told him she'd named him after Miles Standish. He thought that a mistake.

My last column. I played with headlines. "The Lone Kidnapper." "Mob Rule." But I settled finally on "Reservations at the Union Hotel."

Jottings: the circumstances of circumstantial evidence. Lynch law. Trial by street mob. The roar of the crowd. Kill Bruno. Witnesses who failed to convince. An old man, admittedly with failing eyesight, recalls Hauptmann driving by Hopewell years back. I was reminded that the *New York Daily News*, walking around Hopewell and showing photographs of Fiorello LaGuardia and Judge Crater, found folks who insisted these men roamed the grounds the night of the kidnapping. A so-called scientist of wood who talked of wood grain with the fervor of someone deciphering Egyptian hieroglyphics. A telephone number scribbled in a tight closet that only a contortionist could maneuver. Circumstantial—made-up evidence—questionable. Dr. Condon's telephone number written inside Bruno's baby boy's closet—such a small space you'd have to remove a shelf to step in, turn to face outward, have a flashlight to see clearly.

Bruno Hauptmann didn't have a telephone.

Someone in Nellie's Taproom whispered that Tom Cassidy from the *New York Daily News*, allowed to roam the apartment, admitted that he scribbled the number there, then photographed it, incriminating Bruno. The piece of the ladder that was found in Bruno's attic? Detective Lewis Bormann rented the apartment after Anna fled. Although the rooms had been torn apart, including the attic—a difficult space to reach, a hatchway in the ceiling off a small linen closet that required you to lift yourself into the cramped, slant-roofed, dark space—and a dozen cops had inspected it, suddenly Bormann found a missing board, which was found on the ladder. Sawdust no one had seen before in the attic.

Why would Bruno, a carpenter with lumber in his garage and two blocks from a lumber yard, hoist himself into an almost inaccessible attic and cut off a long piece of wood? That was evidence? What to believe?

Reservations from the Union Hotel. Indeed.

Doubt.

An awful word when a man's life is at stake.

Doubt. A deadly sin.

Engrossed in my desultory note-taking, I didn't hear Aleck behind me. "Ferb." I looked up. "Ferb," he repeated. I pointed to a chair.

"The *Times* has a sense of humor," he began, dropping into a chair.

"Who would have believed it?"

"You're not happy." A statement of fact.

"Aleck," I said slowly, "I refuse your simplistic image of me."

He laughed out loud, the high-strained cackle I found so infuriating. "And what is that?"

"I resent your referring to me in your diatribe."

He signaled to the waiter. "I mentioned no names."

"Sob sister. I'm one of the sniveling sentimentalists?"

That piercing giggle. "Choice words, no?"

"I have reservations about what is happening in Flemington. You don't."

"Damned right, Edna. You are a mollycoddler."

I measured my words. "And you have chosen to make a judgment before the trial is concluded. Do you think that ethical?"

His voice got shrill. "I write opinions."

"No, no, you condemn with your words, which is the nature of your bombastic rhetoric."

"Which is equal to your sentimental posturing."

"Still and all…" I paused. "As friends, I expect you not to join ranks attacking me."

He ignored that. "Did you hear Winchell on the radio? He mentioned you by name."

"So I heard. That foolish prostitute."

He sucked in his lips, angry. "You have taken a dangerous position, Edna."

"I have taken no position—except doubt. A position any sane man should have. I'm writing articles that describe the people here." I forced him to look into my face. "And I'm exploring the story of Annabel and her murder and the arrest of Cody Lee Thomas and the mystery of what happened that night in Hopewell. And, I might add, the elusive story of Blake Somerville and Dwight Morrow. Pieces of a puzzle, somehow connected."

His eyes flashed anger. "There is no story there. Just a lot of foolish speculation. In the face of *all* the evidence—piles of it. You indulge in wild goose chases because of the rambling of a dead girl. Now I've humored you, Ferb, but really now."

"As I have you—for decades."

His cheeks flushed crimson. "Let me tell you one thing, Edna, and I'll be done with all this. I see the way you and other women look at Bruno Hauptmann. You and the other ridiculous women. Dorothy Kilgallen telling me that Hauptmann 'is definitely a hit,' in her words, with his mesmerizing stares at the female jurors. I can tell that the fat one, Rosie Pill, is drunk with him. Adela Rogers St. Johns is talking of his 'sex appeal,' the 'weak, handsome man who stirs either some sympathy of sex or of motherhood.'"

"I am not those women."

"No, but you lead the pack of the saucer-eyed mob. Sorry, Edna, but your...advocacy makes you one of the lonely and itchy women who see Bruno as so physically attractive as to be above all suspicion of doing anything unkind." He reached inside a breast pocket and withdrew a sheet. "As I will say in tomorrow's column, 'If he did not have a wife, you would all be flooding his mail with offers of marriage. An old maid's foolish fantasy.'" Steely-eyed, livid. "Why do you embarrass yourself, Edna?"

Livid, I slammed my palm down on the table. "How dare you!"

"A jury of twelve women as yourself would never convict that murderer of *anything*. He's a baby-killer, Edna. Yes, you say the man might be naughty enough to take the ransom money, but—no, no, no—never a kidnapper or a murderer. He's not the knight in shining armor that struts the boards in *Show Boat* or settles Oklahoma with the Sooners. Perhaps you should stick to the claptrap that pays your bills."

I stood. "Aleck, you're simply a New Jersey Nero who mistakes his pinafore for a toga."

His mouth dropped open, and he stammered, "Go kneel at the shrine of Bruno."

Irrationally, I picked up my coffee cup and slammed it down. The pieces flew across the table, a shard into Aleck's lap, the rest onto the floor. From the corner of my eye I spotted young Miles, wide-eyed and delirious, watching and listening. All around us folks stopped to gape. I didn't care.

Aleck carefully picked a piece of pottery off his lap, examined it carefully, and spat out, "You behave like a common scullery maid."

"And you, dear Aleck, like a horse's ass."

With that, I spun around and walked out, colliding with Walter Winchell who was strolling in, followed by his worshipful claque of sycophants. He shifted to the side, but I managed to throw him off balance, even as I tottered against a wall.

"Miss Ferber," he sputtered, "how strange to bump into you like this."

I stared into his face. "And they say God doesn't have a dark sense of humor."

# Chapter Twenty-three

The hotel clerk called my name and handed me an envelope. He looked nervous, his fingers trembling. Not surprising: the creamy white envelope bore an embossed name in the upper left corner: Colonel Charles Augustus Lindbergh. Augustus: emperor. Ruler. I flashed stupidly to another surname: Hauptmann. Hauptmann: head man. Ruler. I eyed the desk clerk eyeing me, anxious. But I thanked him—he appeared disappointed I didn't share the contents with him—and I went to my room. I sat on the edge of the bed, the envelope resting on my lap, and then I carefully unsealed it.

An invitation to luncheon the next day—Saturday—at the farm outside of Flemington where the Lindberghs resided during the trial. There was no expectation that I might refuse—rather, the handwritten note ended with a notation that a car would call for me at the hotel at twelve noon, sharp. Signed: *C.A. Lindbergh*. Beneath his parochial-school penmanship a gracious entreaty: *Please*.

My inclination was to refuse, but that *please* charmed me.

But, of course, on reflection—and a chance hallway encounter with a distant and sputtering Aleck Woollcott—I concluded I was going to be eaten alive. I'd heard through the journalistic grapevine, mainly Walter Winchell who raised his voice as I passed by him, that my *New York Times* pieces on the trial had rankled readers, especially my last piece in which I railed about state police malfeasance, the questionable evidence presented, the compulsion to leak every tidbit of information immediately to the press. Winchell, I knew, sat in the cat seat, jotting down notes he then handed to Attorney General Wilentz in the middle of the interrogation. The knee-jerk good boy at summer camp.

Aleck, sneering, started to walk by me but stopped. A sarcastic edge to his voice. "Someone in Nellie's Taproom—where another bitch in town blocks the entrance way—said that you've been invited to an Inquisition. Colonel Schwarzkopf, I've heard, talks too much. I may never see you again."

"You don't sound unhappy."

He blew cigarette smoke into my face. "Your absence will be conspicuous."

I slatted my eyes, menacingly, I hoped. "Thank you."

"God, that oxymoron cannot be new to you."

I smiled. "Of course not. All your witticisms are borrowed."

He bustled by me, huffing, a trace of cigarette ash dropping onto my sleeve.

"Spontaneous combustion," he said, laughing. "Ferber in flames. I'd pay to see that opening—and closing."

"Only if the Methodist women catered it." I slammed my door behind him.

◇◇◇

Judge George Lange's farmhouse was nestled in a small dale, surrounded by a grove of towering hemlocks. Overnight, sleet had fallen and now, at midday, the cold sun was melting the ice that blanketed the boughs, creating a shimmering crystal palace. As the car pulled in front of the barn-style doors, a dog raced around the yard, howling, gleeful, until an unseen voice called a name—Ike, it sounded like—and the German shepherd disappeared into the backyard. The front doors swung open, and a uniformed state trooper peered suspiciously as the driver opened my door and I stepped out. "Miss Ferber?" A question.

I nodded.

He stepped aside and pointed me inside where, in a rigid but calculated line, three men stood shoulder-to-shoulder. The dark night of the soul. The three colonels: Colonel Lindbergh, Colonel Breckinridge, and Colonel Schwarzkopf. The Roman tribunal facing the whipping girl Rebecca.

Lindbergh was the first to speak. "Miss Ferber, thank you for visiting me." A half-bow as he reached for my hand. His grip was soft, though he held onto my fingers too long.

"An unexpected invitation."

Lindbergh glanced at Schwarzkopf. "It was my wife Anne's idea."

Colonel Breckinridge threw him a hasty look as he hurriedly added, "She mentioned reading your *Cimarron*. With great pleasure."

"I haven't had that pleasure yet," Lindbergh interjected. "Too busy…"

"Of course."

"But we have read your columns in the *Times*," said Schwarzkopf, unsmiling.

"Which, I assume, is why I am here."

The owner of the farm, Judge George Lange, was nowhere to be seen. A local banker and president of the County Bar Association, he'd been added to the state's consul table, sitting next to David Wilentz. His wife, a well-known society dame, hovered in the gallery, watching. She was also missing from the table before us.

A maid walked into the room, nodded, and Lindbergh said, "Please join us." He waited until I walked near, and he grasped my elbow, very gentlemanly, the escort at the high school cotillion.

As we settled around a long mahogany dining table, set for four, I sensed movement in a hallway and caught the fleeting figure of Lindbergh's wife, Anne, as she began climbing a stairwell. Lindbergh noticed my staring into the hallway.

"I'm afraid Anne is under the weather."

I smiled. "Yes. I'm sorry." A pause as I looked into his face. "Of course, Colonel Lindbergh, I would like to extend my

sympathies for all you and your family have gone through…
these past years…it had to be so hard…so…painful…"

Schwarzkopf grunted, cutting me off. "Yes, yes, we know."
He shot a look at Lindbergh. "Let's get on with this." Unpleasant, brusque.

I frowned at him. A martinet, this Colonel Norman Schwarzkopf. In his late thirties, thin and wiry like a chained dog,
a military crew cut, a sliver of a matinee idol's waxed blond
moustache, this man who was head of the newly minted New
Jersey State Police, a Great War West Point man, someone whose
only policing experience was as a floor detective at Bamberger's
Department Store in Newark, a man suddenly thrust into the
spotlight of police authority, fumbling, forced to follow the lead
of Colonel Lindbergh when the kidnapping first happened.
Lindbergh called all the shots, directed, ordered imperially, and
Schwarzkopf, intoxicated by the glow of Lindbergh's persuasion,
salaamed and obeyed. Of course, once the baby's body was discovered, he assumed control of the investigation. Because then,
to be sure, it was a case of murder. A backseat to Lindbergh
until those two men found the decomposed body of a child
four miles from the estate.

Schwarzkopf drummed a finger on the table, ready to pounce.

Colonel Henry Breckinridge, Lindbergh's lawyer and close
friend, leaned in. "Colonel Lindbergh is by nature a shy man."

A contrast to the bulldog Schwarzkopf, Breckinridge was tall,
slender, patrician, dignified with gray hair, the easy countenance
of a moneyed attorney. Princeton elite. Assistant Secretary of
War under Wilson.

Lindbergh squirmed. "I'm right here, Henry." A deprecating laugh. "Miss Ferber, my friends treat me like a milk-fed lad
from a hayfield."

Schwarzkopf wasn't happy. "We're here for a reason, Miss
Ferber."

Lindbergh held up his hand. "A moment, Norman. Let Miss
Ferber at least enjoy her lunch before you castigate her."

"Thank you," I told him. "I prefer my reprimands to be received on a full stomach."

He smiled at me sweetly. "We're all on the same side, of course."

Schwarzkopf broke in. "No, we're not."

"Norman, please." Lindbergh waved a long finger at me. "Colonel Schwarzkopf wants the world at military attention."

"That must have been difficult when he was a floor detective nabbing shoplifters in the women's wear aisle at Bamberger's."

Schwarzkopf let out a bark, but Colonel Lindbergh, tickled, laughed out loud. Breckinridge's head moved back and forth, his eyes wary and uncertain.

Lunch was served, quietly and efficiently, the young woman approaching the table as if in fear of thunder and lightning. No one spoke for a while. A honey-glazed ham, deftly sliced, boiled potatoes slathered in sour cream and butter, and green beans so brilliantly green I feared they'd been dipped in an artist's palate—or, perhaps, arsenic. No one spoke for the longest time, but, peculiarly, no one really ate. Yes, Lindbergh stabbed at a string bean, missed his elusive quarry, and sat back, arms folded, that same beatific smile plastered on his lips. Schwarzkopf cut the ham into one-inch squares, regimented, moved the sections around as though plotting a military campaign, and the lawyer Breckinridge drank two glasses of water and then frowned at the empty glass.

At first, watching the men, I was nervous, my heart racing, but as I contemplated my own dish of food and the silent men, something shifted within me: an overpowering sea change. My nervousness dissipated. One minute I quivered, the sacrificial lamb at the aviator's feast, the next—a perfect wash of serenity.

Because I knew, in that delicious burst of epiphany, that I held control. These three men were boys playing a game, huddled earlier as they strategized and schemed and assembled an agenda. A war plan. Now, perforce, they realized they forgot to bring the ball to the playground. They'd simply assumed their words would flow naturally, the game easily scored. But Edna Ferber faced them, and my few comments had alerted them to the dangers of an unexpected player. Perhaps they understood that I was not a woman to be trifled with.

Schwarzkopf cleared his throat. "I'm afraid you've been a thorn in our side."

Wide-eyed, thrilled. "Me?"

Lindbergh broke in, still smiling, albeit dumbly. His lips were thin, drawn. "Miss Ferber, I agree with what you said in one of your recent columns. The circus atmosphere, the rich ladies in furs in their limousines, the..."

I finished for him. "The packed crowds outside the jail, yelling 'Kill Bruno.'"

He winced. "That, too. Yes." Still smiling. "Mankind at its worst. I don't want a lynch mob."

"I'll say."

He closed his eyes for a second. "My fame in the air brought me notice I could have done without. People always at me, demanding. When I built the house in Hopewell, I chose a secluded spot, hoping, but..."

Schwarzkopf was speaking over him. "We *all* agree it's a zoo in Flemington. That can't be helped. But"—a long pause as he caught my eye and held it—"your last column talked of the bungled investigation, the way police and reporters trampled on the evidence, a thousand hands on that ladder, on rumors that Hauptmann was beaten severely by the New York cops, all the rumors that can only enflame." He stopped because Lindbergh was making a clicking sound, like a small child who was unhappy with his present.

"Colonel Lindbergh," I started, "I assume you understand that in America—in a democracy—it's crucial to have an intelligent opposition—questioning, vigilant."

His snarl surprised me. "I know what it means to be an American, Miss Ferber."

"I wonder about that."

He caught his breath. "I beg your pardon?"

"It's just that I believe any citizen has the right to probe, question, demand. Just as every citizen deserves a fair, unbiased trial."

He threw out, "Bruno Hauptmann is an illegal alien."

"Yet he is being tried in an American courtroom with American jurisprudence."

The lawyer laughed. "Miss Ferber for the defense."

I went on, heated. "All we need to do, sir, is look at Germany today."

Lindbergh sat up. "What?" A quizzical smile.

"Hitler and his band of thugs. Surely you've been paying attention to what's going on there. These days I don't believe Germany, led by that bellowing madman, would grant a soul a fair trial. Bruno Richard Hauptmann would not have his day in court in Germany—he'd be standing before a firing squad." I added loudly, "I don't want to see the equivalent of a firing squad in the country I love."

Lindbergh reflected, "You need to be careful of propaganda, Miss Ferber. I think Germany and Italy, for that matter, are the two most virile nations in Europe these days—the decency and morality of the Germans outdistances our values. In Germany I witnessed the efficiency and lovely symmetry of the Luftwaffe, an air command that…"

"And the current treatment of the Jews?" I said. "Certainly you…?"

Lindbergh made a face, unpleasant. "Yes, that is a problem. But you know, a few Jews add strength and character to any country, I buy that, but too many create—chaos."

"Do we have too many in America?"

He shrugged. "Well, they are, well, other—not really American."

Enough of this madness.

"There can be no good that comes of Hitler," I said.

Schwarzkopf frowned. "Germany has nothing to do with us. Nothing to do with America."

I tapped my foot. "Not yet. Tomorrow."

Charles Lindbergh grinned. "A pessimist, Miss Ferber?"

"A realist, sir."

Breckinridge fussed. "But to the matter at hand, Miss Ferber. Your articles suggest"—He struggled for the right words—"suggest a hidden story, a…a conspiracy."

Lindbergh sucked in his breath. "Violet Sharp."

Two words: explosive, raw, hanging in the rarefied air like a death sentence.

Breckinridge went on. "'Violet Sharp: A Cautionary Tale' was an inflammatory piece."

The reason for this visit, I knew: my column on Violet Sharp—yes, the column had garnered considerable attention—and anger. A storm of irate telephone calls and heated letters to the *Times* office.

And yet I'd said nothing untoward, a simple recapitulation of the questioning, suspicions, and ultimate suicide of the sad British girl. All I'd attempted to do was to remember a life lost in this whole tragedy. No accusations, no summations, no connection with—with her cousin Annabel Biggs and that woman's murder. I'd left all that out. A memorial to a casualty of the drama. Violet Sharp, an exemplum of how a simple life, lived quietly, suddenly exploded in the shrapnel of a wartime blast.

"I made no accusations."

Schwarzkopf hissed, "Yet bringing up her name in such a way can only start tongues wagging."

"Her name will be part of the trial."

Schwarzkopf bit his lip. "Your columns are a distraction. Listen to Winchell—*you* he's talking of. Do you believe there should be sympathy for—for Bruno?"

"I want sympathy for Violet Sharp."

"Of course her name will be mentioned, Miss Ferber," said Lindbergh. "But hasn't my wife's family suffered enough? I never wanted those servants questioned"—Schwarzkopf shot him a mean look—"but it had to be done. I trusted them all. The focus must now be entirely on Bruno."

Something happened as he delivered that plaintive line. For a second that innocuous smile had the ah-shucks bumpkin demeanor so beloved by Americans, the bashful boy aviator I remembered *Time* magazine named the 1927 Man of the Year, so wholesome and *nice*. But then it was as though a switch had snapped on: the lips became razor-thin, hard and white, a look of utter contempt covering his features. That face closed in, angry. I fairly lost my breath.

"Colonel…"

His voice cracked. "Violet Sharp had nothing to do with the horrors I've been through. As I've said, I'd expressly told the authorities"—he glanced again at Schwarzkopf—"not to bother the servants at the Morrow estate."

"I made no accusation."

He spoke over my words. "But you *do*, Miss Ferber. We're not stupid. To bring up the dead girl now—to suggest a *secret*. She was an hysteric, you know, a gal given to fits of spleen, of…"

"Surely you know reporters want to probe all aspects of your…your tragedy."

"Yes, and damn them."

"Colonel…" Breckinridge began.

But Lindbergh raged on. "What exactly do you want to know, Miss Ferber?" But it wasn't a real question, spoken as it was through clenched teeth.

A lock of his blond hair fell onto his brow and he threw back his head.

I chose my words carefully. "Violet Sharp liked to go to speakeasies."

He looked puzzled at my sentence. "I know, I know. And so she lied to my mother-in-law, something of a prude, so she wouldn't know about her running around."

"Rumor has it that she was taken with Blake Somerville."

Silence at the table.

"Who?" asked Breckinridge.

"What are you talking about?" From Schwarzkopf.

Only Lindbergh didn't flinch. "From the nearby Somerville family?"

"Wealthy neighbors, no?" And then, "A close friend of your brother-in-law, Dwight."

He deliberated what to say. "I'm not talking about this. Violet Sharp was the help. Dwight and this…this Blake…"

"You know him?"

"Actually I never met him. I *heard* of him. If you must know, the Morrows and the Somervilles are not close and, I gather, Blake is a black sheep, someone Dwight probably met at Amherst College. I understand he'd visited Dwight at New Day Hill, the Morrow mansion, but Mrs. Morrow stopped it." He looked dazed. "What are you getting at?"

Schwarzkopf broke in. "Enough, Colonel. Miss Ferber is searching for tabloid fodder for a column. Why tell her anything?"

He shot back. "Violet Sharp was a servant. She had nothing to do with Dwight—or this…this Blake Somerville."

"Dwight found her body," I noted.

"She fell at the foot of the stairs after poisoning herself. Someone called for help."

Breckinridge interrupted. "I'm not following this. No more, Charles."

But I saw something in Lindbergh's face. "Rumor has it Violet was seen with Blake at a speakeasy." I purposely omitted Dwight's name.

No one said anything.

The maid tiptoed into the room and began clearing dishes. She looked at Lindbergh. "Sir?"

He waved her off. "Not now." A coldness in his voice.

She rushed away.

I waited a heartbeat. "I gather that Blake is a troubled man. He spent some time with Dwight at an asylum."

Lindbergh stood. His fingers drummed the table. "My brother-in-law has some emotional problems that have nothing to do with Violet Sharp."

Breckinridge said at the same time. "Miss Ferber, if you pursue this line of thought in a future column, you'll be in trouble. Not only that, you'll hurt an already grieving family."

"This is just conversation," I offered.

Colonel Schwarzkopf slammed his fist down on the table. "Like hell, lady."

I jumped.

Breckinridge motioned to Lindbergh. "Sit, Charles."

Lindbergh debated what to do, but finally sat back down.

Calm now, I watched the three men who'd planned an inquisition at luncheon, but I'd refused: I hadn't planned on introducing—hinting at—the stories that Violet Sharp had written about to her cousin Annabel, but…so be it. Out there. Purposeful. Deliberate.

For a few seconds we watched one another. Lindbergh relaxed, though his eyes were hard.

A phony laugh. "Miss Ferber, you *are* a fiction writer."

I nodded. "I am that. But I'm also a journalist."

His lips quivered. "Bruno Hauptmann stole and killed my baby boy, Miss Ferber."

I said nothing.

"Charles…" Breckinridge began.

Schwarzkopf snapped at me. "Charles is my friend, Miss Ferber. There is nothing I would not do for him. There is no oath I would not break to help him."

"Would that include lying?" I asked, and smiled.

Lindbergh held up his hand, his chin quivering. "Can you imagine what it is like to stand outside the cemetery wall and hear that monster call to Dr. Condon, 'Hey, Doctor'? That miserable German accent. Two and a half years ago, and I hear it echo in my head every day. Every night. 'Hey, Doctor.' 'Give me my money.' And he knew my son was already dead. People say to me—how can you identify a man, send him to the chair, based on two words? 'Hey, Doctor.' I wasn't close by, they say. It was night, they say. I was in a car with the windows closed." His voice seethed with fury now. "They are etched on my heart, Miss Ferber."

"I'm so sorry, sir. I mean no…"

A bitter laugh. "Oh yes, you do. Look. I want it all over. Over. Done with. For me and for my poor wife. Over."

"Of course."

"Do you really understand? Over. My wife, my new son, my family. Over. I want him dead and out of memory. I want to leave this country and hide away with my wife and son. Exile from a land that claims to love me."

"Charles..." Breckinridge said softly.

Lindbergh shook his head. "You're not out for justice, Miss Ferber. I've read all your columns. Every one. You're out for sensation. You write romantic novels about heroines who fall in love with ne'er-do-wells. My wife told me that. She warned me. You've taken Violet Sharp, that pitiful girl, and turned her into one of your heroines. And who will be the villain, Miss Ferber? I ask you that." His voice roared across the room. A vein on his pale neck jutted out.

He stood. Schwarzkopf signaled to me. I stood.

Lindbergh's hand fluttered in the air.

"Goodbye, Miss Ferber. Do your dirt as you will."

"Colonel Lindbergh."

His eyes narrowed as he stared down at me. Six feet tall, towering over five-foot me. "Ferber." He waited a heartbeat. "A Jewish name, no?"

"Charles," said Breckinridge.

"You're Jewish." A smile that broke at the edges.

I stepped away from the table.

# Chapter Twenty-four

The trial was almost over.

The jury was out, deliberating.

The final summations were over. Edward Reilly pleaded that the jury use "horse sense," "motherly intuition"—how could one man do this foul deed alone? He blamed Isidor Fisch, Betty Gow, the butler, and—Violet Sharp. "Colonel Lindbergh was stabbed in the back by those who worked for him." Bruno was a "mastermind" one minute—gloves and no fingerprints in the nursery—and in the next—a "dumb man who talked face-to-face with Dr. Condon." "Servants Slew Baby, Defense Charges"—a headline. "Turns Guns on Violet Sharp"—another.

Prosecutor Wilentz screamed out that Hauptmann was "a fellow that had ice water in his veins, not blood, the filthiest and vilest snake that ever crept through the grass, lower than the lowest form in the animal kingdom, Public Enemy Number One of the world." Hauptmann killed the baby in the cradle. "Money, money, money." He pointed at Hauptmann. "Murderer! Animal! Evidence, evidence, evidence, mountains of evidence, evidence which shrieks to heaven and this murderer of a baby cries, 'Lies!'"

Judge Trenchard had given his final instructions—seventy minutes long—to the twelve men and women, a lengthy summation of the evidence and, it seemed to me, wonderfully skewed to convict the hapless Hauptmann. Over and over he stated one bit of evidence, followed by a dramatic pause and stressed: *Do you believe that?* That struck me as undercutting the work of the defense. Translated, in my mind: *Can you believe the defense would try to offer such twaddle as evidence?* In earshot Damon Runyon mumbled, "He just strapped Bruno in the chair."

Bruno was led out, his face pale as a ghost, his deep-set eyes hollow. Bloodless.

The watch was on, reporters lolling in the rooms, cigarettes and cigars stinking up the corridors.

At one point Aleck Woollcott sidled by me and hissed in my ear, "Hangman, where is thy noose?"

A jibe that was made worse by Marcus as he drove me late that morning into the city. "Mr. Woollcott demands my services at five this afternoon," he announced as I sat in the backseat and we sped out of Flemington.

"What fresh new hell is he planning tonight?"

Marcus glanced in the rearview mirror. "You don't sound happy, Miss Ferber. I thought you two were close."

My voice snippy. "You thought wrong, young man." Then I relented. "We've had a falling out. We have them periodically, our celebrated feuds that delight the tabloids. He can be—acerbic."

Marcus chuckled. "And you?"

"Insightful."

"I thought so."

We shared a soft, welcome laugh, and I was grateful my leisurely drive into Manhattan wasn't provided by the garrulous Willie. Marcus would talk quietly, if asked to. Silent, if demanded. I watched his attractive profile as he turned to check an intersection: The hint of a new moustache, very dashing and manicured, very John Garfield. He removed his chauffeur's cap and placed it on the seat next to him, a gesture not allowed. But I approved—he was telling me something about his ease with me. I liked that.

"The jury is out," I said to his back.

He nodded. "Not for long."

I smiled. "You know the verdict."

"So do you."

"Well, that's true. Bruno is doomed."

"Probably not justice but a form of justice."

His words surprised and intrigued. "What do you mean?"

He waited a long time, his head tilted to the side as though unsure of his answer. Finally, softly, he avoided my question. "This was a spectacle I would not have missed."

"A circus, really."

"If you will."

"Do you think he's guilty, Marcus?"

"I'm not on the jury."

"But everyone else has an opinion. I've heard from Willie over and over. He…"

Marcus swung his head back. "Willie believes whatever the newspapers tell him."

"And you don't?"

"I'm a driver." A chuckle. "For important people like yourself." A flip of his hand. "I hear what important people say in the backseat of this car."

"And they all say the same thing?"

He gripped the wheel tightly, leaned forward. "All except you."

"Really?"

"You don't believe he's guilty."

"You've heard me say that?" I asked him.

"No, you never did, in fact, but Willie and I talk about your—excursions. Montclair Manor. Hopewell. He's heard Mr. Woollcott discussing you with Kathleen Norris."

"I can just imagine that chat."

"He thinks you can't put all the pieces together. A mystery that bothers you. Something missing. And it has nothing to do with Hauptmann."

"He's going to die."

"Of course."

"But why?"

"Somebody has to die for the crime. It might as well be him."

I laughed an unfunny laugh. "My, my, the younger generation is more cynical than I thought."

"That's because we read Hemingway."

I tapped the back of the front seat. "You read Hemingway?"

"Being a driver means you gotta sit and wait long hours. Willie reads the *New York Mirror*. Walter Winchell is his god."

I grumbled, "Well, he's worshipping a false idol there."

Marcus chuckled. "I was in Europe after the war. I saw the lost generation."

"Are you lost, Marcus?"

"I hope so."

He sped up, wove his way though a snarl of traffic, and mumbled about the weather as a sudden sweep of sleet covered the windshield. He switched on the wipers. He peered through the opaque window, his lips moving in a silent curse. He was through talking.

In Manhattan, I sipped bad coffee at the *Times* offices with the young woman who coordinated the columns on the trial, and I listened patiently as she eagerly spoke of the response my work had garnered. "Controversy," she hummed, ecstatic. "A brilliant idea to publish your work and Mr. Woollcott's next to each other. We hadn't expected such brouhaha."

"A wonderful idea," I said, but my sarcastic tone made her eyes pop.

"What?"

"No more columns," I told her.

"But…" she sputtered.

I held up my hand. "My work is done. The jury is probably returning with a verdict as we sit here. I watched them file out, heads averted from that poor sap."

"Mr. Woollcott, I gather, has agreed to write the captions with commentary for a series of photographs for *Look* magazine."

"Yes, well, once his vitriolic faucets are turned on, the bile runs forever."

She smiled thinly. "He has become quite adamant."

"A madman, that one."

"I wish you'd reconsider. I thought your portrait of Violet Sharp, as well as your paragraphs on Anna Hauptmann, well, they were touching. Invisible women made eerily visible."

"Thank you but—no." I stood. "I have to get back. Loose ends. I'm checking out tomorrow morning. Frankly, I hope never to return to Flemington, New Jersey."

"A quaint town."

"A phrase used over and over in the press." I looked into her face. "To me, it has the power to incite a digestive surprise."

Before I left she handed me a burgundy accordion file. "You got more letters, Miss Ferber. Our readers have things to tell you."

"Oh, joy." I took the file from her and glanced inside: perhaps fifty handwritten or typed envelopes. *Miss Ferber, New York Times. Important*, said one. I'll bet. Harangues and threats and recriminations and—and maybe a few heartfelt congratulations and huzzahs. Bedtime reading as the sun went down in Flemington.

Outside Marcus opened the back door and reached for the file. "No," I said, "it's not that heavy, although the contents may weigh me down."

He laughed. "They give you homework at the *Times*?"

I laughed back. "Only detention, young man. A dunce cap in a corner."

That puzzled him but he shrugged and slid into the driver's seat.

I debated reading the mail, but thought—no, why ruin a pleasant ride? But as Marcus adroitly maneuvered the car out of the city, cruising through northern New Jersey farm fields, swamp land, and pitiful industrial blight, I found myself dozing off, exhausted, spent.

I startled myself awake with an embarrassing yelp, and heard Marcus chuckle. A rush of nightmarish images flooded me, traces of snapshots from my subconscious: a locked room with a door that wouldn't open, a snow shower that blinded me, pellets of sleet that turned to stones, screaming from the walls of an asylum. A kaleidoscope of frightful images that smashed together, clamored for attention and then dissipated.

Then, like a blow to the face, I felt that I knew something—right there, nagging at the edge of my consciousness. But what? Something revealed in that mishmash of nightmares. What? I knew something, but it was out of reach. The car cruised along, hit a bump, jarred. Whatever it was slipped away.

As we neared Flemington, I got restless, angry that I couldn't pinpoint whatever I understood that I *knew*.

"You looked like you were far away, Miss Ferber," Marcus commented, staring at me through the rearview mirror.

I didn't answer.

Idly, watching the stream of cars headed into Flemington, doubtless to await the verdict—I assumed the jury was still out, given the lack of horn tooting and celebratory fireworks and picnics in the empty courtroom—I rifled through the file. I tore open one long crumpled envelope and glanced at the block letters: YOUR NOT AMERICA ARE YOU. CANT YOU SEE THAT MONSTER IS A KILLER A GERMAN. I pushed it aside. No, not this. God, no.

A long manila envelope was mixed in with the rest. A note from George Kaufman scribbled on it: doubtless he sent it via messenger to the *Times*. *Edna, someone remembered your man, played a bit part with him, and knew his real name. Stage name rang a bell. Had his agency send info. Hope it makes you happy. Cheers. George.*

Big bold lettering across the envelope: ELIOT TANNICK TALENT AGENCY. And an address on the seventh floor in a building on Forty-first Street. I never heard of it.

Marcus was mumbling. "Look at this traffic."

I glanced up. A steady stream of cars headed toward the courthouse. Marcus slowed down and inched along. "Lord." He glanced into the backseat. "Hope you're patient."

"What choice do I have?"

I ripped open the envelope and slipped out an eight-by-ten black-and-white glossy photograph of an actor named Danny Winter. Someone had scribbled at the top: Blake Somerville.

I caught my breath.

Marcus skirted the traffic and pulled over to the curb, braked. Glancing up, I could see a crowd of people gathered in front of the Union Hotel and the courthouse, a block away. Quiet, though—a crowd that waited. The street was blocked.

Marcus turned to face me. His eyes drifted down to the photograph in my lap.

"I was waiting, Miss Ferber. It was just a matter of time."

"Marcus," I managed to choke out.

"You can call me Blake." He laughed. "Or Danny Winter. Or Summer."

"But…"

"I knew you'd finally put it together."

"I don't understand." Wildly, I looked back toward the Union Hotel.

"Of course, you do."

Then, in a flash, that growing seed rushed back at me—that inkling I'd had as I struggled to wake up. Riding in the car… yes…riding in the car with Marcus during the first days of the trial. Now, in a small, faraway voice, I said, "England. You mentioned England. When I asked you about Annabel's murder and the piece in the local paper, you said she should have stayed in England. The article said Chicago. No mention of England."

Grinning, he pointed a finger at me. "Very good. I slipped up. I didn't catch that myself."

My mind roiled. "Then…then." Yes, a flood of snapshots that came together. "You were avoiding Dwight Morrow, weren't you?"

"Of course."

"That time he was on the corner when he was with his sister. You turned off the street, that shortcut that wasn't. Had we driven by slowly, he might have looked into the car and…"

"And seen me. Of course."

"Montclair Manor." My voice shook. "You backed out of being the driver."

"Very good. Old friends there, dangerous to be seen chauffeuring you and that fat fool. 'Hello, Blake. You driving famous people now?' No, no, no."

"But why come here?"

A piercing, harsh laugh, a little crazy. "This is a spectacle hard to miss, true, but I had to be sure I could keep my party going."

"Your party?"

"The thrills." His face hardened. "And that greedy bitch Annabel threatened that."

It all made sense—or did it? I snarled, "Well, I'm afraid the party's over, Marcus or whoever." I reached for the door latch, but Marcus' hand suddenly jutted between the front seats. He was holding a revolver, and it was pointed at me.

"I suggest you not move, Miss Ferber."

A chill ran up my spine.

"Marcus, you cannot think that you can do this in broad daylight—people all around."

"Shut up now." A nervous twitch to his voice. Then an insane giggle. "You're gonna have to die, I'm afraid. I *have* found you amusing, you and that fat piece of taffy, Woollcott." A pause. "You more than him. I appreciate cleverness, the way your mind works. You're probably the only intelligent woman I ever did battle with. Most women wilt—I don't think you allow that in yourself. Noble, really. As for Woollcott—he's like a box of soft candy you want to step on."

"Should I thank you for the compliment?"

"You can do whatever you want."

I tried to remain calm. "Tell me what this is all about. At least let me know what brought it all about."

I glanced out the window, anxious to see someone walking by perhaps. Anyone—a stranger. I planned to pound on the window. If I could roll down the window—yell to the crowd at the courthouse. Maybe. Or, if Marcus got distracted, fly out of the car. Something. Anything. I had no intention of ending my life in the presence of a lout.

"Well, quite simply, Violet Sharp."

"Tell me." I kept my voice firm.

"A foolish maid, easily prey to flattery and promises of impossible love. Quite pretty, really, though too plump for a young girl."

"And Annabel?"

"Well, of course, I knew that Violet wrote constant letters to Annabel in Chicago, telling of her lovely position in the Morrow household, of this pleasure, that grace. Lah-di-dah crap. Intoxicated with wealth and status, of which she had none. Nor would she ever have any. But she could be fun. Illicit visits to speakeasies, forbidden moves in the rumble seat of a car, all things Mrs. Morrow would never tolerate. Such vampish conduct. Oh, my. So be it. I told her not to write to Annabel, made her promise, but I knew she did."

"But this kidnapping?"

He scoffed. "Oh, that. A foolish prank, gone wrong. An insane prank, but then"—he grinned widely—"I was confined to a nuthouse for a bit by my myopic family."

"You and Dwight?"

"Ah, misguided Dwight, so easily maneuvered into foolishness. 'Nobody likes me, nobody likes me. Everybody likes that damned aviator.' Tiresome, that mantra. And Colonel Lindbergh had no use for the namby-pamby brother-in-law who doted on his sister."

"Lindbergh played pranks on him?"

"All the time. Lindbergh is himself a simple farm boy, cagey but simple, a dictator to his family. Happiest when he's off the ground."

"But a little baby…?"

"I convinced Dwight to do it. A lark. I mean, Lindbergh toyed with the baby—an emotionless slob. Christ, one time he dropped the baby in the tub—and laughed." Marcus lowered his voice. 'Make him a man.' Another time he hid the baby from Anne. Yes, for a few minutes, but that gave me the idea."

"But why would you do it?"

"Simple. I needed the money. As you've discovered, my family disowned me. I like to gad about, travel, live it up, fool people. I'm a schemer, Miss Ferber. The only joy I have. Of course, some would say I should be locked up in a loony bin, but I disagree. They already *tried* that. I add spice to prosaic lives."

"A little *baby*," I stressed.

"We had it worked out. Or, at least, I convinced Dwight it would work. He did whatever I said. He didn't want to *hurt* the baby, of course—just the Colonel."

"You took the baby?"

"Who else? Hauptmann? Really? A stranger in a dark room stumbling over furniture and screen? At nine at night? I'd been to Hopewell with Dwight when they were building it. I'd been in that nursery. I knew that shutter wouldn't latch. I heard Anne complaining about it. I knew the routines of the Lindberghs. They're simple people, though I only met Anne once—I avoided the Colonel."

"The ladder?"

"Some old thing I found in the family barn. Not even a real ladder—a handyman made it for our childhood games years ago."

"But I don't see..."

"Violet called to say the Lindberghs were at Hopewell that night. After all, security at Next Day Hill was impressive. So I drove there. Dwight was at Amherst, of course. He didn't know that was the night, if he even really believed we'd actually do it. He liked to talk about it. A mind game we played. I was going to take the little fellow, and Violet's sister, Emily, would watch him for a week, maybe more—Mrs. Chilton was traveling in Europe that winter and the house was empty—until the ransom was paid—to me."

"But the baby died."

"Unfortunately. The rung of the ladder broke and all fall down, as they say in nursery rhymes. The baby's head was crushed."

I shuddered. "So the plans shifted."

"Dwight panicked, hid away in his rooms, cried, saw the devil wagging a finger at him, said never never never call him again. Violet cracked under the pressure. Especially because after the third interview I knew she'd give us away. So I told her she'd be getting the electric chair anyway—buzz hiss bang—and, well, it's best if you check out, darling. Taste the silver polish. That's a nice girl. It'll only hurt for a second."

"But she'd already written to Annabel. She'd described the prank."

He banged the back of the seat. "Exactly. I knew she'd written letters—and one *last* letter in which she talked of the whole damned scheme."

"And so you came here."

"As I say, I don't want my life interrupted."

"I don't understand. The ransom note sounded like it was written by a German immigrant. And the meetings with Dr. Condon in the cemetery—he described a German or Scandinavian immigrant."

Marcus pointed to the glossy photo that still rested in my lap. "Danny Winter. And the agency said I was a lousy actor. I played a German immigrant in that dreadful farce, *A Fraulein in Blue.* A small part, failed. But I had to employ a vaudeville German accent. *Achtung, honeybunch.* After the war I lived with my father in Berlin, rebuilding that horrible country. I was young, and frankly I made many an impoverished *fraulein*, well, blue. The Germans are a miserable people, cocky, nasty, even though they lost a war. Christ, you look at them the wrong way and we are back at war. They should be exterminated. To a man. And every frau and fraulein. Frankly."

"So you posed as a German. You wrote the note—you met Dr. Condon in the cemetery."

He bowed his head. "My best acting performance."

"And poor Hauptmann is not guilty of murder."

"Well, he's probably guilty of something. Everyone is."

"But not the murder of the Lindbergh baby."

"Well, I wouldn't call it murder. A dropped child. An accident."

"Murder," I thundered. "And you are responsible for the murder of...Bruno Hauptmann."

"Calm down, lady. Your last moments should be serene." A deep chuckle. "Bruno—one more expendable immigrant. And an illegal one at that. They're all over the place. They have to have some use, no? Why not die for a rich boy? It's happened before."

"So you had to kill Annabel?"

"That greedy girl wrote a letter to Dwight. It began with a dramatic paragraph: 'I know.' Lovely girl. She wanted lots of money to shut her trap. Foolishly she said she'd be here, in Flemington, assuming he'd be a part of the trial. She'd meet him here. Make arrangements. Christ, she gave him her address! Or she could have a few words with Colonel Lindbergh! Of course Dwight was running scared, and called me. He told me she was here, but he warned me to stay away. I could tell he immediately regretted telling me. 'Please stay away, Blake. For God's sake. Enough. Enough.' Not—not enough. The play still had another act or two."

"You had to come here?"

"Of course. I lied—told him, sure, I'll stay away. He foolishly thought she'd drift away. Maybe he'd give her a few bucks—I don't know. He was rattled. No one knows a thing, he said. Except Annabel, I thought. That's why I didn't want him to spot me driving the car. You were clever with that, Miss Ferber. He'd have caused trouble for me."

"So you were the shadow watching her."

"Yes, in fact, I saw you that fateful morning. You really are a nosy woman, Miss Ferber."

"Yes, I've been told that."

"You also became a dangerous woman. But Annabel was more dangerous. She could mess up my life."

"Where is the money?"

That surprised him. "Well, that was a wrinkle, especially when Roosevelt called for the gold certificates to be turned in. I was sitting on cash difficult to unload. So I sold a bunch of the gold certificates to Isidor Fisch, a man who played that game. I got my share, and away I went. He was greedy, too. And so he left them with Bruno. Or maybe Bruno was in on it all along—money in his pocket. Another greedy man. Lord, I'm surrounded by poor folks demanding money. What kind of world is this?"

"Annabel's greed didn't mean she should die."

"Of course it did. Not an unpleasant chore, I might add. She never knew what hit her." A sickly smile. The gun wavered in his hand. "Well, I guess she did, after all. It was just fortuitous that she had that hillbilly boyfriend and that they fought all the time."

"The letters?"

"The letters," he echoed. "I got all but the one that was most important. A cagey woman, that one. To be sure, I didn't break into that room. After she was dead, I couldn't take any chances. I *watched* the building."

"What do you mean?"

"I had help. Another acolyte who did my bidding. He searched for that lethal letter."

"And who is that?"

He laughed. "You ask too many questions, Miss Ferber. Someone else in town, a nameless soul who bowed before my commands."

"But you never got that last letter, did you?"

The hand on the gun twitched. "Of course I did. Dear Peggy Crispen, a wanderer onto the stage who wasn't even aware that there was a play going on. It's amazing what a gun pointed into a chest will do." He waved it at me. "Case in point, no? Anyway, she handed over the letter and pleaded for her life."

"But you killed her."

"Well, I couldn't have another murder. The hillbilly was in jail. 'Get your coat, Peggy. Let's go for a drink.' I walked her to the fields, made her take off her coat, let her wander away, terrified, crying, until she stumbled from the cold, fell. A bottle of booze poured down her throat. And I waited until she fell asleep in the snow. A quiet, peaceful death, most desirable compared to Annabel's. And, I might add, Little Lindy, the boy Eaglet."

"You're a horrible man."

"But a clever one."

"A murderer."

"Confession time. I tried to run you over when you were snooping around the Bronx, talking to that Ernie Miller. You came this close"—with his free hand he held forefinger and index finger together—"to solving the mystery. You started to know too much. I could hear it in your comments. Your little excursions out of town. Sooner or later you'd point the finger at me." He pointed to the glossy photograph with his gun. "I knew that moment would come." He smirked. "As I say, you are a dangerous woman."

My hand grazed the door latch.

"Don't try it, lady. And now we have to say good-bye."

A scream caught in the back of my throat. A banging. Someone rapped on the window of the car. So rapt was Marcus in his confession that he'd failed to notice Aleck Woollcott shuffling up to the car, out of breath, peeved.

Aleck was peering at me through the window. "Really, Edna. You know I need the car. Are you going to sit and yammer with Marcus all night? I told you I need the car. Your love affair with this…this lady-killer gigolo is a little embarrassing." He went on and on, pounding on the window.

Marcus, bewildered, had pulled back the gun, rattled, but in that instant, he shifted into first gear, released the clutch, and pressed on the accelerator.

He shot me a look. "I think it's time I disappeared from this town."

He maneuvered the car off the street. Suddenly he threw the car into neutral, pushed open his door, and he bounded out. The car moved forward.

Aleck, startled, jumped back, toppled against a pole. "What in the world?" he shouted.

Helpless, bouncing in the backseat, I struggled as the car plunged forward, jumped the curb, gained momentum as it hit an ice slick. Marcus had parked up from a brick-and-cement municipal gas station, a huge block of deadly stone situated down a small incline. I cried out as the car careened across the sheet of ice and slammed the building, the left side of the car crumbling. A window shattered, glass shards ripping into my arm. Frantic, bleeding, I pushed against the door, which was jammed.

A red-faced Aleck, breathing hard, his eyes ablaze with confusion, struggled with the door, wrenched it free, reached in and grabbed my arm. "Edna, what madness…?" He tugged at my arm, and a wash of blood covered his forearm. Using both hands he pulled me from the backseat and he reeled, dragging me a few steps.

"Move," I gasped. "We have to move."

We staggered toward the sidewalk, hobbling, hanging onto each other, my blood smearing his clothing, but then I heard a violent whoosh and pop. Turning, I watched the car burst into a ball of flame, an impact that caused the two of us to topple into a snowbank. Aleck lay on his back, blubbering, while I lay, bloodied and panting, straddling his tremendous belly.

I opened my eyes to face Aleck's astonished glare.

"Really, Edna," he managed to get out, "don't you think this is a little forward of you?"

# Chapter Twenty-five

Marcus Wood disappeared that afternoon, and he was never seen again. There were rumors that he'd sailed to Europe under a different name, which was possible. But I know that no one ever pursued him. I learned that he was spotted boarding the afternoon Black Diamond Express of the Lehigh Valley train, leaving Flemington—no suitcase, only the clothing on his back—headed for New York City. A few days later the livery company received a cursory note, scribbled on lined schoolboy paper, saying he'd not be returning to work. He was "embarrassed"—his word—by his own cowardly behavior. After all, it was his fault the car had inadvertently been left in gear. *Mea culpa*. Forgive me. I can't show my face. Alas. Thank God, Miss Ferber is a trooper. No one cared, *tsk*ing about the young man who almost killed the famous novelist.

No one followed up on it because, alarmingly and devastatingly, no one believed the story I told that afternoon.

The accident was a back-page story in the *Hunterdon County Democrat*—even less attention than Annabel's murder warranted, I noted. Immediately afterwards I was rushed to the clinic behind the jail, patched up, scrapes on my face and arms, an unsightly black-and-blue lump on my forehead, but otherwise intact. Dazed, I demanded that the sheriff of the county visit me, but that never happened. Deputy Hovey Low stopped in, listened to my story, lit a cigar, and left. Doubtless, he thought I was crazed or stunned by the accident. Woozy from the morphine.

Aleck became a hero, of course, with his wide-eyed face beaming from a photograph that appeared in the *Times*. "Celebrated Raconteur Saves Novelist in Fiery Mishap." He wrote the copy and insisted it be run.

Mishap, indeed.

That picture and the accompanying article rankled.

Because no one listened to me. Through my narcotic haze, I mumbled, "I want Marcus Wood arrested for kidnapping and murder."

No one listened. A few nurses' heads shook back and forth, as they nodded to one another. The woman is delirious.

Well, I was. And rightfully so.

But my story was lost in the chaos that greeted the decision by the jury later that evening. The case had gone to the jury at 11:23 that morning, and at 10:45 that night they read the verdict. The thirty-two-day trial had ended. Bruno Richard Hauptmann was convicted of first-degree murder and, in short order, Judge Trenchard sentenced him to the electric chair during the week of March 18, 1935. There was no other news story. To be sure, I didn't know the story until the next morning when I read it in the newspaper. But groggy, lying in a hospital bed, I could hear the hoopla and roar of the street life as celebrants chanted and applauded and howled their pleasure that Bruno would die. A cry for blood. Horns blared, whistles blew, the sound of banging on walls. Pandemonium. Dimly I heard the horrible chants: *kill him kill him kill him*. I drifted off with those words echoing in my brain. I woke, still dazed from the medication, surveyed my bandaged arm and head, and waited.

A radio in the lounge was turned up. There was a popular broadcaster I sometimes heard—and lamented. He'd sing the news, the more horrible the more melodic he waxed. Now, to my horror, I heard his lilting voice: "I read in the papers that Hauptmann's gonna die." Someone hurriedly switched off the station.

I waited for Aleck to visit me, but he never did. Bruised, tired, I left the clinic later that morning. I checked out of the hotel, and a driver I'd never seen before delivered me safely to Manhattan.

Then began my long campaign to be heard—to be believed. Days later, I sat with Sheriff Curtiss in his small office and told him my tale, my words sounding preposterous as I said them. The murder of Annabel Biggs and Peggy Crispen, Marcus Wood being Blake Somerville—"That's a rich family, ma'am"—and even a careful mention of Dwight Morrow, Jr. As I watched him, his eyes got cloudy and faraway, and I knew my visit was futile. "Are you listening?" I begged. That stiffened his posture but not his resolve. After my recitation, admittedly a little hysterical and repetitive because my head still swam, the sheriff nodded politely, and dismissed me.

"I don't think we should talk about this with anyone." His exit line, which infuriated me.

"But there is a miscarriage of justice. Bruno Hauptmann."

"Is a convicted killer, Miss Ferber. He's sentenced to die."

"For a murder he did not commit." I drew in my breath. "And Cody Lee Thomas, sitting now in a jail in Trenton awaiting trial, is innocent of Annabel's killing. Marcus Wood admitted to me…a prank gone bad, the ransom money, the ladder that wasn't really a ladder…"

"And this disappeared Marcus is really Blake Somerville, a guy whose father is a banker in Newark and was lieutenant governor some years back?"

Helpless. "Yes."

He scratched his head. "Ma'am, I mean no disrespect, and I know you're…like famous and all, but this is a little bit crazy talk. Let's you and me not talk about this anymore." Like everyone else in Flemington—perhaps even in New Jersey, indeed, all of America—he was glad the Lindbergh kidnapping case was finally over, the blood-letting finished, the headlines gone, though a sour taste lingered in the mouth, ashes on the tongue. Leave it alone. Bruno was guilty.

I wrote long letters to Governor Hoffman, pleading my case, asking for a meeting with him. Our clandestine meeting was polite but not productive. Governor Hoffman had his own serious reservations about the fairness of the Hauptmann verdict, believed the trial had been biased, evidence fabricated or tampered with, and had hired his own detectives to get to the bottom of it. A sensible, decent man who risked his political future—he was predicted to be a candidate for President of the United States one day—he even met with Bruno Hauptmann for one hour on October 16, a meeting that garnered censorious comment and reprisal. Bruno begged for a lie detector test, for truth serum. "I am innocent."

Hoffman became convinced Hauptmann was a fall guy, perhaps for someone in the Lindbergh or Morrow households, but, as he told me, evidence was not forthcoming. He interviewed trial witnesses, including the old man who claimed he spotted Hauptmann's car near Hopewell, but the old man mistook a vase in the room for a person—he was, indeed, blind. Hoffman suffered a dismal fate—threats of impeachment, editorial condemnation.

"I'm sorry, Miss Ferber," he told me sympathetically, "I'm up against a brick wall."

"Do you believe me?" I pleaded.

"It no longer matters what I believe."

Worse, what was intended as a confidential conversation was leaked out, and the news-hounds had a joyous time of it. Though they lacked details and someone actually made the connection of Annabel Biggs with her cousin Violet Sharp, the tabloid chatter was brutal. "Edna Ferber's car crash allowed her to have hallucinations." That was a mild response.

Walter Winchell, not a fan of me to begin with, chortled and bellowed on his radio program. "Miss Flubber," he termed me. Another time: "Miss Fibber." Fannie Hurst was overheard mocking me at a cocktail party attended by George Kaufman. She did a mean-spirited impression of me after the accident, exclaiming, "I know the name of the killer. I know the name of the killer. It's...it's Aleck Woollcott."

Aleck himself refused to speak with me for over a year, though he routinely enacted his brave rescue, a farcical pantomime done in Manhattan parlors, the rotund man shuffling his feet and yanking a resistant and yammering Edna Ferber from the back-seat of a burning car. "Save me, oh save me, my chivalric hero."

I found none of it amusing. *Liberty* magazine survived for a few years on a wealth of articles written by everyone involved in the Lindbergh case, though most were ghost-written by some hack. Probably Woollcott. Garish headlines and gripping paragraphs lit up the journalistic skies. Inevitably someone penned a semi-serious piece about the various conspiracy theories that attended the trial. There were folks claiming the dead baby was not Charles Lindbergh, Jr. The real baby was being raised somewhere in America. Of course, Attorney Reilly had never challenged the identification of the baby's body. Or the Nazis had orchestrated the kidnapping to get Lindbergh to support Hitler's regime. Anne's sister, Elisabeth, a sickly woman who suffered her own attack of fancy, had smashed the baby to the floor in a rage. Lindbergh himself killed the baby because it was deformed, and he believed in eugenic purity, especially befitting an American hero. Or the baby was deaf, the result of Anne flying in those rattletrap airplanes. We also learned that Lindbergh was partially deaf from those early flights—which made me wonder about his facile identification of Hauptmann's distant voice. "Hey, Doctor." Or the Mafia was involved. The President of the United States played a role. Japan killed the child to deflect attention of her invasion of China. Julius Streiden in *The Storm Trooper* was certain Jews nabbed the baby for blood sacrifice.

Crazies slithered out of the woodwork. Fortunetellers and clairvoyants and tarot card readers and those who entertained visions—all provided cheap amusement for the sensation-hungry masses. And, according to the author of the *Liberty* piece, one of the most bizarre was from Edna Ferber, an otherwise estimable novelist, whose traumatic head injuries compelled her to slip into the land of carnival sideshow and circus acts at the Hippodrome. His sub-heading: "The Chauffeur Who Tried to Kill Me—and Everyone Else."

Lindbergh fled America with his family to England, an exile he blamed on Governor Hoffman's harassment.

I wrote more indignant letters, maddened, but finally, waking up one morning and realizing it was all folly, I stopped.

Yet a month or so later I received a letter from Alice Jamison, the nurse at Montclair Manor. Included with her brief note was a photograph torn from the pages of *Look* magazine, a photographic essay of the Hauptmann trial with appropriate—bombastic, cruel and dismissive—commentary from Aleck Woollcott. The clipping showed a panoramic shot of the reporters and hangers-on at Nellie's Taproom, with Walter Winchell in the foreground, his supercilious mug dominating. But Alice had drawn a red circle around one of the onlookers, standing to the side, his back up against a wall, not really a part of the larger group, his arms folded across his chest, his head tilted to the side.

It was Joshua Flagg.

Her note said that she was stunned to see him, that grainy image flashed to a memory of his stay at the Montclair Manor, the young, jittery man who'd followed Blake Somerville around, doing his nasty bidding. A disturbed young man who begged the slick Somerville for favor. Joshua Flagg, whose real name was Ezra Cilley, the youngest son of a Chicago editor and heir to the Myer Chocolate Syrup fortune. A young man who was released shortly after Blake disappeared. His family claimed he never returned home. They didn't seem too bothered by his absence.

"I always thought him dangerous," she concluded.

In the middle of a hot August I stepped out of a taxi on Fifth Avenue, headed for Passy's Restaurant with my nieces, when I spied Horace Tripp sauntering by. I waved at him, and he realized who I was. "Ah, Miss Ferber. The famous resident of the Union Hotel."

"Mr. Tripp, the erstwhile manager of the café."

He drew his lips into a thin line, unhappy. "Bitter day."

Dressed in a flashy summer suit, white linen with oversized gold buttons, a flamboyant scarlet handkerchief peeking from his breast pocket, a slicked-back haircut that betrayed his increasing baldness, Horace took a step away from me, his hand raised as though hailing a cab.

"The last time I saw you, well, you'd been axed."

He thrust out his lips, a little-boy pout. "And abandoned by my faithful wife."

"Did Martha ever follow up her story to the sheriff of how you left the hotel the night Annabel was murdered?"

Nervous, he looked over his shoulder, frowned at a woman who glanced his way as she passed. "Yes." But he laughed. "He asked where *she* was."

"So nothing came it of."

A smug, satisfied look. "Well, so far as I know, Cody Lee Thomas was the one they convicted of first-degree murder."

With that, he sailed forward, and I watched his retreating back. At the corner, standing in the shadow of a news kiosk, a woman called out to him. He hurried up to her, and they hugged. He whispered something in her ear, and suddenly both turned to face me, shoulder to shoulder, their look accusatory. Feebly I waved, though I don't know why. I found him a slimy concoction of the male species, and she looked vacuous and flighty. A snap judgment, of course, but probably on the money. Both scurried across the avenue, against the light, and a taxi almost sideswiped them. The woman's high shrill laughter and his throaty rumble of joy were drowned out by a bus that backfired as they passed.

Bruno Richard Hauptmann, prisoner number 17,390 in Cell 9—ten feet from the electric chair—was electrocuted on April 3, 1936, at 8:47 p.m. Despite the intervention of Governor Hoffman, despite delays and appeals, despite outcry from so many others, he was killed, protesting his innocence to the end. "*Gott! Gott! Gott!*" he'd cried when the last visitor left. He sobbed in his cell. Clarence Darrow telegraphed the governor: "No one should be executed on such flimsy evidence." The *London Star* labeled it "vulgarity, publicity, insult, and irrelevance." Eleanor Roosevelt said: "The entire trial left me with question in my mind," though she didn't declare Bruno innocent. Even the *Times* rued the trial—the failure "to present positive evidence." The *American Mercury* called it "Tabloid justice." And the *Boston*

*Herald* lamented, "What a miserable mess New Jersey made of the Bruno Hauptmann case."

None of it did any good. I watched a Hearst Metrotone Pathé newsreel in the theater one night, but had to leave—the shots of Anna Hauptmann and her little boy, Manfred, were too heartbreaking.

On the night he died, crowds massed at Trenton, anticipating the death. In his cell, with his writing desk, cot, sink, toilet, and photographs of Anna and Bubi on the wall, he'd been kept apart from the other six inmates waiting for death…He spent days pacing, pacing, pacing. His head was shaved, his khaki pants leg slit. His skin was pale, his eyes sunken, a skinny cadaver now. He prayed on his knees, and told the guard: "I am at peace with my God and I am not sorry to leave a world that does not understand me." They walked him out, a dead man walking, strapped him into a chair, covered his face with a mask to hide facial distortions, and the executioner turned the wheel. Three electric shocks of 2,000 volts. A sudden snap of straps cracking. A wisp of smoke. He was dead.

The *New York Times*: "Hauptmann Remains Silent to the End."

At the Stacey Trent and Hildebredt Hotels nearby, people partied, sang, danced, got drunk.

That night I didn't sleep.

◇◇◇

I'd kept in contact with Cora Thomas; the two of us chatting on the phone, a warm regard developing between us. She was always hesitant in our brief telephone talks, and she always thanked me too much. But over time we developed a careful and wonderful liking for each other, and I understood how important our talks were.

In June Cody Lee Thomas went on trial for murdering Annabel, and the young lawyer Amos Blunt stayed with the case, though his calls to me were pessimistic and disheartening. The prosecutor was a rabid firebrand, a hell-and-brimstone yeller. The defense managed to cast some doubt on the two witnesses who insisted Cody Lee was at Annabel's room that night, but it wasn't enough. And the old farmer who swore that he saw Cody Lee pulling into the driveway of the farmhouse just before seven was subjected to intense and scattershot cross examination.

"No, I seen him," the old man said. "With my own two eyes."

But the prosecutor hammered at him, attempting to blemish his life.

"You were in a mental hospital, right?"

The old man nodded. "Yes, a short time after the war. The Spanish-American. I was with Roosevelt...I..."

'How many times?"

"A couple."

"That's two?"

"Maybe three."

"Three."

He became so rattled he blubbered on the stand, and his hesitations doomed his testimony.

When Cora testified about being with her son, the prosecutor was deferential, but managed to convey to the jury that a mother's love is blind and false and—ruthless. Cora wept on the stand, babbled that Cody Lee had his problems, yes, but he was a good boy. A good boy.

I wanted to testify—to introduce what Marcus Wood had told me, but I realized, especially after talking with Amos, that my words would only make matters worse. The crazy lady from the Hauptmann trial. Folks recalled the incendiary *Liberty* article that talked of my own hallucinations. *Hang her. Hang him.*

The jury convicted him.

◇◇◇

During the first week of December I booked two rooms at the Stacy Trent Hotel in Trenton, one for Cora and one for me. Early Monday morning, despite a swirling snowstorm that shut down the roads, Cora and I took a long walk around the hotel. A cold morning, no one out. A snowplow lumbered through an intersection up ahead. Freezing, silent, we walked. At eight o'clock, chilled, we sat in my room having coffee and biscuits.

At ten o'clock, Cora went into the bathroom and changed into a black dress, old-fashioned, with filigreed lace around the bodice, a dress that sagged at the knee on one side, a tear at the hip that revealed her silk slip. She sat opposite me in a chair by the window as we watched the furious snow falling. Wind slammed the windows of the seventh floor. Though the room was overheated, I shook from the cold.

At one point I stared out the window. Drifts swept up the side of the buildings, buried the fenders of parked cars. A cold morning. Dumbly, I thought of that first morning back in Flemington when I walked behind the Union Hotel and spotted Cody Lee and Annabel having their quarrel in the parking lot. A shadow haunted me. Watching, watching. Blake Somerville planning and loving the horrible moment. Well, Bruno was dead.

Now, looking back at Cora, I trembled. When I closed my eyes, I imagined a shock of electricity piercing my head, my soul. I cried out loud.

At twenty minutes after ten o'clock my phone jangled.

Cora Lee watched me closely, her breath short.

I heard Amos Blunt's sad and dreadful voice.

I hung up the phone as Cora stood, tugged at the ill-fitting black dress, her body spinning like a dervish, her eyes wide with pain and fright, as she fell into my arms.

To receive a free catalog of Poisoned Pen Press titles, please provide your name, address, and email address in one of the following ways:

Phone: 1-800-421-3976
Facsimile: 1-480-949-1707
Email: info@poisonedpenpress.com
Website: www.poisonedpenpress.com

Poisoned Pen Press
6962 E. First Ave. Ste 103
Scottsdale, AZ 85251

$26.95     3/21/16